NEVER FORGET

Acorna put her hand to her mouth and made a hushing noise and they listened again to the broadcast.

"It was a call for help," Aari said, "what you call a mayday." He turned to the Anscam and went back to work. Once the static had cleared, a Niriian face appeared and began speaking. After a few seconds, Becker asked what it was saying.

"It is the ship's log. I believe we are receiving the last entry first."

Acorna's expression became intense. "We'll check all of the fragments of the ship and see if they provide any useful information about who attacked them and why. Meanwhile, we can translate as best we can the entire ship's log."

On the Anscam, the monologue broke off, there was a screech of static, and then, suddenly, there were images on the screen once more.

Horrifying images.

"Holy cow!" Becker said. "Who the hell are the big bugs and what are they doing—oh no—Cosmos on a crutch! They're torturing that—Aari?"

"Those are the Khleevi, Joh." Aari spoke in a very calm, controlled voice. "And that is me. The Khleevi transmitted the images of my torment to this ship."

Books by
Anne McCaffrey and Elizabeth A. Scarborough

ACORNA'S PEOPLE
ACORNA'S WORLD
ACORNA'S SEARCH

by Anne McCaffrey and Margaret Ball

ACORNA
ACORNA'S QUEST

And Coming Soon in Hardcover by
Anne McCaffrey and Elizabeth A. Scarborough

ACORNA'S REBELS

ANNE McCAFFREY
AND ELIZABETH ANN SCARBOROUGH

ACORNA'S WORLD

HarperTorch
An Imprint of HarperCollins*Publishers*

This is a work of fiction. Names, characters, places, and incidents are products of the author's imagination or are used fictitiously and are not to be construed as real. Any resemblance to actual events, locales, organizations, or persons, living or dead, is entirely coincidental.

HARPERTORCH
An Imprint of HarperCollins*Publishers*
10 East 53rd Street
New York, New York 10022-5299

Copyright © 2000 by Anne McCaffrey and Elizabeth Ann Scarborough
Excerpt from Acorna's Search copyright © 2001 by Anne McCaffrey
and Elizabeth Ann Scarborough
Cover illustration © 1999 by John Ennis
ISBN: 0-06-105984-6

First HarperTorch paperback printing: October 2001
First Eos hardcover printing: August 2000

HarperCollins®, HarperTorch™, and ♦™ are trademarks of HarperCollins Publishers Inc.

Printed in the United States of America

Visit HarperTorch on the World Wide Web at
www.harpercollins.com

10 9 8 7 6 5 4 3 2

To Andy Logan, for feeding bodies as well as creative spirits with her care and attention and delicious dinners while she listened to first draft readings!

Acknowledgments

Thanks again to Ryk Reaser for science and salvage consultation. Thanks also to Denise Little for her many suggestions, which helped to launch the various spaceships from their docking bays, as well as her hard work, which helped launch the book into print.

ACORNA'S WORLD

One

oughly six weeks after she had joined the crew of the *Condor*, flagship of Becker Interplanetary Recycling and Salvage Enterprises, Ltd., Acorna sat on "salvage watch" at the helm of the ship, surrounded by the softly glowing console lights in the cockpit and the billions of stars beyond. She felt contented, almost as if she were once more home — back in the first home she could really remember, the mining ship she had shared with her adopted uncles. Behind her for the moment were the intricacies of Linyaari society and culture. Before her instead were the intricacies of the universe as recorded in the notes, tapes, and files of Captain Jonas Becker and his illustrious parent, astrophysicist and salvage magnate Theophilus Becker.

To give herself something to do during the long watch, she was charting those notations methodically so that the planets, moons, wormholes, black holes, "pleated" space, "black water" space, and other locations visited by the Beckers could be easily relocated, and the sites where they had once been could be revisited if the need arose.

Becker had grumbled at first when she started this chore. Since the death of his adoptive father, Theophilus Becker, from whom he had inherited both the *Condor* and the salvage business, Jonas Becker had been lord and master of the *Condor*, with only Roadkill—or RK for short—the huge Makahomian Temple Cat he had rescued from a wreck, for company. Becker didn't like his belongings tampered with or moved. But Acorna had found plenty of evidence that RK periodically made nests out of the hard copies of the notes, often shredded them when he felt the urge, and, in a few sorry instances, had added his own personal—and remarkably pungent—contributions to them when he was displeased with the state of his shipboard toilet. Though she could easily eradicate the odor and the stains, nothing could make the shredded notes legible again. It was high time *someone* charted the notes before RK had his way with the lot of them. After a few "reasonable discussions," Jonas had stopped grumbling and let Acorna get on with her task.

At first RK had stayed at the helm to assist Acorna with her job, but later had wandered off in search of food or a sleeping companion, probably Aari, the only crew member other than Becker currently aboard.

Like Acorna, Aari was Linyaari, a race of humanoid people with equine and alicorn characteristics—including a flowing, curly mane and feathery hair from ankle to knee, feet with two hard toes each, and three-fingered hands with one knuckle on each digit instead of two. The most striking characteristic of the Linyaari, to humans anyway, was the shining spiral horn located in the center of their foreheads. But in Aari's case, the horn had been forcibly removed during tortures he'd suffered while he was a prisoner of voracious bug-like aliens—the Khleevi. While Aari's other wounds had been healed on narhii-Vhiliinyar, the world to which the Linyaari had fled when the Khleevi had invaded their original homeworld Vhiliinyar, Aari's horn had not regenerated.

This was an appalling wound for a Linyaari. A Linyaari's horn had amazing—almost magical, even— properties. The horns had the ability to purify anything—including air and water and food, to heal the sick, and also acted to some extent as an antenna for psychic communications among the Linyaari.

Acorna had learned a great deal more about the powers of her horn and about her people when she had returned with a Linyaari delegation to narhii-Vhiliinyar. Unfortunately, once she had arrived, her aunt and two other shipmates had been dispatched into space again to deal with an emergency, and Acorna had been left among strangers to try to adjust to her native culture, a culture she'd left behind while she was still a baby.

Her only two real friends on narhii-Vhiliinyar had been the eldest elder of the Linyaari people, Grandam Naadiina, and Maati, a little girl who was the *viizaar*'s messenger and the orphaned younger sister of Aari.

When Becker had made his unauthorized landing on narhii-Vhiliinyar to return Aari and all the bones from the Linyaari graveyard to the new Linyaari home planet, Acorna, Grandam, and Maati had been in the greeting committee. Aari at that time had still been terribly deformed from his ordeal with the Khleevi, and the *viizaar* Liriili and some of the less sensitive and compassionate Linyaari had not made his return easy.

Acorna, perhaps because her own loneliness had helped her identify with his, had been drawn to Aari. When an emergency signal had called Becker away from narhii-Vhiliinyar, Acorna and Aari had shipped out with him. They had been able to help in a crisis that had threatened some of Acorna's human friends as well as the Linyaari. As a result of their intervention, a branch of a Federation-wide criminal organization had been destroyed and many off-planet Linyaari, including Acorna's beloved aunt, had been rescued, along with all the other captives of the criminals. Acorna, Becker, Aari, and Acorna's Uncle Hafiz, who had also been on hand for the rescue, were now in great favor among her people.

Acorna could have stayed comfortably on narhii-Vhiliinyar once her aunt and the other ship-bred and ship-chosen Linyaari returned to the planet. But she had decided instead to leave with Becker and Aari.

She wasn't sorry. She might have been born on a peaceful planet populated by beings who had the ability to understand one another telepathically, but her upbringing had made her different, and that was sometimes a problem, both for her and for her people. Space was familiar to her, and its diversity of races, species, and personalities stimulated her. Of course, right now, just being here, quietly charting coordinates, resting her eyes by watching the stars, wasn't very stimulating, but the serene surroundings felt wonderful. She was comforted by the routine watch, at peace with the universe.

Perhaps, she thought, *happily ever after, the permanent version, only happened in fairy tales, but happy every once in a while was restful and healing.*

The cabin lights flicked on, bringing the harsh light of the day shift to her starlit world. She blinked a few times until her eyes adjusted.

"Yo, Princess!" Becker said. "Your watch is over. Whatsa matter with you—sitting there typing in the dark? You'll ruin your eyes that way, didn't anybody ever tell you?"

He strode up to stand behind her, peering over her shoulder so intently his brushy mustache, which closely resembled RK's ruff, brushed her horn. Becker smelled strongly of the aftershave he had begun to use about the time he began to shave again, shortly after she arrived. It wasn't that he was trying to impress her in a courtship and mating fashion, she knew. It was simply a rather old-fashioned, by human standards, sign of gender acknowledgment and respect. "Hey, now, how about that? You've charted the whole journey from the time we left narhii-Vhiliinyar the first time, to that moon where Ganoosh and Ikwaskwan held your people captive, and all the way back again! I figured, with all the excitement we ran into, and all the hopping around we had to do, nobody would ever be able to figure that one out. How'd you *do* that?"

"You kept good notes, Captain," she said, smiling.

"Well, it's terrific! And you did it so fast, too. Where'd a sweet young thing like you learn that?"

"Elementary, my dear Becker," Aari said, sauntering up behind the captain and towering over him. Tall, slender, and graceful now that his injuries had healed, Aari was white-skinned and silver-maned. These were traits he shared with Acorna and the other Linyaari space travelers.

Aari had been reading a trashed-out copy of *The Adventures of Sherlock Holmes* lately. Becker and Acorna could see the immediate result of his current venture into fiction in the way that Aari had layered two baseball caps from Becker's collection, so that the bill of one hat stuck out in back above his long silver mane, the other in the front. It was not only a pretty good imitation of a traditional deerstalker, but the hat covered the indentation in Aari's forehead where his horn had once been. Aari also clutched a Makahomian ceremonial pipe between his teeth. It was a bit longer than an antique meerschaum, but with Aari's height, he could carry it off. The Holmesian effect was only spoiled by the RECYCLER'S RONDY '84 logo on the front of the cap facing them, along with an embroidered trash container rampant beneath the lettering.

"Space-bred and space-chosen Linyaari," Aari said, "develop a heightened sense of navigational interrelationships between space and masses, even energy fluctuations. Many of those relationships are imprinted telepathically upon our brains by our parents when we're young. That is partially how I was able to guide you to narhii-Vhiliinyar though I had never been there myself."

"Hmm," Becker said, surveying his shipmate's latest odd outfit. "You make me wonder if my old man might not have been part Linyaari. You're sure finding your way to the planet wasn't simple deduction?"

Aari looked puzzled. "No, Joh. We do not use footprints, types of mud, or tobacco ashes to do this thing. It is a matter of the mind."

"Must be," Becker said. "Acorna's indicated the wormholes and black space with a precision that you don't see on regular charts, given the instability of the features being charted and the dangers of getting close enough to map them thoroughly. Even got the whole wormhole system we ducked back through to blast Ganoosh and Ikwaskwan to kingdom come."

Acorna glanced up from her charting and shrugged. "We were there. The notations of the holes and folds are roughed out in your notes, and made precise in my mind." She paused to consider something else Jonah had said. "About your father—he is probably not part Linyaari. I do not think it is possible for our two species to interbreed. In the pictures you have shown me of your father, he certainly doesn't *look* Linyaari, though I will admit his intuition about such matters as spatial relationships, as well as yours, seems to me to be similar to some of the psychic abilities our race possesses. I can certainly understand that, lacking a crew and managing all phases of your operation alone, as you do now and as your father did when you were a child, you did not take the time to properly collate and chart your observations. But, frankly, only psychic ability would explain how you were ever able to find anything in this chaos." Her spread hands took in the mounds of papers, chips, and recorded tapes scattered around the console.

"I usually know which pile or computer file to access for what I need," Becker protested. "At least, I did once," he muttered. Then he added graciously, "But I'm sure it'll be helpful to have it all nice and orderly."

Roadkill jumped up on one of the piles of hardcopy and sent the papers into an avalanche that slid clear across the deck.

"RK, you silly cat, you already had your chance at these," Acorna said, madly grabbing for the flying papers.

The cat chased the furthest sheets until they settled to the floor, pounced upon one and shredded it with his back feet, then abruptly lost interest and began washing his brindled belly instead.

Acorna bent down and shuffled the papers, somewhat the worse for wear, back into order.

"I'm pleased you approve, Captain. The task needed doing and it keeps me productively occupied."

"Yeah, I guess you must have been pretty bored after you reprogrammed that junked replicator I had in Cargo Hold Two to make all my favorite dishes, so I wouldn't have to eat cat food when I got busy, and after you and Aari turned Deck Three into a hydroponics garden for your own noshing needs, while you meantime inventoried and catalogued all my remaining salvage."

"It was not so much, Captain. It's not as if I am new to this sort of thing. I used to replicate food and help grow my own meals when my uncles and I lived aboard our mining ship. I also catalogued our specimens and assisted with charting. I like to be helpful."

"No kidding! Between you and KEN," he said, referring to the all-purpose KEN-640 android unit that they had acquired, more or less by accident, during the *Condor*'s last voyage, "the way he keeps the ship soooo—"

"Shipshape, Joh?" Aari offered. "I have been reading

the nautical works of Robert Louis Stevenson, and that term is employed to describe a flawlessly maintained vessel."

"Yeah, what you said," Becker agreed. "Between you two and Aari, I could take up knitting or basket weaving in the spare time I got these days."

"A very good idea, Joh," Aari said. "You have some excellent references on crocheting, beadwork, handweaving, pottery making, and origami, as well."

"You should know, buddy. I'm glad you've been getting so much out of the pile of old books I found in that landfill, not to mention the vid collection. But let me warn you—steer clear of the do-it-yourself veterinary books." Becker glanced down at RK who had one leg poised in the air and was looking up at him with suspicious, wide, golden eyes. In a stage whisper Becker continued, "I once tried some stuff out of one of those vet guides on the cat there. Bad idea. Neither of us came out whole."

Aari looked puzzled. "Why would I read veterinary books, Joh? If 'Riidkyii' "—that was as close as Aari's Standard could come to pronouncing Roadkill's name—"becomes sick, Acorna could heal him. We have no need for the invasive measures described in those books."

"Damn good thing, too," Becker huffed. "The problem with using invasive measures on ol' Riidkyii is he can't get it straight who's the invader and who is the invadee. We were both short a few bits of choice anatomy after that little adventure. Luckily, Roadkill and I eventually got put back together, courtesy of the Linyaari." He turned to Acorna and said, "While we're on the subject, you know you're welcome to the library, too, Princess. Anytime."

"Yes, Captain Becker, that is very kind of you, but I already accessed most of the reading selections you have available during the time I lived with my uncles and guardians. I was raised by humans—unlike Aari, who had no previous exposure to human culture until he met you. So I won't be using the books. The vids are another matter. However, I regret very much that we have only vid goggles available to view the films. It would be such fun if we could all view them together."

Becker gave her a sly look from under his brushy eyebrows. Her psychic powers had been increased while she lived among her own people, but she didn't need them to know that he understood what she really meant. Teasing, he said, "Of course, really, only two people oughta watch at a time because somebody should be on salvage watch."

He knew that she wished to share the books and vids with Aari so that he wouldn't spend quite so much time alone, and so that they would have something to enjoy together. She blushed a little. "I simply thought it would be more companionable."

"Yes, Joh," Aari said, "and, as far as salvage watch goes, you once performed all the ship's duties alone, and your metabolism requires that you sleep for long periods. You must have let the ship's computers take over occasionally then. You could certainly do so now. I do not see the difficulty of sharing these vids."

Becker chuckled and shook his head. "What is it with you guys? Mutiny? But, okay, we'll keep an eye out for something we can convert to a full screen setup for vids instead of the goggles."

"Thank you, Captain," Acorna said. She believed Aari would be much better off if he didn't spend nearly all of his time on his own. He had spent years alone in a cave on the deserted planet Vhiliinyar, hiding from the Khleevi who'd tortured him, before Becker had found and rescued him. Aari hardly knew how to speak to people anymore. And every time he disappeared while she was not on watch and Acorna decided to go to him to try to initiate a conversation, Captain Becker always seemed to have some task he needed her assistance with or some errand for her to run. RK, too, tried to deter her. His claws and piercing cries could be quite eloquent, even to one who possessed no higher understanding of cat language than vulnerable skin that could be spoken to with fang and claw. She sensed her friends were possessed by some sort of male protectiveness toward Aari. She was sure it was not a reasoned response to her actions, but she was hard-pressed to understand it. She meant her fellow Linyaari no harm, and sought only to lead him to a deeper healing than had been necessary with the wounded she had previously treated.

She was also as perplexed as she was amused by Aari's "literary disguises," as Becker called them. They were funny and sad at the same time. As he adopted the headdresses and costumes of various characters in the books and vids he was exposed to, Aari looked less like a maimed Linyaari and more like an interesting, if rather oddly dressed, human. Of course, she herself had at times donned disguises that covered her horn and feet so that she could pass for human, and it had been a useful skill. But in Aari's case, she sensed a huge chasm of loss underlying his attempts to be someone else. It was as if he no longer considered himself fully Linyaari. The horn transplant the doctors had attempted on narhii-Vhiliinyar had not taken. A living horn transplant from a close relative might be possible with a specimen from Maati when she was older, but could not be attempted just yet while her horn was still growing. They'd have to wait until she'd reached full adulthood before they could risk harvesting enough tissue for a successful transplant for Aari.

The com unit button lit and emitted a beep as Aari replaced the fallen papers on the console, lifted RK to his shoulders, and headed back into the hold to continue his reading.

"You get it, Acorna," Becker said. "It's probably for you anyway."

She flipped the toggle, fully expecting to hear the voice of either her aunt, *visedhaanye ferilii* Neeva, checking to make sure she was all right, or that of the *vüzaar* Liriili, spouting yet another list of instructions and requests that Acorna was to pass on to her contacts in the Federation in general and to her Uncle Hafiz in particular.

Since the rescue of all the off-planet Linyaari spacefarers, ambassadors, teachers, students, scientists, engineers, healers and their families, and the subsequent return of those rescued to narhii-Vhiliinyar, just six weeks before, big changes appeared to be taking place on the Linyaari world. According to Neeva, the governing council had been in almost continuous session, trying to decide if, when, and to what degree the

Linyaari should end their isolationist policy with regard to most of the galaxy, and whether they should open trade alliances with Federation planets and companies.

The council had already unanimously decided on a most favored trade alliance with House Harakamian, the empire Uncle Hafiz had recently handed over to his nephew Rafik Nadezda, one of Acorna's adopted uncles. The Linyaari hadn't yet decided whether or not to allow House Harakamian vessels to enter Linyaari space, however. At this point, the majority of the council favored off-planet trading at some mutually agreeable location. But that wasn't a unanimous view. Some of the more progressive Linyaari space travelers even favored entering the Federation. As they pointed out, isolation had failed to protect their people from the Khleevi or from capture and mistreatment at the hands of Edacki Ganoosh, the Kezdet robber baron. The vocal minority of the council felt that knowledge of other civilizations, both friends and foes, was better protection for a peaceful people like themselves than ignorance and isolation.

Since most of the Linyaari diplomatic corps was currently recovering from their ordeal on narhii-Vhiliinyar, the council was entrusting all of the Linyaari's initial overtures to the Federation to Acorna, who was a newly appointed Linyaari ambassador and also, conveniently, Hafiz Harakamian and Rafik Nadezda's adopted niece. The council completely ignored her protestations that Becker did not intend to return immediately to Federation space, preferring for the moment to search for salvage in the galaxies occupied by the Linyaari and their current trade allies, an area neither he nor any other Federation-licensed salvage company had previously explored. Acorna had passed on the Linyaari council's messages to Hafiz before his flagship, the *Sharazad*, departed from Linyaari space.

Hafiz's last message to the *Condor*, and to Becker in particular, had been suspiciously expansive and nonchalant.

"Of course, dear boy," Hafiz had said, "there is no need for you to hasten your business on our account. By all means stay in this congenial universe. Get acquainted. Find useful refuse. As long as Acorna is happy, her Aunt Karina and her other uncles and I are content. We'll see each other soon enough."

Perhaps Hafiz was really serious about retiring after all? In Acorna's experience, it was very unlike him to fail to seize a business opportunity by the throat and milk it for all it was worth. If he wasn't retiring, he was clearly up to something.

So she had reason to hear from many people of her acquaintance just at this moment. But this time the com unit surprised her. When a face appeared briefly on the screen, it was not her aunt, or another Linyaari, or even the wily Uncle Hafiz. Instead, a heavily bovine face was being transmitted, male and jowly with a curving brownish horn above each ear. It spoke in a language Acorna didn't understand, so she reached for Aari's LAANYE, a Linyaari device that collected samples of unknown languages, analyzed them, then served as both a translator and a sleep-learning device to implant foreign languages into the brain of anyone who wished to learn them. But the transmission trailed off just as she got the machine activated.

According to the LAANYE, the last word the creature had said translated as "Mayday" or "SOS" in Linyaari. The only other words she'd caught in the transmission before the screen turned to white, crackling static were "Niriian" and "*Hamgaard*." She did recognize the race of the creature who'd appeared on her com screen. He was from the planet Nirii—the Niriians were regular trading partners of the Linyaari.

Acorna scanned the frequencies, trying to pick up the signal again, but to no avail. Becker put his hand over hers and pointed. She followed his finger and saw that the screens of the long-range scanners he used to detect possible salvage showed blips of white light in several locations. One of them was backed by a mass of green light. "There," he said. "There's a solid mass under that one. According to the readout, it's a small planet with an oxygen-based atmosphere. If the ship was seeking refuge, that would be the most likely place in this sector of space to retreat to. Let's go see what we can find."

Acorna nodded. "Yes, I see what you mean. Given the direction of the signal's probable source, it is likely that the salvage is the distressed vessel whose broadcast we just received. The LAANYE translated the last word before the message was interrupted to mean 'Mayday.' Possibly the signal we intercepted was a general one sent as the ship's systems were failing during some sort of accident or attack. I feel sure we received it only because we were within range of their emergency transmitters. If the signal had been meant for us, the broadcast would have been in Galactic Standard or in Linyaari."

Becker shrugged. "Yep. That's the way I've got it figured. Don't get your hopes up, though. We're probably not going to find the cowboy who was transmitting the mayday alive, or anybody else. None of those blips on the scanners look like an intact ship. But we may be able to tell what got him from the fragments. The time stamp on the message is a couple of days ago—if the problem was indeed an attack instead of an accident, whatever nailed them seems to be long gone."

"So we will check the situation out and report exactly what happened to the Federation?" Acorna asked.

"Yeah, eventually," Becker said. "But mostly we'll know what to avoid ourselves."

Intricately twisted vines and stems joined and twined, braided, knotted, and separated before bursting into jewel-toned rainbows of richly hued blossoms, reminding Acorna of pictures she had seen of the illustrated borders in Celtic holy books from ancient Earth. Except that this vegetation was no mere border, but a lush tropical jungle so interconnected that it was impossible to tell where one plant stopped and the next began.

At first, the tangle of plant life looked impassible. She, Captain Becker, RK, and Aari had stood on the lowered platform of the robolift, overwhelmed by the sight of it. Becker was fingering the sharpened blade of his machete while Aari held the portable scanner, waiting for it to indicate the hiding place of the large piece of salvage that had shown up on the *Condor*'s screen.

Acorna was busy cataloging the minerals and elements that made up this planetoid. She had already notified the others that no breathing apparatus would be required—the atmosphere was void of any substances lethal to carbon-based life forms and far richer in oxygen than Kezdet or narhii-Vhiliinyar, and the soil was as rich in nitrogen. Of course, that was just her scientific opinion. In practice, once she was actually faced with it, the air was so heavily scented with the aromas of the flowers it felt too thick to breathe, laden with a heady mixture the like of which she had never smelled before. She detected elements of the incenses that had perfumed Uncle Hafiz's palace, like cinnamon, cloves, vanilla, and the kind of human cooking known as baking, and also smells like mint, rose, violet, lavender, gardenia, and lily of the valley, but all were much deeper and mixed together with new scents—things she'd never smelled before. The end result was so intense that it almost took on substance and color.

Captain Becker said the place reeked like a high-priced bawdy house, which seemed to please him. Aari had sniffed curiously. "I have no basis for ascertaining the validity of your comparison, Joh, but I defer to your knowledge of such matters." For their excursion dirtside, Aari had removed his Holmesian baseball caps and pipe in favor of a colorful scarf tied around the top of his head and a plaskin patch, inked black, over one of his eyes. Acorna deduced, Watson-like, that he had been reading *Treasure Island* and was assuming a piratical disguise in lieu of his Holmes persona. Though he was giving the soil a very Holmesian inspection, what he could see of it from where they stood.

Soil was clearly foremost in RK's mind, too. The ship's cat leaped off the platform and hopped through the vines—which parted, almost as if the cat's reputation had preceded him, to allow him to pass easily through them. The roots and trailers along the ground seemed to shrink away as RK pawed the soil, turned his back on his work, and deposited his own ecological contribution to the planet.

Acorna started after the cat but Becker touched her arm and said, "Wait. Let us see if he gets out again okay."

The cat pawed backward to cover his work but the vines and other ground cover were already creeping back across the pile. Roadkill looked behind him, saw that this was happening, gave a little shake that could have been a cat's version of a shrug, and bounded back through the path that had cleared for him on his way in. He then hopped up onto the robolift platform and proceeded to wash his whiskers, as if they had been somehow affected by his previous chore.

"Okay, then," Becker said.

"That way, Joh," Aari informed him after consulting the scanner, and pointed in the direction from which the cat had just come.

"Well, then, onward." Becker raised the machete in one of the dramatic gestures he was fond of and pointed. RK leaped to his shoulder and the four of them dismounted the platform. As they set out, the jungle growth shrank even further away this time, leaving a wide lane open before them. It gave Acorna an odd feeling to see the plants moving and shifting out of their way. Becker walked over to one side and raised the machete to hack at a thick stalk, but the stalk bent in the middle to retreat from him.

"Wait, Captain," Acorna said. "The plants seem to be trying to accommodate us by getting out of our way. It hardly seems right to cut them."

Becker gave her a look. "Yeah, well, we don't know how long it will take us to find the ship. And we don't know what wrecked it. We might be looking at the cause of the trouble right now. How do we know these plants won't close up around the *Condor* and bury it so deep we won't be able to get it loose again? They're several stories high, after all. We wouldn't even be able to see the suns if they had decided not to part for us."

"I think 'decided' is a relevant term in this case," she said. "These plants seem to have some kind of limited sentience, or at the very least the ability to react quickly to stimuli. I think it might be wise to sheathe the machete. Maybe we had better not make them angry. Besides, we could find the ship with the portable scanner, couldn't we?"

"Yeah, but I always like to have a backup plan," Becker said, while putting the long knife away.

Aari dug in the pocket of his shipsuit and pulled out a ball of shining thread. "I have just the thing, Joh." He tied one end to the robolift and held the rest in his hand. "We can leave a trail behind us, like Theseus seeking the Minotaur in the labyrinth. This also works very well in caves when searching for lost cascades of gold and jewels."

"Caskets, buddy," Becker said.

"As you wish," Aari agreed amiably, and began unrolling his ball of string.

"Ow," Becker said as his shoulder was punctured by the claws of the suddenly hyper-alert ship's cat, who hunkered down and switched his brindled gray and black tail, his ears perked and his eyes intently following the gleaming thread as it unwound behind Aari. "Belay that, mister," Becker said.

The cat immediately leaped from Becker's shoulder to Aari's. "Aaargh," Aari said, rolling his *a*s instead of his *r*s. "Avast there! It is my faithful paro, Pol."

RK made a dive for the thread. Acorna intercepted the cat and received a few scratches for her trouble.

"I am sorry, Khornya," Aari said. "I think Riid-Kiiyi does not wish to be a paro."

"It's all right," she said, cuddling RK up close to her body and scratching him gently under the chin. He immediately abandoned his quest to play with the string in favor of purring and rubbing the side of his face against her skin.

The small party set out into the jungle. The vegetation now made a path as wide as the *Condor*, the stalks bending almost flat to avoid contact with the people passing among them. The heady fragrance turned to an acrid stench.

"Sheesh," Becker said, holding his nose. "What are these, skunk vines?"

Acorna looked around. "No. They are the same sort of plants as the rest, but see how the flowers are closing up and the scent they are emitting is changing? It is as if they are afraid of us."

"Hmmm, well, it does smell like the last guy who tried to gyp me out of some money he promised me," Becker admitted. He leaned closer to a stalk and the stench grew stronger.

"Joh, don't," Aari said.

"Just testing," Becker said. "Sorry, plants. No harm intended."

Aari was busy unwinding twine with one hand and holding the scanner with the other. "It should not be far now, Joh," he said. "The salvage is just ahead."

An opening in the canopy was visible before them, and Acorna saw a long cylindrical pod lying among some twisted and charred stalks right in their path.

Becker prodded it and turned it over. Beyond it, they could see other bits of the downed ship visible among the stalks. Although there was nothing overtly useful in the wreckage they could see, Becker decided he wanted to haul all of the pieces back to the *Condor*. "We might be able to figure out why the Niriians sent the mayday," he said. "Maybe find some clue to who exactly they were, what kind of trouble they were in, who attacked them." He scratched his head. "Don't think that this is a normal part of my business, Acorna, because it's not. Finding wrecked ships, yes, but not stumbling on the wreckage before it's cold. And I have a funny feeling about this one."

"Me, too," Acorna said.

Aari looked up, surprised at their words. "I apologize, Joh, Khornya. I did not realize that you had not understood the *Hamgaard*'s broadcast. I would have translated it for you if I'd known."

"*Hamgaard?*" Becker asked.

"That is the name of the Niriian ship that broadcast the message that brought us here. Niriians have been trading partners of my people for many, many years. Like us, they are a nonaggressive race. Before I—before my brother was lost—I traveled on more than one trading mission to Nirii."

He turned away, stepping over nearer pieces of wreckage to retrieve others farther from the ship.

Acorna noticed as she picked up the fragments of ship that they were sticky with some reddish fluid. At first she thought it was blood, but then she saw that it was actually more of a deep amber in color and far too transparent to be either human or Linyaari blood. It was clearly the source of the acrid smell they had noted earlier, and she wrinkled her nose. "Phew," she told Becker. "This is what is causing the stink."

Becker looked more closely at the damaged vines all around them, gleaming with redness that Acorna had not noticed in the plants nearer the ship. "I think you're right. Look there. They're weeping this stuff."

Acorna looked. The redness ran down the stalks, pooled at the base of the stems, and was slowly encroaching on the wreckage.

"We're going to have to give this stuff a good scrubbing," Becker said disgustedly.

Aari was looking, too, and nodding. Then all of a sudden he turned toward them, leaped over the wreckage, and ran back to the ship as fast as Acorna had ever seen him run.

"Hey, buddy, wait up, what is it?" Becker asked as they chased after their friend, but Aari was back on the robolift platform before they could catch him, curled up in a fetal position on the very center of the platform, his eyes tightly closed, and his entire body shaking. Sweat and tears ran off his face and wet the deck beneath him. RK dabbed at him with an experimental paw and then looked up at Becker, wide-eyed.

Becker raised the robolift and he and Acorna shepherded Aari back to his bunk. "You stay here with him," Becker told her. "I'll get the KEN unit to help me load the cargo."

Acorna had leaned against Aari so that he was in contact with her horn all the time they were loading him and he was quieter now. His trembling had stopped and he was no longer sweating. Her healing abilities worked to some degree with mental as well as physical wounds, but she was learning that she had limits. There was only so much she could do with deeply embedded psychological injuries, particularly with Aari.

When he'd been tortured, his survival had depended on being able to escape mentally to a place where the Khleevi tortures couldn't touch him. Unfortunately, when he was in deep pain, he still retreated to that place. Acorna couldn't reach him there, and the healing power of her horn could not touch him either.

She tried, but she could not read Aari's thoughts, which were jumbled and incoherent. But the feelings that rolled from him were all too clear—deep dread, loathing that was *ka*-Linyaari in its repulsion. It was as if Aari had been flung down into some dark and nightmarish place he could not escape from. He no longer knew where he was or who was with him. She could only hold him, her horn buried in his mane up tight against his scalp, trying to exude enough soothing energy to overpower the spiraling horror that gripped him in its vortex. Time seemed to slip away as she tried to give Aari some relief from the mental demons that gripped him. And then, as she reached the point of exhaustion, everything slipped away from her and the world faded to black.

When Becker returned to the main deck, he and the KEN unit both sticky with the foul-smelling sap, he looked in to see that Aari and Acorna both slept, she with her arms wrapped tight around him, he at last relaxed, though his face was still damp with tears. Becker saw that Acorna's golden horn was looking a little transparent, as if the effort of trying to comfort Aari had drained her healing energy. Past experience had taught him that this was how it was with Linyaari who pushed their limits of endurance. He had seen that all too clearly from the effects of the tortures inflicted on captured Linyaari by Edacki Ganoosh and Admiral Ikwaskwan. But normally it took a long time and a lot of injuries to deplete a horn to any degree. The fact that Acorna's horn was already translucent instead of a healthy gold told him that poor old Aari had to be in a world of hurt.

RK, who had spent the time Becker and the KEN unit used to round up the salvage getting the sap off his fur, plopped himself within the tangle of Linyaari feet and buried his face in his own paws. The cat had apparently decided that a vigil was in order.

Becker looked at Acorna lying there, and thought that if her knuckles weren't already so pale they'd be white from hanging on to Aari. She was clutching him like a lifeline. He was hurting, and she was bound and determined that he was going to stop hurting. That was all very well on the surface, but Becker wasn't sure Aari was ready to be out of pain, or ready to let Acorna in to heal him. He wasn't sure that, even with the Linyaari's legendary psychic abilities, Acorna had enough experience of men to understand how complicated her caring for Aari could be for both of them.

He touched Acorna's shoulder gently and woke her, so that she turned toward him and relaxed her grip on

Aari. He didn't need to do anything else. As soon as she saw where she was and what she was doing, she rose, not as if she were ashamed, but like she knew it was the prudent thing to do.

"He was very frightened of something out there," she said. "Khleevi must have attacked that ship, Becker. Aari's mind was screaming about the Khleevi, and he was reliving his torture when they captured him again. It was very hard for him."

"It was no picnic for you, either, Princess. Better hit your berth and strap in. I'll strap him in, too. I've got all the salvage stowed. We can look at it at our leisure once we're back in space. I don't want to sit down here any longer than necessary and give those plants time to get so relaxed about having the *Condor* among them that they decide to make us part of the scenery. Know what I mean?"

It was an image she could visualize all too well. She nodded sleepily and stumbled off to her berth.

Two

W hen at last the *Sharazad* returned to Maganos Moonbase bearing a triumphant Hafiz Harakamian and a host of others, Rafik Nadezda was so relieved to see the old pirate he could scarcely believe it.

While the ground crew tended to unloading the ship and servicing it, Rafik walked beside the Harakamians to the transit lounge, which was the most luxurious of the quarters at Maganos Moonbase. The soundproofed facility, with its deep carpets and soft, comfortable divans and chairs in the lounge, fully equipped business suites and conference rooms, had been designed to make a good impression on visitors, potential employers, and clients for the skills and goods that were being offered by the base's residents. Maganos Moonbase was a mining, manufacturing, and training facility set up to reeducate the former child slaves of Kezdet. The children ran the base as a business, and were responsible for its financial and educational successes. The moonbase had been built with money from both Hafiz Harakamian and Acorna's other benefactor, Delzaki Li, as well as with reparations seized from Kezdet's kingpin of the child-slavery operations, Baron Manjari. But it was the children's job to ensure that the investment was a profitable one.

Now the former child slaves rushed up the gangway connecting the ship and gantry to the transit facility. They greeted the Harakamians and the ship's other passengers with cheerful familiarity that Rafik was pleased to see Hafiz apparently took as a compliment. He smiled and waved and spoke a word or two to some of the children he recognized from previous visits.

Hafiz looked somewhat trimmer and fitter than he had when last Rafik had seen him. It was possible that this new trimness was owing to Hafiz's marital exertions with his bride, but if so, the old man was a considerate as well as an energetic lover. His new bride, her ample form flatteringly draped in an expensive drift of violet and orchid silk embroidered with gold to accentuate her not inconsiderable bustline and hips, had not diminished by one curve or chin, and glowed with contentment.

As Hafiz embraced him, Rafik thought there was a renewed vigor and purposefulness to the old man's step as well, a gleam of reinforced steel in his eye and grip.

"You look well, my uncle," Rafik remarked.

"Nearly being killed a thousand times can do that for a man of action, O son of my heart," Hafiz replied with a dismissive wave of his hand, to indicate that real men of action knew this thing and found it beneath them to make too much of it.

"You were magnificent, my hero," Karina said, and turned to Rafik, white gold carousels glittering with amethysts and blue diamonds swinging from each ear beneath the light veil she wore over her dark hair. She gestured dramatically with heavily beringed hands, and the jewels at her neck and bosom heaved with pride as she lauded her husband. "He was a lion! He saved a shipload of children as well as most of Acorna's relatives!" Her hands fluttered down to cling like plump white doves to her husband's arm. She batted her eyelashes and looked up at Hafiz adoringly—no small feat since she was an inch and a half taller than he.

"So we have heard from the Starfarers, Uncle," Rafik said. "They, too, are here on Maganos, recuperating."

"Are they? That is good. That is very good indeed. It fits in with my plans exactly," Hafiz said.

"Plans?" Rafik said.

"All in the proper time, most beloved of nephews. I don't suppose you have a few small viands at hand to comfort weary travelers?"

After Hafiz and Karina had been comfortably ensconced on a well-padded divan and refreshments ordered, and Rafik had seated himself in the throne-like carved chair opposite them, Rafik asked, "Back to the plans you spoke of, my uncle. Tell me more of them." The old man might have officially retired from the business, but when he stopped scheming, Rafik would know that Hafiz had stopped breathing.

Hafiz clapped his hands together and shook them for emphasis. "They are splendid plans, most splendid plans indeed, O son and heir of my heart! Thanks to your efforts and those of your partners to rid the universe of our enemies, our Linyaari friends and the relatives of our dear niece Acorna are opening their hearts to us, and perhaps their purses as well. But they are, as you know, very shy. And our beloved niece, appointed by her people to represent them in trade, wishes for a time to travel with the estimable Captain Becker and his intriguingly tragic new first mate."

"Ye-es?" Rafik said. "Some of the Starfarers have mentioned another Linyaari—a hornless one. They say he survived the Khleevi, but surely—"

"Survived he has, indeed! A worthy man in many ways, from what I have seen of him. But that is neither here nor there," he waved his hand dismissively.

Karina captured Hafiz's waving hand with her own ring-laden one.

"Actually, nephew of my husband," she said, "the point is, that it is *not* here but *there* that Acorna wishes to stay for a time at least. Your uncle, benevolent and kindhearted patriarch that he is, wisely has chosen—with my help, of course—to view this circumstance not as an obstacle to our future trade with the Linyaari, but as an opportunity."

Rafik raised an eyebrow politely.

Hafiz slipped Karina's hand through the crook in his elbow and patted it. "Can you guess what I intend, scion of my house?"

"I believe there is no need for me to hazard such a guess, O founder of my fortune, as it appears you can barely contain your wish to tell me all about it."

"Even so, my boy, even so. I will give you a hint. Is it not written that if the profit cannot go to the mountain, the mountain shall go unto the profit?" Tea and kaf arrived, along with cool bowls of sherbet that had been flown in from Hafiz's main compound at Laboue in anticipation of his arrival, and many assorted pastries and savory morsels. The lounge began to fill up with people from the ship and those who had come to greet them, among them the Starfarers, many of whom now were young adults. The Starfarers were permanently planetless space travelers, their ship serving them as world, country, state, city, and family home all rolled into one. Rafik waited patiently until everyone had exchanged greetings, then steered conversation back to the matter at hand.

"The profit will go to the mountain. . . . So it is written in the third of the three books by the third of the three prophets, Uncle," Rafik said with a respectful inclination of his dark and handsome head. Then he looked up sharply, a smile dawning on his face. "Uncle, surely you do not intend to . . .? No! I can see that you do." He was not really as shocked as he sounded, but he enjoyed watching his uncle's pleasure in his reaction. "But how? Is not the Linyaari homeworld still closed to visitors?"

"It is," Hafiz said.

"Then how? Surely you would not risk offending them and endangering our business, not to mention our relations with Acorna's people, by violating their privacy?"

"Absolutely not, my son! That would be unthinkable. Inconceivable. We will, of course, wait for an invitation—which will naturally not be that long in coming. In the meantime, however, we will undertake an enterprise so courageous, so farsighted, so monumental, that the fame of House Harakamian will rise like the proverbial djinn from the proverbial smoke of the proverbial bottle, and bring with it all of the riches, the luxury, the beauty, and the bounty that accompany such great good fortune."

"You mean to establish a branch of House Harakamian beyond Federation space, my uncle?"

Hafiz spread his hands this time, indicating his innate generosity. "Someone must, my son. These people are surely lacking all that we have to offer and possibly are unaware that they are even in need of it! How will they know unless we show them what they are missing? And the Linyaari *are* shy. Had it not been for their need to warn other innocent races about the Khleevi, they might never have ventured into Federation space, might never have found Laboue or Maganos Moonbase. While it is true they might one day venture out of their territory again, an enterprising businessman does not leave such matters to time and chance any more than a doting parent would the happiness of his adoptive daughter. We are in good odor with the Linyaari at present—"

"Due to the bravery and innovation Hafiz showed in the rescue of all of their important space traveling people," Karina put in, looking up at her spouse with adoration.

"True, true," Hafiz said. "I covered myself with glory, it is true. But in my experience, gratitude is an ephemeral commodity, and the memory of those who are indebted to one is even more so. Therefore, we must move with the swiftness of a desert storm if we are to take maximum advantage of our past good works. We must organize our exhibitions, the travel for our exhibitors, sales and support staff, security, et cetera, et cetera, et cetera."

"Nadhari Kando might be available for security," Rafik said.

"Excellent! I am glad you concur. She has been traveling with us. She should be joining us here soon, as a matter of fact, but she wished first to oversee certain arrangements aboard the *Sharazad* before we set off again."

Karina placed her silver gilt fingertips to her temples and said, "Ahh—you see, Hafiz? Rafik said exactly what I foretold!"

"Indeed, my dear. Actually, nephew, Karina sensed that you would wish to employ that formidable lady, so I have already offered her command of the outpost's guard and given her full rein to recruit her own staff."

"It is well, my uncle, Madame Karina," he said with a courtly inclination of his head to his 'aunt.' Hafiz's bride had a gift for "sensing" matters that she would have had to be comatose not to know, but she made Hafiz happy, and for this Rafik was prepared to regard her "powers" with tolerance, if not with the awe she seemed to think they should invoke in him.

Hafiz continued. "If we are to be beyond Federation assistance, I will want the best people, even if Nadhari has to lure them away from Federation forces, and naturally she will require the latest and most effective weaponry as well. And she is one who may be trusted to acquire what is needed with the utmost discretion and dispatch."

"True," Rafik agreed.

"Your partner and your senior wife, the ugly one, will be required, as well as your current light of love and her illustrious kin."

Rafik grinned. Hafiz's mention of Rafik's senior, ugly wife was an inside joke. Back when Rafik had been a space miner, he and his partners—Calum Baird and Declan "Gill" Giloglie—had found the infant Acorna adrift in space, saved her from certain death, and raised her. The first time the three miners and Acorna had approached Hafiz together, in order to keep Hafiz from attempting to "collect" Acorna as a "rare specimen," Rafik had veiled and robed both Acorna and Calum and presented them as his wives. He'd told his uncle he had converted to Neo-Hadithianism, a radical fundamentalist branch of the True Faith that permitted and even encouraged polygamy. He had counted on his uncle's respect for his nephew's "wives" to protect Acorna from acquisition. It hadn't worked, and before their visit was over Acorna had been revealed for what she was and Calum for what he was. But before Hafiz could resort to anything too nefarious in his quest to acquire Acorna, he had learned that Acorna was not a one-of-a-kind creature, but only one among many of a populous alien race. Consequently Hafiz had lost interest in Acorna as an acquisition, and learned to value her as an adopted niece. Calum, however, had never quite lived down posing as the senior, very ugly, wife.

"I'm sure they will be most eager to assist in this endeavor, Uncle. However, there is the small matter of Maganos Moonbase to manage, the education of the children . . ."

"Details! Such ideas as mine are as the towering pyramids of the ancients, not to be smothered in the details as numerous as grains of sand. *Bring* the children! Let them learn! They can staff the new businesses, apprentice themselves to the artisans and technicians, provide support. It will be a marvelous experience, an unparalleled learning experience for them!" He considered. "Also, many of the elder ones have already learned how to set up artificial atmospheres and life support systems on lifeless rocks such as this one was prior to its transformation. Their previous training will, no doubt, be helpful—"

"In which case, they should be paid," said Calum Baird, joining them with a mug in his hand, into which he poured a fresh infusion of tea from the tray between Rafik and the Harakamians.

"Like all who join us, the students will be suitably taken care of," Hafiz said. "Food, lodging, travel, richly rewarding associations, toys for the young ones . . ."

Calum rubbed the thumb and first two fingers of his right hand together in a time-honored gesture used for many generations by his canny Celtic ancestors. "The ready, Hafiz. If the children are to learn business, they must also learn to manage their own money. To do so, they need to earn some. If they are to work, they must have a share of the profits. And even at that, I'm not sure we should allow it. To take innocent children beyond the protection of the Federation!"

"Ah, yes," Karina said, regarding him with one of those flashes of sudden shrewdness that lurked like sharks beneath the fathomless sea of mysticism with which she drenched most of her utterances. "I heard how well-protected the children were when they were

employed on Kezdet as child slaves, miners, prosti-
tutes, human fodder for the mills of industry without
decent food or accommodation. The Federation forces
protected them so well then I really doubt the little dar-
lings will be able to bring themselves to part with such
security."

"She has a point," said Khetala, a tall and sturdily
built young woman with dark brown skin and a serious
expression. She had entered from the gangway when
the food had been delivered, accompanied by Dr.
Ngaen Xong Hoa, the meteorologist. Dr. Hoa's shyly
tentative smile and the blazing intelligence in his dark
eyes had kept him from being completely invisible as he
and the girl silently listened to the exchanges between
the Harakamians, Calum Baird, and Rafik.

They were not the only spectators to this conversation, even though Khetala was the first to add her own
contribution to it. As was often the case on Maganos
Moonbase, a good-sized audience of avid listeners
stood around the divan and the chair, taking in every
remark and gesticulation. Which was fine with Rafik
and which seemed to give the theatrical Hafiz and Karina an audience to play to.

Even if the children had not been included in Hafiz's
plan, they would have been welcome to listen. They
were at Maganos Moonbase to learn not only useful
trades but also all of the other survival skills necessary
to living independently and well, skills which could not
be acquired in an atmosphere of adult secrecy or adult
superiority. The kids needed to understand strategy and
self-government, and they learned best by example.
They discovered how to be effective adults by watching

the adults in their lives make decisions, from the beginning of the process to the end.

Khetala, or Kheti, even more than many others, was already respected as a teacher, an organizer, and a leader. As one of the older, stronger children in the mines, Kheti had taken beatings for many of the younger ones and shielded them, lifted loads too heavy for them, and held them together when things seemed hopeless. Toward the end, she had been hauled off to the pleasure houses, and although Acorna had rescued her from that particular pit of despair, Kheti had taken a special interest in helping girls and women who were formerly used in those places regain their self-respect and sense of purpose. Among those who cared about Kezdet she was as much a legend in her own right as Acorna. All of the adults present knew her story.

Hafiz opened his hands, palm up. "I rest my case," he said.

Dr. Ngaen Xong Hoa cleared his throat politely. "I was just discussing with Khetala, Hafiz, which of the children have demonstrated an interest in meteorology. If I am to help you maintain a pleasant atmosphere within the compound at your outpost, energetic assistance from alert young minds would be most beneficial." Dr. Hoa's particular specialty was planetary weather control.

"And we Starfarers will go into action helping set up the communications relays you'll be needing," said Johnny Greene, the computer communications expert of the *Haven*, the Starfarers' ship.

"Good, then I think we are all agreed," Hafiz said

with a universal beam of bonhomie at all who were gathered around him. He rubbed his palms back and forth, "We leave a skeleton staff to keep the moonbase running, and go to seek adventure. It is time to begin gathering what we shall need and, of course, a few small, essential luxuries."

"Oh, goody," said Mercy Kendoro from the edge of the gathering. "Shopping."

In far less time than anyone who had not witnessed the power of House Harakamian in action would have supposed, the initial supplies, provisions, and personnel were acquired, transport was organized, and a flotilla of space vessels, headed by the *Sharazad*, left several respective planets and moons, rendezvoused at a point just outside Kezdet's orbit, and began a long caravan through unmapped space toward the site Hafiz had chosen for his new "trading post."

Three

Since Aari was the only one who really understood the language spoken in the Niriian transmission, Becker hoped the guy would be in a better mood when he woke up from his nap. There was no point in opening the pod until he did. Of course, if there hadn't been anyone aboard who spoke the language, Becker would have opened it, hoped the LAANYE and the computer were up to the task, and tried to figure out its secrets on his own, but right now he could afford to wait. Aari had to wake up eventually.

Becker had other reasons to delay that task as long as possible. Someone needed to note the original location on the planet where each piece of salvage from the wreck had been found, as well as where it was currently stowed aboard the *Condor*, and except for RK and the KEN unit, Becker was the only one awake. Or so he thought.

It had only been a few hours since Becker had left Acorna sleeping next to Aari, totally exhausted. Now she surprised Becker by walking up behind him.

"I can take over again, Captain. Aari is still asleep."

"Don't scare me like that. Clomp a little the next time you wander up behind me, okay? So how's Aari doing? You're pretty sweet on him, aren't you?" Becker asked.

Acorna blushed. "Captain, on narhii-Vhiliinyar people wear shields on their horns, in part to avoid questions just like that. He seems to be resting peacefully now. I am not sure that 'sweet' is the proper term for my feelings for him. I am very interested in Aari, it is true, and I want to help him, as you do."

"Yeah, but *I'm* not his type, " Becker said, running a hand through his grizzled gray and black hair. "I *am* going silver maned, can't argue with that. But I'm not a girl." He grinned at Acorna. Then he had a thought he hoped he was keeping to himself. Aari did like girls, didn't he? Becker figured he did. But there was no evidence here to go on. The guy had not exactly been in any shape for courting during the time that Becker had known him, nor had he mentioned any past loves, which seemed pretty natural considering what he'd gone through and how alone he'd been for most of his life. On the other hand, Aari's treatment of Acorna had been brotherly, though every so often Becker did see him watching Acorna closely, sometimes smiling, sometimes with a troubled expression on his face. If he saw Becker watching him, Aari would look quickly away. And Acorna was probably unaware of Aari's interest, if that's what it was. He always watched her when Acorna was doing something else.

As Becker worried about his shipmates he heard Acorna let loose a big sigh.

"I dunno, Princess, you should probably tell me to

butt out," Becker said, troubled by seeing her lovely eyes cloud.

"Oh, no, Captain, I would value your advice. My aunt intended that I should find a lifemate on narhii-Vhiliinyar but—perhaps because most of the space travelers left early—I did not meet anyone I liked until you came with Aari."

"You really like him or just feel sorry for him?" Becker asked. Why did he feel so fatherly to this gorgeous young woman—well, gorgeous young alien woman—who was taller than he was, probably smarter than he was, and was in full possession of a number of rather spooky powers that were her birthright and had been Aari's, too, before some of them at least were partially looted from him. "You don't have to answer that."

Acorna smiled and patted his hand. "I know you ask only because you care for my happiness, Captain. You are so much like my uncles—"

"Much better looking, of course," Becker said, huffing through his mustache. "*Way* better looking than Baird."

Acorna chuckled. "They say that sort of thing about each other all the time. I do not know what I am supposed to be looking for, to tell you the truth, I have never done this before. I am here because I like to be here and feel that it is time for me to move away from both of my homes, at least for a while. I care for Aari. Perhaps as a healer cares for her patient, but also more than that. I have never decided before to linger beyond the immediate healing I can do. Something in him calls to me. Perhaps he will be a friend of my own species, and closer to my own age than either Grandam or

Maati. Perhaps because of Maati, who is his sister, and is almost like my own little sister, I am here in her stead. . . ."

They locked eyes and he could see that hers were disturbed in a particular way that made his heart ache. He had fallen for a few women over the years, but none of them were willing to live for long on a salvage vessel, though a couple of them had been quite happy to take off with everything on the vessel that wasn't bolted down and a few things that were. They seemed to consider him a little eccentric, too. Mostly he just had his favorite bawdy houses and a favorite girl or two at each when he was in port. But nobody had ever looked at him the way Acorna was looking when she was thinking about Aari.

Roadkill jumped onto his lap and dug all of his claws in, purring madly. Becker sucked in a sharp breath through his teeth and waited for the pain to subside. Then he rubbed the cat's thick brindled fur with his knuckles. "I don't think so, Princess. But you know the guy has a lot of problems. And he probably thinks a classy gal like you wouldn't like a Linyaari with no horn."

Acorna shrugged. "I was raised by men who had no horns. And he will have a horn again some day. But—"

That was as far as they got before they heard Aari's footsteps clanking on the deck plating. He wore no disguise this time, and he said in what was for him a brusque tone, "Now let us see what else the Niriians had to say."

"Okay," Becker said, and reached for a crowbar he kept on the bridge, just in case he wanted to pry or bash one of the second-hand parts that was no longer working. While he was wondering which method would work best with the pod, he heard a series of snaps and clicks.

Turning, he saw that Aari had opened the pod and pulled out what looked—and smelled—like the slimiest mess of cheese Becker had ever seen. It was full of holes, covered in places with green moldy luminescent stuff, and had the fragrance—well, RK had the right idea when he backed up to it and started making shoveling motions with his feet.

Aari grinned up at Becker, showing his rather large teeth in a way that could be intimidating if the guy was pissed.

"What is that?" Becker asked.

"Niriian organic technology," Aari said. "They have developed ways to use products of their own bodies, slightly chemically altered, for functions some peoples achieve with inorganic materials. The biotechnology does not supply all of their needs, of course, but with the properly stabilized balance of biological components and nutrients, quite sophisticated functions, including information storage and retrieval and energy generation, may be performed by . . . lifeforms . . . such as these."

"Yeah, but how do you plug it in?"

Aari laughed. "You don't plug it in, Joh! But it is legible—organically-based arrays can provide a remarkably compact form of data storage. Its contents are accessible in an orderly fashion."

"Oh, sure. Mold and mildew and slime on Limburger cheese—I had an accountant like that one time. Real orderly. Acorna, sweetheart, can you do anything about the stench with—you know?" He was trying to be delicate, pointing at her horn while Aari's head was bent back over the cheesy thing.

"What do you use to retrieve the data?" Acorna asked.

"Yeah, whaddaya use? An ice cream cone?" Becker asked.

Aari rolled his eyes. "No, Joh. The usual scanner the computer uses to examine and analyze objects."

"The Anscan? I don't quite get how that would do the trick, buddy, but whatever you say—hey, you're not putting that thing on my console, are you?" Becker asked. He was not normally all that fastidious, but that smell was more alien invasiveness than he could handle. And the Anscan was expensive.

Acorna set the pod upright and Aari returned the cheese to it.

Then they set the whole gizmo on the console. Aari pulled the Anscan over to where its probe could read the structure of the cheese.

"That is *not* what that delicate piece of equipment was engineered to do!" Becker said.

"The Niriians know that, Joh. Though it is true they have not probably encountered this particular piece of equipment, but they and their trading partners have similar technology and they have developed this device so it will work by this means. There have been many fascinating seminars about how Niriian organic devices can be used with conventional equipment—you should access them sometime."

"Why couldn't they just get electronics like everybody else then?" Becker grumbled. He was getting a little lightheaded, trying to hold his nose so he didn't breathe in those fumes.

"Because this *püyi* is cheaper, more efficient, and entirely homegrown for the Niriians," Aari answered, now using the keyboard to open the interface between the Anscan and ship's computer and com unit.

If Becker wasn't actually astonished to see a bovine two-horned Niriian appear on the com unit screen, he was at least mildly flabbergasted.

"I'll be darned. That cheese *does* work, just like you said."

"It is a *püyi*, Joh."

"It is a pee-yew as far as I'm concerned, but—"

Acorna put her hand to her mouth and made a hushing noise and they listened again to the broadcast.

"Can we stop it and start it so you can translate for us, buddy?" Becker asked.

"Yes. The *püyi* forms a permanent linear archive, but access to information can be controlled by your . . . Anscan."

"Okay. Stop it then. What did he just say?"

"The same thing as before. It was a recorded broadcast, a call for help, what you call a mayday. Their ship was under attack. They identified themselves and gave their location, but the coordinates they listed were far from here and even farther from their home planet."

"Does it say who attacked them and why?" Becker asked.

"Not here."

"Okay, let's see if there's anything else on that monstrosity."

"Undoubtedly, Joh. The *piiyi* is a high-density storage device."

"Dense with stench . . . that I'll agree with," Becker muttered.

Aari went back to work. Once the static had cleared, a Niriian face appeared and began speaking. After a few seconds, Becker asked what it was saying.

"It is the ship's log. I believe we are receiving the last entry first. It is hard to tell, exactly, Joh. This is a different speaker—probably the captain. His dialect is difficult to follow. Wait! Yes! By the Niriian calendar they were transmitting—ummm, you would say, five days ago."

Aari had made his answer quickly, and quietly, keeping one ear focused on the Niriian voice as it droned on.

"Ah, yes." Aari said. "He says that he and his crewmates were on a scouting expedition. You know, Niriians are always looking for greener pastures—like us, they are a grazing people, but they are a rather more numerous race than the Linyaari. He is referring to an earlier entry in the log, something about a very fertile planet and then, disappointingly, signs of previous colonization—no, present colonization. Very, very small signs. One—pod? Does he mean this one? No, he is saying something . . . something about Linyaari."

He shut it down and turned to them, his eyes wide. "Joh, he was saying something about a dwelling place, and a small downed Linyaari vessel, but it was not near where they detected the mammalian life signs. His accent is too thick, Joh."

Acorna said, excitement barely controlled in her voice, "This sounds very important. Perhaps we should forward all this information back to narhii-Vhiliinyar, where some of the Starfarers who have spent time on Nirii can translate it more accurately than we can. In the meantime, we can use Aari and the LAANYE to try to understand the rest of what is being said. I wonder who attacked the ship. . . . And I wonder if the Niriians really found stranded Linyaari outside our normal trade routes and, if so, how our people came to be there?"

"If it was an escape pod, maybe the Linyaari got to the planet in question the same way you told us you reached the human galaxy—you know, ejecting from a ship in trouble," Becker offered.

Acorna's expression became so intense, her mouth so set, and there was such a determined look in her eyes that Becker thought she might be hoping somehow that there had been two life-support pods after all in the space ship her parents had been on, that perhaps they had escaped. He felt obligated to point out to her that it wasn't the most likely possibility.

"We need to get those coordinates and do a little searching ourselves," he said. "They could be people who escaped Ganoosh's and Ikwaskwan's goons when the fake Federation troops were 'arresting' all your people."

Acorna's posture relaxed slightly, dejectedly, at that. "I suppose that's what it must be."

"But you're right. Your people can probably sort this out quicker than we can, and also, maybe somebody who's been to Nirii more recently—wasn't that where your aunt was, Acorna?" he asked. She nodded. "Well, maybe they will know who to notify among the Niriian authorities to let them know the *Hamgaard* ain't coming home no more, no more. And we should probably do a little searching around to find out who is responsible for taking out the *Hamgaard* before we make that report."

If he'd had a hat, he'd have taken it off and placed it over his heart right then. He knew that the cowboy and his crewmates would have families waiting for them in vain back on the old home world. It was one of the hazards of spacefaring that all spacers tried not to think about.

"Yes," Acorna said. "You're right. We'll check all of the fragments of the ship and see if any provide useful evidence. Meanwhile, we can translate as best we can the entire ship's log, and while we're at it, take the coordinates of the place where they saw the escape pod."

"You're sure you don't find anything else about the attack in there, Aari?" Becker asked.

"I will attempt to scan throughout the device for such information." Aari turned back to the Anscan and the *püyi*. The monologue broke off, there was a screech of static, and then, suddenly, there were images on the screen once more.

Horrifying images.

"Holy cow!" Becker said. "Who the hell are the big bugs and what are they doing—oh, no—Cosmos on a crutch! They're torturing that—Aari?"

Acorna's healing must have worked pretty well because Aari spoke in a very calm, controlled voice . . . well, actually, Becker thought, his voice was about as dead as the last fish who tried to swim in a Kezdet river.

"Those are the Khleevi, Joh. And that is me. The Khleevi transmitted the images of my torment to this Niriian ship."

Four

Once the Linyaari space travelers returned, everything should have been fine again. Everybody should have been happy. Maati had thought that she, at least, would be happy. But first Aari had decided not to stay on narhii-Vhiliinyar. And then Khornya, who had begun to seem like a big sister to Maati, had left.

Maati felt left out because none of the space travelers she knew wanted to talk to her about what had happened to them. If she'd been old enough to be able to read other peoples' minds, then maybe she wouldn't have been so lonely and alone, but she doubted it. From the shocked, hurt, and sometimes almost nauseous way those who had not been in space reacted when meeting those who had been, Maati could tell that the spacefarers' experiences had been really bad. You could see in their eyes that the pain lingered inside them, in spite of all the healing Khornya and the Linyaari doctors had attempted to do.

Because so many of the space travelers were seeking out Grandam Naadiina's counsel, since Grandam was the oldest living Linyaari and by far the wisest, Maati couldn't even talk to Grandam. Grandam was much too busy.

It was probably better that way. Maati would have hated to have to admit to Grandam that she didn't feel especially happy to see the others, not when her brother had left and then Khornya had left, too. It might be selfish of her, but it was the way she felt.

If the *viizaar* hadn't been so mean to them, Khornya and Aari might have stayed. Maati had really started to hate the *viizaar*. Hate, she knew, was not a thing a good Linyaari should feel. It was a violent emotion and her people were supposed to be gentle. But the *viizaar* was not gentle. She was mean. She just hid it from everybody, even the people who were good mind readers. Grandam said Liriili was a good administrator because, since she was less sensitive than average for a Linyaari, she could make more objective decisions.

Right. She had made one of those recently, it seemed to Maati. She had decided Maati was an object to be pushed around and sent here and there. Nobody even noticed how nastily she spoke to Maati. Everybody was too busy with the returned space travelers.

When the spacefarers weren't doing some kind of therapy, they were in council, discussing trade agreements and that kind of dumb stuff. Grandam was there, too. At least the council kept ol' Liriili busy so she wasn't always yelling at or for Maati.

Although once, in front of the whole council, just because Maati dropped a piece of hard copy she was bringing from the doctors concerning the wellness of some of the returnees, Liriili had snapped at her.

"Honestly, you are the clumsiest messenger I have ever had! And the slowest! You would have never been given such a responsible position if the council hadn't been softhearted about you being orphaned. And now look at how you repay their trust!"

Everybody was so preoccupied with all the important things they were thinking of that nobody cared when hot blood rose to Maati's face or that her ears rang with *vüzaar* Liriili's hurtful words. She couldn't read their minds, but they could read hers, and in former times people had always been kind. But now nobody cared what one little flunky felt. They were worrying about the grievous hurts their scientists, diplomats, teachers, and traders had suffered.

A hundred faces watched impassively as Maati bent to pick up the paper and hand it to Liriili, who snatched it from her hand. Maati would have been even more humiliated if she thought they were really paying any attention, but clearly almost every single one of them had used the distraction to get lost in his or her own thoughts. Thoughts she couldn't read.

In times past, Liriili would have her stay close by during council sessions, in case messages needed to be delivered to outlying areas, but these days the *vüzaar* couldn't wait to get rid of her. She sent Maati out on the silliest errands, errands that could have been handled easily enough with a beep on the com unit, anything to get Maati out of her sight.

Maati had recently heard *Visedhaanye-feriili* Neeva remark to some of the others, "I wish Khornya and the young man, Aari, had chosen to stay with us. I cannot understand what was so urgent that they had to go collect salvage with Captain Becker."

The notion had crossed Maati's mind that *she* knew exactly who had made them feel like outcasts and made their lives miserable enough to drive them away. Just as that thought crossed her mind the *viizaar*'s voice had cut through her musings like a laser.

"Obviously our Khornya was attracted to the boy and they wished to be alone together without the weight of custom that was unfamiliar to Khornya and that, frankly, the boy is too unstable to deal with at this time. Maati, our water has grown quite stale. Please go fetch some more and see to it that this is disposed of."

Maati barely stopped herself from saying, "What do you think you have a horn on your head for anyway? Freshen it yourself!" But that would really cause trouble. The half-formed thought alone brought a hard stare from Liriili. But Maati was a messenger, not a—a—some kind of a subspecies to be ordered to do busy work because the *viizaar* felt like exercising her authority.

Just when Maati thought it couldn't get any worse, the Ancestors—the one-horned four-leggeds who were one of two species from which, back in the time before the Beginning, the Linyaari had ultimately been formed—sent for Grandam Naadiina. They insisted that she bring with her the space travelers who continued to suffer from nightmares and other emotional ills, despite the healings of their families and physicians. All were to attend the Ancestors in their hilly home. The personal attendants of the Ancestors called the occasion a "retreat." Maati thought of it as an abandonment.

No sooner had Grandam and the others disappeared from sight than the *vüzaar* sent for Maati and informed her that, during Grandam's audience with the Ancestors, the *vüzaar* could not allow a young girl to remain alone in the pavilion she shared with Grandam. Therefore, Maati would be given a guest mat in the *vüzaar*'s tent and would sleep there until Grandam returned.

"That way you will be handy in case I need you," the *Vüzaar* said with a false smile. What she really intended was to keep her own eye on Maati. Every time Maati wanted to go visit with someone, or was asked to graze with a group of other youngsters, Liriili invented some urgent errand for Maati to carry out.

Maati finally realized that the only way she could have time away from the *vüzaar* was if she did what the *vüzaar* was already accusing her of, and dragged her heels on certain errands.

Like her last one. Late in the evening, in the middle of a downpour, she had been sent to the spaceport to take Thariinye, who was on com-shed duty, a basket of hand-plucked greens prepared for him personally by the *vüzaar*. A little note was attached to make sure he knew how he was favored.

When she'd handed him the basket, though, Thariinye had groaned. "Oh, no," he'd said.

Maati shook the water from her mane and peered into the basket. "What's the matter? Don't you like those sorts? Because I'm *not* going to take them back to her. My feet are sore. She keeps me running day *and* night now. I'm tired." She flopped back into the second com-console chair and sprawled.

"I'm sorry, little one. You want any of these? They're

perfectly good grasses. I'm just not, you know, wanting
to accept any favors from our lady leader."

Maati's eyes narrowed and she studied him a moment. Thariinye had changed a little since he and
Khornya first returned from the galaxy of her people.
He had been sooo full of himself when they arrived, and
had boasted that he and Khornya were to be handfasted
as lifemates. But later, oddly, Maati had heard from
many young females to whom Thariinye had also paid
court. They were all complaining that if only Khornya
had no claim on him, Thariinye would gladly ask them
to graze with him forever. But really, as he and Maati
both very well knew, Khornya hardly liked him at all,
much less wanted him for a lifemate. Thariinye was
very handsome, if you liked the tall, slim, muscular
type, but Khornya was somehow . . . older, smarter than
he was, and she didn't like his attitude—Thariinye was
a bit conceited. But Maati had to admit that any male
who could successfully string along so many females
who could read minds had to have something going for
him. A lot of *nyiiri*, Grandam said. Which meant something similar to courage, except that it meant he was
courageous enough to act on things he shouldn't actually be acting on and say things he shouldn't really be
saying.

"Maybe she's just letting you know she doesn't think
you're so bad, even though those ladies complained
about you wooing both of them," Maati ventured, with
a little of her own *nyiiri*, watching him to see what he
would say.

A crack of thunder heralded a gust of wind that sent
rain splashing in huge puddles against the viewports of

the com-shed. In the distance, jagged lightning sliced through the blackened sky, strobing the night with brief but brilliant flashes.

Thariinye snorted and gave her a smile as phony as the one he gave his extra girlfriends. "Such a sweet little youngling you are, Maati. Of course she doesn't think I'm so bad. After hearing all those other girls tell her what a splendid specimen of manhood I am, she's courting me herself."

It was Maati's turn to snort. "You've been away from space too long, Thariinye! You've got ground-sickness!" It was the sort of joke the spacers made about ground people and ground people made about spacers to explain their peculiarities. It was the only thing Maati could think of, other than Thariinye's high opinion of himself, to explain why he would imagine the *viizaar* capable of any softer, more female feelings at all.

"No. No. It's true. She fancies me. Always says so. Told me she thinks I need a more experienced woman to guide me, keep me in line, and yet be able to indulge my little flights of independence. Youngling, that is the last thing I need. No Khleevi will ever scare me as much as that woman!" He shuddered so hard his mane shook and his skin twitched.

Maati was shocked. "But Liriili is really *old*. She's almost as old as Grandam, I bet—as old as Neeva, anyway and you're—well, I'm just a kid and even *I* remember when you were still a dapple gray!"

Thariinye made a wry face. "Maybe you see her as being old, but when I'm around her, Liriili acts like a frisky filly. I don't think narhii-Vhiliinyar is big enough for both of us."

"I know exactly what you mean," Maati replied, remembering her own troubles. She wouldn't tell Thari-inye about them, though. He'd get all adult and bossy on her if she did, she was sure. It was never a good idea to let him have the upper hand. She had figured that out because she knew several of those silly girls he'd been involved with. As long as they didn't seem to notice him, he sought them out and was very polite, even humble, with them. But as soon as they started to like him, he didn't care for them anymore and went trotting off after somebody else. That was part of why he kept after Khornya even though the two of them basically didn't get along very well.

Maati gave him a sly look. "I guess that's what you get for being irresistible! So, all right, I'll help you get rid of your gift if you'll pass me one of those *thülsis*. They're my favorites." He handed her one of the tender yellow-green grasses which smelled spicy and tasted sweet with a little tang to it.

He gnawed absently on one himself. "I should have known what she was doing when she wouldn't let me go with Neeva and Melireenya. Now everybody who was anybody among the space-chosen has had a traumatic experience that will probably bond them forever, and because Liriili kept me planet-bound, I alone was left out."

"I can see why you would be mad at her for making you miss being mistreated until you almost died," Maati agreed.

"You're far too young to understand," he said loftily.

"Receiving transmission from the alien salvage vessel *Condor*," a quiet computerized voice said from the com set. "Please stand by."

The lightning flashed again and again, the thunder crashing just after. Thariinye turned up the volume on the com unit.

"We have just recovered the wreckage of a Niriian vessel," Aari's voice said, sounding strange and flat. "Among the ship's artifacts is a *püyi* containing the ship's log and several other messages. Please stand by to record the material you are about to receive." There was no visual transmission, but Maati was pleased to hear Aari's voice, no matter how fleetingly. This message was evidently sent several hours ago, according to the time stamp, so that real-time exchange of communication now wouldn't be possible. Maati wished she could talk to her brother, but that clearly wasn't going to be possible on this night.

"It is extremely urgent that the information on this *püyi* be fully translated and interpreted immediately by an expert in the Niriian language. It contains evidence that the Niriian ship made contact with the Khleevi"—Aari's voice faltered for a moment—"and prior to that perhaps discovered a Linyaari escape pod and survivors on an uncharted planet. Once translation is made, please respond immediately to the *Condor*." Aari signed off and silence filled the com-shed.

Maati jumped to her feet. "I'll go try to find a specialist." Looking out at the slashing rain, she hated leaving the warmth and dryness of the com-shed.

"Where do you think you'll do that?" Thariinye said. "The spacefarers are on retreat, remember?"

"This is important enough to call them off retreat. I mean, if the Khleevi are involved, we'd better let Liriili know right away. She can call them back."

"I speak excellent Niriian," Thariinye told her. "My first off-planet mission was to Nirii and I have always been good at languages."

"Well, that's good," Maati said. "Get started right away on that broadcast. But Liriili will have my horn if I don't let her know at once."

"I'll let her know. Just stay put for a *naanye*, will you?"

He switched to the domestic com unit. "*Viizaar* Liriili, this is Thariinye at spaceport communications. We have just received a message from Aari aboard the *Condor* concerning a recovered Niriian *püyi* with information about a probable recent encounter with the Khleevi as well as something or other about a Linyaari escape pod with survivors left stranded on an uncharted planet. We are being asked to translate and advise the *Condor* of the contents immediately."

"Then do so," Liriili said. They could only hear her voice. The *viizaar* did not switch on visuals at her end. She sounded grouchy and sleepy. "You speak Niriian, do you not, Thariinye?"

"You wish me to do it, then, ma'am? You don't wish, for instance, to send for Melireenya or *visedhaanye-feriili* Neeva?"

Liriili's voice took on a softer lilt as she woke up enough to realize to whom she was speaking. "I have every confidence in you, dear boy. If Aari's impression that there is urgent information contained in the *püyi* is confirmed by your translation, please alert me at once. If it is indeed as important as Aari says—though you know his experiences have made him somewhat . . . unstable, shall we say, just between us?—

then of course you should send the messenger girl after another expert. But I would prefer not intrude upon the retreat the Ancestors have declared vital to the recovery of our spacefarers unless I feel it is absolutely necessary."

"Yes, ma'am."

"And, Thariinye?"

"Ma'am?"

"I shall expect a personal and confidential report of your findings in my quarters as soon as you have finished."

"Yes, ma'am." He signed off, shaking his head in frustration.

It was a good thing Liriili couldn't see Thariinye's face, Maati thought. He gave the most awful grimace and bared his teeth something fierce.

"You probably should go back and sleep," Thariinye told her pompously. "I'll be too busy to baby-sit you while I have duties to perform."

"You want me to leave? In this stuff?" she asked, nodding to the weather, which seemed to grow wilder by the moment. "No way! I am not bailing out just when something interesting is finally happening. Let's have a look."

"I don't think this material is fit for children," he argued. "If the Khleevi are in it—I have seen them in action. Trust me. They'll give a youngling like you nightmares."

"Aari said 'urgent,' Thariinye. Don't you think you should stop arguing with me and get to work?" she asked.

"Are you sure Liriili isn't grooming you to be the next

viizaar?" he grumbled. "You're very bossy for a youngling."

"The *püyi*?" she pointed to the com screen, tension twanging through her body so hard she thought she'd snap. It worked. Thariinye turned back to the console. She watched the visuals and listened to the Niriian voice speaking as Thariinye began the painstaking work of translating and transcribing the Niriian broadcast from the beginning. Of course, he brought up a computer translation of the broadcast on screen almost immediately. But verifying the translation and interpreting the nuances of the broadcast took time and concentration. He listened to the alien words while watching the accompanying visuals and the streaming machine translation on the com screen. Sometimes he would amend the machine translation, and other times he let it proceed unchanged. Because he was working with a recording, he could halt the broadcast and back it up when he needed to. He was a lot better than she expected him to be at the work, actually. He didn't have to stop very often, and it was clear he took it quite seriously.

When he got to the shots of the escape pod lying in the greenery by the makeshift shelter, Maati got a funny feeling in her stomach. As the shot went by, she felt as if a part of her was still there, with the pod, wherever it had landed.

She was almost sure she knew those markings. In fact, the whole pod looked familiar, though it was hustling by on the screen too fast to be sure. Even though she didn't make a sound, Thariinye hit the stop button on the broadcast and turned to her.

"What was that?" Thariinye said and then she knew for sure that he was reading her.

"The pod," she said. "Whose pod was that?"

"I don't know. And I'll need that information for my report. Go look it up for me, will you? There's no one at the other computer." He gestured to the opposite wall. All Linyaari ships were unique, and it was a simple matter to match the markings to the master list of ships. She also wanted a listing of the people aboard the ship on the date that the Niriian broadcast indicated the shot had been taken. Lists of crews and passengers, projected and actual itineraries, manufacturing and maintenance records—in short, anything that affected the ships throughout their time in the Linyaari fleet could be found in the government computers.

So compelling was her feeling of connection with the pod that she didn't even wait to see what else was on the *püyi*, but did as Thariinye asked and opened the flight records.

She started scrolling through the files, after telling the computer to check the most current entries first. Surely, she thought, the pod belonged to one of the ships whose crew had been attacked by the criminals Khornya and her friends had freed the space travelers from. But the computer didn't list the pod as being registered to any of the ships now in active service and currently in space. That was odd.

She expanded the boundaries of her search. And kept digging, listening to the thunder crash and crack outside while inside the Niriian monologue mumbled away, and now and then Thariinye would say, "To the—sanctuary? No. Hiding place? That's not it either—" as he tried to find the proper Linyaari translation.

Then she heard him say something about "Khleevi" and turned to look. She had never seen a Khleevi. She was curious, in a horrified sort of way. What did such vicious and voracious beings look like?

She turned her chair around to view the screen over Thariinye's shoulder. The bug-like Khleevi were only visible as feelers and legs and shell-like carapaces around the margins of the vid. In the center of the screen was the main subject of the transmission. His face was distorted with blood, sweat, and agony, and his body was even more broken than it had been when she had first seen him. But she could not mistake her brother.

"Thariinye," she said, her voice tight with emotion, "that's Aari! The Khleevi have Aari! What can we do? Are we too late? We have to help him. Where are Khornya and Captain Becker? Have they been killed already?"

Thariinye turned slightly and looked at her, his face as serious as she had ever seen it, and perhaps a bit green, too. "This is an old vid, Maati. Probably a Khleevi broadcast to the Niriian ship. The Khleevi like to do that—send pictures of old tortures to the people they plan to make their next victims. Nobody knows why. But that's what this is. Look there—see—Aari still has part of his horn. Long slices have been carved away, but it's there. This is what happened to him before you saw him."

She didn't recognize the emotion that was making Thariinye's voice sound so strangled. Perhaps he was trying not to throw up. Abruptly, he switched off the visuals.

Maati felt as if her heart had been clutched in a tight fist and then suddenly released to fall thudding to the floor. Her breath came out in a rush. "That's horrible. Horrible. Are the Khleevi—are they coming—h-h-here?" She was stuttering now through chattering teeth and felt cold all over, a reaction that had nothing to do with the temperature in the room, and everything to do with what she'd just witnessed.

"No. I told you. It's an old vid. They sent this to the people aboard the ship that carried this *püyi*. Any luck on that registration design?"

"Not yet," she said, and turned back to her task with a new sense of urgency, widening the parameters of her search. The ordinariness of looking for information steadied her and gradually her hands stopped shaking. And, at last, there it was—the design, the number, and the name of the ship that had carried that pod. And the names of the people aboard when it shipped out on its last flight. A chill engulfed her again.

"Th-Thariinye?"

"I'm almost done, Maati."

"B-but—Thariinye. I found it."

"Good. Just a moment."

"No, now. It's important. The ship the pod was on? It was registered to my parents. To mine and Aari's parents. The people on the Niriian ship found them. I thought they were dead—but if the Niriians are correct, maybe they're not. At least, not both of them, at least not when this pod was found."

"That is wonderful," Thariinye said. "We need to let

Liriili know at once. I thought this *püyi* was bad news, but it seems we have at least one cause for celebration among the information it brought us!" He put the final touches to his translation and uploaded it to the *vüzaar*.

"We have to tell Aari and Khornya and Captain Becker," Maati said. "They can go get our mother and father."

"Yes, yes, but first Liriili must know. It's procedure," he said, going all adult again. Thariinye turned back to the com station.

He hailed Liriili and told her what they had discovered.

"I just thought it prudent," he finished, "to let you know the contents of the message before transmitting my interpretation to the *Condor*."

"Thank you, Thariinye. That is very interesting. In light of your information, I think that tomorrow I shall send an emissary to the Ancestors to let them know what has been discovered. However, there will be no further transmissions from the com station. Not to the *Condor* or anywhere else."

"But, honored lady! Aari, at least, should know immediately—the pod is apparently that of Aari and Maati's parents, who have been missing—"

"I know that very well, Thariinye. I also know now, from hard past experience, that any transmission we send may endanger this planet. If Khleevi are out there, we will not let them know our current location. It is simply too dangerous. The evacuation ships must be prepared, and steps taken for all Linyaari to escape the planet, if necessary."

"Again?" Thariinye said. "Where will we go this

time? And what about Acorna—she and Aari are out there near the source of the message. They sent it to us, in fact. Do they not deserve to know what we've learned?"

"As soon as possible I will consult the *aagroni* and make the decision as to where we must go. Dear boy, I know this is difficult for you to understand," Liriili said. "But you simply must trust my judgment. We cannot send transmissions, and that is that. I will not put this planet in any further danger, no matter what. If anything else pertinent comes in, let me know."

Thariinye ended the transmission with an exasperated snort. "I can't believe that! Can you?'

"From her? Sure," Maati said. "The question is, what are we going to do about it?"

"We?" Thariinye asked with maddening superiority. "*We* will do nothing, youngling. I, however, am going to borrow one of the ships from the spaceport, and fly it to wherever I have to go to so Khornya will know how much danger she and her friends are in, and how much hope there is that Aari's parents are still alive. And then I'll rescue your parents. If Khornya and her friends want to come along, well, so much the better."

"I'm going, too." Maati said.

"No, you're not."

"I am, too, and you can't stop me."

"I can, too. I'm bigger, in case you hadn't noticed."

"As if you'd let me forget. But if you try to go without me, I'll tell Liriili what you're doing in time to stop you."

"You wouldn't do that. You want to save your parents and your brother and Khornya as much as I do."

"More," Maati said firmly, crossing her arms across her small chest. "That's why I'm going. So you don't mess it up."

"So I don't—"

"That's what I said. My family have been spacefarers for generations, just like yours. I will do fine in space. And you need backup. To get it, all you have to do is teach me the controls. Two will be better than one. I think we should leave right now."

"In this storm?"

"The ships are built to handle worse. Once we leave the atmosphere, the weather won't be any problem, will it?"

"It's easy to see you haven't had the parental discipline you need."

"At least I don't tell the same lie to six different girls and expect them all to believe it and like me afterward."

Thariinye didn't say anything to that, and Maati didn't need to be able to read minds to know she'd won.

"Come on, then. We'll take the *Niikaavri*. I've been checked out on her already and she's loaded and fueled and ready to go. We can be out of here before anyone can stop us."

In her quarters, Liriili mentally followed Thariinye as he and Maati boarded the *Niikaavri* and prepared for take-off. She was not ignoring the threat of the Khleevi. But if the information from the *piiyi* was correct, their enemies were at the far end of the galaxy—weeks away even in the worst possible extrapolation of risk, and with many likely targets between them and the Linyaari to slow them down. Tomorrow—today, actually, as it was early morning now, she would send another, more trustworthy messenger than Maati to the Ancestors — one she could control. She would ask for another translator, one she would hand-pick for discretion, and when Thariinye's findings were either verified or modified, then would be time enough to send runners to the general populace, to alert the spacefarers, possibly even to prepare the evacuation ships if necessary.

But at present, she felt sure the Khlcevi did not know where the new Linyaari homeworld was, and she had protected their position by disallowing all outgoing transmissions from narhii-Vhiliinyar. Becker's vessel was hardly a Linyaari ship, and once the troublesome Maati and Thariinye had joined the *Condor* they could all look after each other.

The girl had become a hazard, her very existence menacing Liriili's position by threatening to "expose" her to the spacefarers for alienating Khornya and Aari. The child didn't understand the delicacy of Liriili's task in leading the planet, the careful balance that had to be maintained for the good of all. And, as for Thariinye . . . Who did he think he was, ducking away from her delicate overtures? He, too, was a hazard, disrupting the peace of so many of the young females, and not realizing that he obviously needed a mate who could guide him and help him control his less responsible impulses. He blamed her, she knew, for she could read him even when his horn was shielded, just as if he was made of plasglas. He had wanted to go on the *Balaküre*'s last mission, and he thought she had robbed him of glory. Very well, let him seek it now. Perhaps when — and if — he returned, he would be much wiser, would understand that her counsel had been for his own good. But, as for now, her two most difficult charges were headed off-planet, possibly never to return. She'd sleep well tonight.

She arose the next morning at a leisurely pace, and halfway through cleansing herself, answered the call from the spaceport com-shed. "Yes?"

"*Vïizaar*, I am here to relieve Thariinye, only Thariinye is not here. The equipment is on and there is a strange message looping through the monitor, but Thariinye is absent."

"How strange," she said. "In this weather, where can he have gone? It's hardly fit outside for grazing." Thunder was once more booming outside the pavilion and the cracks of lightning could be seen indistinctly through the fabric of the walls. Liriili shivered lightly, and pulled a blanket across her shoulders.

"Also, ma'am, one of the spacecraft is not in its berth."

"How strange. Was it there yesterday? Perhaps it has been taken for repairs?"

"No, ma'am. I—wait—there *is* a note here from Thariinye. He says that he and Maati—surely he cannot mean little Maati the messenger!"

"Surely not," Liriili agreed.

"—Have gone to look for the girl's parents. He also wishes to warn others of a Khleevi presence detected in this galaxy by a Niriian vessel—that's the message on the com screen."

"How very extraordinary," Liriili said. "Stay at your post, then—is it Iiril this morning?"

"Yes, ma'am."

"Stay at your post, Iiril. Be alert for incoming messages, but under no circumstances are you to answer them. There will be no outgoing messages of any kind from this planet until further notice from me. Do I make myself clear?"

"With Khleevi in the vicinity? Yes, ma'am, absolutely."

"I will send to the hills of the Ancestors and ask those spacefarers on retreat to return for a special meeting of the Council on this matter."

"I'll be right here, ma'am. Even if we're not to respond, Thariinye may report back to us with more information about the Khleevi."

"My thoughts exactly, Iiril," she said, and ended the transmission.

"I don't get it," Becker snapped, glowering at the com screen. "For six weeks that damn thing is squawking at all hours with messages from everyone from your grandma and your aunt, Acorna, to that—woman— who runs the place. 'Pick us up a nice trade alliance when you go home, honey. See if you can get us good terms on joining the Federation. And don't forget a pint of milk and a loaf of bread while you're at it.' "

Aari and Acorna looked at each other and shrugged, then returned their attention politely to Becker's rant.

"And now, when we have something really important to tell them, when we need to hear back from them right away, we get zip for a week and a half. What *is* it with those people, anyway?"

He was not the only one who wanted to know. Aari and Acorna had spent every waking hour with the

LAANYE and the Niriian logbook, then, while sleeping, learning the nuances of the Niriian language from the LAANYE's sleep-learning programs. They listened over and over again to the mayday message and the ship's log entries. If the captain had given specifics about the transmission from the Khleevi, the details of the ship's final hours, or any findings pertaining to the location of the vessel pictured on the verdant planet, they had not found them. They *had* deciphered an entry that was a personnel list of the crew aboard the downed Niriian vessel.

The *Condor* had picked up more of the wreckage of the Niriian ship in the meantime, but very little of the equipment was intact.

All of them had been listening, even in their sleep, for a signal from the com unit, but not a single word out of it did they hear the entire time.

"Well, RK doesn't seem to have any opinion about this, and normally I'd flip a coin," Becker said. "But since I have a crew I guess I better ask—what do you guys think we ought to do?"

"Do?" Aari asked. His voice was a little hoarse from disuse. He and Acorna had been concentrating so hard on the translations he would have neglected to eat if Becker hadn't finally become worried about his crewmates and tromped down to the hydroponics deck to pluck some greenery for them. He had no idea what a tasty or nutritious combination was composed of but figured if they'd planted something, it was supposed to be edible. They both took his offerings, nibbled abstractly, and kept translating. Even after Acorna was as certain as she could be that they had made good sense of the messages, Aari continued to go over and over them.

Acorna could not help but read the anxiety Aari was broadcasting as surely as the com system was not. Her head pounded with the strain he was experiencing, as well as her own pain. She couldn't usually read him literally, but this sense of anxiety was more of an emotional maelstrom spinning around him and enveloping her than a conscious stream of thought. Even Becker and the cat were out of sorts, all from dealing with the heavily charged atmosphere inside the *Condor*.

Becker was continuing. "Yeah, what do you think we should do—you know, as in action? Here's our options, the way I see it. Number one," he ticked off the fingers of his right hand with the forefinger of his left. "We head on out of here, back to Federation space, and warn people about this. However, this area ain't Federation and they aren't going to come all this way uninvited by the locals. Two, we can turn around and go back to narhii-Vhiliinyar and ask 'em face-to-face why they aren't speaking to us. Of course, it could be that the Khleevi's got their tongue—sorry, Aari," he said. "In which case, we'll hope we see some evidence of the damage before we reach the planet and get our own derrieres in a sling or slings, as the case may be. If we do, we will return to option one and call out the posse. If we can round one up in time. Option three happens if there are no Khleevi and everything is cool on the planet. I kick some administrative heinie and make them promise never, ever, ever to ignore us like that again, no matter what. Or option four—we try to figure out what's going on for ourselves, keeping our eyes open so we don't get ourselves killed, and see what's needed before we hare off and run for help. End of options, unless you can think of any others. Aari? Acorna?"

"Joh, we must go back to my planet," Aari said. "They must know. The Niriians must be warned, as well."

"Yes," Acorna said. "You know, it *is* possible we have gone out of range even for a delayed relay to narhii-Vhiliinyar. There are several wormholes and space distortions between us and them, and we *are* very far off the traveled routes where communications are routinely boosted at regular intervals. We cannot be sure they have received our broadcast. The likeliest explanation for their silence is that they have not heard from us. It's essential that they be aware of the presence of the Khleevi in this part of the world, and also of the possibility that Aari and Maati's parents are still alive somewhere. If the Khleevi are in the neighborhood, our people need to have the evacuation ships ready, and a plan to board them prepared. After we warn the Linyaari, we should return to Federation space and alert the authorities that my people, who have been considering applying for membership, will possibly soon be under attack by the Khleevi. The Federation has already seen the nature of the Khleevi—after the battle on Rushima they're aware of the sort of creatures we are dealing with here—and know that they pose a threat that cannot be ignored. Also, we should consult with Uncle Hafiz and the others and ask them to prepare a new haven for my people, should it be necessary to evacuate, some temporary place where they may stay until the situation is resolved."

"That makes sense," Becker said. "But somehow I can't help but thinking that they're okay for now and it's that snotty lady-dog of a leader of yours who is behind this."

"You could be right," Acorna said, "but we cannot risk it. If our people are to be safe, they must get those ships ready, and that will take time."

RK, who had been sleeping with one eye open, idly flipping the end of his tail up and down, suddenly yawned and stretched. In a casual way his outstretched, kneading claw hooked Becker's arm.

"Ow!" he said. "Okay, the fourth member of the crew has voted. We're changing course."

Five

Thariinye tracked the *Condor*'s erratic course from the data sent with the transmission. Maati watched him while he made his computations. Maati took to space travel like a *kidaaki* to water. Her favorite hiding places back home had been the techno-artisan village and the spaceport, and with a child's curiosity she had examined the interiors of all the ships, even the big evacuation vessels. She'd asked questions constantly, so many that she was afraid the workers would tell her to leave, or call Liriili and ask her if the government didn't have something better to do with its messengers than have them bother people.

But actually she had made friends with most of the people she talked to. Aarliiyana, a motherly techno-artisan, had explained all about the colorful designs on the hulls of the ships, how they were based on the banners of the most distinguished Linyaari clans and individuals. Aarliiyana had also told her that the techno-artisans had developed a new and more advanced cloaking technology for Linyaari spacecraft. The very craft Maati was now riding in, named after her dear friend Acorna's grandmother, was the first craft to incorporate the new system.

Hidden among the brightly pigmented coatings used on the hulls were a field generator that could create the illusion of invisibility and a radiation absorption matrix, or RAM. The two would, between them, defeat sonar, radar, infrared, and all other traditional detection methods used to trace the location of a spacecraft. These systems could be turned on and off at will. In addition, the techno-artisans had developed ways to deal with the engine exhaust, the ship's communications, and so on, so that the ship's location could not be determined by any means. Even the ship's locator beacon was routinely cloaked to both friends and foe, unless the ship's captain made the decision to turn it on. That had to be done occasionally so that the craft could move through crowded shipping lanes without running the risk of being rammed by vessels that had no idea she was there.

It made Maati feel odd, knowing that nobody could find them out here in space, unless they chose to be found.

Being on shipboard when the vessel was in space as opposed to being inside it when it was docked at the techno-artisan's village was very different. For one thing, the air was drier, and it smelled peculiar, almost canned. Perhaps because of the drier air, she found her sense of smell was diminished, blunted in some way. It gave her a curiously light feeling. And also, consequently, the grasses in the hydroponics garden — many fewer varieties than grew dirtside—were not as tasty as they were at home. Well, the tastes were subtler, maybe. She figured she'd get used to the change soon enough.

With her sense of smell reduced, her sense of sight seemed to be more important, somehow. The inner surfaces of the ship were made of brightly colored materials softer to the touch than metals, and the crew's quarters were designed to look like small traveling pavilions. Sort of cozy, really. At first she missed the horizon, and the sweeping vistas of grass and town and distant hills she was used to at home, but when she went to the bridge and looked out the viewport into the stars, her homesickness faded. How could those grassy fields compare with the beauty of deep space? She was lost in wonder. The galaxy gleamed like a jewel box before her. And she'd barely begun to taste the joys of space travel. How would it look at night on a planet with one moon? What about a planet with rings—how would that look from the ground? How thrilling to think she would soon be seeing for herself! Even with the looming threat of the Khleevi hovering in the back of her mind, she felt freed, somehow, for the first time in her life.

And if she was going to have adventures, she'd picked the right ship to have them in. In addition to being comfortable, the *Nükaavri* was equipped with all of the newest devices her techno-artisan friends had demonstrated. Maati already knew that because Thariinye had shown off the ship's features when he returned from his first brief flight, greeting the *Condor* and the many Linyaari ships when they returned carrying the spacefarers from captivity.

"Does this ship have any weapons?" Maati had wanted to know then.

"What would you know about weapons?" Thariinye had asked in that tone that made her feel like a total child.

"Grandam told Khornya that her father had developed a defense weapon that would destroy our enemies if they attempted to capture one of our ships. Grandam said it was how Khornya's parents were killed—when their ship self-destructed along with the Khleevi chasing them. She thought Khornya's folks must have used it on themselves after Khornya's pod was ejected. The force of the blast was the only way to explain how far away Khornya was when she was found by the men who raised her." Maati had been wondering at the time if that was how her parents died, using a similar weapon to destroy themselves and their ship before the Khleevi could capture them.

"Yes, the *Nükaavri* is equipped with the defensive system," Thariinye said. "But no offensive weapons. That would be *ka*-Linyaari, against everything we believe in. The ship does have all the very latest innovations, of course. You ask too many questions."

Why, of all the people she'd ever met, did she have to be on the ship with *him*? Nobody else among the spaceport personnel, the techno-artisans, or the spacefarers treated her like she was inferior just because she was younger and shorter than they were. In contrast to Liri-ili and her political friends, the spacefarers had, with rare exceptions, treated her with respect.

But she was stuck with Thariinye and supposed she'd have to make the best of it, at least if she wanted to get to Khornya and Aari, and maybe, just maybe, her parents. It was an unfamiliar feeling in her heart, the thought that there was a possibility they were still alive.

When Maati wasn't arguing with Thariinye, she watched the tutorials that came with every new ship's complement of programs and she took herself through a simulation of Captain Becker's course.

The human employed unusual navigation methods, diving into unplotted wormholes and through unexplored folds in space rather than following conventional spaceways. If she and Thariinye were going to manage to rendezvous with the *Condor*, they would have to do the same. Thariinye confirmed her hunch, when she asked him point-blank about their course.

Now Thariinye looked nervous as the entrance to the wormhole loomed before them, but then he grinned and got a strange gleam in his eye. He shifted to manual controls. "Strap down, youngling," he said.

"I *am* strapped in," she said. "Hurry up, will you?"

"Okay. Yeeeeeeeheeee!" he cried, a little anticlimactically. She really didn't notice much. There was nothing to see. One moment the opening was ahead of them and the next it was behind them. The stars were in different places. That was all.

And—something else.

"Well, look at you, little girl," Thariinye said, when he turned to glance at her and the glance became a stare. "You are now a bona fide star-clad spacefarer."

She was! She really was. Her skin had been getting a little lighter since they left, and the pale spots in her mane broadening to overcome the black parts, but now, her hands below the cuff of her shipsuit were white!

Completely. As white as Thariinye's, or Khornya's, or Aari's. She wanted to run for the nearest reflective surface but got tangled in her safety restraint straps, her fingers fumbling as she tried to release the catch. At last she got free and was able to examine herself in the grooming device. Her face was as pale as the second moon, her mane pure silver, and her horn golden, though still of a childishly stubby length. She frowned at her reflection.

"Does this color make me look plumper?" she asked Thariinye, and immediately regretted it.

He laughed. "Of course not. And even if it did, there's nothing to be done about it. You're star-clad now, youngling."

"How come it happened so fast?" she asked.

He shrugged. "I don't know. Usually the change is more gradual. Maybe the shift of light inside the wormhole accelerated the process."

"There wasn't any light—was there?"

"Of course there was *light*. You're confusing your basic physics. That was a wormhole, not a black hole."

"I *know* that," she said. "I'm just young, not stupid. But I didn't see any light till we came out on this side."

"You probably blacked out," he said. "Fear will do that. Your first time in space and all that."

"I *did not*," she told him. "I just didn't see any light. Did you? Honestly?"

"Well, no, but then, probably I couldn't pick it up. We were travelling so fast and it—"

"Forgotten your basic physics?" she asked sweetly. "What's next on the course?"

"Cross this planetary system from here," she put her

finger on a purplish planet that was farthest from its sun, "to over here," this was past the seventh planet from the sun, "and then there's a sort of funny part of space—bumpy, as if it's pleated. . . ."

"You can see that?" he asked, peering at her finger as if it had eyes.

"I did the simulation, silly. Maybe you should, too. Oh. I forgot. Experienced Starfarers don't need to do that stuff."

"We'll have no insubordination out of you, youngling."

"Fine. You asked. I told you."

She left him alone on the bridge and stomped down to the hydroponics area to do some serious grazing. And pouting, if the truth be known. The *Condor* had been gone for six weeks before the *Nükaavri* launched. They had only been in space for ten sleep periods. Maati tried to think about what she would say to her parents if she saw them again, how she would convince Khornya and Aari to let her stay with them instead of returning to narhii-Vhiliinyar. But even her vivid imagination began to run out of ideas after a while. She thought about it, analyzed the jittery feeling that made it hard for her to sit still. That wasn't all. Her attention wandered at any excuse, and everything Thariinye said was sounding even stupider than usual. She had a thousand questions about how everything on the ship worked, but lacked the patience to listen to Thariinye's lectures on the subject. She wanted to climb behind the panels and see how things worked instead of just sitting and waiting. And waiting. And waiting.

She was bored. Here she was on the greatest adventure

of her whole life and she was sooooo bored. She was used to having the run of Kubiilikhan, keeping so busy she was exhausted at the end of the day. To having conversations with people from all walks of life all over the city and surrounding countryside. Here on this ship she mostly sat. And talked to Thariinye. Who treated her like a baby. By the Ancestors, something had better happen soon!

Her wish was granted in seven more sleep periods. She had been using the LAANYE Thariinye brought along to brush up on Khornya's language—Standard. She wanted to be as fluent as possible when she saw Khornya, Aari, and Captain Becker again. If she could speak the language, maybe they wouldn't fuss too much when she announced she intended to stay with them, wanted to go back with them to that moon Khornya had mentioned where all the children lived and learned new skills.

It was her watch and she was tired of studying.

If only the *Condor* weren't still so far away! Linyaari ships were faster than those of the humans, so they should be overtaking the salvage vessel before long, but she wished fervently that they were *there* already. She ran the course simulation again, wondering if maybe she could plot a more direct route instead of simply following Thariinye's extrapolation of the *Condor*'s course.

As she calculated and plotted her various trajectories, she noticed some familiar-looking coordinates among her calculations.

"Thariinye?" she said, speaking into the onboard hailing system.

He huffed and snorted, from which she gathered that she'd awakened him.

"If we just deviate two degrees from Captain Becker's course for a few hours, we'll be at the point where the Niriians saw the planet with my parents' escape pod on it."

"Hmm? Oh. Good."

"I think we should alter our planned route and find my parents before we go see Captain Becker and the others. Shall we change course?"

"Oh, yeah, okay. Fine, kid. Don't bother me," he said and then before she could draw another breath said, "*What?* No, no, Maati, wait. Don't you *dare* touch anything! I was asleep. I'll be right there!"

She shook her head when she saw him, rubbing his eyes, his mane all flattened on the left side. He stumbled a little when he walked.

"You—didn't touch anything, did you?" he asked.

"No. That's technically your job. That's why I called. But I do think we should try to get my folks since they're sorta on the way." She tugged at his sleeve, and pointed to the screen where the course she had been plotting intersected with the familiar coordinates.

"Absolutely not." He looked again, tapped a button, compared her course with the original tracing of the *Condor*'s. "What's this all about?"

"I was trying to make our trip shorter and faster. The *Condor* is just looking for junk. They are not in any hurry, and they are rambling all over the place while they are looking. They are not trying to take the most direct route through space. But we do not have to follow their path. We could reach them faster by plotting a more direct course."

"Oh, we could, could we? I suppose now that you're

star-clad, you think you know as much about navigation as seasoned spacefarers, do you?"

"It's not that. It's just that if those horrible things that hurt my brother are out here too, I don't want them to find my parents all stranded on some deserted planet. I wanted to come with you so that I could help you save them. And if we keep on our present course, it will take forever to reach where the *Condor* was. Then we'd have to try to find it from there and, meanwhile, my parents could die."

"Ummm," Thariinye said again, tracing each route simultaneously with both hands. "If we take this shorter route, we could rescue your parents on our way and still rendezvous with the *Condor* in half the time I figured." Maati looked up at him with wide, approving eyes but inwardly she was laughing about how he was making this whole thing sound like his own idea. "Very well then. I'll change course now."

He did, putting on quite a show for her benefit—embellishing his movements with graceful little flourishes, humming to himself the "Hero's Gallop" song. He evidently thought that, instead of being grounded for life when he returned to narhii-Vhiliinyar, he would receive a hero's welcome for the rescue of her parents, his account of which would no doubt be as embroidered as his current implementation of the course change, or maybe even more so. Let him be the biggest *fraaki* in the pond if he wanted to. Maati didn't care. She would finally get to see her parents again.

Maati was at the helm once more when the ship prepared to enter the orbit of the planet whose coordinates matched those described by the Niriians. The planet was a pretty one from this distance. Overall it was the color of the small lavender flowers that grew in the best grazing grounds. Large pools of deep indigo appeared through the powdery blue clouds that swathed the world. It even had several blue moons. She wondered what they would look like from the surface. She'd find out soon enough. . . .

Maati was about to summon Thariinye when the com unit came alive. She heard, not words, but sounds like rocks being banged together, "Klick Klack, klick-klick-klickety-klack-klack-klack."

Thariinye must have been on his way to the bridge already because suddenly he was beside Maati. The color completely drained from his horn and he looked like he was watching something terrible. "What's the matter, Thariinye? We're here!" she said.

"Yes," he whispered, nodding at the com unit. "And so are the Khleevi."

Six

"Captain Becker, look," Acorna said, when he arrived on the bridge for his watch. She pointed out to him their present course back to narhii-Vhiliinyar, and a slightly altered one. "If we deviated here slightly, we would intersect with the coordinates the Niriians mentioned in their vid. The ones where the escape pod was seen. Do you wish to make that detour? From the looks of the vid, at least one person survived. Even if that's no longer the case, perhaps you would find the pod valuable salvage?"

Becker beamed and patted her on the shoulder. "You're gonna make a junker yet, Princess. That's a great idea. While we're at it, we'll see if there's anybody there who can tell us more about the wrecked Niriian ship, and if so, we'll see if they'd like a ride. If not, we have salvage that looks like something your people would like to have back. Even if they don't, I bet your uncle Hafiz knows somebody who would want to buy it as a curiosity."

Slight as the course change was, it had a profound effect on Aari, who stared at the *püyi* broadcast continually while he was on the bridge, and particularly focused on the picture of the pod.

He had gone over the broadcast so many times that Acorna was surprised he could still stand to look at it. He didn't even flinch away from the scene of his own torture anymore. True, he went into an apparent trance while watching, but since he could be distracted from it if necessary, Acorna decided he was simply thinking deeply about his experience, trying to face up to it and process it, which surely meant he was growing stronger and healthier and better able to deal with it? She hoped so.

Becker rolled his eyes now whenever he looked at Aari. He had tried some conversational gambits with no success. Aari would answer a polite "Yes, Joh" or "No, Joh" and return to staring at the screen. Acorna usually met with the same response.

Had it not been for the cat and the KEN unit, the situation might have never been resolved.

Once his initial curiosity about the *püyi* had been exhausted, RK paid no attention to it for several days. As the same images playing over and over on the screen meant that Aari, who was one of the cat's favorite people, would be on the bridge, RK started spending more time there. But enough, in RK's opinion, was enough. When Aari refused to focus exclusively on the cat, RK, tail lashing, began watching the screen, too. Acrorna noticed that every time the Khleevi appeared on screen again with Aari at their mercy, the cat would enlarge himself to twice his already considerable size, flatten his ears, and hiss. The first time Becker had witnessed RK's reaction, he'd laughed until he fell out of his chair. The cat then hissed at Becker, too.

Even Aari couldn't help laughing.

But RK, as his apparent understanding of what he was watching grew, became even more agitated when the scene appeared on the screen. One day, when they were all on deck and the scene appeared, the cat flung himself at the screen, claws and teeth bared. The force of his collision with the hard, smooth, and totally uninjured surface of the screen knocked RK onto the deck, where he lay for a moment. Then he sat up and licked the fur on his left side as if that had been his intention all along.

Aari picked the cat up, stroked his fur, and laughed.

"You got yourself a defender there, Aari," Becker said.

Acorna reached over and scratched RK under his chin. The cat graciously permitted her ministrations, though he did not go so far as to actually purr.

During the long hours when she was not on watch and the others were busy or sleeping, Acorna undertook to "educate KEN," as Becker put it.

The android was being underutilized, she told Becker. Though he was programmed essentially as a servant or at least an employee, he had a vast amount of unused memory.

"It would greatly expand your ability to collect salvage, Captain," she told Becker. "If you landed on a world rich in salvage but with an unbreathable atmosphere, for instance, the android could collect your salvage for you long after the limited oxygen supply in your pressure suit forced you to return to the ship."

Becker nodded. "Sounds good to me."

"I'll need access to the *Condor*'s memory banks."

"*Mi casa es su casa,*" Becker said.

"Is that Standard?"

"Only to the Pallomellese," Becker said. "It means 'my house is your house, my ship is your ship.' Go for it."

During most of this programming, the KEN unit was turned off, but during the rest, he remained conscious and participated in the work. Acorna was surprised at how natural he seemed. He was not, after all, a particularly new model.

"Were you originally programmed to feel or display emotion?" she asked the robot.

"No," he said. And then, half a beat later, he asked with seeming anxiety, "Was that the wrong answer?"

She smiled to reassure him. It seemed silly to think that someone who was basically a machine needed reassurance—but, on the other hand, she had heard her uncles talk to their ship, she'd seen Becker talk to the *Condor* in the same way he spoke to RK, so there was really no reason to think that machines didn't respond in some way to emotional input. Particularly machines which appeared to be human. "I do not think that there is a wrong answer to that question," she said. "But I'm interpreting your responses as being emotionally motivated. This makes me more comfortable with you."

"I hope you are comfortable with me, miss," the KEN unit said. "You have taught me a great deal these last few days. I know many more things. I understand a great deal more about the people here, this ship, this universe. Kisla Manjari did not wish me to think for myself."

Acorna frowned. "Kisla Manjari was a very troubled person. And she had the unfortunate habit of passing her trouble around to everyone she met."

"She was a very difficult user, miss. I believe I perceive what you mean. Captain Becker, on the other hand, keeps me shut off most of the time. This recharges the batteries but does not add greatly to my knowledge."

"I don't think the captain realized your potential, KEN-640," Acorna said. "I'll ask his permission to leave you on continually while you are assimilating the data I have added to your banks."

"Miss, I note that the captain, and you, and the other being like you, and even the fur-bearing creature call each other by casual appellations. KEN-640 is my model number. But it is not the same sort of appellation."

"I'm sorry, KEN-640. You may call all of us by our given names. Although Aari calls me Khornya, as do others of my race, my original name is Acorna and I prefer it. Do you wish to be known by a different appellation than KEN-640 yourself?"

"Yes, Acorna. I have scanned the selection of names for humanoids of Terran origin, which I resemble, and have decided it would be appropriate for me to be called MacKenZ. Mac means son of, which sounds more human than modeled by, does it not?"

"It does."

"And although my model number indicates that I was not the latest or most sophisticated unit made to date, I feel that your programming has put me on a par with the most recent and updated of my series. And if an "A" indicates the first or earliest model in the Standard alphabet, then Z surely means the most recent upgrade. Hence MacKenZ."

"Fine, MacKenZ. If you'll accompany me to the bridge, I will reintroduce you to our crewmates."

She did so. After that, Becker readily agreed to leave the MacKenZ operational most of the time and began some programming of his own, teaching MacKenZ some of the important points to remember in collecting salvage. "I think Mac is self-programming to some extent anyway," Becker said, scratching his head. "Otherwise, I don't see how he could come up with some of the stuff he does."

Becker was nonetheless reluctant to trust MacKenZ at the helm alone, although he didn't mind tutoring him in Becker Enterprises navigational methods when he stood his own watch.

MacKenZ spent much of his time on the bridge, when Becker didn't have any other specific assignment for him. Acorna was glad of the company. She used the time to input more data, using the books that Aari had now abandoned in favor of studying the *püyi*.

She discovered, as she came on watch to relieve Aari, that MacKenZ, too, had taken an interest in the broadcast.

Aari was involved in the liveliest exchange he had engaged in since they recovered the pod. He and MacKenZ were conversing in Linyaari. Acorna had programmed the android for Standard. The Linyaari was either the android's own idea, or perhaps Aari had taught him.

"From observation," MacKenZ was saying, nodding

at a frozen frame of the Khleevi torture scene, "I have deciphered the meaning of some few of the utterances Khleevi make by rubbing their legs together, Aari," MacKenZ was saying in a puzzled tone. "But these sounds, while they have a definite pattern and twenty-one thousand four hundred fifty-two distinct combinations which can predictably be determined to have specific meanings, are not translatable with the use of your LAANYE device, which I find odd. Can you enlighten me as to the meanings of these clickings? Are they the only form of communication employed by these beings?"

Aari sat back in the command chair and closed his eyes, rubbing the area around the cavity where his horn once grew. He looked very, very weary. "They use thought-speak," he told MacKenZ, sighing deeply. "I didn't realize it at first, but they touch their antennae together and thought transference takes place. The audible communication they perform with their leg rubbings is apparently a code for more complex thoughts they are able to transmit in full by antennae contact. This is what has made it so difficult for the LAANYE to make sense of their verbal communication in the past. I suppose I am the only living being who has spent enough time with them to comprehend their mode of data transference." He paused, then added dryly, "I suppose that dubious distinction also means I may be the only Linyaari qualified to try and program the LAANYE to decipher the Khleevi utterances."

"So the Khleevi have to be physically present to employ such a mental means of communication," the android said. "So they use the clickings of their legs rubbing together as an audible means of communication for longer distances, such as ship-to-ship transmissions. Fascinating. What else did you learn while you were with the Khleevi?"

"How loudly I could scream. How long before my voice gave out," Aari said. "How I could be reduced to a mass of searing pain, with no thought, no higher purpose than to make it cease."

"And yet, clearly, from what you say, you were able to withhold the location of narhii-Vhiliinyar, as well as your brother's hiding place. Was that not an act of will?"

"Willful memory loss perhaps," Aari said with a very faint smile.

"What meanings did you attribute to these various clickings?"

"Perhaps on my next watch we will attempt to interpret them, Maakinze. Here is Khornya, come to relieve me."

He smiled at her, but she was looking beyond him, to the screens that were, as Becker would say, lit up like pinball machines. "Look, Aari! Signals from everywhere! And we are nearing the coordinates of the lost pod. Perhaps we should alert Captain Becker."

"I'm right here, Mac!" Becker called out from down the corridor, his bare feet clanking as he jogged across the grated deck plating. "What's up?"

"A diffuse sonar signal is emanating from the area around the planet where the Linyaari escape pod is located, Captain," Mac replied.

A strange feeling came over Acorna as she looked at the thousands of tiny blinking lights spread across the sonar screen. She had seen this pattern before. "I know what that is, Captain!" she said. "It's the sonar-blocking signal given out by cloaked Linyaari vessels. One of the techno-artisans showed me how it worked recently."

"So," Becker said. "If it's a cloaked Linyaari vessel, what's that?" He pointed to a substantial and solid blip rapidly entering the sonar array.

As if in answer, the com unit began a "Klick-klack-klick-klack-klick-klack" noise.

"Khleevi," Acorna and Aari whispered, while Mac said the same word in a matter-of-fact, almost cheerful tone.

"Those guys?" Becker asked, peering at the dot as if he could make out the shape of the ship from it.

"Scope," Acorna said, and the viewscreen suddenly zoomed so that the mantis-shaped Khleevi vessel was indeed readily identifiable, though still quite distant.

"So that's what one of the little buggers looks like." Becker said, quietly, as if afraid they would hear. Meanwhile the klickings and klackings continued. "We seem to have intercepted one of their transmissions. Anybody have any idea what it's all about?"

"Klickety-klack," the Khleevi vessel's message seemed to be tapping directly onto Maati's spinal cord. She sat for a moment with her eyes squeezed shut.

"You don't have to close your eyes and pretend they can't see you," Thariinye said, but not as scornfully as he might have. "We're cloaked."

"What does the noise mean?" she asked.

"I don't know. I didn't hear a lot of their language when we were up against them on Rushima. And I wasn't alone. So far, nobody has gotten enough of a sample into the LAANYE for reliable translations. All our contacts with them have pretty much been at the wrong end of a weapon. Maybe it's Khleevi for 'come out, come out, wherever you are.' But don't worry, youngling. We may not be coming out, but we're moving out right now. I'm putting us into the nearest wormhole and—"

Maati's eyes blinked open and she reached to intercept his hand on the controls. "But . . . my parents! They're still on that planet! The Khleevi will get them." A brief struggle ensued, which Thariinye won.

He gave her a pitying look and reached again for the navigation controls. "I'm sorry, Maati, but we don't know for sure they're still alive. If so . . . well, they've escaped the notice of the Khleevi so far. Perhaps they can continue to do it until we can find help. We—"

He never finished his sentence.

A heavy blow thudded against the *Niikaavri*, knocking both of them forward, straining the straps that held them into their chairs. At the same time, the lights on the control panel flared and two blinked out.

"Oh, no!" he cried, and punched frantically at the board again.

"Oh, no, what?" Maati asked.

"Somehow, in that little maneuver of yours, we turned our camouflage off. They know our position now."

"Put the cloaking device back on and move, then!"

"I'm trying to, but the ship is not responding!"

A bolt of light shot in front of the viewport and they were once more rocked by the force of some sort of energy weapon striking their starboard bow.

Suddenly the egg-like ship was spinning dizzily, and the blue planet grew larger and larger in their viewscreen.

Thariinye grabbed the com unit and yelled, as if it could carry across space, "Mayday, Mayday, we are the Linyaari vessel *Nükaavri* and we are under attack from a Khleevi vessel."

Maati thought he had lost his mind. Surely no one would hear them, but then she cried, "Tell them who we are, Thariinye. In case my parents can hear us. Tell them it's me, so they'll know what happened. Tell them to hide!"

"I am Ensign Thariinye of clan Renyilaaghe. My second in command is Maati of clan Nyaarya. We are under attack by a Khleevi vessel. Our coordinates are . . ."

Maati thought she was hearing things for a moment when the klickings and klackings and sound of failing systems were replaced suddenly by a familiar comforting voice.

"Thariinye, Maati, it's Khornya. You've been badly hit. Use the escape pod. We'll pick you up and get us all out of here."

Another, harder thud and the ship was spinning dizzily, the blue planet looming larger with every revolution.

Maati floated up from her seat. "G force has been cut."

"Khornya, the Khleevi! Save yourselves!" Thariinye bellowed into the com unit. To Maati he said, "No time to deal with it, youngling. Unstrap. Climb into the pod!"

The pod was located behind the command chairs. Maati snapped her restraint open and did a handstand on the back of the chair, flipping herself down to the top of the pod and popping its catch.

"No sweat, sport," Captain Becker's voice was saying. "We got 'em covered."

"Thariinye, the escape pod," Khornya said again.

Maati climbed inside the pod. She suppressed a nervous giggle. The zero G popped her up to the top.

"Oh," Thariinye said, and she saw the top of his head as it swiveled to take in the wildly flickering console lights, the sparks flying from the board at many points.

Maati waited. It felt like forever. She felt sick from the spinning and thought that the stars swirling past the viewport looked like what she'd thought she would see in the wormhole.

She heard the snap of Thariinye's restraint, and saw his feet, then his legs as he bounced over the top of the chair and off the deck.

Maati held on to the pod lid with one hand and grabbed his foot with the other, pulling him in. He was barely inside the pod when all of a sudden the canopy slapped closed and locked, and they felt a bump as gravity returned, but increased fivefold, pressing the pod against the deck.

Thariinye pressed the release button to eject the pod and activate the recirculating oxygen supply. Oxygen flooded the pod with a hissing sound, but they were still stuck inside the ship. The ejection mechanism was malfunctioning, just like everything else on the ship! And the gravitational force was so strong they couldn't pop the hatch again to see why the pod had failed to eject.

Thariinye's heart boomed against her ear.

"It's okay, Thariinye. The pod will help protect us during a crash. They're amazingly resilient, you know."

His breath rasped in and out a few times.

"Unless, of course, the ship burns up on entering the atmosphere or we're smashed in the wreckage when it slams into the planet," Maati said, and realized that what she was voicing was Thariinye's thought. He hadn't said a word. What a time for her psychic powers to kick in!

The pod insulated them a bit from the noises around them, but she knew they were still inside the ship because she hadn't felt the explosive acceleration that would indicate the pod had separated from the mother ship. They were still stuck.

(I could open the hatch and . . .) she thought she said aloud.

Thariinye hugged her close to his chest. "Not if it's stuck, you can't. I'll keep hitting the firing mechanism. We'll just have to hope that the relay decides to engage before the crash—or maybe even during."

(Oh, no, we're trapped!) Panic welled up inside her and tears began to flow from her eyes. She couldn't spend the pitiful fraction left of her life cooped up in this tiny shell. She couldn't. She just couldn't.

Then suddenly it was as if they had hit a bump. They felt themselves sliding and then their pod was launched so that at first they were flying, then dropping.

(It will level out, won't it?) she asked. Or did she? They were wrapped so closely in each other's arms that it was no wonder she could suddenly hear his thoughts and he could hear hers.

(Yes,) he said. (But I am doomed anyway. Even if we survive the crash and the Khleevi, Liriili will kill me for stealing and losing her newest ship.)

Becker jerked his thumb backward, gesturing for Aari to surrender the command chair. The *Condor*'s hiding place behind one of the moons kept it out of range of the Khleevi ship's sensors, giving the crew a little breathing space to make plans.

Aari got up, but gave the captain a level look. "I am fine, Joh. The Khleevi no longer freeze my ability to think."

"I know that, buddy, but you don't know my bird like I do." He clasped his hands, intertwining his fingers, straightened his wrists and flexed his knuckles, then shook both hands out and applied them to the buttons. "Let's deploy those Winding laser cannons we picked up last year."

"Sorry, Captain," the computer said, "but you have not yet found the right mountings to affix them to the gun ports."

"Oh, yeah. Then fire the Apatchipon micron splitters."

"You have not been able to fashion suitable ports, Captain, to accommodate both the micron splitters and your latest hull modifications."

"Well, I've had all these people around and—okay, so we'll just go for the plain old atom blasters Dad installed years ago."

"You removed those and stored them, Captain, when you traded for the Windigi laser cannons."

"Fraggit! So what have we got? Spit? We fired the

last big load of cargo into Ganoosh's bird and we haven't acquired enough new stuff yet to do any good." He shook his head and said, "I guess we could board 'em and go *mano a mano* with the side arms and laser rifles. It worked on Rushima."

Acorna leaned forward, "You used the tractor beam before, Captain. How much will it hold?"

"A bunch more than we've got to throw at these buggers," Becker replied. "This was supposed to be a nice, simple cargo run. . . ." He and Aari exchanged long looks. Acorna did not care for the grim set of Aari's jaw or the glazed, doomed look in his eyes. Nor could she bear to think of Thariinye, much less Maati, at the nonexistent mercy of the Khleevi. She had sensed some difficulty with the pod before their ship crashed, but she had no true reading of what it was.

"Joh, listen to me and do exactly as I say," Aari commanded, interrupting Acorna's train of thought. His voice was clipped and hard and she was amazed to see he had appropriated Becker's side arm, and was raising it in Becker's direction. "You have an operational shuttle in Bay Two. You will take Khornya and Riidkiiyi and board the shuttle now. I will give you five seconds to clear and then I will ram the *Condor* into the Khleevi ship."

"Over my dead body," Becker growled, whipping around in the chair to face Aari. "That's mutiny."

"Over your stunned body if necessary, Joh. Khornya, you understand this is the only way to save Thariinye and my sister, don't you? The Khleevi killed me long ago. I live only to prevent them from doing to others what they did to me. So unless you wish to lose your horn to them as I did, and worse, you and Mac will take Joh and Riidkiiyi now and evacuate."

"You're not gonna crash my ship!" Becker said belligerently, his jaw stuck out.

"If you will all just listen to me for a moment," Acorna interjected. "Aari, give the captain back his weapon. We will need the *Condor* to rescue Thariinye and Maati and your parents. I have a better idea. Remember in that old vid, when the evil western agricultural workers dragged the good quick-draw warrior the indigenous inhabitants had hired to save them? They dragged him through cactus, and over hardened trails, and he was much the worse for wear as a result. I remember thinking that actually it was highly unlikely he would have survived, especially maintaining his headgear as he did, had the event been an actual occurrence rather than a fictional one. Well, it seems to me that we could do much the same thing here. The atmospheric rim on this planet is quite dense and the gravitational pull strong. If the tractor beam will hold the Khleevi ship . . ."

"Gotcha, Princess! You're brilliant!" Becker spoke to the computer. "Okay, Buck, engage the tractor beam. Hook onto that big, nasty piece of salvage off our starboard bow." He chuckled and said to his crew members. "Heh-heh. This is a great idea! They can't shoot us or anybody else while they're locked onto the tractor beam's gravity well."

The beam locked onto the Khleevi ship and hauled it toward the *Condor* until it vanished from view beneath them.

"At least, I don't think they can, unless they got some

new technology that lets them." Becker continued in a slightly more worried tone as he maneuvered the beam so that the Khleevi was in tow behind and at an angle from the *Condor*, riding between the salvage ship's belly and the planet's rim.

The klick-klack noise on the com unit was now loud, angry, and very obviously intended for the crew of the *Condor*.

"They are telling you to surrender, Joh. They have us in their pincers," Aari said. He was baring his teeth, and it was not a friendly grin. Acorna reached up without thinking to wipe the sweat where it was suddenly dripping off his chin. He touched her hand lightly, his fingers stroking hers once, regretfully. She knew from the touch that he still could not imagine they would come away from this encounter alive, much less unscathed.

"Strap down, crew," Becker said.

Acorna grabbed RK and strapped him in with her. Aari and Mac did likewise in the seats Becker had scavenged so that the entire crew could be together on occasion—though none of them had thought that such an occasion as this would ever arise.

"Buck, give us a visual of the cargo in the tractor beam," Becker told the ship's computer. Once he could see the Khleevi ship, Becker accelerated and the *Condor* shot toward the blue planet, past where the enemy vessel had originally hovered while watching the crash of the Linyaari craft. The screen showed the mantis-like ship dangling beneath the *Condor*'s belly, while the klicking and klacking from the com unit rose in volume and variation. Threats, no doubt.

Becker dove and the blue planet grew larger and

larger, until its vaporous cover seemed ready to swallow the *Condor*. "Manual," Becker said, and pulled back on an actual lever among the buttons of his control panel, with the effect that the *Condor*'s nose swooped up, slinging the Khleevi ship behind it.

Acorna felt a bump as they changed course, and on the screen the Khleevi ship jumped and shook as it dipped into the atmosphere and was pulled out again. Becker did this three times. Diving and swooping, and—at the end of each swoop—a bump. As they pulled up, the pressure of acceleration pressed all of them to their seats. RK's lips pulled back from his teeth in a fierce grimace, as did Aari's. Acorna would have laughed but her teeth were bared, too. Only Mac's face remained just the same, robotic flesh impervious to the force. Acorna's stomach could not decide whether to go into her throat or her legs, and the variations in gravity made her lightheaded and giddy.

Just as the Khleevi ship bumped the third time, Becker commanded, "Disengage tractor beam, Bucko. We're gonna play a little game of crack the ship."

The Khleevi ship was flung wide from the *Condor* and skipped three more times against the resistance of the outer atmosphere, almost as if the ship was a flat rock and the atmospheric rim was a pond. But the ship wasn't solid, and the *Mantis*'s legs and antennae broke off with the first skip, while large cracks appeared with the next before it plunged spinning toward the surface. It disappeared into nothingness as the *Condor* flew deeper into space.

"Whoa, Buck," Becker said.

When the *Condor* had slowed, Becker returned to the

atmosphere and reversed thrusters. The *Condor's* screens were picking up signals from the Linyaari escape pod as well as several from the Khleevi ship.

The planet appeared even bluer than it had from the air as the ship approached the surface.

Acorna didn't know she was humming until Aari asked, "You are singing—is it your death song?"

"Gill used to sing it sometimes," Acorna said. "It is an old Terran folksong of military origin."

Becker laughed and sang in a gravelly and tuneless voice, "Off we go, off into the wild blue yonder."

Seven

"Thariinye?" Maati said. "Thariinye, we've landed. My arms are pinned. Can you open the canopy?" His heart still beat in her ear — slow and steady. He was alive, anyway. "Thariinye, are you okay?"

He blasted her other ear with a loud snore. She elbowed him in the ribs. "You fell asleep! We could have been killed and you fell asleep!"

He stirred and groaned. "Not asleep. More like unconscious, I think."

"Unconscious people don't snore. You were snoring."

"Where are we, anyway?" he asked, changing the subject.

"I don't know. But it feels like we landed. That was too much of a thump for us to be still in space. Can you open the canopy?"

"What if we have landed on some hostile planet where there is only nitrogen to breathe?" he asked. "If I open the canopy, we die."

"Look at the sensors, you dope. The air's fine. Remember, my parents lived here for long enough for the Niriians to find them. They must have breathed the air and still survived. And if you don't get us out of here, I wet my pants now and we both die of hunger or worse later anyway," she said. "Do you just want to sit here and wait for the Khleevi to snatch us?"

"Okay, you've got a point." He opened the hatch. While he was at it, he turned off the locator beacon. "Don't know who'll be looking for us, do we?" he asked. Through the open hatch, they saw periwinkle blue sky, lacy fronds of vegetation, one sun and half a dozen moons simultaneously, and some large and very beautiful birds with blue and green iridescent plumage soaring above them.

"How could you fall asleep when the Khleevi were after us and maybe even got Khornya and Aari, too?"

"I couldn't do anything about it, could I? When you are older and more experienced, youngling, you will learn to utilize whatever quiet moments you can grab from the constant excitement of a spacefarer's life to conserve your energy and mend any damage done by life's travails."

"Right," she said, and tried to sit up. The pod moved under her, bouncing up and down. "Whoa, stop!" she said, and looked over the edge to see what was causing the motion. Lacy, fernlike growth held them in the air. "Thariinye, look. These are the tallest bushes I have ever seen!" All around them and high above them, blocking off the view in most directions, other lacy fronds fanned briskly back and forth.

He sat up, too, and the pod rocked even more perilously.

"They're not bushes, youngling. These are treetops. Can you climb down? If the branches support your weight, then maybe they'll support mine. I don't think we're up very high. All of the other trees appear to be higher."

She leaned over the edge and touched something solid, big enough it let her spread her whole hand. Thariinye leaned against the opposite side of the pod to balance it as she felt her way along. When she was sure the support was wide enough for her to step out on, she did, slithering her belly, pelvis, and legs over the side to follow her outstretched hands and arms. She crawled along the limb on hands and knees, peering through the fronds to try to find more sturdy branches. When she reached the trunk, she had to lift more fronds to find the way down. "No wonder it wasn't very tall," she crawled back to Thariinye.

"Be careful, you'll . . ."

"Oooops!" she cried, windmilling her arms as she let her legs shoot out from under her.

"Maati!" Thariinye cried, and toppled the pod reaching for her. It fell from the nest of fronds and landed below—about three feet below. Thariinye had covered his head with both hands anticipating the crash.

Maati laughed and laughed, and stood up. The fronds and the part of the trunk still in the ground rose only as high as her waist. "Gotcha!" she cried, clapping her hands. "We broke the tree when we landed and its branches cushioned our fall!"

"Brat," Thariinye grumbled, extricating himself from the pod.

"Now what, O experienced spacefarer?" Maati asked cheekily.

"Standard protocol is to stay near your pod," Thari-inye told her. "Which would be a good idea if Khornya and her crewmates are looking for us."

"But a bad idea if they lost out to the Khleevi, and it's the monsters who are looking for us," Maati said.

"Yes," he admitted.

"I know what we can do," Maati said.

"Oh, you do? Who put you in charge of the mission?"

"The same power that put you in charge," she replied. "We're in this together. If I get saved, you get saved. If I get caught, you'll—"

"If I get caught I'll try to make sure they don't know you're alive," Thariinye told her with unexpected gravity.

"Right. Well, all I need to do is climb up one of the taller trees, if it's climbable, and look around. I can maybe see where the wreckage of our ship is and if anybody is checking it out. That is the first place anyone will look for us, and it isn't like we can't tell our friends from our enemies in this situation. One look, and we'll know what to expect."

"Why, that's a very good idea. You learn quickly, youngling."

Climbing these trees was easier said than done, however, unless you were one of the small blue-furred scampering things constantly running up and down trunks and through the underbrush. The trunks were smooth and thick—it was the broken off end of the trunk that Maati had crawled along when she first left the pod. But the frond branches were not very strong and snapped under the pressure of even Maati's small feet.

She made it halfway up one of the trees, and that was

as far as she got. She felt around for handholds or footholds but found none.

Thariinye called up to her from below, "Keep going."

"Can't," she said.

"Well, what do you see from there?"

"More trees. But I think the ones over that way," she pointed to the west, "are on a hill, maybe. And there is some kind of clearing at the top. If we could go climb that hill, we could see more." When she'd pointed, she'd let go of the tree with one hand, and transferred all her weight to her other hand. That put more pressure on her grasping hand and the frond she was holding broke. While she was searching for another, her feet bore too heavily on the fronds she stood on, and those broke as well. She slid precipitously down the trunk, catching her shipsuit several times on protruding fronds on the way down. It was a sturdy synblend and didn't tear, but Maati wasn't so sure the skin beneath the suit was as undamaged.

"It'll take us farther from the pod," Thariinye said with a sigh. "But that might be a good thing."

"I don't think we ought to talk so loudly anymore either," Maati said. "In case the monsters hear us."

(We wouldn't need to talk at all if you weren't such a baby,) Thariinye grumbled.

She punched him lightly in the side with her balled-up fist. (I heard that.) Then after a beat, (Hey, do you think we could contact Khornya and my brother mentally from here? Or maybe even my parents? I can do that, can't I, now that I'm able to send and receive?) The last was thought quite proudly, and Thariinye received an image of a grownup Maati.

(Not if they're still too far out in space or too busy to listen—engaged in battle with the Khleevi, maybe,) Thariinye sent a withering thought. Maati realized that this was a frequent behavior with him. The idea had not been his and therefore he was trying to make it sound worthless.

(It doesn't hurt to try, though,) Maati pointed out.

(Unless, of course, the Khleevi can read our thoughts and find us from them,) Thariinye said. (In case they followed us down here.)

(Oh,) Maati said. (Yeah. Okay. I'll shut up. Back to the hill, then.)

They were nearly there when they heard the whistling, roaring sounds. They scrambled quickly to the top of the hill and found the clearing in time to see the wreckage of the Khleevi ship falling from the sky, splashing into a sea some distance from them. They could make out the wreck of their own ship on the shore.

"At least if we lost our ship, they did, too," Maati said.

"I suppose that's some consolation," Thariinye agreed. "The Khleevi ship was wrecked—maybe Liriili can blame the Khleevi for the whole mess, instead of me, if we live long enough to have to confess it." And then he pointed. For once, even he was speechless. Maati could see why.

Also tumbling down from the sky, but in much better shape than the larger ship had been, was a small Khleevi shuttle. As it fell, two figures could be seen emerging from it, trailing some sort of membrane behind them that caught the air and sailed them gently to the ground.

Maati, seeing the bug-like creatures alive for the first time, even at a distance, was filled with horror and loathing. Tears began trickling down her cheeks as she looked up at Thariinye.

"They landed somewhere over there," he said, pointing toward the beach. "So I think we should run in the opposite direction as far and as fast as we can."

"Yes," she said, "But-but-Thariinye?"

"What?"

"If their ship is crashed and in pieces and only two of those creatures are getting out, does that mean the *Condor* won?"

"We can't take that chance, youngling, though by the Ancestors I hope it is so. We are no match for even two of those creatures. Quickly now."

He didn't have to tell her twice.

The Linyaari ship lay broken in two like a giant egg that had hatched its chick. It was nestled deep in a beach of aqua blue sand, beyond which cerulean blue waters stretched to the horizon. Wreckage from the Khleevi ship was scattered like bits of large and particularly ugly seaweed on the surface of the water and along the beach, carried in by the waves. Behind the beach was a range of blue dunes and, beyond them, the fronds of a forest of graceful fern-like trees beckoned the *Condor* to land.

Once the ship had done so, Acorna released her restraint and RK's.

"Conditions are hospitable, Captain," the Buck Rogers voice of the ship's computer told him. "That blue stuff that looks like sand, is. The other blue stuff that looks like the water is. Salt water, though, so take your desalination and purification unit. The temperature is sixty degrees Fahrenheit with moderate winds at three point two knots. The air is breathable, even fragrant, by human standards."

"Are there—life forms?" Aari asked.

"Other than here? How should I know? I'm a ship's computer, for heaven's sake, not an anthropologist. My heat and motion sensors are picking up something, but it could just be all that wreckage out in the water."

The scanners showed what Buck was referring to more precisely. Becker salivated at the sight of all that salvage.

Aari was more sober. "Does it show if there are any live beings there?"

Becker shook his head. "Don't know. My scanners are for salvage, mostly."

"I hope Thariinye and Maati were able to make it to the escape pod," Acorna said with a little shiver that made her skin twitch. "I don't think anything else would have survived that crash."

Becker said, "Look at the ship. I don't see any obvious signs of them or the pod in the wreckage. They're here somewhere. And if that's the case, Princess, we'll find them. What I'm hoping is that none of those stupid bug things made it to a pod."

"Their ships don't have pods, Joh," Aari said. "Their carapace protects them against many things that would kill others."

"What about that large shuttle-shaped piece of debris over there, captain?" Mac asked.

"Rrrrrowwsst!" RK responded.

"Cat says it's Khleevi," Becker told them.

"We heard him, Joh," Aari said soberly.

"Well, from here I'd say it's not as badly wrecked as the Khleevi ship." He indicated the fragments of the ship floating in the water. "We can at least hope that any occupants are in the same fragmentary state as their transportation," Becker said.

RK bolted for his personal exit and they heard his claws scrabbling as he slid down the cat chute to the ramp that led to the robolift.

"We better get moving," Becker said. "Cat seems to have to go real bad. Must be that pretty blue sandbox out there just itching to have a Makahomian cat scratch in it. Aari, you get that Khleevi earthmoving weapon you brought along as your dowry. I've got the locator and laser rifle," he said, hefting a sleek and deadly looking weapon the length of his forearm.

"And I have my own array of attachments, Captain," Mac said, opening his forearm to display the corkscrew, can opener, knife blades, scissors, magnifying glass and other small equipment that were standard with his particular model.

Acorna made a side trip of her own. Taking a slight detour to an otherwise empty storeroom, she gathered up a lightweight titanium cargo net she had spotted earlier in the journey.

"Good idea, Princess," Becker said when he saw it. "We'll be able to net us some salvage from that Khleevi ship for sure."

Thus armed, they boarded the robolift and headed down. Acorna felt something sticky on her shoes. She took a closer look at her shoes, then at the source of the problem. "Mac, when we get back here, I want you to scrub the lift down. It's a mess from the plant sap on that planet where we picked up the *püyi*."

MacKenZ looked surprised—probably because she was talking about minor housekeeping matters now, when so many more important things were at stake—but didn't say anything. Clearly the robot had never learned the trick of keeping fear at bay by concentrating on the trivia of life. Maybe robots didn't ever feel that kind of fear.

Once the robolift set down, however, Becker regarded the outside of his ship with disgust, too. "Those damn plants slimed my hull! Look at that! What a mess."

"Joh," Aari said softly, nodding to redirect the captain's attention to the halves of the Linyaari ship. "What if Maati and Thariinye are in the wreckage?"

"If they're there, they'll be easy to find. We'll know soon enough what the situation is. No sense borrowing trouble. Princess, anything to add here?"

"I was—receiving some impressions toward the last, before we picked up the Khleevi, that the pod might have become stuck in the ship. If so, they could still be alive but trapped in the wreckage in the pod."

"We must reach them before the Khleevi do," Aari said.

"If there are any Khleevi left," Becker said. "Come to think of it, maybe we'd better try to head the bad guys off at the pass even before we check the wreckage."

"There *are* Khleevi here," Aari said. "I can feel them."

RK, back up and tail brushed, apparently agreed with him.

They made their way cautiously down the beach,

weapons at the ready. Acorna felt a little foolish trailing behind, preoccupied by the feeling that she knew Maati and Thariinye were here somewhere—alive—but she couldn't tell where. She only had a vague sense of them. Why couldn't she at least reach Thariinye? She couldn't shake the feeling that her friends were alive, but in trouble.

They saw wrecked Khleevi shuttlecraft lying in the dunes, broken up but considerably more intact than the Khleevi ship, lying in the dunes further up the beach. Something brown lay crunched around the edges, and a green fluid tinted the blue sand turquoise.

"Any Khleevi who survived were most likely in that shuttle," Becker pronounced. "Look at their ship. I doubt they could live through a wreck like that. The ship is toast, but the shuttle—well, that looks like it was spaceworthy till the last minute. No convenient vacuum or decompression to kill all the occupants for us."

As they drew nearer they saw movement and heard a sound that made Acorna's skin twitch—the klick-klack she had heard so often on Aari's video. The light wind carried a terrible stench—rot combined with vomit. RK stopped, dug his claws into the ground, and hissed like a tea kettle. Aari's steps slowed. Becker surged ahead like a missile, Mac outpacing him with nonchalance in the face of danger that only an android—particularly one who had once been the face of danger himself—could achieve.

"It appears we've got a live one," Becker growled as he rounded the dune where the shuttle lay. "Though it's half buried under that shuttle. It's not going anywhere fast. I'll just put this cockroach out of its misery."

"Please, wait," Acorna said. "We must question it. Aari knows their language, at least enough to get something useful out of it. Perhaps we can get more from the LAANYE. We have to find out if this ship was alone or if others will be coming, where the main swarm of Khleevi is now, and where they are heading next. If my people are threatened again, they must know at once."

Aari found his voice and his feet, and in six more strides stood beside Becker. Acorna approached cautiously, curiously. The creature snapped its mandibles and reached for Becker with its pincers but the captain sidestepped smartly and beckoned for Acorna to give him the cargo net.

She wondered suddenly why it had occurred to her to bring it. Then she glanced at Aari and saw him smiling at her with both approval and triumph. That was it, of course. Aari had sent her the suggestion. He thought he couldn't intentionally send any longer, but he was clearly mistaken. He had certainly just done it. Why hadn't he asked her aloud, she wondered? It would have been a reasonable request. How odd.

Aari was carrying the very large and heavy weapon which he'd retrieved when his torturers fled the death throes of Vhiliinyar. He trained it on the monster. Maybe that was it. Acorna had been the logical one to bring the net—but, still, he usually communicated with spoken words. She looked up at him again, frowning this time, but he was concentrating on the Khleevi.

"Okay," Becker said. "Aari, Acorna, and I are going to capture this thing. When we have the net over it and solidly anchored, Mac, you maneuver the shuttle off its leg and thorax, okay?"

"Yes, Captain."

Acorna was the only one who could use two hands, but fortunately the creature was trapped and rather badly injured by the crash. Much of its back end was crushed beneath the shuttle, from what she could see. It still gave her cold chills to be this close to a live Khleevi, no matter how much was wrong with it. When the android lifted the broken piece of the shuttle from the back of the Khleevi and tipped it aside, the Khleevi struggled mightily against their titanium net, but in vain. Mac then aided his crewmates in finishing netting the monster's hind parts. The monster klicked and klacked and gnashed its mandibles at them as best it could through the impediment of the net, but they paid it no attention. Finally it was well wrapped enough that they could risk transporting it.

"Now, then," Becker said. "We'll put him in the brig and Mac can stay and guard him while the LAANYE collects language samples. As mad and as noisy as this beast is, we ought to get enough stuff to be useful. As long as he doesn't have any friends to scream for, we should be fine. I'm told they kill their wounded, so the fact that he's alive means he's probably alone. Then, Aari, buddy, while that's going on, you and me are going to excavate that egg ship and make sure your little sister and that idiot punk she's with aren't trapped inside."

"I'll start searching through the debris while you're gone, and I'll broadcast that we're here, Captain," Acorna said. "If our friends are nearby, and conscious, Thariinye will hear me and he'll let me know where they are."

"Good idea, Princess. We'll be right back with the plasma cutters."

Acorna climbed inside the half of the egg that should have contained the bridge. She could see the lower edge of the crushed viewport sunken deep into the damp sand. The sea was licking at the wreckage now, wide wet fingers teasing loose bits of smashed equipment and carrying them out and back with each wash of the waves. She wondered about tides—was the wreck in danger of being flooded? Perhaps, with so many moons arrayed about the planet, that wouldn't be an issue. Maybe they would all cancel each other out, gravitationally, instead of amplifying the movement of the seas. She could hope so, anyway.

The shadows were growing long now. Becker and Aari would not have much more daylight. She began throwing everything she could over the side of the ship facing away from the water. Becker would certainly want his salvage. Nothing faintly resembling the bridge was visible yet. Fragments of burnt and ripped pavilion fabric passed through her hands, as did a mane comb, and the shards of a mirror. Acorna saw her own slender face reflected back in the device. She hadn't realized she was weeping until then.

(Thariinye? Thariinye, answer me if you can!) she thought as hard as she could. But everything within the ship was still. The only movement was the settling of the rubbish as it shifted beneath her feet, and the lapping of the waves against the ruined hull of the ship.

She heard the *Condor*'s robolift descend again. Becker and Aari soon arrived carrying the plasma cutters with them. At Becker's signal Acorna climbed back out of the shell. Becker gave her an inquiring waggle of his eyebrows, but she shook her head sadly. She had been unable to make contact.

The men worked until well after dark, seeing by the light from their cutters. At one point, Acorna went up on the robolift and turned on an exterior floodlamp Becker had rigged above it for nighttime salvage expeditions. The shadows it cast made it look as if the two men were mining the pits of darkness, their grunts and the raucous scorch and sizzle of the saws adding to the general impression of demonic digging. The tide had risen and the wreck was beginning to flood. The men were waist-deep in water, so that they had to dive as well as cut. Meanwhile, Acorna carried salvage to the robolift.

She made mental calls to her friends from time to time, pleading for Thariinye to answer, but she felt nothing, heard nothing. Not then.

When the men were up to their necks in water, Becker finally threw his plasma cutter onto the beach over the broken hull of the shell ship and hoisted himself out. "C'mon, Aari. We're going to have to wait for the tide to go out. If there's anything there to see, it's too far under water now. Maybe the tide will shift some of the junk still there so we can see more."

"My little sister might be in there, Joh. A child."

"Maybe, but I doubt it," he said. "I'm betting that she and Thariinye were smart enough to get out." He looked toward Acorna but all she could see were the whites of his eyes and his teeth. "You sense anything from in there yet, Princess?"

She shook her head. "Nothing," she said. "It is possible the pod broke free while we were discussing how to destroy the Khleevi ship. Thariinye and Maati could have escaped then."

The three of them climbed onto the robolift. RK had stayed aboard the ship during the salvage operation. "Our new guest better hope they escaped, or be prepared to tell us where they are. Aari, I've got a few questions I want you to translate into their *klick-klack*."

"Certainly, Joh. I can ask questions, but I do not think the Khleevi will answer. They have never answered questions. The Linyaari sent ambassadors to them and the only answers we ever received to our questions were vids of the ambassadors being tortured as I was. But those ambassadors never escaped. Our people met their deaths in those vids."

"Nasty stuff. Well, maybe your people asked the Khleevi the right questions, but didn't ask in the right way. You Linyaari have got a few scruples that don't particularly apply to me. Aari, I want you to give Mac a little language lesson. He learned how to ask questions when he worked for Kisla Manjari. I'm betting our guest will be real happy to tell us anything we want to know before Mac is done with him. But we're still going to need you to translate. You folks are pacifists, I know. Is this going to bother you?"

Aari bared his teeth until they were whiter than his skin in the light of the two moons. "No, Joh. It will not bother me."

The sole Khleevi still alive and free on this planet cut a swath through the fern-like trees. At first it was a low swath. The creature was a bit stunned from his emergency departure from the shuttle, but it managed to properly decimate the undergrowth in the approved style. The Khleevi scoutship crew had expected that the strange craft that destroyed theirs would come for them on this planet, trying to protect the fragile little one-horns in the decorated space-borne food container. But the strange ship hadn't been fast enough. The Khleevi had made short work of the one-horn ship, and would have done the same to the strange ship had it not taken them by surprise and used unfair and totally uncalled for tactics to wreck them and cause the deaths of all of the other swarm members but the navigator and the self of the Khleevi who now ate its way through the forest floor.

That self—the inquisitor—had heard the klickings of the navigator for miles and miles, but the inquisitor was not about to go back. The navigator had been half squashed when the shuttle fell on him. The navigator would be recycled into food soon. The inquisitor would see to it.

The inquisitor had a communications device. It would be difficult to activate without the ship's power to fuel it, but organic activation could be implemented in an emergency such as the current one. It had only to reach a high point on the planet, arrange indigenous ingredients in a certain proportion, and chew, and the resulting chemical reaction would provide carrying power for the message the Khleevi wished to transmit.

The mission would not fail. The Khleevi swarm would come to this planet and find plenty and prosperity for another short time, and then all of the neighboring worlds and all their viable foodstuffs would also fall to his race's relentless mandibles.

Meanwhile, the other scout ships would search out other areas. But the inquisitor's sole purpose now was to notify its swarm of its own location, the location of the food, and the loss of the ship.

That, at least, was its sole intended purpose until, after eating its way through the undergrowth, it found at its very jaws a one-horn device, small and compact and shaped like a food container. To the inquisitor's regret it was empty, but the one-horns who had occupied it had left a trail of broken plant matter, scent, and vibrations. The inquisitor chomped its way after them up a steep hill and down it.

At the top of the steep hill, it looked at the seashore below it and saw the navigator being lugged down the beach by two hornless two-leggeds into the strange ship. The navigator was still alive and klicking. Not for long, the inquisitor was certain. That information would be noted when the inquisitor broadcast the next report to the swarm. It continued eating, tracking the missing one-horns.

As nighttime fell, the inquisitor was very full, but unsatisfied. It had a need to smell alien one-horn blood. To see it flow. As it ate its way downhill into a little valley, it saw how to fulfill that need, too. Leaning against a tree, apparently sleeping, was a one-horn. The inquisitor closed on its prey.

Eight

The healing retreat in the hills of the Ancestors, under their gentle, probing care, was meant to erase all pollution, all contamination, all taint, all pain, all shame left behind from the dreadful ordeal the Linyaari spacefarers had faced. The process could go on for days, weeks, months, years, by Standard reckoning; a *ghaanye* or many, by Linyaari reckoning.

However, the deep healing had barely begun when personal attendants began handing the supplicant pilgrims their wraps and saying, "Go home. You are needed in Kubiilikhan."

Grandam had never known of such a thing to happen in all her life.

"Have we done something wrong?" one of the younger crew members from the *Iülüra* asked. "Are we being cast out because our taint is too great?"

"Don't talk nonsense, child," the personal attendant said. "Didn't you hear Us? You are needed. And as for being cast out, how can We possibly be casting you out when We are coming with you?"

Back in town, Liriili had been fidgeting, forgetting to graze, pacing until her feet were quite rough and sore, walking up and down the road to and from the space-port. The *viizaar* had no messenger since Maati had van-ished, though she had little to do for the moment except wait. Wait for the Khleevi to find them again. She did not know what to do. Now recovered from her anger, she told herself she had done a service to Thariinye and Maati. When the Khleevi came here, those younglings at least would be spared. *If they hadn't already been consumed*, a small voice inside her head pointed out. She ignored it.

Walking down the road from the spaceport, where she had once more been checking with the com-shed of-ficer of the day, refusing to believe that the remote re-ports to her office were frequent or rapid enough to alert her in time for an attack, she saw the stream of her people, two footed and four footed, flowing down from the hills on the opposite side of the bowl-shaped valley containing Kubiilikhan.

Alarmed, disturbed, frightened, and yet, somehow, relieved as well, she returned to her office to await the return of the pilgrims—and of the Ancestors.

The thought of questioning of the Khleevi prisoner bothered Acorna. Despite her fear and loathing, she knew she would not be able to watch without wishing to heal any hurts inflicted upon the Khleevi in the line of questioning. She also knew that trying to heal the de-structive monster was not reasonable.

She could, however, feel its pain from two decks away. Despite Becker's threats to the contrary, no one had touched it since it had been brought aboard and its net locked into place where cargo nets were normally strung up. It hadn't been necessary to lay a hand on the creature. It was answering their questions sporadically, in between spasms of pain. But it was dying. She could feel it dying.

The feeling was so intense, it was as if she could feel herself dying, too. She couldn't stand it any longer. She had to leave or she'd be forced to interfere with what Becker was doing. And they needed the information he was extracting. She abandoned the bridge for the robo-lift, stopping on the way to tell the others what she was doing—that she was going to see if the tide was out yet, and if it was, she'd load some more cargo. She'd also continue calling for Thariinye and Maati while she was at it.

She got a "Yeah, ummm hmmm, okay," from Becker. Aari and Mac were totally absorbed by the Khleevi's rapid-fire *klick-klacking*.

The door edged open for a moment and the impression of the pain within staggered her. RK pushed himself through the door, flipping his tail up along his back as the hatch automatically snapped shut behind him. With a light leap, he was on her shoulder.

She scratched his chin. "Thank you, my friend. It will be good to have company."

Ghostly blue vapors billowed across an indigo sky and the turquoise light of two of the planet's moons strobed across the sea, the beach, and the forest beyond. Sand skidded against Acorna's ankles and calves.

Out here she could still feel the captive Khleevi's pain, but distance helped attenuate it. It also helped knowing that none of her crewmates was inflicting the terrible torture; they were only taking advantage of the monster's agony to obtain answers that might save her people, and any other creatures whose path the Khleevi crossed.

She breathed deeply of the night air. The fragrance of the sweet and spicy grasses and the fernlike trees, exotic and citrusy, filled her nostrils. She realized she hadn't grazed yet that day, and was hungry. She didn't worry about venturing beyond the dunes. Her Linyaari navigational instincts gave her an excellent sense of direction, and the light of the two moons above her was sufficient to see her way to the grasses between beach and forest.

She was relieved to put some distance between her and the *Condor* now. When she had eaten, she would return, see what progress her friends had made, and, if they were finished, ask them to let her examine the prisoner and tend to its wounds. She had not offered to tend to it so far out of fear that once she healed the thing, one of her friends would then have to reinjure it, in all likelihood, to obtain the vital information they needed. This could well be one of the very same Khleevi who had caused the death of her parents, but it was against her nature to cause or endure the suffering of another living creature. It was against Aari's nature, too. Despite what the Khleevi had done to him, she could not help but feel that participating in actual torment of another creature, even one of the species who had all but destroyed him, would impede his inner healing, perhaps even prevent it altogether. He, more than she, was born and bred to the Linyaari way, which was nonviolent.

Back on the beach, Aari had brandished his Khleevi weapon with authority and deadly intent, however. She didn't blame him or judge him for that, but it worried her that he had undergone such a tremendous change, one that was completely contrary to his upbringing.

She tested the grass with her horn—it was suitable for her to eat. So she took a mouthful of grass. It was peppery, not quite what she had in mind. She searched for another plant and found, growing sparsely among the peppery sort, a little reed with nodes on the stem. The nodes had a pleasant sour tang that offset the sweetness of the reed. They, too, were edible, and much tastier. She searched selectively for these, while RK slithered through the grassland as though he were a large jungle cat stalking prey.

She visualized Maati, who had been practically her only friend from narhii-Vhiliinyar. The child was just approaching puberty—funny, enthusiastic, lively, hardworking, inquisitive. She pictured Maati's soft pale brown skin and white and black spotted mane and feathers, her brilliant smile, short nose, and wide golden eyes below her little spiraled horn. She thought of Maati's immediate acceptance of Aari and her unquestioning love of her long-lost brother. The child's sadness and disbelief at being left behind by the *Condor* when it had taken both her newly found brother and her friend away. They could have brought her along, even though Liriili had objected violently when the subject came up. If they had done so, Maati wouldn't now be lost, maybe dead, along with poor Thariinye, who, although he was about the same age as Acorna, had not had as much experience or adventure in his life as she had, and so was still rather callow. Irritating, conceited, and arrogant, but not a bad fellow, really.

Her thoughts were anguished and regretful. She especially worried about her little friend, so sensible and knowledgeable about Linyaari ways but more willing than any to help a stranger. (Oh, Maati, Maati, I am so sorry, youngling. I thought you should stay with Grandam. I should have listened to your own thoughts more and not tried to decide for you. . . .)

(Khornya? Khornya! You're here! Oh, Khornya, come quickly. I can't find Thariinye and there is something awful out here in the bushes. Please, Khornya. I'm scared.)

(Maati! It's all right. I'm here. Where are you?)

(Looost!) The thought was a long wail.

(I'll come and get you. Just keep sending and I'll find you and bring you back. Can you see the beach from where you are? Can you see the *Condor*?)

(No, I'm in the woods and it's dark and Thariinye was *right here* standing guard while I slept. Now he's gone and the noises are terrible, Khornya.)

(Can he read you? Have you tried?)

(No. I think he must be unconscious. Knocked out, maybe.)

Acorna was galloping through the grass now and into the trees, following Maati's thoughts as if they were spoken words, tracking them to their origin.

The footing was treacherous in the dark but she leaped over bushes and roots. She had to pause frequently, however, to listen again for Maati's thought.

(Keep sending, Maati. I can't follow you unless I can read you.)

(I'm sooo tired, Khornya. And I'm almost afraid to think too loud for fear whatever it is that's thrashing around out there will hear me like you do.)

(I understand, dear, but if I'm to find you, you have to keep sending. If whatever it is hasn't bothered you yet, it probably can't read us.)

Acorna was halfway up a steep hill when she slipped and fell in a trail of slime. As she picked herself up again, she saw that she had fallen on the broken branches of what must have been brush. The raw ends of the branches were sharply severed at just above ground level for a long swath as wide as Acorna was tall. Where the foliage had been, a trail of foul-smelling slime covered the ground.

From the smell, she knew this was a Khleevi trail, the creature eating, digesting, and excreting as it went. No wonder they could trash entire planets in such a short time!

Had the wind not been from the sea, and blowing the smell of the slime away from her, she easily would have picked it up earlier. Now she had a spoor to follow and she lost no time scrambling after it.

(Maati, I think it is a Khleevi who has Thariinye. Stay right where you are and do not make a sound unless you know it is me. Have you moved since he disappeared?)

(No, I was too scared of the things out in the bushes.)

(Okay, then, that is good. Just stay put. Somewhere right near you there is a trail of broken brush and smelly Khleevi slime.)

(Eeewww, is that what it is? I thought maybe this planet just smelled really bad in some places.)

(No, that's Khleevi spoor. They excrete as fast as they eat, apparently. You sound stronger. I'll be with you in a bit.)

Acorna scrambled further up the hill and down it, following the trail until, though she hadn't heard from Maati in some time, she suddenly caught a very loud thought.

(Ouch! You stepped on me!)

Looking down, at first she saw nothing but more pale blue brush but then she saw, white and lustrous among the leaves, a face. She stared.

(Maati?) she asked uncertainly.

"Yes, it's me, Khornya," Maati whispered, and rose to her feet and threw her white arms around Acorna's neck so that Acorna's nose was buried in the girl's silvery mane.

(But you look—)

"Oh, yeah!"

(Think it, youngling. We don't know how near danger is.)

(I'm star-clad now. Like the new me?)

(Why should I not? I liked the old you. You are beautiful! So let's keep you alive, shall we? I need you to follow the slime trail back down the hill and through the woods—your nose will help you if you get off track. When you get to the beach, you'll see the *Condor*. You need to get Aari and Captain Becker's attention and have them come to help Thariinye and me—)

(And leave you alone? Thariinye won't be any help. I can't read him at all. Something's happened to him. If that's a Khleevi, you need me.)

RK bounded up to them and sat down, seemingly to wash, though he kept his ears cocked slightly back, as if he was listening to their nonverbal conversation. At some point in their journey, he had departed from Acorna's shoulder and taken off on his own explorations. Probably when she began galloping.

(It *is* a Khleevi. And it will be no trick to find it and Thariinye. The trail is extremely clear. Just go back and tell the others that we'll need their help. Meanwhile, I will try to keep the Khleevi from harming Thariinye anymore.)

(What if there are other Khleevi?)

(Captain Becker will know if there are. He has been questioning an injured Khleevi that we captured. He'll be able to tell us how many of these things we're facing. I need that information very much before I tackle freeing Thariinye. And I'd like you somewhere safe from this one,) Acorna said simply. And turned toward the slimy trail. But Maati wasn't done yet.

(You said you'd come for me,) Maati reminded her. (You were thinking all those nice things about me, and how you and Aari should have let me come with you. I'm not just a kid, you know. I'm smart. I could help you. What if I get caught on the way to get the others? What if I get lost?)

(Just follow the trail.)

(You're only one person. You need help, too. You know Thariinye won't be much help. We could hear him if he was in a position to help us. You know, you didn't treat me like such a child back home.)

Acorna hesitated. She didn't want to put her young friend in harm's way but, then again, maybe that

thought was a little ridiculous. Maati had already survived the wreck of her space vessel and eluded capture
by the Khleevi once today. It was entirely possible, if
the Khleevi were on this planet in force, that the ship
was no safer place than trooping with Acorna through
the forest.

(Very well. You can come with me. But thought-
speak only. And stay behind me.)

(Okay.) Acorna felt Maati searching for RK, but the
cat had vanished. Maati was a little worried, so Acorna
sent her the calming thought that if anyone on the face
of the blue planet could look out for themselves, it was
that cat. Then they pushed forward, along the broken
trail the Khleevi had left behind them, hoping against
all hope that Thariinye was still all right.

Nine

The Council meeting was brief. Liriili had been questioned. The accusations against her by com-shed personnel and by Thariinye's many mourning soon-to-be-lifemates were verified, and a proposal was made for her dismissal. The evidence was examined, including a copy of the broadcast from the *Condor* that Liriili denied had ever been received. One of the com-shed officers, who was also one of Thariinye's lady friends, had concealed copies of the *piiyi* transmission and Thariinye's translation of it, which she had taken from the com-shed before Liriili had given orders to have them destroyed. That was right after the *viizaar* had told the com-shed officers to stop transmitting anything at all from the planet for any reason. Not only did the young officer realize that Liriili had for some reason allowed Thariinye and a child to go into space alone, but she recognized that the *piiyi* had great implications for the Linyaari, and that the people must know about it. The com-shed officer had been about to set off for the hills herself to fetch the space-farers when the pilgrims came streaming home.

The Council had not been kindly disposed to having the warning of a possible Khleevi threat withheld from them for any reason, no matter what Liriili thought.

After the matter of Liriili had been discussed, the Council was expanded to include Neeva, Khaari, Melireenya, and several of the ambassadors and high teachers and merchants and officers from the returned fleet.

In lieu of Liriili, Grandam now presided over the Council. Liriili faced them from the opposite side of the table where she'd sat for so many years, wearing her "Everything is in order, business as usual" face.

Grandam could not help but smile. "Liriili of Clan Ri-ivye, *Vüzaar* of Kubiilikhan, you stand accused of trea-sonous acts against your people and your world. We will not ask you how you plead. You of all of us are most skilled at concealing your thoughts, one reason we felt you would make a good administrator. But you have betrayed not only the trust of your people, but my personal trust to you of the life of a young and parent-less child, as well as the life of a brave officer of our fleet."

"It was not my fault!" Liriili said. "I told them not to go. I told them—and this is perfectly true; any of you can read me—that we must not transmit further com-munications to the salvage ship that sent the *püyi* mes-sage to us, for fear of the Khleevi tracing the signal back to us. It is perfectly standard procedure. I have saved us all by my actions and this is the thanks I get? That you hold me responsible because two feckless and rebellious young people stole our newest and finest vessel and took off on a pointless and dangerous joyride against my express orders?"

"Enough!" Grandam bellowed. "You knew very well that the *Condor* had sent the *püyi* here for translation — a translation Thariinye completed before the children departed. There is a record of the conversation in which he informed you of his translation. You knew at that time that there was a good chance of communicating with the *Condor* so that Captain Becker, as well as securing the safety of his ship and crew, could warn our allies of the impending threat without. You did nothing."

"Allies!" Liriili snorted. "Look at the Starfarers if you think we have allies! Did our so-called 'allies' not turn over our finest ambassadors and officers, teachers and traders, to enemies who imprisoned and abused them?"

"They were deceived," Grandam said. "But you, Liriili, were not deceived. You knew that the *Condor* and our allies could have been notified of the threat long before the Khleevi were likely to be close enough to trace them. You knew that Thariinye also knew this, and that neither he nor Maati would allow harm to come to Khornya, Aari, or to Captain Becker if it was in their power to prevent this. You even knew, Liriili, that the *püyi* contained evidence of the probability of the survival of Kaarlye and Miiri of the Nyaarya clan, Maati's and Aari's parents. All of this information was problematic for you. And so you deliberately ordered the children to do nothing, knowing that they would be forced to disobey you, and that they — and all those who depended on their information — would be lost."

Liriili felt a sharp pain in the middle of her back and she was jabbed forward so quickly she fell to her knees. "I didn't *know* that. How could I *know* for certain? All of you spacefarers, as usual, were off someplace else when decisions had to be made immediately. I did what I thought was best for the people. Including you. And is this the thanks I get for my dedication to duty? Some thanks . . ."

She was weeping now with rage, with fear, with indignation, for she half-believed what she was saying herself, as Grandam well knew, or she could never have said it.

"Oh, Liriili, my poor granddaughter," Grandam Naadiina said, pushing past the Council table behind which she had been sitting and kneeling to put her hands on either side of Liriili's wet face. Liriili stared rebelliously back at her. "We have been aware of the flaw in your makeup since you were very young, you know. You, of all of us, are best able to conceal your thoughts. You alone are capable of, if not lying, at least twisting the meaning of your thoughts to a degree that makes them difficult to read. We decided when the old *Viizaar* passed on to the land of the Ancestors that this—difference—in your makeup need not be a flaw, but could be used for the greater good of all. And you are correct. In general you have been an excellent and conscientious administrator.

"Much of the fault lies with us for not realizing that your—specialness—separated and isolated you, not only from the rest of your people but from the truth within yourself. Now we do not punish you, child, but seek to recompense you for the harm we have allowed you to do to yourself as well as to others. You must face the truth of your actions, if not within yourself, for you seem to be incapable of doing so, but by seeing for yourself the consequences."

Liriili was very easy to read now. Caution was trying to displace fear and disbelief in her mind as Grandam retreated to her official position, sat, then rose again, in unison with the other Council members.

"Liriili of clan Riivye, you are relieved of your duties as *Viizaar* of Kubiilikhan and administrator of narhii-Vhiliinyar by the High Council after consultation with and in accordance with the advice of the Ancestors. You are reassigned to duty as a junior shipman on the *Balakiire*, under the command of *visedhaanye-feriili* Neeva and Melireenya. Your mission will be to pursue the information obtained from the *piiyi*, to attempt to warn the *Condor* of the peril contained in it, to ascertain the whereabouts and ensure the safety of Thariinye and Maati and the *Nükaavri*, to determine the whereabouts of Kaarlye and Miiri and rescue them or at least retrieve the data in their landing pod, and to warn our allies of the Khleevi danger, even if by issuing such a warning you allow the Khleevi to trace a signal back to the *Balakiire*. *Visedhaanye-feriili* Neeva and her crew have volunteered for this mission, and have agreed to take responsibility for you. They are prepared to make the ultimate sacrifice, if necessary, to accomplish this mission. You are hereby dismissed into the custody of the Neeva, her crew, and the *Balakiire*, and may the wit of the Ancestors and the Grace of the Friends preserve you all from harm."

*　　*　　*

The prisoner was in unbearable pain. Aari had decidedly mixed feelings about the fact. His need for revenge was at odds with his hatred of seeing anything, even a Khleevi, suffer so. But there was one comfort to be found in the hold of this ship, as terrifying a place as it was right now. The prisoner was klacking out all the information Aari demanded, but neither Aari nor Becker nor even Mac, who had been quite prepared to "slowly disassemble" the Khleevi, had laid a finger on the creature. Whatever was causing the Khleevi so much agony, they weren't responsible.

Instead of disassembling it, Mac was rapidly processing the information he was given about Khleevi klackings by Aari and the LAANYE to help interpret Aari's and Becker's questions into simulated klacks and to interpret the answers.

The thing lay within the cargo net on the deck, and the net's couplings were securely fastened to the bulkhead. The monster was going nowhere. Aari was grateful the despicable creature's form was somewhat obscured by the grid of the net. Its titanium strands pulled tightly across the creature's protruding eyes, restrained its pincers, and bent one antenna flat against the side of its bulbous head. The putrid smell Aari had first noticed out by the Khleevi ship now filled the hold and seemed to grow worse and worse as time went on. Becker remarked on the green icor draining from beneath the netted Khleevi.

"It's messing itself, it's so scared," he said.

"Scared?" Aari asked. "A Khleevi? Scared? Of us?"

"Sure. You were scared, when we found you for the first time, weren't you?"

"Naturally, but I am not a Khleevi."

"Let me tell you a little something about people, buddy, any kind of people," Becker said. "These creeps," he gestured to the Khleevi, "they like to hurt anything they come across just to watch it squirm. It's how the buggers think. So when one of them gets caught and put in the same position as its victims, of course it's going to figure we'll do the same to it. Only difference is, we're after information. According to you, when you were a Khleevi captive, they didn't seem to care all that much if you said anything or not. They just liked to hear you scream, right?"

"Yes, Joh. I never understood any of that."

"Well, understand this. As afraid as you were, this critter is even more afraid. Because to do to someone what the Khleevi did to you requires being a real lily-livered son of a gun at heart. Yessir, these Khleevi may look like bugs, but they're all piles of pure cowardice with legs, if you ask me. Cowards and bullies, every one." Becker threw his arms around and let his voice ring to make it heard above the piteous but irritating high-pitched sound the Khleevi was making. Aari had never heard the bug-like beings make that sound while he was among them. Though perhaps he might have heard the sound, or a variant of it, coming from himself.

"Now, Aari, if you have any more questions, ask away. Mac, you follow and see if you can fill in any blanks for him."

"What will *you* do, Captain?" Mac asked mildly.

"I'll be thinking up threats and—uh—persuasions," Becker said.

"Very well, Captain. Aari?"

"Mac, ask it what it was doing here, how many others like it there are close by, where the main fleet is, and the location of the homeworld."

Mac manufactured the klacking sound of the Khleevi, using his mouth alone. Aari was impressed.

The Khleevi let forth the high-pitched whining sound once more.

"Tell it we'll stop the pain if it gives us the data," Becker instructed Mac, his jaw clenched tightly, his teeth bared in what was an indisputable display of hostility—a hostility Becker seemed to be reveling in.

Aari, on the other hand, was not enjoying his position. He had certainly thought he would enjoy giving back to a Khleevi what the Khleevi had done to him, but instead he felt filled with loathing—for himself. He was now doing a Khleevi thing. He might as well be one. But the information was important. He put the thought on hold when he realized Mac was speaking, and not in klacks this time.

"Theirs was a scout ship. The Khleevi have many such ships. Their mission was to locate a likely world with the proper atmosphere and nutrients for consumption by the horde. The horde's main fleet has already been notified that this being's ship had located a large number of suitable worlds, including this one, due to a lucky conquest of a scout ship of a two-horned race."

Mac turned to Becker and said, "That would be the Niriians, surely? You understand, please, that many of the concepts this creature expresses can be interpreted only loosely. Fortunately, because of the remaining programming from my former user, I am quite conversant with the basic content of this creature's thought and language patterns and can assure you that my interpretations are fairly accurate. The Khleevi have a lot in common with Kisla Manjari."

And so it went. To minimize the misunderstanding or chance of lying on the part of the Khleevi, ("Well, for pity's sake, Aari," Becker said, "any critter who would do to you what these guys did is certainly not going to stop at a little *lie!*") Becker insisted on asking the same questions over and over in many different ways.

Mac said, "You are very good at information extraction, Captain Becker. Have you been in the business before yourself?"

"No, but my dad was great at giving pop oral exams on the subjects I was supposed to be learning when I was a kid," Becker said. "I never could put anything over on him. Who knew it would come in so handy? So let's go over it all one more time . . ."

Aari found himself sweating during the questioning, remembering himself in the Khleevi's place and hearing the squeal ooze out of the creature along with the stench.

At some point during the questioning, Khornya stopped by. When she left, Aari noticed that RK was no longer in the room with them. By then, among them, they were trying to explain to the Khleevi that they wanted the coordinates of the horde fleet and of the Khleevi home planet, as well as the codes that would allow them to crack Khleevi communication devices.

The thing had just given them a useless string of babble that none of them could decipher when the stench suddenly became much worse, the klacking much more muffled, and the squeal thinner, higher, shriller. Then, suddenly, all was still.

Mac kicked at the creature. "I think it is unconscious, Captain."

"Sissy," Becker said. "We never touched it. Some people will do anything to get out of having to answer a few simple questions."

"Joh, you told it we would stop its pain if it told us what we wished to know," Aari said.

"Looks to me like the pain has almost stopped," Becker said.

"No, it is worse. The thing is dying. We must have Khornya heal it. I would but — I cannot."

"Ain't it just too bad for old klacker here that they took out your horn, then?" Becker said, and Aari felt a flash of anger toward him.

"We must call Khornya back in to save it, Joh. It may have — more information."

"Hmm, true. You look like you can use a break anyway, buddy. Go ahead then. Get her."

Aari left quickly. He was surprised to see that he had to call the robolift to return to the deck for him to descend. Its deck was stickier than ever, despite the heavy traffic, and when he tried to move his feet made a sucking sound. The patches of sap were — yes, they actually *were* larger than they had been when he and Becker ascended to the ship with the prisoner. He bent down, curious, to touch the stuff. It seemed innocent enough, but when he tried to right himself, he found that the hand he had been using to steady himself on the deck stuck to it. He lost his footing and fell, getting sap all over the front of his shipsuit. He unstuck himself and regained his balance with some difficulty. He also resolved to clean the deck as soon as they had disposed of the prisoner.

As the lift continued to descend, he saw that the bright blue day had become indigo night, lit only by the pale blue moons. The wind soughed through the tall sapphire grasses. Khornya was nowhere to be seen, but as he looked, he suddenly heard a raucous "Mrowl" and saw RK bounding across the field between the beach and the woods.

As soon as the cat saw him, RK turned and leaped back in the direction from which he had come. Sprinting a few steps, RK turned and stared meaningfully, his gleaming eyes twin molten gold coins. He mrowled again and Aari followed, reluctantly. He had planned to take a slight detour and try to clean off the sticky, irritating sap with sea water, but the cat was trying to lead him to Khornya, of that Aari was certain. "Where is she, Riid-Kiiyi?" he asked.

RK ran another few feet and glanced back again, mrowling for Aari to follow him. The cat was conveying a sense of urgency that worried Aari. Through the long grass and to the ferny trees, Aari followed the cat's lead. Khornya. The cat was leading him to Khornya. She was in some sort of trouble, perhaps wounded, or maybe she had found Maati and Thariinye and they were wounded and she had sent the cat back for help and—

Aari smelled the Khleevi spoor before he was actually upon it. Old and cold, it had hardened to a nasty shiny trail. The Khleevi. The Khleevi had Khornya.

He vomited what little food he had eaten that day into the underbrush. Returning for Becker now was out of the question. Every moment counted—he remembered what the creatures had done to him and his blood ran cold at the thought of Khornya in their clutches.

Precious time would be lost if he went back to the ship—moments Khornya would pay for in unimaginable pain if the Khleevi did indeed have her. Somehow, somehow he had to find her, to free her, to protect her. No one must go through what he had. Especially not Khornya—beautiful, graceful, gentle Khornya. So kind. So caring. Practical and intelligent too and very strong, but no one could hold out against the Khleevi. That they should have a chance to break her into pieces as they had him was unthinkable.

Perhaps he couldn't yet feel what he sensed she would have liked him to feel for her—he still felt hollow inside, numb and cold, when he wasn't filled with pain and fury. He had nothing to give to someone like Khornya. But he owed it to her to make sure she lived to receive it from someone else someday.

He followed the spoor uphill and down again and then into another section of forest, up another hill. He did not notice when the cat disappeared once more.

But when he heard the screams, the steady jog with which he was following the sign lengthened to a full gallop.

Ten

As far as Acorna could see, the problem was not finding the Khleevi. The thing was not stealthy. Its excremental trail led straight to it. The only problem was how to get the better of it before it could harm Thariinye.

They found Thariinye first. He was at the end of the trail, wrapped up in the end of the trail in fact, pinned by a hardened twist of it to a tree. In the chill of the night air, his breath made a vapor, so they knew he was not dead. But neither of them could pick up any thoughts from him, not even a snatch of dream.

The Khleevi stood slightly uphill from him, its moon-drenched shadow falling over them, mingling with the shadows of the trees. Its bug eyes were lifted to the moons, its head bobbing. Two of its legs tended what seemed to be some sort of electrical contraption. Sparks flew periodically between its legs and the machine, while two more of its legs burned a bit of the excrement, with predictably nauseating results. After each set of legs had gone through the ritual, the pincers made a series of klacks, much like the Morse code Acorna had learned on the mining ship.

Maati and Acorna thought at the same time, (It's calling the mother ship. We have to stop it.)

(Free Thariinye first,) was their next simultaneous thought. Maati saw Acorna's teeth shining in the dark—humor and hostility mixed.

(Work your way behind the tree, Maati. See if you can get him loose from that stuff. Here, take my laserknife. I'll see if I can create a diversion.)

(Okay. Be careful, Khornya.)

The two split up, and Acorna circled wide in the forest and up the crest of the hill to one side of the Khleevi, who was actually within a slight clearing. Peering at the creature through the trees, she could see that it was busy with its work. Still, she had the feeling it was only trying to make contact, not that it had achieved its goal. Its pauses were to adjust the machine, not to listen. The Khleevi creature must be stopped before it brought an entire invasion force down upon them.

She needed to draw him off, away from whatever it was he was using to communicate and away from Thariinye and Maati. And she needed to have a plan to get away herself, if possible, once they were a safe distance from her friends. She thought for a second, took a deep breath, and started moving.

She picked up a stick, flung it at the creature, and raced off down the hill at a diagonal from Thariinye's position.

"Neener neener neener!" she yelled at the Khleevi, using an expression she'd picked up from the kids on

Maganos Moonbase as she galloped down the hill. She glanced back to see if it was paying attention.

It gave two hops and was almost upon her.

She took off at a dead run, thundering down the hill, screaming at the top of her lungs, with the Khleevi hopping behind her, covering two or three yards with each hop.

(Khornya, run!) Maati cried inside her head. (I can't get through this stuff without Thariinye's help. And I can't wake Thariinye.)

(Try harder. Use your horn if you have to.)

(What if I hurt Thariinye?)

(Better that than what the Khleevi will do to him.)

Thinking and running at the same time was not easy. Acorna stumbled across a broken tree and fell sprawling among the branches. In two short hops the Khleevi was practically upon her. She dove under the fronds and wriggled her way to the trunk, then hopped up and tried to run again, only to find her leg wouldn't work. Sharp pains were running up it.

The heat and stench and klack of the Khleevi were all around her as she tried to squirm and touch her horn to her leg.

The huge bug appeared nightmarishly dim through the fronds as it jumped—and landed on her hurt leg.

Acorna had not cried out for help, mentally or aloud, because she did not wish for Maati to run to the rescue and try to fight the Khleevi. But the sudden pain was so intense she let out a piercing scream.

"Hey you! Big old bug!" Maati sang out, followed by Thariinye yelling, "I'm over here, you slimy hulk of a feces machine!"

The Khleevi stepped back for a moment, uncertain. Then Acorna could swear it bared what passed for teeth in that gaping maw, and deliberately brought its foot down again on, well, on the area where her leg had been, because she had pulled the broken limb out of the way.

"Maati, you silly child, *run*!" Acorna cried.

"Don't you hurt her again, you dung-eating pile of— of dung!" Maati yelled. Footsteps ran in closer.

"Maati, *no*," Acorna screamed. And so did Maati. Acorna couldn't see what happened, but she heard a crunch and a yelp, then a sound as if the air was being let out of something.

"You pick on little girls, you bag of excrement!" Thariinye hollered. "Why not tie me to a tree with your slimy trail again!" He profited by Maati's example because his voice grew a bit fainter and Acorna heard the sound of his feet crushing brush as he retreated. The Khleevi gave a hop—and she was free. At least for a moment.

Bending from the waist she rubbed her horn against her leg once she had the bone properly aligned. The pain eased at once, but she was forced to concentrate on the healing of the limb rather than on anything around her. She had no idea, for a precious few moments, whether or not Maati was living, whether Thariinye had escaped capture while leading the Khleevi from her, or even if the Khleevi was about to step on her head this time.

As soon as the pain stopped and the bone had knitted, Acorna raised herself up to see the Khleevi grab for the dancing Thariinye with its front pincers. Thariinye screamed, and Acorna grabbed the nearest object—a rock from the ground beneath her—and threw it at the Khleevi.

The big insectoid was not so quickly fooled this time. It grabbed Thariinye and began slashing at him with its razor-sharp pincers, leaving gruesome wounds on Thariinye's upraised hands and arms. Acorna leaped across the fallen trunk of the tree and pounded on the carapace of the creature with her fists while her old shipmate's heart-rending cries rang in her ears.

"Let go, let go, let go!" she bawled.

The Khleevi did let go, and Thariinye, bleeding from many wounds, fell like a limp doll very close to Maati's still form. Acorna turned and ran.

The Khleevi rounded on Acorna, its pincers snapping. Only a single tree hung between them. Then, with a chomp and a noisome burst of gas, the tree was gone. Acorna turned and ran, leaping over the fallen tree this time, putting it between herself and the Khleevi. She dashed past frond after frond, only to have them vanish down the Khleevi's maw to reappear behind the creature as another smelly bit of trail.

The Khleevi seemed to smile as it took its last bite from the tree trunk, taunting her with its deliberate progress as it ate away her only barrier. She kept moving, mentally calling to Maati and Thariinye, hoping to hear a response but urging them to lie still.

The Khleevi finished the tree trunk. Acorna backed up against another tree. It followed her slowly, taking first one chomp and then another from fronds she thrust between them. It was clearly enjoying the game.

She shrieked as a pincer came within a centimeter of

her face. The Khleevi snapped at her, then brought its pincers up again, close to her horn. She dodged and tried to dive between its lower legs.

All at once, from the corner of her eye, she saw a white blur. The Khleevi fell over backward, a Linyaari form bearing it to the ground, surrounded by its flailing legs and pincers.

(Khornya, run!) Aari's voice was mental, but far from a whisper. *(Get Joh. Get weapons. I will keep it busy as long as I can, but you must save yourself and my sister.)*

(You can't fight it alone, Aari.)

(No, but I can delay it. Go!)

(It will kill you!)

(I am carrion already.)

She ran through the woods screaming for Becker, screaming the names of her fallen friends.

Much to her surprise, Becker and Mac, brandishing weapons, bounded toward her through the woods, Becker yelling, "Where is he? Point and duck!"

She turned and ran back toward Aari, who, much to her surprise, was raising himself unharmed from among curled Khleevi legs and pincers. The creature made no attempt to stop him or damage him. Instead it stayed on the ground, emitting the same high-pitched "eee-eee-eee" sound their prisoner had made back on the ship. Becker paid none of that any attention at all. As soon as Aari was clear, Becker pressed his rifle against his hip and fired. A huge crackling hole opened up in the creature and it was still.

The echo of the shot had not yet faded when a pair of Linyaari figures carrying what looked like strips of metal came running over the hill. (Maati? Aari? By the ancestors, are they *dead*?)

Acorna grabbed Aari's arm and heard the mental call when she touched him. (Mother? Father?) he said, stunned.

Maati sat up, groggy. "Did somebody call me?"

Acorna released Aari and moved to kneel beside Thariinye. Her old shipmate did not look up, but she could see he was breathing. His shipsuit was a bloody mess. One of his hands dangled from a scrap of skin protruding from his sleeve. A chunk was missing from his right cheek and one of his eyes was swelled shut, the lid and brow lacerated. His horn was an inch or so shorter than it had been.

"Thariinye!" Maati cried, and rose to her hands and knees to do a very fast crawl to Thariinye's other side. "Oh, no, look at his hand."

"Maati? Baby, is that you, all grown up?" the male Linyaari who had appeared during the fight asked.

Maati's face rose to look at the two tall Linyaari strangers. Once she got a good look at their faces she ran to them, crying. "Mother? Father? Help us! Thariinye's hurt bad. He made the Khleevi fight him so it wouldn't kill me." She dragged her parents back to Thariinye's side.

"My goodness," her mother said. "The young man certainly is in a bad way, but this young lady is doing a fine job of healing him. Maati?"

The male Linyaari gently shoved Acorna aside and bent his own horn to Thariinye's hand. "Allow me, my dear. This boy was little more than a toddler when we left narhii-Vhiliinyar. And now he's been wounded protecting our little girl."

Acorna willingly surrendered Thariinye's care to the man. She was weary beyond belief from her own ordeal, but she needed to see to Aari. He hadn't appeared to be greatly harmed by his own encounter with the Khleevi, although he had been locked in its multilegged embrace. But there had been something odd about their "parting."

Becker and Aari were both bent over the corpse of the Khleevi, studying it.

"The Khleevi was dying when you shot it, Joh. It could not hold on to me. See how its legs are curled?"

"Lead poisoning will do that to you," Becker growled.

"Lead poisoning? Where was the lead?" Aari asked. "You used the laser cannon."

"Figure of speech," Becker replied.

"Aari, are you hurt?" Acorna asked, looking him over careful. "The front of your shirt—it's a mess."

Aari looked down and said with satisfaction, "Khleevi blood, mostly. You or Thariinye must have wounded the creature before I reached it. I had no weapons."

"Neither did we," Acorna said. "We weren't expecting trouble here." She knelt to examine the dead Khleevi. Gingerly, she touched its chest along the edge of the wound made by Becker's laser cannon. "What is this? It's not the same color as the Khleevi blood."

"Oh—that's from me," Aari said, "I fell in the sap on the robolift when I left the ship. It was all over the front of my shipsuit."

Acorna tried to remove the sap with her finger but it had actually sunk into the Khleevi's carapace. In fact, she saw as she pulled some of the sap aside, it had eaten away a portion of the creature's shell-like protection.

She looked up at the two men who were frowning down, watching her. "What became of the other Khleevi?"

"It was dying when we left the ship," Aari said. "I came to get you to heal it."

"Did you harm it?"

"No—no, we did not have to harm it. It seemed to . . . believe we were harming it, though, and we let it think so," Aari said.

"We really were going to let you heal it up, honest," Becker said. "As soon as we got all the information we needed. Figured maybe the scientists could study the thing—" He tried to sound innocent. Acorna knew that Becker had just thought of the scientists studying the Khleevi. He had been very much against healing its wounds. "Maybe it was hurt worse in the crash than we figured. It told us what we wanted to know and then— really, pretty conveniently—it keeled over. Aari was coming to get you to see if you could maybe heal it or something."

Both men looked very uncomfortable. Acorna looked from one to the other. "I don't think it was the injuries in the crash that killed that prisoner—and I suspect this one was mortally wounded from the moment Aari jumped on him."

"You *jumped* that thing, buddy?" Becker asked Aari, clapping him on the back. "Way to go. I didn't think you had it in you. Not bad for a pacifist."

"You miss the point, Joh. Khornya just said I killed the Khleevi. How did I do that, Khornya?"

"The sap on your shipsuit," Acorna told him.

"Ye-es," Aari said. "Yes. That makes sense. I remember the first time we saw the sap. It killed small insects preying upon the vines in the homeworld."

"Yeah, the plants thought we were a bug, too," Becker said. "They slimed the *Condor*, trying to get through its shell. Lucky us, it didn't work."

"The sap probably only destroys selected organic substances. Judging by the results, I would guess that the polysaccharides in the Khleevi's chitin carapaces are susceptible to it, Joh," Aari said.

"Good. Anything that eats up Khleevi shells is fine by me," Becker rejoined.

Acorna glanced over and saw Maati and her parents were helping Thariinye stand. His clothing was still bloody, but he was moving the fingers of his formerly injured hand, and all of the gashes and gouges were cleaned up. His horn, however, remained shorter than it had been.

Aari deliberately turned his back on the Linyaari quartet as he, Becker, and Mac began pulling another of the titanium cargo nets around the dead Khleevi. Acorna, panting and catching her breath, stared at his back, and shook her head. He was clearly not going to fall on the necks of his long-lost parents and rejoice at their presence. In fact, it looked like he was going to avoid dealing with them at all, if he could.

Miiri—Maati and Aari's mother—was the first to discover the rash on Aari's hands. While Aari's palms were now mostly cleaned of sap, they were red and itching, swelling in places. He kept pausing in the journey to rub his palms on the legs of his shipsuit. His mother, who had been trying to run along beside him to talk to him, noticed.

Aari tried to ignore his mother but Acorna stopped

him, turning to rest a hand on his arm, raised his palm and examined it. "I had an itchy red place like this on my finger just now, from where I examined the sap on the edge of the Khleevi's wound, but I put it up to my horn and it healed. Let me see if I can help you," she said, lowering her horn to Aari's palms and touching them lightly, first one hand and then the other. The pain he was in was all too evident in his rigid posture and the look in his eyes. Finally he let out a sigh of relief and gave her a look half of irritation, half of gratitude.

"That sap, which eats into the Khleevi shells and kills them in short order, apparently merely causes an allergic reaction in our species," Acorna said. "It's irritating, but the sap doesn't appear to be lethal to us."

"Mac," Becker said, "when we get back to the ship, priority one is for you to scrape all that sap off the robolift and collect it, then stow it in one of the unpressurized cargo bays. I want samples of it analyzed as soon as possible. This stuff could be useful."

The next few hours were a blur of activity. Maati and Aari's parents thought-spoke with the other Linyaari while everyone worked, telling a little bit of their adventures while stranded on this planet. Their survival here was a testament to both their courage and cleverness. But Maati had so much to say to her mother and father that she chattered away like a magpie, using her newfound telepathic abilities. So, consequently, most of the conversation centered on Maati's recent escapades, rather than on her parents doings since they left their homeworld in search of their children. And, despite the need to reconnect with the wanderers, there was too much to accomplish to truly do justice to the occasion.

All the Linyaari, as well as the remaining crew of the *Condor*, bent their backs to the tasks at hand. They wanted to load both the crashed Khleevi shuttle and the remains of the *Nükaavri* aboard the *Condor*, as well as any other cargo they could reach or Mac could wade out to retrieve. The main Khleevi ship was simply shattered, most of the resulting fragments of debris too small to be of interest even to Becker, though they salvaged what they could.

(Why are we bothering with this trash right now?) Kaarlye, Maati and Aari's father, asked Maati. (Don't we need to get in contact with our people? The Khleevi were here.) The parents, without time to sleep-learn standard Galactic from the LAANYE, could make no sense of Becker's or Mac's thought patterns, though RK—as always—managed to make himself understood.

(I will see what I can find out,) Maati told him.

"Captain," Maati said in Linyaari, following Becker down the beach until when he turned back to pick up another piece of salvage he nearly stepped on her. "If the Khleevi are scouting this area and the swarm is near, shouldn't we leave this stuff until later and return to narhii-Vhiliinyar to warn the people—"

Becker tried to answer, first in Standard, then in the broken Linyaari he had picked up from Aari. Before Kaarlye's confusion became total, Acorna hurriedly translated Becker's answers as physically transmitted by Maati.

"Well," Becker said, "except for finding you and Thariinye here, we haven't had any communication from your planet since we sent the *püyi* data, honey. We told 'em to get back to us with a translation, remember? I don't think they're listening to us, and I'm sure they're not talking to us. I don't imagine that's going to change now, even though we've got things to tell them. I hate to say it, but for all we know, the Khleevi could be there already, maybe even been there and left.

"That monster we were able to question only knew the position of the fleet as of the last transmission he'd received, which was days ago. If it helps, as far as the prisoner knew, the Khleevi weren't on your world yet at that time. But we don't know what's going on at your home, nor can we give them any solid information other than the warning about the Khleevi maybe being in the neighborhood that we already sent—you know, the one that made you and Thariinye go hurtling into space? We gave your people that warning when we transmitted the *piiyi* contents—though from what you've told us about that horse-faced *vüzaar* of yours, it might not have done any good. All we can really add to our first broadcast is that we've found your parents here. Whatever's happening back at your planet, our help's too far away and will arrive too late to change anything. That's why I'm not in any hurry to talk to your planet.

"Right now, I'm more worried about us. That bug we talked to told the rest of the bugs exactly where this planet is, and how rich it is in Khleevi food. The swarm could be on their way here, for all we know. We could have a lot of time, or we could have very little, before they arrive. My scanners don't show anything, but that's not conclusive. So that's why I want all the salvage we can manage to get aboard the *Condor* before we take off. If the com system in the Khleevi shuttle is undamaged—it looks pretty good to me—and if we can turn it on and get it working, there's a chance it could still be getting signals from the fleet, which would tell us where they are, and maybe even where they're going."

So everyone pitched in and worked for hours gathering the cargo and transporting it to the ship. After they got it all stacked ready to stow, they watched Mac open his forearm and extract a paint-scraping tool. Then the android punched a button just under the skin of his wrist that switched him to what looked like a holovid on fast forward. With rapid sweeps, he cleaned the robolift of sap and stored the sticky stuff carefully in one of Captain Becker's ceramic yogurt containers—after first evicting the yogurt and cleaning the dish, of course.

"What am I to do with this, Captain?" Mac asked.

"Stow it in one of the outer holds, not a temperature-controlled one. The sap was doing just fine out there in the cold vaccuum while we traveled here. I don't want to mess with a working system. Great stars and asteroids, will you look at my hull?" The *Condor* was normally a silvery metallic color but now was covered with broad trails of the yellowish sap as vines would cover a quaint cottage. "I guess this stuff was frozen in space and is having a field day here thawing out."

Acorna stopped relaying his words to the non-Standard-speaking newcomers, and suggested, "Captain, we should make certain none of the sap is left behind since it is alien to this ecology, and may greatly damage it."

"I was gonna say that next," Becker told her.

Once the lift was cleared and they were sure no sap remained on the ground, everyone helped load the cargo. Mac returned from stowing the sap and carried the heavier items such as the nearly intact Khleevi shuttle. Becker cast a regretful glance at the hull of the Linyaari vessel. "I really want to take that with us, but I can't justify the time it would take to grab it, disassemble it, and stow it. Well, I guess since you guys came with it, it's not really salvage anyway."

Acorna thought he was going to cry in his mustache at leaving such a valuable item behind, so she patted his arm and said, "When the crisis is over, Captain, we can always return for it."

"That's right," he said, and brightened up immediately.

She translated for the newcomers again and Kaarlye said, "Yes. Perhaps when he returns the captain could retrieve our escape pod as well. We're very fond of it. It saved our lives, you know."

Eleven

I think we'd all like to know how you came to be here and what has happened to you since you left narhii-Vhiliinyar," Acorna said much later to Kaarlye and Miiri. Becker, RK, and Mac were manning and catting the helm. Aari and Acorna led their new guests to the hydroponics gardens to graze.

"There's not much to tell really," Miiri told her. "We left as soon as Maati could be cared for by someone else." She ran her hand over Maati's mane. "You do understand, my dear, that we didn't think we would be gone long, and we didn't wish to endanger you, should the Khleevi still be in the area of our old home. We hoped somehow our boys—you, Aari, and—"

"Laarye died, Mother, while I was a prisoner of the Khleevi," Aari said. "I'm sorry. I couldn't save him."

"Yes," she said simply. "I felt it."

(Did you feel me, too, Mother? Did you feel my suffering?) At his mother's shocked look, the stolid, mildly bored look Aari wore as a mask left his face and he, too, looked shocked. "I didn't say anything," he said a little pleadingly to Acorna. She let out the breath she had sucked in when he spoke to his mother.

(You used thought-speak, as you did with me earlier when the Khleevi attacked me.)

(I—did not think anyone could hear me. I did not realize—)

(I heard you,) Acorna said. (I heard you this afternoon when the thing was attacking me. It gave me courage, knowing you were coming.)

"I heard you, too, my son," his mother said. The light in the hydroponics gardens was dim now, simulating nighttime to give the plants a rest. The air smelled sweet and fresh down here. The rest of the ship'd had a very pungent odor when the six Linyaari boarded. Even though Mac had dragged the Khleevi corpses into another outer hold, and cleaned the sap and the Khleevi blood from the decks, the *Condor* reeked. Of course, the Linyaari horns cleansed the air. But it still seemed like the dead Khleevi could stink up the place a little faster than the Linyaari horns could clean it.

This area of the ship was something of a showplace, one Acorna and Aari had worked hard to bring into being. They had draped drop cloths from the bulkhead above the space so that they resembled clouds and sky. The ship's artificial lighting now shone down on them, filtered gently by the "sky." All six Linyaari were squatted in grazing posture, in a circle, staring at each other through eyes shining with the reflection of the simulated moon. A little enclosed pond Acorna had created to make the area nicer as well as to maintain the humidity needed for optimum plant growth sent rippling shadows across the billowing drop-cloth clouds.

"I heard you across the galaxies, Son. I heard your brother die and I heard your screams," his mother said. "Why do you think we left Maati with Grandam and returned?"

"To join me in the Khleevi torture chamber?" he asked. Aari's bitterness was all too visible then. He could not choke it down, and Acorna knew that this was some of the buried pain she'd been unable to touch in him. "What a waste that would have been. You would have done better to have parented Maati, even if you hadn't given up on Laarye and me."

"Read me," his mother said. "I heard you. We came when we could."

"She heard you," his father said, his face solemn and his eyes deeply sad. "She screamed at night along with you. She lost all sleep and appetite as she endured with you what you endured. Did *you* not hear *her* as our enemies killed not only your brother Laarye, but the twins she lost before she carried Maati?"

Acorna gazed at Miiri more closely. She was very thin, but then, Linyaari were inclined toward slenderness as a rule. Her eyes were a beautiful copper color, but set deeply in her head. The color and texture of her skin were not good. Not sickly—her lifemate would have healed her if it had been merely an illness that troubled her—but unhealthy nonetheless. Strain had etched deep lines from her nose to her mouth, and other lines formed a diamond with points at the base of her horn and the bridge of her nose.

"And you, Father?" Aari asked. "You felt nothing."

"You know I have very little of the empathy that is both your mother's gift and her curse. I concentrated on sending. Sending you the directions to our new world, suggesting ways to escape, and praying to our ancient friends that somehow you would be saved, that Vhiliinyar itself might cast out the invaders and preserve my sons."

Aari looked aghast. "But—I did know how to get to narhii-Vhiliinyar. Were we not all programmed that way?"

Kaarlye shook his head, his mane flying and settling again, briefly silver in the lamplight, a slight whuffling snort emitting from his nostrils and lips. "Of course not. I am a strong sender."

Aari looked abashed for a moment, then defiant. He inclined his head briefly in acknowledgment.

"But—you had *me*," Maati said, almost wailing.

"Yes, youngling my own," her mother said, stroking her cheek with the back of her fingers. "We had you. It was your birth that delayed us. Grandam would not permit me to move, she kept me sedated with good herbs and sang me soothing songs through the night and a circle of women laid horns on me for hours a day until you were safely into the world. But then, oh Maati, my love, we *had* to go. With you there to carry on the clan name, safe with Grandam, we had to go find your brother. I heard him no longer, you see, once you were born. And yet I had not felt his death. As terrible as his torment had been, I knew what it meant while it continued. It told me Aari lived and he felt and that I was in contact with him. But then he was lost and I did not know what to think. I could not feel him, I could not—"

"My horn," Aari said, touching the slightly indented scar on his forehead. "They had taken my horn. It nearly killed me. No doubt the loss also . . . lessened . . . my ability to transmit to you, Mother."

"Yes," his father said. His mother could not speak for the tears choking her. Acorna was rapidly wiping away her own. Maati sniffled and snuffled. Thariinye, strangely quiet, put his arm around her. Maati's mother also held her daughter close. Acorna laid a hand on Maati's knee and one on Aari's. He lifted her hand and held it against his face for a moment, bending his head to press it between his jaw and his shoulder. His face was damp, but she thought it was perspiration rather than tears. This confrontation was very painful for him, but a good pain, she hoped, a healing pain. Aari's nerve endings burned with life again.

"To lose a child to untimely death is almost the worst thing there is for a parent. To know a child is being deliberately and terribly injured is even worse. But when I lost you, when I didn't know where you were or what was happening to you, to know you were there but not to feel you—that was unbearable. Had it not been for the twins, and then Maati, we would have left to find you long before we finally departed."

Miiri reached out to Aari, but he flinched away from her touch. She withdrew her hand and rested it on her knee. Raising her chin, she continued her tale. "When we could, we flew back to Vhiliinyar. We maintained radio silence lest the Khleevi trace the signal. But our old home planet had been violently altered, and it seemed it was now fighting back. From our vantage point in low orbit we could see that the beautiful greens, blues, and purples of our world were gray and black now, with angry red sores and craters all over. The seas had dried up, leaving behind cracked and broken soil, and where once streams had flowed through mountain meadows the barren riverbeds flowed instead with magma from the ravished peaks. Indeed, many of our mountains had hurled themselves into the heavens, erupting violently. One of these eruptions destroyed our spacecraft before we could raise our shields. It came from nowhere. We took heavy damage. Knowing that the ship was likely to break up at any time, we headed toward the nearest habitable planet. As we approached the atmosphere of this world, we barely had time to slip into the pod and eject before the ship was destroyed. We landed here, much as Maati and Thariinye did, the pod's sensors guiding us to a safe landing. Here there was food and water, and breathable air. We survived and waited for rescue, so that we could continue our search for our son." Miiri's voice grew small and stilled, her hands clasping and unclasping on her knees, her eyes dropping from Aari's.

Acorna, her hand still in Aari's, with her other hand took one of Miiri's and joined it with her son's. They did not clasp hands, but they touched. Miiri raised her eyes again and searched Aari's.

Kaarlye took up the tale. "There was little we could do but survive, and wait, and hope that you would somehow free yourself from the Khleevi. And here you are."

He ruffled Maati's hair. "And here you are, too, our beautiful daughter, starclad and a young lady now."

Aari's hand clutched his mother's now, and Acorna

slipped away as the family reunited. Thariinye sat there watching, so quiet it was hard to believe he was Thariinye.

Acorna joined Becker on watch. Mac had shut himself down to conserve his batteries. RK sat cleaning himself, warming his underside on the lights from the console. The *püyi* that had played constantly on the com screen was blessedly shut off for the moment.

Becker looked around as Acorna slid into the chair beside his.

"Family reunion stuff, huh?" he asked.

Acorna nodded, feeling happy but subdued. The emptiness that was in Aari was filling in like a dry spring after a dam had broken, and to a lesser extent, the same thing was occurring with Maati. It made Acorna feel wistful, wishing that perhaps her own parents had escaped somewhere, could rejoin her. But no, she did not feel that would happen. She had not known them, had missed them as a baby only long enough for dear Gil, Calum, and Rafik to learn her Linyaari baby names for mother and father, and then she had been wrapped in the loving care of her three "uncles" who were actually her fathers, and all of her other new friends, who were her family. Now she had an aunt and a planet and so much more—and she did not begrudge Aari finding his parents and learning of their continued love for him and Maati. And yet—

Becker leaned over and patted her shoulder. "Makes you wonder, doesn't it, Princess?"

"What?" she asked. Becker was better at reading thoughts than she'd realized.

"What your own folks were like, what it would have

been like to be with them, you know. I knew my mother a little—she was a scientist someplace, I'm not really sure where. I was about three when there were a lot of explosions and gunshots and she fell down with blood all over her and then I was taken to the slave farm on Kezdet. Maybe it's because I was only three then, but what I remember most about it was, it was boring being with my mom. And one thing about Dad—Dad Becker, I mean—there was nothing boring about him. I don't reckon I've missed anything, come to think about it." But she saw, in his heart, where that creek in him was still dry, waiting for the dam to break and water it.

And she knew that in spite of all of her friends and her adopted parents and her real Linyaari kinfolk, she had a similar dry creek inside herself. But dwelling on such things was pointless. Besides, she had work to do. She looked out at the stars and asked, "Where to now, Captain?"

Twelve

For the *Balaküre*, tracing the signal to the blue planet was not difficult. The coordinates had been on the *püyi*, and the *Nïkaavri*'s ion tracings led straight to the planet. But none of the crew was prepared, as the *Balaküre* began to home in on the beach where once the *Condor* had landed, for the site of the *Nükaavri*'s broken shell, lying open to the elements as if some massive chick had hatched from it and abandoned it there.

They saw wreckage bobbing in the sea as well, and washing up onto the beach. After a closer look at it, Neeva recognized some of the fragments as coming from a Khleevi vessel. A quick trip back to the ship to consult the scanners gave no indication of a continuing Khleevi presence on the planet. From there it was just a matter of figuring out exactly what had happened. Beginning at a debris-littered indentation in a sand dune, they followed a trail of Khleevi excrement. Liriili was given the honor of walking in front, which she did with the poor grace Neeva expected of her. The broken trees, the large, coagulated pool of blood surrounded by many other blood-stained fronds and ruined trees and crushed leaves, drew a low, painful groan from all them. They followed the trail further up a hill, until they came to a place where a tree was surrounded by broken heaps of the solidified dung. They searched farther still, and found that beyond this last hill, the woods thinned once more into a low marshland of reeds, and beyond that stretched the wide blue sea. Only a few pieces of debris bobbed on the waves on this side of the landspit. But tucked up next to the trees, in a small clearing that showed signs of occupation, lay an egg-shaped vessel covered with a symbolic design. Liriili gasped as if this came as a surprise to her, which of course it should not have done.

The Linyaari made their way to the shuttle and examined it.

"This is the design registered to the . . . the ship Kaarlye and Miiri took when they went in search of their sons?" Neeva asked.

Liriili nodded reluctantly.

"You are sure?"

Liriili's eyes were reddened and slightly bulging, as they had been since the return of the pilgrims and the ancestors. She had not been a pleasant shipboard companion. No number of Linyaari horns could cleanse the atmosphere of her energy field, which was so discordant as to upset the harmony of even such a close-knit crew as the Balaküre's.

"I should know," she said hollowly. "I watched that transmission and checked over the information Thariinye had gathered from the files over and over again. It's not as if I made my decision lightly, you know. I was doing as I always have done, acting with the good of our people in mind, and this is the . . ."

"Yes, yes," Khaari, who was not a diplomat, said shortly. "Thariinye and Maati's ship lies in pieces, and we have found traces that indicate the *Condor*, containing Khornya and Aari, was in the vicinity of the armed Khleevi ship that wrecked the *Nükaavri*. Khleevi spoor is all about, and here is the pod belonging to Kaarlye and Miiri, but this whole situation is still all about how badly misunderstood *you* are."

Liriili gave her a sullen look and sniffed. "Whatever . . . but since everyone you've mentioned except the Khleevi who made these trails are no doubt dead, perhaps we could end this futile mission and return home?"

"I'm surprised you want to," Neeva said. "In your place I would be considering a long mission that sent me to the farthest galaxy imaginable, preferably one where no one ever heard of me."

"That is your nature," Liriili said. "It is not mine. I am not a spacefarer."

"You are now," Melireenya said. "I can't believe you can look at all of this without some feeling of compassion, some sadness perhaps, even remorse in the case of Maati and Thariinye."

"If you think the arbitrary decision of a council influenced by an influx of my enemies is going to make me feel guilty, you are very much mistaken. I did what I thought best for the good of the planet. If harm befell anyone because of my decision, then it is the Khleevi who are at fault, not me."

Khaari rummaged in the pod and pulled out the tiny capsule that kept a record of its flight.

In the ship's shuttle, they did a low flyby circling the planet. Though they looked carefully, they never found another biped lifeform on the planet's surface, dead or alive.

Back in space once more, they discussed what should next be done.

"We must warn our allies of the impending Khleevi threat," Neeva said.

"The same way they warned us of the fake Federation troops?" Khaari asked with a trace of bitterness lingering from that betrayal.

"Those enemies were only human beings," Neeva said. "Bad ones, admittedly, but still merely human. And they tricked our allies. It wasn't right, what happened to our people as a result, but letting the Khleevi overtake any civilization without warning would not be right either."

"I suppose not. Should I begin a broadcast?"

"No!" Liriili said, "You will lead them straight to us, and from us to narhii-Vhiliinyar."

Neeva sighed. "I'm afraid I have to agree with you, Liriili. No, silence is still necessary this close to recent Khleevi depredations. I'm afraid we must deliver at least the first of our warnings personally."

They returned to their ship, docked the shuttle, and plotted a course that would take them toward the inhabited planets closest to their homeworld.

The *Condor* transmitted broadcasts on all channels to all worlds and spacecraft within range about the Khleevi threat. The Linyaari response to their message proved to be typical—not a single reply came from any of the planets they'd targeted. But three days and two wormholes away from the blue world, Acorna was startled and delighted to see Calum Baird's face on the com screen and to hear him say, "This is the *Acadecki*, *Condor*. Read you loud and clear. Acorna, what in the cosmos are you and that junk ship up to now? Didn't we teach you better than to play with the Khleevi? They're not nice."

"Roger, Calum," Acorna said, baring her teeth at her beloved foster father, who was likewise baring his teeth at her. Before they could say more, however, other faces and signals replaced Calum's in quick succession.

Becker, hearing the unfamiliar voices, came running to the bridge, followed quickly by Aari and their Linyaari guests and Mac.

"Damn, are we back in the Federation already?" Becker bellowed. "We musta taken a wrong turn at the last wormhole. I told you that was a left, Aari."

Aari, who was used to Becker's odd expressions, had picked up a couple of them himself. "I am sorry, Joh," he said. "I must have done the wrong thing while attempting to determine which turn signal to activate."

Maati stared wide-eyed at the faces on the screen, while Kaarlye and Miiri looked alarmed and Thariinye began translating with only a trace of his former pomp.

The younger male had changed his attitude quite a bit since being captured by the Khleevi. At first, right after he'd been rescued, he had retreated into himself, uncharacteristically tremulous and reticent. All Maati's goading, Becker's scolding, and Acorna's kindness couldn't reach him. But Aari had been wonderful with him, encompassing him in an exclusive wordless empathy extended from the first and heretofore only Linyaari to survive capture by the Khleevi to the second. Thariinye had responded to Aari's help with relief and something like hero worship. He'd had a taste of what the Khleevi were capable of, and couldn't begin to imagine what Aari's ordeal had been like. The bond was clearly healing for them both.

Aari had begun to speak with his parents and Maati of his time alone and with the Khleevi on Vhiliinyar. Some of what he described was new to Acorna and even to Becker. Now that all of them had had such a close shave—Becker's description, but an apt one—with the Khleevi, everyone understood Aari's experiences much more fully. They were horrified for him, of course, but their reaction was one of grim comprehension, not shock or squeamishness.

With his new air of self-assurance, Aari faced the parade of faces on the com screen with a degree of comfort he'd never exhibited in the past.

Once everyone had been hailed, Acorna switched back to Calum. "Delighted as I am to see you, what are all these ships doing here?" Acorna said.

"We're en route to join Hafiz and his caravan at the House Harakamian Moon of Opportoooonity," Calum said, deepening his voice into a parody of a Scottish brogue. "It's on that moon you used as a base of operations to rescue the folks Ganoosh and Ikwaskwan captured."

Becker chuckled. The wily Hafiz's lust for trade reminded him of his own for salvage. "His timing coulda been a little better," Becker told Calum. "According to—uh—our informant, this whole sector will be crawling with Khleevi before long. On the other hand, if the old pirate had waited till later, there wouldn't have been anybody to trade with, so we'll just have to deal with it, I guess. I presume you're up for a bit of haggling over rescuing the galaxy once again?"

Thirteen

*C*aravan Harakamian had come to rest at its destination after sailing through vast distances of space. Along the way it stopped at various watering holes and oases to refuel and pick up a few forgotten but essential supplies, experts in various fields, security personnel, and general shopping. Its space-going "camels" were fat with the finest cargo by the time they arrived at the desolate moon.

In less time than it took the genie to build the castle of Aladdin, Hafiz and his colleagues in commerce had erected a gigantic trade center. Hafiz used his own hologrammatic magic to disguise the envirobubbles as giant Linyaari pavilions, such as those described to him by Acorna and Aari. From the inside the bubbles were all blue sky and flying birds, waterfalls and forests and mountains in the distance. In the foreground was the flowering vine of goods and services, the commercial center that House Harakamian erected solely to attract the Linyaari and their allies to what Hafiz fondly hoped would be an exclusive trade agreement.

Calum Baird had taken charge of leading a second expedition of technicians who set up relays between the new sector and the old one, specifically Laboue and Maganos Moonbase.

Rafik, Gill, Mercy, Judit, Pal, Johnny, and Ziana ensured that the kids who came from Maganos Moonbase and the crew of the *Haven* were given all possible learning opportunities. Some of the older children were now of age for university training. Those whose brains had been damaged by deprivation or who had been kidnapped into slavery so young that they were still catching up on their educations remained on Maganos Moonbase in the care of trusted teachers and some of the more gifted older children. They would help coordinate future supply caravans, and the transmission of orders from the new Moon of Opportunity, as Hafiz had dubbed his trading colony.

Dr. Hoa's weather wizardry created a climate both varied and pleasant, cycling through a temperate change of weather every thirty days. With the resident botanists, he came up with species well adapted for several days of warm rain with intermittent hard rain, interspersed with brilliant warm sunshine, followed by crisp autumnal days that caused the special trees to turn bright red and gold and drop their leaves before the snow that fell only on the lawns and in the mountains on the recreational portion of the moon, where residents and guests were provided with skiing, snowboarding, ice skating, sledding, and ski lodge activities.

In another part of the resort area, specially tailored

palms swayed above a white sand beach onto which
surfable waves glistened and slid under sailable winds.
Provisions were made for the alien recreational activities Hafiz had knowledge of as well, vine swinging (for
the Limurian jungle dwellers), mud-rolling (for the
Porcinian beings of the Greater Ursine constellation),
and of course, high and low gravity events—long
distance jumping sports and soil diving among them.
Hafiz's brochure promised that more exotic entertain-
ments would be offered later.

His hologram wizardry also made the hotels play-
grounds for both the children and the sophisticates, of-
fering a variety of fantasy-oriented suites and facilities,
even holographic houris. He was a bit surprised that
Khetala, who had been reeducating former pleasure
house employees, took it upon herself to visit the holographic harems of the houris. While there she attempted to convince the denizens they were being
exploited and should perhaps take up courses in ac-
counting or business management to empower themselves.

That was his first inkling that perhaps his colony was
beginning to seem a bit too frivolous for some of his as-
sociates. But of course, the guest facilities had to be in
place before the university and healing centers could be
completed.

Karina ordered up the initial hologramatic ambience
for the healing center. She also spent a fortune on crys-
tals, candles, gauzy draperies, drums, incense, amorphous music, and real greenery and fountains. Hafiz
was allowed to embellish her setting with his holograms, but she insisted on the genuine article as far as

plant life and water features went, "for the ozone and the extra oxygen, beloved. One doesn't get that from a simulation."

A large portion of that pavilion was kept barren however, awaiting the arrival of the first Linyaari trade partners, who would of course have their own specifications.

Thus was all in readiness for the first trading partners. Hafiz and his staff waited. And waited. And waited.

Signals had been sent on all frequencies to all planets in the sector. Calum Baird and his technicians finished their work installing the appropriate links and relays to allow swift communication with Maganos Moonbase, Laboue, and all other previously known Federation worlds, moons, and space stations. But until Calum and his fleet intercepted the *Condor*'s signal, not a single response did the newly created facility receive.

Finally these last ships docked and by the time their crews were welcomed and rested, the *Condor*, its sides virtually bulging with cargo and expanded crew, waddled into port to squat beside the other, sleeker vessels.

Becker gave a low whistle as the crew, including RK, descended on the spanking clean robolift.

"Will you look at this spread?" Becker asked. "Your old uncle has done himself proud, Princess."

Acorna wasn't listening. She didn't even wait until the robolift touched the ground before jumping off and flying into the collective arms of her uncles and old friends from Maganos Moonbase.

Hugs, kisses, tears, and exclamations flowed freely

and to Maati, seemed to sadly contrast to her own reunion with her brother, mother, and father.

Finally, Hafiz Harakamian, mindful of the presence
of four horned Linyaari and Aari, whom he had met before, detached himself from the storm of sentiment and
greeted his new guests.

He was flanked by Karina on one side and Nadhari
Kando on the other. As chief of security, Nadhari considered it her job to be with Hafiz in any crowd and put
herself between him and harm.

"Welcome to my pavilion, and to this Moon of Opportunity, honored guests, Captain Becker, and er —
crewman?" Hafiz said with a glance at Mac.

RK leaped onto Nadhari Kando's shoulder.

"It's that Makahomian warrior lady again. Hello,
there," Becker said, perhaps a bit eagerly.

Nadhari gave him a slow smile and stroked RK's
plumed tail. "I see the sacred cat has brought you safely
through another journey, Becker."

"Yes, he was a lot of help," Becker said, reaching over
to stroke RK too, and incidentally brush his fingers
against Nadhari's sculpted cheekbone resting against
the cat's side. RK growled and batted at him. "The hero
of the whole thing actually," Becker continued. The
growl lowered. "In fact, if he hadn't alerted Aari to the
fact that the Khleevi was after Acorna, and then come
back to lead me and Mac to where the Khleevi and Aari
were duking it out, we probably would not be the hale
and healthy party standing before you now."

RK was purring now.

Hafiz, who had been trying to ignore Becker to court
the Linyaari, suddenly turned to him, very pale despite

the artificial sunlight in his offices. "Khleevi? You encountered *Khleevi*!"

"Yeah, got a couple of dead ones up top," Becker said, jerking his thumb toward the *Condor*.

Acorna rejoined the crew, her friends and relations surrounding them all now as they strolled off the robolift and toward the sumptuously appointed reception area. "Uncle Hafiz, we will need to establish some sort of laboratory to study the dead Khleevi and to analyze a substance we discovered on another world."

"You need establish nothing, O flower of my family tree," Hafiz said. "We have the best of all laboratories here at your command complete with all the most advanced devices and equipment."

"And we have some top Linyaari organic chemists in our crew, Uncle," Acorna said with a nod to two of the newcomers. "Allow me to present Kaarlye and Miiri, father and mother of Aari and Maati."

"We are honored," Hafiz said. "And our laboratories of course are at your disposal. Just across the garden of a thousand succulent sweetgrasses and flowering fountains you will find luxurious pavilions designed with Linyaari tasks and requirements in mind." He clapped his hands and porters appeared. "When you have rested from your journeys, we will dine."

"No time to rest," Kaarlye said brusquely. "We must analyze this substance at once. When it is warm, it spreads rapidly."

Becker stopped the porters at the robolift. "Wait a minute, folks. We didn't come with a lot of baggage and I think my crew and I had better unload the sap and the—uh—prisoners. You might want to stand back.

They stink. A lot. As for RK, Mac, and me, we're staying aboard the *Condor*."

Nadhari lifted an eyebrow and made a very unconvincing pout with her mouth. RK laid his ears back and wrapped his tail possessively around Nadhari's neck. "Unless of course the cat has other ideas," Becker finished lamely.

That night a sumptuous meal was laid before them.

Under an open canopy, silvery platters of meats and sweets nestled among opulent arrangements of flowers and plumed grasses upon a long low table nestled within a bank of tufted divans covered with poufs of paisley silks and velvets. These topped thick soft rugs of various harmonious patterns and jewel-like hues.

Becker and his new crew sank into the divans and following Hafiz's lead, Becker, Karina, Dr. Hoa, Acorna's non-Linyaari family, and Nadhari Kando plucked succulent items from the trays on the table. Meanwhile Acorna, Aari, Maati, and the parental units grazed on the flower arrangements. Becker was a little startled until he realized that this was the intended purpose of what he had thought of as an overabundance of centerpieces. The old man had simply seen to it that the Linyaari "dishes" were arranged as appealingly as the savory morsels offered to the other guests.

"Uncle Hafiz, you are amazing," Acorna said. Becker was pleased to see that after the strain and danger and hard work the girl had recently endured, she looked as fresh as some of the flowers she was eating, glowing with happiness at being among her old friends again. "How long did it take you to build this installment, anyway?" Her eyes took in the gently lit garden with its fountains and mountainous background, the spired and domed palaces that formed Hafiz's chief residence and several of the hotels and office buildings besides. Overhead stars twinkled—not any stars Acorna had ever been among but artful stars, placed with an artistic interpretation of constellations and formations Karina had deemed auspicious.

"Little more than the twinkling of an eye, dearest child, that and many, many, many trillions of credits, of course."

Becker was seated on the end of one divan, Nadhari Kando on the adjoining end of another, the *Condor*'s first mate still wrapped complacently around her neck like a living fur collar. Every once in a while a forkful of fish eggs or meat didn't make it all the way to Nadhari's mouth, however, as a paw or a set of feline teeth intercepted it.

"But enough of my little pastimes," Hafiz was saying while Becker was admiring the line of Nadhari's jaw and the curve of her neck, "I am consumed with curiosity to know how it is that you actually have two dead Khleevi with you?"

"Oh. Them," Becker said. "Well, they're survivors. I mean, they were survivors. From the crash of their ship. The one we caused since, you know, they had just finished shooting the kids' ship out of the sky."

"And by kids you mean . . . ?"

"Maati and Thariinye," Acorna put in. "They apparently decided at almost the same time we did to search for Maati's and Aari's parents on the blue world. But the Khleevi had the same idea, and had already launched an attack when we arrived."

"Tell me, Captain, I am intrigued," Nadhari said. "What powerful weapons do you carry on that salvage ship of yours that vanquished a Khleevi vessel?"

"Yes," Hafiz said. "Please, tell us. If they are that effective, I will order many for the protection of our moon."

Becker gave Nadhari a smile that urged her to wait a moment and answered Hafiz, "Well, sir, it is true that I have a bunch of very lethal weapons on the *Condor*. Some of them even work. Or would, if I had them assembled and installed. Which I didn't. So then Acorna here says, what about using the tractor beam?"

A smile played at the edges of Nadhari's mouth, which was the only thing about her with any extra flesh—her lips were sculpted but pleasingly plump, at least they were when relaxed. He seemed to recall seeing that same mouth set in a hard grim line above the jut of that firm and shapely jaw. It would have had him quaking in his gravity boots, if he thought she had any quarrel with him. But she didn't, and RK's tail tip flitted playfully from her shoulder bone to jawline to eartip, as flirtatious as a courtesan's fan.

"Captain, surely you have not acquired enough cargo by now to act as another slingshot bomb with which to fell your enemies?"

"Oh, no, ma'am. Not slingshot this time. We—uh—skipped 'em like a rock and then played crack the ship with their sorry carcass. Worked good, too, didn't it, crew?"

"Yes, Joh. Good," Aari said.

"Except for the survivors. We didn't know there were two at first," Becker said.

He regaled the table with the story of the questioning of the injured Khleevi while interweaving the story of Maati and Thariinye as if he had understood every word they spoke of their ordeal or had been with them while it was occurring. He gave it a few flourishes here and there and ended by saying modestly, "So I blew a hole through the bugger, but Aari here had already pretty much finished him off."

"How?" Karina Harakamian asked.

"Why, by giving him a great big old hug. See, that Khleevi was so purely mortified by all that Linyaari sweetness and light Aari was extending to it just because he's of such a highly evolved nature, that I figure the Khleevi came down with a monstrous case of sugar diabetes on the spot and it was such a shock to its system it curled up its toes and died."

Karina clasped her plump, beringed hands over her heaving amethyst-veiled and amethyst-encrusted bosom and sighed, "How thrilling! And what a triumph for the light!" Then she glanced around at the stolid Linyaari faces, and at Becker's determinedly innocent one. He was trying to keep his mouth from twitching. "Wait a moment. Is that true?" she asked.

"Not a word of it!" Becker exploded with laughter. Karina was exactly the kind of audience he loved. Gullible. "Well, the thing did curl up and die and it was because of something sticky as sugar, but not sweet. It was this sap stuff we picked up on some planet full of vines. But I had you going there, didn't I?"

Nadhari shook an admonitory finger at him, "Naughty, naughty, Captain. But I must say, I'm very impressed. You and your crew of pacifist warriors vanquishing such formidable foes without so much as a real weapon among you—"

"You're forgetting that I blew a hole the size of the cat through that thing," Becker said, slightly offended at being lumped with the pacifists.

She shrugged like a panther rippling its muscles in preparation for a longer stretch. "Oh that. A mere coup de grace. But your ingenuity and wit amaze me. Anyone can win by force of muscle or superior firepower. But winning because of strategy and the ability to turn whatever you have at hand into a weapon, I find that— very, very impressive."

"You *do*?" Becker was surprised at first, then amazed, followed by stupefied. Him? Impress *her*? She was absolutely the most impressive woman he had ever seen in his entire life and fascinated him at the same time she scared the bejesus out of him. He hadn't done anything she couldn't do with both hands tied behind her back, but it was nice to hear it anyway.

"Absolutely." He couldn't tell if it was her or RK purring. Both of them were regarding him through slitted eyes.

"I certainly do. You and I should discuss—strategy."

He was flummoxed. The truth was, he never stuck around for courtship or seduction much past the brief encounters in the pleasure houses—hadn't since he was younger and encountered all the ladies who wanted a good time but thought spending any part of it on a salvage ship beneath them. Nadhari Kando knew where he lived. She'd been there. "I—uh—I'd really like that. I need to check in with Mac though—that's the KEN-

640 unit—he's repairing the com unit on the Khleevi shuttle so we can maybe monitor their movements—"

"By the sacred whiskers, you think of everything, don't you?" She moved closer and offered him an olive. He held out his hand but she held it with two fingers and her thumb and waved it teasingly till he opened his mouth, then she popped it in. He could definitely get used to this. Her scent was a mixture of musk and citrus, and something like a forest after a rain. He liked it. He held out an olive for her.

"And I—uh—I guess I should get RK back, too. He hasn't had his usual eighty hours of sleep today."

"Oh?" she said. "That's funny. He's been communing with me. He wants to stay with me tonight."

"Well, if that's not just like a cat!" Becker exclaimed, dropping the olive back onto his plate in his consternation at his first mate's defection.

Nadhari smiled. Her smile reminded him of RK—he just hadn't realized that was what a cat smile looked like. "What's that?" she asked as the cat rubbed against her cheek. "Oh, yes. He wants to stay with you tonight, too."

"Divided loyalties?" Becker asked.

Nadhari swung her sturdy but very shapely legs down from the divan with a sinuous slither and stood looking down at him. "Hardly. RK is a sacred temple cat. His wish is my command. If he wishes to be with me, and with you . . ." her hand reached down to cup Becker's chin and with slight pressure on it, raised him to his feet. "I am not the one to gainsay him. Are you?"

"Disappoint my old buddy?" Becker asked, slipping her hand through his crooked elbow. "Perish the thought. Mind telling me where he wants to spend this time with us tonight?"

"Aboard your vessel," she replied, and he was surprised to see that she actually had to look up at him. How did she do that? He could have sworn she was taller. "In the hold where you questioned the first Khleevi."

"Really?"

"Yes. The sacred cat thinks I would find that environment rather — stimulating."

"Kitty knows best," Becker said.

Fourteen

*H*afiz would not hear of the Linyaari remaining aboard the *Condor*. Acorna was
glad, particularly when she saw Becker,
RK, and Nadhari strolling arm in arm in the direction
of the ship.

A self-contained trio of pavilions triangulated around a
garden/grazing area. Kaarlye and Miiri were billeted in
one, and although Maati could have stayed with her parents, she asked if she might share a pavilion with Khornya
instead. This left Aari and Thariinye to share the third.

Acorna spent most of the rest of the evening with her
adoptive fathers/uncles, describing what had befallen
her since they had last seen each other.

"This Aari guy," Gill said. "You and he . . . ?"

"We're friends," Acorna said, off-handedly.

"Evidently, if he's willing to wrestle bug-eyed monsters on your behalf," Calum said.

"We were all in danger," Acorna said, reasonably
enough. "And Aari was trying to save us all."

"He didn't know that stuff smeared on his shirt would kill the thing though?" Gill asked. "He just dove right in and tackled it?"

"Well—yes."

"Sounds kinda suicidal to me," Calum said.

"I don't really think he is—at least, not now," Acorna said.

"But he was before?" Gill asked.

Acorna suddenly felt more uncomfortable than she had ever before felt in the company of these beloved men. "Why are you questioning me this way?" she asked.

"Why do you think?" Calum asked, exasperated. "Because we care about you, of course, and we've talked it over and it looks to us like you care about him."

"But we wish to make sure," Rafik said, "that—well, you're not just feeling sorry for someone who cannot be a good mate for you, to put it bluntly."

"You must admit, pet, that we know a few more things about men than you do," Gill said, smiling.

"Human men, yes, but Aari is Linyaari," she said. "And we are friends. Nothing more."

"Not—yet?" Gill asked.

"No, nor will we be until he's—"

"Until *he's* ready, darlin'?" Gill pressed. "What about you? Are you going to crew on a salvage ship until the guy makes up his mind whether or not he could stand being mates with a beautiful, intelligent, funny, talented, warm, and loving girl? You must excuse us, but it's a no-brainer. Which makes us wonder about how intelligent or warm *he* is."

"Frankly, we thought you'd get snatched up by some young stud the minute you landed on your homeworld," Calum said. "We're a bit surprised at this turn of events."

Acorna dimpled at them suddenly. "Is this one of those situations where you are going to ask me when I'm going to settle down and give you grandchildren?"

"Yes," Rafik said. "Usually mothers do it, well, used to, but you have no mother and we weren't sure your aunt would think of it, besides which she's not around, is she? So we thought—that is, Calum and Gill thought—maybe between us, we should discuss this."

"Hafiz started it, really," Calum said. "Hey, we did pretty well, I think. Gill was all for calling the guy outside and asking him what his intentions were when we saw how he—how you—how things were. But then we figured a guy who tackled a Khleevi bare-handed might be the sensitive type, so we decided asking you—"

"Was safer," Rafik finished with an impish grin.

Acorna laughed. "You've asked. We've discussed it," she said, giving them each a hug. "And I have nothing more to say—honestly, there *is* nothing more to say right now. Meanwhile, when am I going to get to give my fathers away in marriage is what I'd like to know? Judit and Mercy will not wait forever while you busy yourselves speculating about *my* love life."

"Actually," Calum said. "We um, have an announcement to make. But I will wait until she can—"

The other two started thumping him on the back. Talk turned to how the nuptials were to be handled and then all of them began to feel the need to talk to *their* mates and Acorna slipped away, back to her assigned pavilion.

Maati was not there. Acorna thought perhaps the girl was spending more time with her parents. That was fine. It would be nice to be alone for a while. As light as she had made of her dear friends' questions, they echoed questions in her own mind, and she didn't want a youngling new to thought-speech to read her, even accidentally.

Did she care for Aari simply because she had pitied him, or was there more to it than that? How would she know? She had never chosen a mate before. She knew her uncles had only her best interests at heart and it was quite true that she hadn't noticed all *that* much difference between human and Linyaari males. And she felt, being raised by men, that she understood them as well as a female could. At this point in her life anyway. But she couldn't say she understood Aari at all. She could read his mind when he let her and she knew he cared for her. She could empathize with his pain. But she hadn't a clue why he behaved as he did. She wished Grandam Naadiina or Aunt Neeva were here to consult with. She would have asked Gill, Calum, or Rafik about the matter but they seemed to be predisposed against Aari.

With a sigh, she settled down to an uneasy and dream-filled sleep in which she was being courted by a Khleevi.

Aari, on the other hand, was getting no sleep, nor was he able to progress very far in the book he had chosen from the *Condor*'s ancient hardcopy library, a collection of ancient European literature by various authors. Aari was currently reading an excerpt from a play called *Romeo and Juliet* by William Shakespeare. The language was not easy but Aari had read another book that referred to Shakespeare as inventing the language of love, so he thought it might be interesting to see what the Bard of Avon had to say. Although he could not imagine why a cosmetics firm from the twentieth century (the ship's library also contained a number of small brightly colored pamphlets from this company) would choose to sponsor an ancient poet unless it was because he was also an actor and they, as Aari was learning, also used makeup.

But while he was struggling with the language, Thariinye was chattily giving him the benefit of Thariinye's spectacularly successful career (according to the young male) as a wooer of females. Aari had not had the heart to ask him to be quiet, as he knew that the loss of the tip of Thariinye's horn had made him feel disfigured and the younger fellow was relating his past exploits simply to bolster his own confidence.

But in that estimation, Aari was using the projection of his own feelings about the loss of his horn and empathy for Thariinye's distress, not thought-reading, which he found impossible to do while he was trying to unravel Shakespeare's *thee*s and *thou*s. So he was taken aback when Thariinye suddenly rolled over on his own pallet and poked Aari playfully in the ribs.

"That Khornya is quite a reed, isn't she?" Thariinye said with a wink.

"A—reed?" Aari asked, looking up from his book at the mention of Khornya's name.

"A—slender and succulent desirable mate, to oldtimers like you," Thariinye translated with a tolerant wave of his hand.

"I—yes. Maati mentioned that you had considered yourself pledged to her. Is that—still true?" His voice was steady and controlled.

"Me? No! No, no, no. By the ancestors, no! Oh, I was smitten, of course. She is beautiful—quite a reed, as I said. But, well, it really was just that I was the first Linyaari male she met and she was so dewy eyed and innocent I felt protective, so I wanted to warn off other males lest they not . . . appreciate her finer qualities . . . properly. No, now that I know her better, she is not for me."

"No? And why not?" Aari asked, suddenly feeling protective himself, and rather angry at Thariinye dismissing Khornya. Who *wouldn't* want Khornya?

"Frankly?" Thariinye said. "She's too smart for me. And well, a bit too idealistic. And a little too strange, being raised by humans and all. She has peculiar ideas about things so I can't begin to guess what she's going to do next. That makes me nervous around her."

"I admit I am nervous around her, too," Aari said thoughtfully.

"I noticed. But you're crazy about her, aren't you?" Thariinye's voice was insinuating and his eyes sly. "You want her, don't you?"

"I . . . have no right," Aari said. "She deserves a mate who is whole in mind and body. And horn," he said, a bit cruelly, since Thariinye was being cruel and discourteously invasive, to his way of thinking.

"Ouch," Thariinye said. "I guess I deserved that. But I'm told *mine* will grow back, in time."

Aari was quiet. Thariinye had responded to cruelty with cruelty of his own. That was one reason why the

Linyaari usually eschewed cruelty. It was not only unkind, it was unwise to start the spiraling descent that would lead to all parties having fallen to a lower level.

"Sorry," Thariinye said again. "I'm trying to tell you something here and I keep on upsetting you. You're pretty touchy, you know that, don't you?"

"Perhaps it is because for so long, when anyone touched me, it was to cause pain," Aari said through gritted and bared teeth. Then he relaxed, "I am sorry too. I have begun to think of you as a friend. Grandam says friends come together to teach each other. I sense you are trying to teach me something. Proceed."

"What I'm saying," Thariinye said, "is no matter what YOU think she deserves, the females I know seem to feel that what they deserve is whatever their little female hearts decide they want. I think it's pretty clear she wants you."

"No," he said. "She is a kind and loving person. She feels sympathy for my injury, for what happened with the Khleevi. When she is sure I am as healed as possible, for she is a healer above all, she will return to her human people for good as our ambassador—stopping by narhii-Vhiliinyar to communicate with the government perhaps. By then Joh and I will be far away so I—" *so I will not have to watch her leave again*, he thought to himself.

"You're just making that assumption!" Thariinye said. "Why don't you ask her? Talk to her? Take her some of these beautiful, delicious flowers! Recite Linyaari love poetry to her! She's never heard it, you know. I was going to try it out on her but I could tell she wouldn't believe me."

"What would it tell her that I bring her flowers from a garden that is also hers to graze?" Aari asked, shaking his mane.

"That you brought her breakfast in bed?" Thariinye suggested. "No, no, go back to your book. Forget I said anything."

But the next morning, Thariinye slept in while Aari went to see if he could assist his parents in the laboratory where they were analyzing the sap that had killed the Khleevi. Upon awakening, Thariinye saw the book Aari had left behind. His journey with Neeva, Khaari, and Melireenya to collect Khornya from her human foster parents had given him a superior knowledge of Standard, he felt. With the help of the LAANYE he had carried with him from the *Niikaavri*, he was able to translate one of the stories, although the words fell in odd places. This particular tale, by a human named Rostand, told of a fellow with a disfiguringly long nose—which sounded perfectly attractive to Thariinye, since long noses were considered elegant by Linyaari tastes. The long-nosed chap was in love with a female also desired by a more attractive male, a friend of the long-nosed chap. Finally, because he was a kind person and wished to see both his friend and the female he loved happy, and also because it allowed him to speak his own words of love to the female, the long-nosed male hid and spoke his love words while the handsomer male pretended to speak them to the female.

Thariinye knew that it obviously would never work out. There were a few similarities in the personalities involved of course, but considerable mutation would have to occur before such a solution would in any way serve the present situation.

Maati was a youngling, but in her capacity as a messenger, she had been receiving a great deal of vicarious experience since she was very small. The only other females available to discuss this with, unfortunately, were Khornya and Aari's mother, who was quite busy and besides, Thariinye didn't know her. Maati would have to do.

Maati was thrilled to find herself among human younglings approximately her age. They had been alive much longer, as Linyaari children developed very rapidly and, once adult, maintained a healthy maturity of great longevity. The youngest of these children had been alive at least eight years, which was much longer than Maati's single *ghaanyi*. A *ghaanyi* was about one and a half years, by Standard time, which was how these humans measured their days.

But the younglings were barely sentient for a very long period in their early lives, so their experience, while different, was not much greater than Maati's own. Certainly none of them had been messengers for their governments, although Laxme, one of the boys, had developed unusual skill with the com units. Nor had they been shot down by a Khleevi ship, fought a Khleevi hand-to-hand, and lived. But the Maganos Moonbase children, she was sorry to hear, had all endured horrible lives as child slaves. The Starfarer children of the *Haven* had watched their parents die at the hands of hijackers, had defeated and dealt decisively with the same hijackers, and now were in command of their home ship, with only a little help from a few adults. The thing all of the children had most in common was that they loved and admired Khornya, though the human children called her "Acorna," "Lady Epona," or "The Lady of the Light" and regarded her with worshipful adoration Maati found strange.

"She's just a really nice girl, like us, only a little older," Maati told them.

"Like you, you mean," Jana corrected her. Jana was really nice and had been asking Maati lots of questions about healing. At first Maati had been unwilling to answer. Linyaari did not usually let outsiders know they healed directly through their horns. Doing so could lead to incidents like the one where bad humans took many Linyaari ambassadors prisoner and tried to force them to heal and cleanse water and air under horrible circumstances. Linyaari raised on the homeworld knew this, but Khornya had not.

"Don't be so cagey," Jana had said when Maati tried to play innocent. "We know all about how you can heal people. Acorna healed all of us when we were in the mines and other bad places. If it hadn't been for her, most of us would be crippled. I don't know why you wouldn't want people to know what you can do. It's wonderful! I wish I could do that. I want to be a doctor."

"I'm going to create holograms, just like Mr. Harakamian," Annella, a redheaded girl from the *Haven*, said. "He's shown me a lot of what goes into it. It's not as hard as you'd think but then, he says I have a natural talent for it." Then she realized they weren't talking about careers, they were talking about Acorna's ability to heal and she added, "But it must be wonderful to be able to heal the way your people can."

Maati made a wry face. "It comes in pretty handy, like when the Khleevi attacked us. Thariinye got hurt real bad trying to save me and Khornya. He probably would have died if he wasn't Linyaari and we hadn't been there. Or at least lost a hand."

"That was really brave," Jana said. "Kheti is brave like that. And Acorna is, too."

"My brother was the bravest though."

"Which one is your brother? Thariinye?" Annella asked.

"Oh no—Thariinye is a friend, sort of, when he isn't being a *biinye*."

"I don't know what that means," Jana said, "but I bet it's not good."

"No, it's not, but he's not that way as much anymore. My brother is the one who doesn't have a horn. The Khleevi, um—" Maati found she had trouble saying it, even now. "When they captured him they tortured him and, you know—"

"We get the picture," Jana assured her hastily, hearing the choke in the voice of the Linyaari girl. "Your brother must be very brave. We heard he tackled that monster bare-handed."

"He did. But the monster was about to get Khornya. That was a fatal mistake," Maati said with satisfaction unbecoming a member of a nonviolent race.

"I've seen how Lady Epona looks at him," Jana said with a sigh.

"Everybody sees but him!" Maati said. "He is so smart and so brave but he just thinks because he doesn't have a horn, Khornya would be getting a bad deal — that she might not accept him, even though everybody can see she really likes him."

"Why doesn't she tell him?" Annella asked.

"Cause she's afraid that even though he likes her, he would still maybe reject her and I think, well, *actually*, I sort of peeked. She is afraid that rejecting her would cause him more pain and she doesn't want to do that. Grownups are sooooo complicated."

"You'd think they'd realize that life is pretty short to be so backward about *good* stuff," Jana said wistfully. "Everybody is being so careful of everybody else's feelings they're *never* gonna get together."

"That's what Thariinye said," Maati agreed, heaving a deep and dramatic sigh. "He was talking about some male with a large nose who did the talking for some other male to a female they both cared for. Do males with long noses play the role of go-betweens in your society? Are there any of them here we could get to talk to Khornya for Aari — or the other way around?"

"Nooo," said Jana. The other kids shook their heads too. Their educations on Maganos Moonbase had tended to the practical and technical and neglected the arts. Their former masters hadn't exactly provided them with cultural opportunities either.

However, Annella's mother, before she had been spaced by the invaders, had been very fond of theater. "He's talking about a character named Cyrano, Maati. It's from an old earth tale."

"I see," Maati said wisely. But she didn't.

"I think he's hit on something," Annella said. "Maybe they need a go-between."

"A matchmaker," put in Markel, another of the kids from the *Haven* who had been listening carefully to what went on. He considered himself a very special friend of Acorna's, since it was with his help she was able to save herself, Calum Baird, and Dr. Hoa and help the youngsters of the *Haven* overthrow the hijackers. "Only, it sounds like a lot of people have tried to be one from what you say, Maati."

"Yes," Maati said. "Khornya's foster fathers talked to her about it and she didn't want to talk, Karina Harakamian can't read her mind, Thariinye said he knows she won't talk to him, and she thinks I'm just a kid and can't understand. But I *do*. I understand they are both being dumb not to talk to each other. They don't really need to talk to some third person because neither of them will believe anybody else. They need to talk to each *other*. Aari needs to talk to Khornya and Khornya needs to talk to Aari or they won't believe it." She shrugged. "Not even a long-nosed male could help."

"Maybe there's a way for that to happen, kind of," Annella said slowly.

"Are you thinking what I'm thinking?" Markel asked.

"I think so. Do you think we could pull it off?"

"Maybe. It can't hurt to try anyway. Hafiz isn't going to care. He probably will even find a use for them later."

"What?" Maati asked. The other kids looked at the two Starfarers as well.

"Come with us to the holo lab. We'll try to show you. It'll take a while, though."

Fifteen

I n the days that followed, Becker staggered around the ship humming marching songs. While Nadhari was on duty, RK stayed on the ship. She was on duty a lot, but still found time almost every day for a little visit. Becker was chronically surprised that she really seemed to like him, and the *Condor*.

And of course, Mac was conducting, under Becker's guidance, an extremely critical security operation. He could now receive signals from the main fleet, although he could not yet send them. While Mac was working, Becker regaled him with cute stories about Nadhari. The captain figured if he was going to be crazed about the woman, the android was the perfect party to hear his jabbering. That way he wouldn't make a fool of himself to anyone who was likely to gossip.

He was just getting to the part where Nadhari, in a fit of passion, had inadvertently reintroduced him to somersaults and handsprings, when Acorna arrived, looking bemused and distracted, but as usual, determined to be useful.

"Any luck with the com unit, MacKenZ?" she asked.

"I have had some contact with the main fleet. They are wondering where this scouting shuttle is. They apparently received some communication before the crash onto the blue planet. However, these beings are on the whole unperturbed by peril to individual members or even vessels, from what I have learned from our captive, from what Aari has been able to tell me of his experience, and from what I have gleaned from their communications."

"Where are they? What are they doing?" Acorna asked urgently, hunkering down beside the thoroughly exhausted Becker and Mac.

Acorna looked down at the com unit, still mounted on the control panel, and at a mess of other hardware from the shuttle. "What did you do with the rest of the shuttle?" she asked.

"Smells like Khleevi," Becker said. "Without you and the others on board, the smell was enough to gag a maggot. Maybe the smell *was* a maggot, for all we know. Khleevi are bugs. They could have maggots."

"Ye-es," Acorna said. "We really should investigate their life cycle. We would have a better idea of their vulnerabilities if we knew more."

"True," Becker said. "Wonder if Hafiz has got any entomologists in this bunch of settlers he's imported."

"From what I can tell, Khornya," Mac said, "The fleet may be en route to the Niriian homeworld — where the *püyi* came from."

Acorna nodded. "The Niriians have been warned already that their ship was intercepted and that the Khleevi are in this general area and still at large. Surely they will have taken defensive measures."

"In case they haven't," Becker said, "Nadhari was going to get Hafiz to dispatch a light drone with a pre-recorded message to broadcast from space—well away from here. We still haven't heard from narhii-Vhiliin-yar, Princess, but it looks like the bugs haven't got there yet."

"What's needed is technology that prevents transmissions from being traced back to their origins, at least by Khleevi devices," Acorna said. "Do you think we could do a diagnostic that might help some of the engineers develop something within the near future?"

"Yeah, if we survive that long," Becker said. "Anyhow, it won't hurt to ask Hafiz about it."

"If the Khleevi find the drone and destroy it, that would give my beloved uncle an economic motive anyway," Acorna said. "He just hates to lose something he'd hoped to make a profit on."

"You know, me too," Becker said. "Your uncle and I have got quite a bit in common."

Acorna smiled mischievously at him. "I know."

Becker gave her a sideways glance from under his bushy eyebrows. "Seen much of Aari lately?" he asked innocently.

"Not too much," she said, feigning lightness. "He has been assisting his parents in the laboratory, from what I can tell. They've determined that the sap contains a spore which, when it comes in contact with an insect's carapace, metamorphoses into a fungal infection of great virulence."

"I knew it had to be something like that," Becker said. He didn't mention that she'd changed the subject away from Aari. "So all we gotta do basically is lure them to the place where we got the sap and tell them to eat their fill." He chuckled. "I'm getting good at this decoy business. We faked Ganoosh into thinking the Federation Outpost was the Linyaari homeworld and now all we have to do is convince the Khleevi fleet that whaddayacallit—vine world—is full of yummy bug food and let them and the plants fight it out to see who eats who. Piece of—you should pardon the expression—cake."

"First, however," Mac said, "I must fix the transmitter on this unit. While I have no problem with concentration or distractions, Captain, you do happen to be sitting against the access panel. Perhaps you would consider moving?"

"Mutiny!" Becker grumbled. "C'mon Acorna, I'll treat you to a bouquet or something dirtside."

They ate together in one of the little bistros Hafiz had set, one to a building, circus, or block, for times when people did not want to meet in one of the several great dining halls. All of the ones in the main compound, which contained the Linyaari compound, opened onto gardens for al fresco mixed human and Linyaari grazing.

"Have you tried any of the activities around here?" Becker asked Acorna casually. "Nadhari and I are going to take a room in one of the fantasy suites at the hotel. Complete holo landscapes in every suite." He sighed. "She's an amazing woman, Nadhari."

"You really like her, then?"

"That's a little mild. I mean, there's not many women

I'd let take RK with them while they're working, but she said he wanted to see what she did. She's the first Makahomian he's been around since the crash. He likes being worshipped. I guess everybody ought to try it once. Being worshipped, I mean."

Becker did not need RK. He himself looked like the proverbial cat who had swallowed the unfortunate proverbial canary.

"I am pleased for you, Captain. Have the two of you made any long-range plans?" Acorna asked.

"It's a little early yet," Becker said complacently, "But I figure after we save the universe as we know it, what with her brawn and my brains . . ."

Acorna didn't warn him, but Nadhari herself, clad in her green security forces uniform, crept through the garden until she was directly behind Becker, where she caught his head in a hammerlock, "And then what, oh brains of the outfit?" she asked. RK, slipping through the weeds behind her, stopped at her feet and wound around her ankles.

"Whatever you want, babe," Becker said, removing her arm without difficulty and distributing kisses up the crease in her uniform sleeve.

Nadhari actually wrinkled her elegant, if oft-broken nose at Acorna. "Isn't that cute? He called me babe. Nobody ever calls me babe. If most men did it I'd have to break at least a finger. But from Jonas, it's not lack of respect, it's protective." She put both arms around his neck and gave him a half-comic noisy smooch before melting back into the garden as if she were one of the plants, the cat's plumed tail the last vestige of their presence.

Becker sat there with a silly grin on his face. Acorna remembered the word used for someone whose internal dam had broken so that the banks of their dry stream were filled to overflowing. Besotted. Becker and Nadhari were besotted and Acorna was glad for them.

But she had to excuse herself before she choked on the lump in her throat.

Maati made Thariinye close his eyes as she led him by the hand into the holo-lab. Opening them, he saw a number of the youngsters from the station grouped around Aari and Acorna.

He looked confused. "Is this some kind of an instructional meeting or what? Where's Becker and the cat and your parents?"

"Look closer," Maati told him, now letting go of his hand and herding him in among the children. "Aren't they awesome?"

He saw now that Aari and Acorna were standing in little pools of light. Neither of them greeted him and once in a while, though very seldom, one of them would flicker slightly.

"Holograms?" he asked.

Annella Carter beamed at him. "Yes! What do you think?"

Thariinye scratched his chin and circled the two familiar figures. "Well, they do flicker sometimes. What are they? Tourist attractions?"

"Noooo," Maati punched him lightly on the forearm. "'Course not. They're to, well, be go-betweens for the real people."

"Go-betweens to what?" Thariinye asked.

"What's the matter with you?" Maati demanded. "Have you gone soft in the head from too much easy living? Go-betweens to each other, of course!"

Thariinye groaned. "I was afraid of that. You don't think it will actually work, do you? These things wouldn't fool either of them for more than a moment or two if they have their wits about them."

"That's why we wanted your help," Maati said. "You're the one who made me think of it. How do we make it work?"

"Work?" he asked. "Why ask me? I don't know anything about holograms."

"No," Maati said, "but according to you, you know *all* about looooove." She drew the word out mockingly and he gave her a look that would have sent older and more susceptible girls running away in tears. She just laughed back up at him and the other children giggled.

"Of course I know more than a lot of infant younglings," he said. "What is it that you need to know about it? And how does it concern your little holo dollies?" He flipped his fingers at the life-size holograms as if they were no bigger than his foot.

"We need to know what Khornya should say to Aari and what Aari should say to Khornya to get them together, of course!" Maati said. She did not seem to be getting the idea that she was a mere child being put in her place. She acted as if he was the one who was being stupid. He didn't much care for it, but as her words sank in, he did see what the children were trying to do.

"Oh," he said. "Well, she should tell him that she loves him and why and he—er—should do the same."

"But how would they say it without sounding

corny?" Jana asked. Maati and Thariinye had both
been speaking in Standard for the benefit of the others.
Maati's Standard was quite good by now, he noticed, no
doubt the result of her prolonged association with the
other younglings.

A young male the others called Laxme tapped some
keys on his control pad and the Aari figure swung
toward the Acorna holo and said, in a comic mockery of
Aari's own voice, "Oh, kiss me, my sweetie pie," and
made sounds like hooves pulling out of a mud puddle.

Thariinye was indignant. "Stop that at once!" he said.

Laxme shrank back into himself as if he expected to
be hit.

"He was just playing, showing you how it worked,"
Jana said softly.

"I know, but Aari is a brave man, the bravest man my
people have ever produced probably, and I'll not have
him and Khornya ridiculed, not even by friends."

"That's why we wanted your help," Maati said. "To
make them do and say the right things."

"What right things?" Thariinye asked.

"You know—to get them together. You say you're
this big expert on luu-uuve. So you should know,
right?"

He glared at his former shipmate. "I know how to attract a girl to *me*," he said. "But, uh—" he lowered his
voice and spoke out of the side of his mouth so just
Maati could hear, "as you'll remember, it didn't work
with Khornya."

"Maybe not, but she's already attracted to Aari. We
just have to have his hologram to encourage her, and
vice versa. So what things should they say?"

"First of all," Thariinye told her, "you'll have to have the holograms appear to them after they've been sleeping for a while so that they're groggy and won't notice the shimmering."

"That's what we were going to do," Annella said. "But they don't shimmer *that* much."

Thariinye ignored her. He was thinking hard. "I know," he said. "I think I can find just the thing. Wait a bit."

He returned about a half hour later carrying the book of ancient European literature Aari had been reading.

For the next several hours, Jana read aloud and the others argued the use of this passage or that, while Maati and Thariinye, with the use of the LAANYE, attempted to translate the agreed-upon phrases into Linyaari. Once they decided on the phrases, they had to program the holos to move properly.

"They should look seductive, but mustn't touch a real person, of course," Thariinye said. "They should lead Aari and Khornya to a real place together to continue in person . . ."

"Or a holo place!" Annella said, "None of the holo suites in the hotels are filled yet, since we haven't had a single new guest, just the people who came with the caravan and they all have their own quarters."

Mac's performance and function had been greatly increased by his recent upgrades and education, and he knew the captain was pleased. Becker had puzzled him somewhat when Mac had shut himself down in the captain's absence with Nadhari Kando. "I thought you'd keep working on the shuttle, Mac," the Captain had said. "Not exactly a self-starter, are you?"

"No, sir, though I do shut myself down to conserve energy."

"I want you working on that shuttle day and night, whether I'm here or not. So program that and don't worry about conserving energy. There's energy to burn in this place and I don't think Harakamian will begrudge you some if it saves our butts in the long run."

"Yes, sir," Mac had responded. And he had of course been following instructions ever since. If he could have felt regret, it was that now most of his social interaction was in the Khleevi fashion. He had repaired the transmitter some time ago, though he had not used it yet, as he had not been instructed to do so.

But he practiced, nevertheless, imitating, interpreting, assimilating, and integrating the klicking and klackings until he used them—if only to himself—quite as easily as he conversed in Standard and Linyaari.

He was left alone a great deal these days. The captain and the cat spent increasing amounts of their time with the denizens of the Moon of Opportunity, particularly with Ms. Kando. Sometimes they had their get-togethers aboard the *Condor*, but since Ms. Kando needed to be available to her staff, many times the three of them shared her off-duty time with her in her quarters or in one of the hotel rooms available in the compound. Aari and Acorna were busy elsewhere as well, and the few times when any of the Linyaari had come aboard, the initial smell, the noise emitted by the shuttle, its com unit's volume on high so Mac could hear it as he moved about the ship, seemed to distress them and they left again quickly, particularly when Mac accidentally greeted Aari with Khleevi klackings.

So it was that he was alone when he heard the ships sounding off, a roll call of attack, heard the staccato klickety-klack-klack of orders passed from one unit to another. The essence was that the planet of Nirii, around which the fleet had been gathering, was now being attacked, the fleet swarming down upon it much as hungry insects were said to do on some particularly appropriate foodstuff.

Mac listened with interest. Had he been capable of it, he might have been excited. He was still listening when Becker returned.

"Hi, Mac, can you turn that damned thing down? It sounds like an army of tap dancers landing on a flat wooden planet."

"Oh, no, Captain, nothing like that. The sound is simply that of the Khleevi invading the planet of the two-horned bovine beings. They are passing communications among their various ships, attempting to first conquer major cities and defense outposts, and to an extent prevent any possible escape by inhabitants. Their efforts are concentrated primarily on the attack however."

"Great galloping gravity, Mac, why didn't you say so?"

"You did not instruct me to do so, Captain."

"Do I have to tell you everything?"

Mac was pleased to now be able to employ one of the captain's own idiomatic phrases, "Yes, sir. Pretty much."

"Right. Okay. You keep monitoring that thing—remember everything you hear. I gotta go see a man about a drone."

*   *   *

Hafiz was explaining why the drone was not yet in space as he had assured Becker it would be with all possible dispatch. "I was preparing my message, dear Becker."

"Your message? How long can it take to say, 'The Khleevi are coming, the Khleevi are coming, lock and load or get the hell out *now*?' "

"You don't understand, my boy. Even such public service messages carry delicate nuances. And of course, we did not know exactly when or where they were coming, did we?"

"Now we have a pretty good idea, though. They're chowing down on the cowboy planet right now."

"Cowboy planet?"

Becker stuck a forefinger from each hand up beside his temple and wiggled them. "Two horns like cows, get it?"

"Ahh, the Niriians. Yes, I have heard they have excellent organic technology."

"It stinks, if you ask me, but nobody deserves to have the bugs on top of them and that's what's happening right now. So, is the drone going up or do I have to take the *Condor* up and make like Paul Revere?"

"Paul who, dear boy? And what was he revered for, exactly?"

"Getting his drone up before the enemy had a chance to eat every planet in the galaxy, that's what. Now then, do you think you can finish your message?"

"Certainly."

"Good. I'll just wait then and carry it out to the drone for you."

Hafiz turned on his recorder and rewound. "Let me see, where was I, oh yes, 'This urgent humanitarian warning is brought to you through the kindness and beneficence of the Federation's foremost philanthropic economic ambassadorial firm, House Harakamian.' "

"A *commercial*?" Becker demanded. "You held off putting the drone into space while you made a *commercial*?"

Hafiz spread his hands with an elegant shrug. "I am in commerce after all, dear boy."

"Not for long if the bugs attack us," Becker said grimly.

"Ah, an excellent point. Very well, I shall continue."

The message concluded, "The dastardly insect creatures of torture, doom, and enormous appetite, the Khleevi, are known to be attacking the Niriian homeworld. Any who dare assist the Niriians, feel free to do so, please, with our commendations and blessings. All others in the same quadrant might think seriously about evacuation or defense, as your culture dictates."

Becker gave him a disgusted look, but said only, "Good. Now then, that should be translated to all of the languages of the nearby races. I don't expect, since we're making first contact here, more or less, their Standard is going to be really up to par."

"Ah! A good point." He clapped his hands. A servant appeared. "Please fetch our Linyaari guests—all of them. Ask them to bring their clever translation devices and tell them it is a matter of some urgency."

Hours later, which seemed like months to Becker, each Linyaari had contributed a translation of the message in all of the languages each of them knew. Since all but Maati and Acorna had spent considerable time visiting nearby planets at some point in their lives, they felt they had pretty much covered it.

Meanwhile, Nadhari and her staff went on red alert, and to the whine of the sirens, the first evacuation drill began, just as the drone was shot into space.

The *Balaküre* had not yet landed on the first planet on the list of those to be warned when they heard a broadcast that at once made their mission and their caution futile and provided them with a new mission.

Oddly, this new mission began in a similar fashion to their present one.

"Mayday, Mayday! This is the Niriian vessel *Fossen* broadcasting a Mayday to all worlds and ships in the area. Our homeworld is under attack. The Khleevi have landed. Our ship escaped before the invasion. Mayday! Come in, please." With a glare at Liriili, Neeva picked up the communication device.

"Please give us your coordinates, *Fossen*. The Linyaari ship *Balaküre*, is reading you loud and clear."

The Niriian gave the *Fossen*'s coordinates. "Hurry, *Balaküre*. We are nearly out of fuel and air. We were on our way in for both when the Khleevi attack commenced. The Khleevi have covered our cities like sweetbugs converging on their hive."

"We are coming, *Fossen*. Please do not send additional communication unless we request it or you are in further distress. To do so may alert the Khleevi to your — and our — position. Signal that you have understood and then please, silence unless we contact you."

"Understood, *Balaküre*. Be swift, be swift, please."

Liriili snorted. "I suppose we will join them just in time for a Khleevi attack."

"Perhaps," Neeva said. "But I, for one, hope not. At

least their signal should be heard by nearby worlds and other craft, so our personal warnings to those worlds will not be necessary."

"I wonder what they will make of it on narhii-Vhiliinyar," Liriili said with a bitter smile. "I warned them."

"Yes, you did, and fortunately, with you no longer in charge, they will probably ready the evacuation ships, refuel the fleet, gather the lifeforms, and prepare to leave narhii-Vhiliinyar in the direction farthest from the Niriian world. I suspect they may fly into Federation space. That will be the recommendation of those of us who have been in contact with the peoples of that alliance."

"Yes, and they will come with their weapons, disrespecting the principles the Ancestors taught us."

Melireenya turned in her seat and stared at the former *vüzaar*. "What is it with you? You are not satisfied one way or the other. Would the destruction of our people please you now that you have been deemed unfit to lead them?"

Liriili gave her a superior smile but didn't answer. Neeva was becoming alarmed by the woman's attitude. Instead of helping her heal, this entire experience was driving her more and more into herself. She was so aloof there was no question of touching her with a horn to try to heal her and besides, she seemed to be resistant to the usual bonding that cohered the Linyaari.

The next hours were spent in preparation to take the Niriians aboard. The *Balaküre* had no fuel to give them, and their ships were fueled somewhat differently. Extra berths were prepared, the gardens hyperplanted with varieties of plants the Niriians were known to favor.

The Niriians were pathetically glad to see their Linyaari allies, and also somewhat shame-faced. "*Visedhaanye-Ferúli* Neeva," the captain of the Niriian ship began. "We heard you and your crew had been taken into custody by false authorities. Please know that our lives are yours from this day forward and we will defend you always to any—"

She choked, sputtered, swallowed, and continued. "I was about to say, to any who seek you on our planet. But it is unlikely we will have a home to return to."

"Which brings up a good question," Khaari interjected. "Where should we go now? Return to narhii-Vhiliinyar?"

"Yes, but we should emulate Captain Becker and take evasive action, don't you think, rather than returning directly? In case the Khleevi have spared any ships to follow the *Fossen*."

"A lot of good it did the junk man," Liriili sneered.

"How do you know what good it did him?" Khaari demanded. "We don't know what became of anyone yet."

But they were to learn very shortly. On the other side of the wormhole, they picked up a broadcast.

The first portion was in Standard, and while the *Balaküre*'s crew were putting their heads together trying to remember enough of that language to decipher the message, it was rebroadcast in other languages.

The Niriians became agitated, "They know! They know about the attack! Perhaps they will send help. They are speaking our tongue!"

Neeva looked up. Khaari said, "I know that voice! That's Thariinye speaking!"

"He's alive!" Melireenya said.

"Of course he is," Liriili said. "I told all of you that he would be perfectly all right, and no doubt the brat is as well."

The language switched again, this time to Linyaari, and Neeva smiled widely. "That's Khornya."

They recognized other voices as the broadcasts were repeated in other languages—Aari's and those of Miiri and Kaarlye, which made Khaari, who was related to Kaarlye on her mother's side, sigh with relief.

When the Standard broadcast was repeated, Neeva said, "I know that voice, too. Doesn't that sound like Khornya's kind and generous uncle Hafiz? He spoke before we parted of starting a trade colony on that moon where we went to recuperate after—"

The other two nodded, indicating she needed to be no more specific. "That must surely be where they all are now."

"I have the coordinates right here, Neeva," Melireenya's voice practically sang. "Perhaps he can contact the Federation and they will drive the Khleevi away." She smiled up at the Niriians. "Your world may be saved yet."

They clasped each other so tightly their horns locked. "Only let it be so," the captain said fervently.

Acorna was awakened by a brilliant light shining in her eyes. She opened them wide. She was very tired, having spent the day formulating evacuation plans for the children. The first shipload carrying the youngest ones was to leave in two days' time with Calum on the *Acadecki*. The crew of the *Haven* would send their youngest along too, but the older ones insisted they would stay and fight. Acorna had also done translations of follow-up messages to broadcast in the languages she knew—Linyaari of course, but also Federation-based languages. The Khleevi had invaded Federation space once in search of Linyaari, who was to say they would not do it again?

The tension and her efforts both had wearied her until she had fallen onto her cot too tired to say goodnight to Maati.

Now the light awakened her and her first thought was that she was being wakened because the compound was under attack.

Aari knelt beside her, a few feet from her sleeping pad. He looked rather odd, but not especially alarmed. Maati, on the other side of Acorna from her brother, was rolled onto her side and covered completely by her blanket. She did not seem to notice the light. Acorna rubbed her eyes. "What is it, Aari? Is something the matter?" she whispered.

"Hark!" he said.

"What?" she asked, thinking for one ridiculous moment that he might break into a holiday carol, though she had no idea why he would unless he had been inspired by something he had been reading. But the archaic term was the only word he uttered in Standard. The rest was in Linyaari.

"What light is breaking through the pavilion flap over there? It is the suns and Khornya is the moons!" he asked in a very soft version of their rather nasal native language. Evidently this was not, then, an alarm, unless it was perhaps in some sort of code.

Otherwise, oh dear, she had to wonder if perhaps he might have a fever? An infection perhaps? Or a poisoning? She had no idea really which dangers he might be more susceptible to, without his horn, than the average Linyaari.

"Aari, are you all right?" she asked. "You look rather—well, no pale, but see-throughish. I don't like the texture of your skin. And what you are saying does not entirely make sense. Here, let me feel your pulse. . . ."

But he backed away a bit, babbling, "A reed is a reed by any other name and would still not smell very much but be as graceful and delicious as Khornya." He beckoned her to follow. Which she did because whether his strange utterances were a code for danger or because he was ill, she could hardly ignore them.

Aari thought at first he must be dreaming. Khornya knelt a short distance from his sleeping mat. She was surrounded by a very bright light, as if perhaps she'd taken radiation, and was looking at him with a yearning that echoed what he felt whenever he looked at her.

"Khornya!" he said, when she did not speak. "Khornya, is something wrong? Are the Khleevi attacking?" He looked for Thariinye, to waken and warn him, but the other man was not on his mat. This was not unusual for Thariinye. He had been gone a great deal lately, working on translations and evacuation procedures and also apparently chatting up females, even if they were the wrong species, just to keep in practice, as he said.

Khornya did not answer him directly but instead said

something very strange. He thought it might be code, but if so, no one had given him the key.

"How do I love you?" she asked in Linyaari. "Let me count the trails! I love the very ions scattered behind your vessel. I love the fragrance of the grains on which you sup. I love the—"

"You do?" Aari asked, comprehending that what she said was complimentary if not particularly coherent, evidently not code, but her own pent-up feelings. Her tone of voice was rather declaiming and he could not read her at all. But then, there were times when that happened to him. "But—I have no horn."

"I love the horn you do not have and the horn you used to have and the horn you will have again," she continued, rather than answering him. "Come, my love, let us wander into a secluded bower and there take our ease, if you know what I mean?" Very un-Khornya-like, she waggled a silver-white eyebrow and winked at him. He wondered if perhaps Hafiz's gardens had inadvertently been planted with a stand of what was called "loco weed" in the ancient Zane Grey novels of the wild western America.

Either that or it was some peculiar female mating ritual his mother had neglected to tell him about. Well, there was no time to consult her now. Khornya was wafting away and he could not let her wander around this huge alien compound in such a state. Someone might take unfair advantage of her. He rose to follow her.

She flitted ahead of him like one of the ectoplasmic entities of the wraith-haunted ruined world of Waali Waali his parents had taken him to as a child. Back in the early days of terraforming technology, a powerful company had rapidly terraformed planets, raised great cities upon them, and settled whole transplanted civilizations upon their surfaces, where they thrived and bred, loved and warred for several eons. And then the terraforming destabilized, the ice caps melted, the seas froze, the mountains erupted, and the ground opened and buckled. The cities were ruined and the people were killed, but the heavy gravity kept them bound to the surface, which had an indelible memory of the former grandeur of its cities imprinted upon its ruins. A similar, more tangible memory of its inhabitants, now bodiless spirits seeking some solid vessel in which to be reborn, flickered about the ruins in the same way Khornya's white form was now kindled, now quenched, as she wound her way through the ornamental back alleys of Hafiz's compound.

He could only follow, the winds and rain of Dr. Hoa's climactically generated monsoon soaking through his mane, his steps clicking quickly up cobbled steps leading through narrow passages and by doorways shrouded with night-velveted rugs and blankets, their patterns picked out golden with the light of the holotorches from the main thoroughfares. Suddenly he saw Khornya's white form disappear through a doorway and he found it, concealed by a waterfall of luminous beads, then he too quickly entered.

He threaded through what seemed a maze, except that instead of blank walls, there were more often curtains, blankets, rugs, beads, and once, the side of a large gray beast with flapping ears, long curving fangs, a nose like a snake, legs like pillars, and small, disinterested eyes that regarded him mildly, then returned to contemplating the infinite. Aari passed the beast, but when he looked back, all he saw was blackness.

He began to wonder and to fear. Perhaps he was still in the Khleevi torture machine, and his mind was playing cruel tricks on him, all of this a mere illusion to build his hope, to give him a dream they could cruelly dash? But—well, no. He didn't hurt. That was a sure sign there were no Khleevi. When he had been with the Khleevi the pain was always with him and now there was nothing but his body, feeling whole and quite astonishingly alive, and the night, and Khornya flickering ahead of him, a beckoning candle.

Abruptly, her white form twinkled out ahead of him and then, much farther than he thought she could have gone in such a brief instant, he heard her call, "Aari?" in a rather plaintive and childish voice. He rushed forward.

"Khornya?"

"Aari, where are you?" She sounded not frightened but anxious.

"Right behind you. I'll be there in a moment," he called, and he was. Suddenly he found himself facing her across not a room, but a moonlit field, much like the ones he remembered from Vhiliinyar when he was a boy. The moons shone down through mist rising from a free-flowing stream, and night birds crooned softly from the boughs of scattered trees. Khornya stood near one of the trees beside the stream, and noted his arrival with relief.

"There you are!"

"Of course I am." He went to her. He was relieved to

see she seemed healthier and more substantial than she had at first appeared in his pavilion. Her skin radiated warmth and the sweet clean floral smell she carried with her. But there was another more enticing scent emanating from her as well. She looked up at him with her eyes wide and shining as the moons and her mouth moist.

"I feared you wouldn't come back," she said softly.

"Against love's fire fear's frost hath dissolution," he said.

"Excuse me?"

"It's something I read recently," he told her, his hand running through her mane, the backs of his fingers stopping to feel the curve of her cheek. "It seemed appropriate."

She sighed. "It sounds better in Standard."

"I will ask my parents to tell me Linyaari love poetry and fill your ears with it, if that's what you want," he said, realizing that the language of love must have been what she'd been trying to speak when she was in his tent. She was right, even with the meaning rather unclear, the poetry from the books he'd been reading did sound much better in Standard.

"That is not *all* I want," she said, her voice husky and her breath sweet.

He felt parts of himself he'd thought dead rushing to fill his veins with life as hot and strong, as urgent as magma seeking to escape a volcanic fissure. She lifted her arms, almost as if in a trance, and he took her into his own and held her. Her sweet musky scent swept over him as they slid together into the wildflower sprinkled grass, which was not damp and dewy as he expected, but as warm and comforting as a blanket.

＊　＊　＊

Annella and Maati let out a sigh at the same time. Jana pulled them away from the control booth for the holo suite. She had Laxme by the ear. Thariinye lingered a little until Maati reached back and snagged his arm.

"They deserve a little *privacy*," she said.

"I maybe should have given him a few more pointers before we started this," Thariinye said.

"There was no time," Laxme said. "They're going to make us leave pretty soon and we had to finish it—get them together before whatever is going to—happen, happens."

"Looked to me like he was doing—they both were doing—just fine, without your advice," Maati told Thariinye. "And we should leave them to do it."

Jana grinned at her. "I think you're wise beyond your years, Maati."

"Someone has to be," Maati said, with a meaningful look at Thariinye.

Feeling quite pleased with themselves and considering their good deed a job well done, the group of young people emerged from the Spanish-Moorish castle that housed the grandest of the holo hotels. The curtain swags and bead-draped maze of back streets through which Aari and Acorna had followed each other's doppelganger was the hotel lobby. The suite Aari and Acorna occupied now was on the second floor. The field of fragrant flowers and grass was actually a rather nice Turkomoon carpet, the stream an en suite lap pool, in case they wanted to bathe after their . . . activities.

No sooner had they emerged however, than Maati realized the air smelled subtly different—she recognized the smell too. It was the smell of ships landing. Linyaari ships. She recognized it even before she heard the boots pounding in concerted double time down the street from the spaceport.

With each stroke of the hand, each gentle nip of teeth or lap of tongue, Acorna felt more and more bonded to Aari, as if they were exchanging their very molecules, which of course, they were, romantic as the thought might sound. It didn't feel unromantic however. The urges that had been mysteriously rising in her, troubling her dreams, thrilling her at inappropriate moments, were all about *this*. This exquisite agonizing ache that made her feel as if she would burst from her skin if something didn't happen. She knew Aari felt the same way and yet, he hesitated.

"If we—continue," he said. "There will be no going back."

"Why would I want to go back?" she asked. "You are my lifemate. I think I've always known that."

"Really? I didn't think—I couldn't hope—"

She shushed him with a kiss and they moved so that she was poised above him, his hands on her waist.

"Now, beloved?" he asked.

She bit her lower lip and nodded emphatically, "Yes. Now."

The double-quick pounding boots rounded the corner and the security forces halted with two quick and perfectly synchronized stomps. Nadhari Kando paced effortlessly at the head of the cadre and Captain Becker pantingly trailed behind the buff and ready cream of planetary militia from Federation worlds.

Nadhari glared at the children. "It is long after curfew."

"What curfew?" Jana asked, innocently.

"Were you not at the briefing at twenty hundred hours this evening?" Nadhari asked. "We have a red alert situation and a curfew is in effect until further notice."

"So what're you gonna do, shoot us?" Laxme demanded. He liked being free after his childhood in the mines. He did not take kindly to orders, even from the good guys. Or gals.

Nadhari pursed her lips and regarded him seriously. "No, but you could ask Becker's friend Aari how much fun it is to not be where you're supposed to when the evacuation starts and be left behind when the Khleevi attack."

None of the kids said anything and Nadhari continued. "Now then, Maati, Thariinye, you are to report to the reception area. The *Balaküre* has just landed and they are very anxious to see that all of you are alive and well. I need to find Aari and Acorna, too."

Becker grimaced and told Maati, "That witch of an administrator came on the *Balaküre*, too. I bet the Linyaari couldn't take her on the planet anymore. But Neeva really wants to see everybody and make sure you're all okay."

"I'll go tell her Khornya is okay," Maati said. With a wicked grin she added, "Thariinye can fill Liriili in."

"No, that's okay," Becker said. "Just tell us where Acorna is and I'll get her."

Thariinye's glance strayed toward the hotel entrance and Becker asked, "Are they still in there? Why didn't you say so?"

"Good. I'll fetch them," Nadhari said, and before anyone could stop her she pushed past them and entered the hotel.

Moments later she emerged, looking most uncharacteristically embarrassed and shame-faced. "Why didn't you tell me they were—uh—occupied?" she demanded. "I thought you had all been playing a game or having a meeting or something! What were you doing, using their rendezvous as a training class?"

Maati's face fell. "Noooo, we were trying to get them together. And we did, too. And now it's all ruined!"

"Uh—not entirely," Nadhari said. "Not from what I saw. But I certainly spoiled the mood."

Annella groaned. "It took us weeks to set that up."

"Set what up?" Becker asked suspiciously, but Annella, Markel, and Jana were shaking their heads slightly that Maati should say no more.

In a few minutes, Aari and Acorna walked purposefully from the hotel, as if they *had* been interrupted in nothing more personal than a meeting, except that every once in a while one of them would steal a look at the other one. And smile. Or sigh. Or get lost in looking and stumble.

Nadhari said nothing as she led the way back to the spaceport. Becker talked rather a lot.

Sixteen

The Niriian refugees endured the Linyaari reunion and the subsequent confusing introductions as well as they could, until at last they met someone whose name they recognized. "And this," *Visedhaanye-ferilli* Neeva said, "is Mr. Hafiz Harakamian."

"*The* Hafiz Harakamian of the message?" they cried, and faced him with broad smiles. "Ah, it is *you*, exalted sir, who will save our world and our people. But it must be done quickly. Many die even as we stand here wasting time with these formalities."

Neeva translated and Hafiz smiled broadly back at his guests. "I am very sorry for the plight of your planet, dear alien beings, but you see, I am a merchant. While it was within my power to provide you and the neighboring worlds with a warning about the Khleevi menace, I am not a warrior or a warlord, merely a humble tradesman."

This was the point when Khornya was sorely missed.

Neeva understood Niriian very well indeed, but she missed many of the nuances of Hafiz's speech.

"He says he can't save them," Neeva said. "He is no warrior, merely a rich merchant."

Hafiz caught her look and saw that he had fallen somewhat in her estimation. The Niriians weren't buying it, however. They set themselves even more squarely in front of him and stuck their round jaws out a bit and smiled even more broadly and determinedly.

"Sister-child's father's sister-brother Hafiz," Neeva said, for had he himself not said he felt as if he were related to the Linyaari as he was to Khornya herself—therefore he would naturally also be related to Neeva. "I must tell you that these Niriians are very stubborn people. Once they put their minds to a thing, they do not budge until they have achieved their goals."

"Most admirable," Hafiz said nodding and smiling still. "But their tenacity cannot change the facts."

At this impasse, Nadhari Kando and Captain Becker and the little cadre of security troops Nadhari commanded marched into the reception area. With them were a gaggle of children including Maati, as well as Thariinye, Aari, and Khornya.

"My husband is a merchant, as he has explained to you elevated alien beings," Karina Harakamian now addressed the Niriians with an apologetic flutter of lilac-and-violet draperies and a sparkle of amethyst-jeweled hands. "Surely you would not wish him to subject himself and those he protects to the same fate your planet has met? Hafiz is a genius at accumulating and distributing useful things and services. The idea of the sort of mass destruction the Khlecvi wreak is abhorrent to him, but also totally incomprehensible. I don't know how you could possibly imagine he could be of assistance."

Liriili had a fine curl to her lip and to Neeva, said in Linyaari, "It is as I suspected. Your great hero—our adopted 'uncle'—is perfectly willing to trade with us but as far as being a true friend of anyone but himself—hah!"

Neeva tried valiantly not to let the disappointment show in her eyes as she murmured to the unflinching Niriians.

Acorna was roused from her bemusement by this exchange, and separated herself from Aari and the others to go stand next to Hafiz.

To Liriili she said, "That is not fair. Uncle Hafiz is responsible for the lives of all of the people here and their welfare has to be his first consideration. And he and Captain Becker have been making some strides in perhaps finding a way to combat the Khleevi without risking more lives."

"Is that so?" Liriili demanded. And before anyone could stop her, she translated a version of what Acorna had said to the Niriians. The result of this was that one of them, following Acorna's glance to where Becker stood beside Nadhari, reached out a muscular arm and hauled Becker into a great crushing hug.

Liriili smirked. "Our allies say the junk man is their hero and surely if he knows a way to fight the Khleevi, he will use it quickly to save what is left of their world."

Acorna translated to Becker, "They want you to use the methods we have discovered to fight the Khleevi *now*, Captain, to save the rest of their world."

"Okay, okay!" Becker hollered. "Just tell them to let me go! We'll talk."

This time Thariinye stepped in to translate, adding his usual flourishes.

The Niriian did not loosen its grip on Becker.

"What did you say?" Aari asked Thariinye. "It's not working."

"I told them the captain was a great hero and had already slain many Khleevi and would save their homeworld with the help of the philanthropist Uncle Hafiz."

"Tell them they have to let Captain Becker go before he can help them," Acorna suggested.

Thariinye spoke to the Niriians again and the one who held Becker released him with such an enthusiastic clap on the back that the captain staggered into the arms of Nadhari Kando, and stepped on the cat's tail as he stumbled.

RK rewarded him by opening his leg from kneecap to ankle.

Nadhari patted Becker absently and shoved him gently aside to pick up the cat and croon to it. "Your servant meant no disrespect, sacred feline. Is your magnificent tail broken?" She looked at the nearest Linyaari, who happened to be Liriili. "Please heal the tail of the sacred temple cat."

Liriili, much to the surprise of anyone who was paying attention to her, abandoned her goading behavior of the rest of the humans to add one of her hands to Nadhari's in RK's thick fur, cradle his tail in the other hand, and gently lowered her horn to touch it. The cat immediately began purring and rubbed his cheek against Liriili's.

"If *that* isn't adding insult to injury!" Becker yowled, clutching his bloody pant leg.

Aari scowled at Thariinye, who quickly stopped jabbering to the Niriians and knelt beside Becker. "Sorry, Captain, allow me." He placed Becker's foot upon his own bent knee and ran his horn the length of the cat scratch.

Becker let out a long sigh of relief.

Liriili was crooning to RK. "I had a little *pahaantiyir* once and you are very like him, sacred temple cat, yes, you are, you lovely creature!" Tears were actually coming to her eyes now. "Oh, how I wish he were with me now, my little friend, when I am surrounded by ill-wishers."

RK purred as if he had found a new best friend.

"Traitor," Becker growled.

"Come, my friends, let us refresh ourselves in the gardens and discuss this brilliant plan of ours." Hafiz waggled an eyebrow at Becker, but the eye under the brow was extremely skeptical.

Of course, Becker didn't really have a plan. Acorna knew that. But between the experiences the current crew of the *Condor* had and the skills and resources of Hafiz Harakamian, Acorna saw the components of a rather good plan taking form. All it took to formulate was for everyone involved to pool their resources.

As the others trailed off behind Hafiz, Acorna fetched Mac.

"The captain told me I should remain here, Acorna, and monitor the Khleevi broadcasts."

"You are recording them, aren't you?" Acorna asked.

"Yes."

"Then you can listen to the recordings when you return. We need you now, MacKenZ. Captain Becker is going to explain to Uncle Hafiz how we can defeat the Khleevi."

"Oh, that would be most instructive. I am grateful you thought to bring me, Acorna."

She smiled and eased him away from the Khleevi shuttle. He had spent so long with it the smell had permeated him and she had to stop and give him a once-over with her horn to erase the unpleasant odor.

"Of course you must come, Mac. Without you and your skills, we would not have a hope of defeating the Khleevi."

"Now then, Captain, we are all eager to hear your plan," Neeva said.

"Ye-es, dear fellow," Hafiz said. "Please enlighten us."

"Oh, you're part of it, too, Uncle Hafiz," Acorna assured him. "In fact, we can't do it without Uncle Hafiz's holographic magic can we, Captain Becker?"

"Uh—no, of course not," Becker agreed.

They sat on low cushioned chairs positioned near the fountain. Servers brought delicacies for the humans, while the Niriians and the Linyaari were invited to pluck whatever appealed to them from the bounty of the lush gardens surrounding the pool into which the waters splashed from the horn of a unicorn, rampant. The Linyaari who had not yet seen this fountain regarded it with wonder, even Liriili. This was not the usual way in which homage was paid to the Ancestors, but no doubt the Ancestors would approve.

"And as I was telling Mac, we can't do without his skills. Of course, if Aari had not made an effort to recall

all he knew of the Khleevi, had not concentrated so hard on the *püyi* that was, I am sorry to say, Toroona and Byorn, the legacy of one of your brave crews, we would never have learned their language or anything about how they function." The Niriians were actually a mated couple, female and male, rather than two males as those unacquainted with the species had assumed. Becker was surprised to find that his ribs had almost been broken by Toroona, the female.

"Yeah," Becker said, "Aari found out about another important part of the plan too. Namely that a substance we discovered while on a salvage mission is toxic to the Khleevi. And what Kaarlye and Miiri have been doing is analyzing the damage to the corpses as well as the effects of the substance on other things. What have you folks come up with anyway?"

"We are still exploring possible ways to synthesize the substance, Captain, and to utilize it in a controlled fashion outside its native environment."

"That's okay," Becker said. " 'Cause the truth is, there's nothing wrong with using it in its native environment. See, it's this vine world, full of these big plants that secrete the sap that eats through the Khleevi shells. The way I figure it, if Hafiz here can make use of his holos to make the vine world appear to be like a Linyaari outpost or something, and Mac can persuade the Khleevi that he's one of their guys who survived in the shuttle we've been—well, Mac's been—studying, and we can set up drones and such to make it seem inhabited, then the Khleevi will maybe leave the Niriians to come to the vine world, and the vines will attack 'em, sap 'em, and no more Khleevi."

Everyone agreed that it was a brilliant plan. Almost all of it could be carried out by remote control, once the vine world had been prepared to look inhabited. The only danger was that the vine world was closer to both the Moon of Opportunity and to narhii-Vhiliinyar than the Niriian homeworld, but they could not, of course, let that weigh too heavily against the lives of any Niriians still surviving the initial Khleevi attack.

The Niriians listened anxiously to the translations, their faces stoic, but when they spoke at last their words sounded urgent.

"Time is of the essence," Neeva interpreted. "They implore us to begin implementing the plan immediately."

The Moon of Opportunity shut down its recreational functions and trade centers. Personnel were reassigned to emergency functions. If the plan worked as everyone hoped it would, security, medical, and reconstruction teams would be sent to Nirii following the destruction of the Khleevi.

Aboard the *Condor*, Mac reassembled the Khleevi shuttle.

Kaarlye and Miiri continued their experimentation with the sap and their studies of Khleevi anatomy and physiology in the laboratory.

The children were assigned to either the *Acadecki* or the *Haven* for evacuation. However, Annella Carter, Markel, and Jana were remaining as long as possible in order to help Hafiz prepare the necessary holograms.

"We must simulate a civilization sufficiently luscious to induce salivation among the Khleevi," Hafiz instructed his pupils. "We shall transfer the holos of Linyaari pavilions to nestle them among the vines. We will also need to use the *Balakiire* as a model for simulating other Linyaari vessels of different designs."

"Oh, goody," Annella said. "It will be like decorating giant Easter eggs!"

"Also, we must have holos of individuals—Linyaari and the Niriians. We can do several sims of each of the Linyaari guests and hope the Khleevi will not be aware of the duplication."

"We already have done ones of Aari and Acorna," Annella told Hafiz.

"*Have* you?" Hafiz asked. "That is excellent. Excellent indeed."

"Yes, and we can do me and Thariinye next," Maati said. "Except I want *my* holo to be really large and fierce."

"Why bother?" Thariinye said. "All they have to do is make an unaltered holo of Liriili and she'll probably frighten the Khleevi into leaving a slime trail all the way back to their homeworld."

Seventeen

T he first invasion of the vine world was both human and Linyaari. Acorna, moving gently among the fragrant vines, felt remorseful for what her people were about to bring upon this self-contained ecology.

The plants felt far less alien this time, and far more friendly, now that she knew what their sap could do to Khleevi. She had scarcely noticed before how exquisitely beautiful the flowers were, with their petals shaded from cream to ivory to milky white and translucent, with the barest hints of pink near the stamen.

The scent did not seem so overpowering as it had before. Instead it was rather hypnotic, permeating her other senses so strongly that it seemed to be a color, a taste, a voice, as well as a smell. As technicians and scientists barged through the vines so quickly the plants whipped back and forth as if in a strong wind, Acorna merely held her hand aloft and the ropes of leaf and flower parted for her like a curtain. Perhaps she was thinking of these vines as saviors, champions, defenders of her kind against Khleevi kind, but they were altogether more attractive to her than on her last visit.

Kaarlye and Miiri led teams of volunteers in the harvesting of the sap. They brought containers, of course, but all they really needed was their own footwear and gloves, which collected plenty of the sticky substance as the people plowed through the vines.

Technicians carefully placed the drones that would transmit signals to lure the Khleevi away from the Nirians. These would be overlaid with holograms of Linyaari ships and pavilions being projected by other technicians while the programmed Linyaari holos began milling around among the holo-structures like so many ghosts.

Acorna found it quite startling when she parted the vines with a small gesture to face herself on the other side of them, a self apparently kneeling to collect sap and murmuring odd-sounding words. Acorna retreated two careful steps and the vines closed back over the projection.

"Hmmm," she said to herself, and returned to where the ships that had brought the technicians, scientists, and equipment were almost totally wrapped in vines.

"Captain, I think I may have learned something about these plants," she began.

"Yeah, well, save it, Princess. We got us a situation here. Most of the holos are being hidden by the vines. Except for the projections we can make from above, of the tents and the ships, and only the tops of them are showing, this is still looking pretty much like what it is, a vine world. It's going to take either some earth-moving machines or some heavy machete work to clear spaces for the holos and then these things have a way of growing back. The only good thing about it is that mowing a few of them down will produce more sap. But how it's going to work for a decoy, I dunno." He scratched his mustache in a thoughtful way.

"Wait, Captain. Perhaps that won't be necessary. Perhaps we can communicate with them."

The Captain looked at her as if she were insane. "Acorna. Darling. Sweetie. Princess. Honey. Excuse me. You're a real bright kid, but *they* are *plants*. You eat them. You *don't* discuss strategy with them."

"Perhaps not. But if you use heavy equipment or even machetes to clear the area around the holos, then won't that defeat the purpose? Especially if the vines do *not* regenerate quickly enough in this area? Then the Khleevi will simply land in an area filled with holos, and once they discover that the bait is indeed, merely a collection of holograms, they will go back to the Niriians, or what will be worse for all of us, follow the projections back to the source and prey on the Moon of Opportunity instead."

The mustache bristled and Becker scratched it again. "OK. Guess we better have a council of war here."

Acorna made the same speech to Rafik, Gill, and via transmitter to Hafiz, orbiting the planetoid in the *Ali Baba*, one of his more modest vessels. Karina Harakamian, who had come along as the mission's "spiritual adviser," answered for Hafiz. "Of course, Acorna, dear, you are quite right to try gentle persuasion first. I will have the first officer transport me to the surface at once so that I may assist."

"How kind," Acorna said, quite insincerely, but there was no point in hurting Karina's feelings. Fortunately, her new "auntie" was a mind reader only on very sporadic occasions, and those were never the ones Karina predicted or anticipated.

At Acorna's signal, the *Balaküre* landed beside the holos of the other Linyaari ships, some of them decorated with bunnies and flowers as well as the more usual rococo designs that symbolized the great families and heroes of the Linyaari people.

Thariinye and Maati, who had been setting up the smaller holos and who had also noted the problem of the vines obscuring them, responded to Acorna's mental summons, and Aari, who had been keeping her within sight as much as was possible, joined them.

"I don't suppose the LAANYE will be of any help here," Acorna said. "But I think we must try thought transference with the beings on this planet."

"The vines?" Aari asked.

"Yes," she said. "It came to me while I was out among them that they may communicate by their scent. Remember, the first time we came here, it was almost overpowering."

"It still is right around the ships, and where Captain Becker and the scientists are working," Maati said. "But I noticed as we got a little farther away, planting some of the holos, that the smell was actually kind of pretty."

"Sexy," Thariinye said.

Maati put an elbow in his ribs. "Trust you to think so, even about vines!"

Aari shrugged. "I don't see what help I can be. I'm not very psychic without my—"

Acorna had to turn to face him as he was behind her, one hand resting lightly, reassuringly on one of her shoulders. "Aari," she said, staring, not into his eyes, but slightly above them.

The other Linyaari, including his parents, who had just arrived, panting, hefting their collection bags, followed her gaze. "Aari, what is that on your scar?" she asked, a little breathless with hope as she reached up to touch, thinking realistically that she would probably encounter a piece of a petal from one of the vine flowers. Her finger and his touched the little white protuberance at the same time.

"It's horn!" he said. "My horn is regenerating. The graft is finally taking."

(And I'll bet I know why,) Thariinye whispered, laughing.

Both Acorna and Aari blushed and Maati, who also picked up the whisper, stomped hard on Thariinye's foot.

Acorna embraced Aari and his parents and Maati touched him briefly.

Karina arrived. "I suppose we should start by everyone forming a circle!" she said brightly.

"Why?" everyone else asked, almost in unison.

"The better to commune, of course!" Karina said.

"With our species or yours maybe," Acorna told her gently. "But I think perhaps with these beings we might need to use different methods. One thing I do feel we must do, however, is to distance ourselves from the main part of the camp. The odor given off by the vines is the most overpowering and noxious near the ships."

Acorna led them into the vines, which parted almost

politely before her and the others. They walked perhaps a half of a kilometer from the ships before Acorna stopped and inhaled.

"What do you smell?" she asked.

"It's nice here," Maati said. "Does that mean the plants here aren't as upset as the ones near the ships?"

"I don't know really," Acorna said. "It's just something I thought we might try."

"It sounds pretty silly to me," Liriili said, though she had been unusually quiet until then. "How ever can you imagine that something can communicate with smells?"

Miiri laughed. "What do you think we do when we're ready to mate, Liriili? Or other species for that matter? With pheromones!"

"It's not unheard of for species to communicate with something other than sound, after all," Neeva said. "Many do by sight, or touch, or, as we do ourselves, by thought alone. Had you spent more time investigating the universe around you, Liriili, you would know that."

Acorna said, "Now I remember! Ants! Little ants communicate by pheromones too—a fairly complex set of smells to give each other signals, indicate pathways, that sort of thing."

"Ye-es," Liriili said, sounding almost pleasant, "of course. *Pahantiyürs* also leave scent marks on their territory, or for mating. I just never thought of it as communication before."

"Yes, well, live and learn," Neeva said as diplomatically as possible, clearly not wishing to discourage Liriili's willingness to consider for once that something someone else said might actually contain merit. "The problem is how we should interpret the scents given here."

"That probably won't be as hard," Acorna said, "as somehow managing to communicate with the plants themselves. But I wondered—if the scents symbolize their thought forms, perhaps we can find some common ground to teach them something about ours."

"Why?" Thariinye asked.

"There are many good reasons why one would wish to communicate with a new species, Thariinye," Neeva said. "But the specific one Khornya has in mind, I suspect, is so that we might ask the vines to part and allow the holograms to be seen by the Khleevi."

"But first we must find a common vocabulary," Khaari said. "What do we know about the vines? How could we show similarity?"

"We-ell," Maati said, "If we want them to part, maybe she should start with that. They come together and they spread apart. Maybe we can show that with each other."

"But they don't communicate by what they see," Liriili said, and for once she was using a reasonable, if impatient, tone that only slightly hid the fact that she was as puzzled as any of the rest of them. "They communicate by smell."

"But they convey a thought, sort of," Maati argued. Acorna thought the girl had matured a great deal since she had stopped being Liriili's messenger. She was much more confident now.

(Showing off for her parents,) Thariinye, catching Acorna's thought, whispered to her uncharitably. But Aari scowled at him, as if he read the thought too, and Thariinye looked away as if the thought had been sent by someone else.

"Yes," Acorna agreed with Maati. "It is a thought form, however they express it and who knows? Maybe to the vines, we exude a scent too when we are thinking certain things. Only we'd be a lot more complicated for them to read, maybe, than they are for us. Let's try to simplify it for them. Everyone spread apart and concentrate, as we do so, that we are spreading apart."

"Our essential apartness," intoned Karina.

(Move gently, spread wide,) Acorna whispered. "Karina, think, 'Move gently, spread wide.' "

"A mantra! I love it!" Karina squealed. "Move gently, spread wide. Move gently, spread wide,"

"Softly," Acorna said. "In fact, don't say it, think it."

Karina nodded gravely and only moved her lips to the words.

The whisper was taken up by the others, in unison, (Move gently, spread wide). Their line spread until they could not touch outspread hands. As they moved at first the plants only parted to let each individual pass but gradually, as the people kept whispering, the vines softly lay themselves down upon each other until there was a large rectangular area open around the Linyaari and Karina.

When this concept seemed to be understood, Acorna said softly to Karina, who was on her right, while whispering to the others, (Close up, gather together, twining, tangling, plaiting).

The others took it up and gently came together, then pressed themselves in closer, joining hands, lacing fingers, wrapping knees and feet around legs, hips, and waists as tightly as possible—and then more tightly as the vines locked in around them, squeezing until

Acorna gasped, "Move gently, spread wide" again and the others picked up the thought. It took the vines a breathtaking moment to realize that this time, they must spread first, but their scent lightened from the suffocatingly close aroma it had become while holding the Linyaari, and the vines spread once more.

"These plants are definitely sapient beings," Neeva said approvingly—and apparently somewhat fragrantly. The vines swayed gently back and forth, as if pleased, and emitted a light, sweet aroma.

"Good," Acorna said, "because now we have to tell them about the Khleevi."

"Why?" Thariinye asked.

"And *how*," added Maati.

"Because," Aari said. "We are bringing the Khleevi among them to be killed, but the Khleevi may also kill many of the vine people. When we thought they were not possessed of intelligence, then it seemed good to let the Khleevi graze here and be killed by the sap. But now that we bring this evil upon these beings, the least we can do is warn them."

"Where are they going to go if they object?" Liriili asked archly.

"That is not the point," Neeva said. "Now that we know they are beings who would suffer from the Khleevi as we would, we naturally will continue Captain Becker's plan only with their cooperation."

"Which we will obtain how?" Liriili demanded with the same archness.

"My collection bag!" Miiri said suddenly. "Where is it?"

"There—among the vines," Kaarlye said. "Mine too.

They're open. Do you suppose the plants mind that we are taking the sap?"

"Perhaps they don't mind so much as—wonder what we are doing with it," Acorna ventured. "After all, they know what function it serves for them, but it must be hard for them to understand why we would wish to take some away."

"Mother, Father," Aari said, "I know of one smell that is very evocative—that might demonstrate to them exactly what we are trying to convey. Do you have anything with you that smells like the Khleevi?"

"Oh no," Miiri said. "We bathe very carefully after our laboratory work."

"I'll bet MacKenZ does," Acorna said. "The ship still reeks horribly of Khleevi when you first board it, no matter how many times horns purify the air. That shuttle has the stench hardwired into its structure, I believe."

"I'll go ask him," Maati said.

She returned a short time later holding a peculiar looking object at arms length in one gloved hand, while she held her nose with the other.

"I guess I'm not old enough yet to purify it," she said.

"Good. Don't anyone else try to erase the smell till we can show the vine beings what it means," Acorna said. "Now then, set the thing down, Maati, and let us all allow ourselves to react as we would to a Khleevi with it—fear, disgust, horror, anger, feel them as hard as you can and send. Work yourself up into a sweat if possible."

They all did as she suggested. Aari grew particularly rank with sweat and the stench of fear so that even she could smell him, though usually the Linyaari had only a pleasant odor, if any.

The vines shook and trembled at first and then all at once they swept past the people and converged on the Khleevi object, pouring sap over it, almost shooting the viscous fluid from their stems and blossoms until the thing was entirely covered.

"They get it!" Thariinye cried. "They understand."

"Either that or they're simply acting from self-protection," Liriili said.

"Maybe we should make a holo of the Khleevi to show them?" Maati suggested.

"If they communicate by scent, they'll know the Khleevi when they smell them, and apparently they know what to do with them too," Melireenya said.

"We need our collection bags back," Kaarlye said.

Acorna frowned. "Perhaps they'll understand now. Try to take it back. They know we are afraid of the Khleevi and they have probably noticed that we can't exude sap as they can. That might be clear enough to them—we fear something they have a defense for that we don't."

Kaarlye reached for the sack and met with no resistance as he reclaimed it and then Miiri's from the vines that had been curled protectively over it.

"Back to the original problem of the holos. I suggest that we simply go to the various holos and ask the plants to spread apart where they are. We will have to work on suggesting that they remain that way until the Khleevi are among them."

Neeva shook her head. "The initial problem isn't the main question now. With beings as intelligent as these, we have no right to sacrifice them to spare the Niriians, or ourselves for that matter."

"So, let's show them the *püyi*," Thariinye said.

"If they can't see it, how can they judge?"

"Can they smell it?" Aari asked. "Becker was complaining of the smell of the *püyi*. We still have the capsule in which we found it. Perhaps the smell of that will convey information to the plants that it does not to us."

"I suppose it's worth a try," Acorna said. "Though I hope we're not giving them the wrong smells."

Thariinye and Aari duly boarded the *Condor* and emerged with the *püyi*. They were trailed by RK, who ignored the smelly organic communications device to sniff the plants, after which the cat turned his hoisted tail to the nearest vine and, with a mighty shudder of his magnificently furred appendage, let fly a bolus of *eau de chat* that momentarily overpowered the scent of the flowers.

The vines bent down and for a moment Acorna feared they would perhaps attack RK, but they seemed instead to be bowing to him.

"Look!" Maati cried. "They recognize his scent! They know he's a sacred temple cat! It's like he's blessed them!"

Neeva wrinkled her nose. "If that is the blessing of the sacred temple cat, I should hate to smell the curse!"

The *püyi* was attached to a portable scanner and played for the plants. The vines reacted to nothing until the Khleevi appeared on the *püyi*. Then, to everyone's surprise, the plants sprayed the *püyi* with sap.

"Well," Acorna said, "they clearly recognize the Khleevi. Even when Captain Becker behaved aggressively toward the plants, they didn't spray sap at him or us, but just the image and the klacking of the Khleevi cause the plants to attack."

Aari nodded. "Yes, I think it is because the Khleevi seem to the vines to be larger versions of the insects their sap is created to destroy. That first time we were here—when I—when I had to return to the ship? I saw the resident insects in the sap and they reminded me of the Khleevi. Very much."

Neeva frowned. "If the plants regard the Khleevi as natural enemies, and respond aggressively automatically, then I think perhaps this plan will work and still be within the bounds of diplomatic integrity. Now then, all we have to do is get them to spread themselves away from the holos."

With the communication they had already established, this did not prove difficult. Even Becker was impressed by the cooperation of the vines. When the last drones were planted, the crew of the *Condor* looked down to see a little frontier outpost of the Linyaari, nestled among flowering vines. Tall unicorn people scurried to and fro among the buildings and vines.

"That ought to be enough to fool the Khleevi," Becker said, and turned to Mac. "Are you ready to transmit from your shuttle?"

"Aye, Captain," Mac said.

"Then stand by. As soon as the area is cleared, you can invite your friends to our garden party," Becker said, his mustache bristling as he bared his teeth in what Acorna decided was *not* a show of friendship.

"Uncle, I thought we agreed that the children were to be evacuated here to the Moon of Opportunity immediately," Rafik Nadezda reminded Hafiz.

"Ah, but that was before the excellent Becker devised his excellent plan," Hafiz said. "And Ambassador Neeva and the eminent Linyaari scientists Kaarlye and Miiri assure me it will succeed, as does our own beloved Acorna. So why send the kiddies home? And if they go, why not all of us? And if we go, so goes a large portion of the assets of House Harakamian, which I have invested in the establishment of the Moon of Opportunity." Seeing his nephew's eyes snap and his mouth open, Hafiz added hastily, "I know, dear boy, I know, of course, that human—and Linyaari—life is not to be measured against mere profit. Naturally. But is it not true as well that these people, Acorna's people, have come to rely upon us for a certain measure of protection—well, perhaps, *support* is a better word? And if we begin sending away our own children, indicating that we believe danger still exists, does this not imply that ours are more important than *their* loved ones? Such an implication hardly sets the right tone, you see?"

"Tone be damned!" Rafik said. "These kids have already been through a thousand kinds of hell and we have definitely promised them our protection. The Linyaari are home, as are their children. Our kids should return to Maganos Moonbase and stay there until the Khleevi are no longer a problem. And the *Haven* has no business here either."

"The *Haven* is free to go whenever it wishes. Thus far the Starfarers have decided to remain with us."

"You can't allow it, Uncle Hafiz. It's much too risky."

"Nephew, dear boy, listen to me. *Life* is risky. Business—successful business—is even more so. We are pioneers, son of my heart. If we are to tread the surface of planets which have never known a human footprint, if we are to trade in currency as yet untouched by human hand, risks are necessary."

Rafik's eyes narrowed and his tone was filled with disgust he didn't bother to conceal. "You say this to me, you who cowered in the underground shelter of your compound at Laboue when you first saw what the Khleevi did to their prisoners?"

Sweat broke out on Hafiz's forehead despite the sweet and mild day Dr. Hoa's weather magic had provided. "The shock of first contact, dear boy." Hafiz blotted the moisture with a monogrammed scarlet synsilk tissue. "But, very well, if you insist, your aunt and I will personally escort the children back to Federation space, while you as my heir and representative will naturally conduct business as usual until the crisis has passed and it is safe for us to return. At which time you will see the wisdom of your old uncle's counsel and realize how hasty you have been."

Rafik smiled ruefully, to let his uncle know he had been outmaneuvered. Hafiz could now take Karina and the children and retire from the field, leaving others to face danger for the sake of his profit. On the other hand, with the old man and the kids safely out of the way, Rafik could command the dismantling of the Moon immediately if it looked like Becker's plan to eradicate the danger from the Khleevi might fail.

Hafiz knew this, of course. And furthermore, he knew that Rafik knew that he knew. But it was much easier to handle matters this way, allowing Rafik to make the decisions that would preserve or risk life, determine profit or loss. After all, Rafik was now head of

House Harakamian, while Hafiz was technically retired. But these things were very difficult and must be handled delicately. If the Moon of Opportunity failed, it would be on Rafik's head, and not Hafiz's.

Thus as soon as the holo team returned from the vine world, the *Acadecki* and the *Haven* were loaded with the children of Maganos Moonbase. As a mark of his faith that he would be returning shortly, Hafiz left the *Sharazad* on the Moon of Opportunity and submitted himself and Karina to the far less commodious accommodations of the *Acadecki*. Rafik had suggested the gesture, both because the plans were already in place to use the *Acadecki* for evacuation and also because, should general evacuation become necessary, the *Sharazad* was larger and would hold more personnel.

With Aari translating, Kaarlye and Miiri approached Hafiz just before he boarded. Miiri spoke first and Aari said, "My mother implores you to take my sister with you and the children. My parents vow to remain here and continue searching for a way to exploit this biological weapon the vine world has provided, although you understand of course that no Linyaari can actually deploy it as an implement of aggression, even against the Khleevi. However, they say they can work better if they know that Maati is safe. They wished for me to join her, but Khornya and I wish to remain with Captain Becker. My sister is young and longs for new experiences, and would very much like to see the Federation worlds. So take her with you. Take Thariinye as well so that one of her own kind bears her company." He looked back to his mother for further words but she was swallowing hard and looking away.

As Maati and Thariinye transferred ships, Thariinye complained that he wanted to stay with the *Condor* but he drew only a stern look from Neeva, who silently indicated he should obey.

What no one said, or even whispered, was that if the Khleevi prevailed, despite the plan, and once more attacked narhii-Vhiliinyar, at least there would be one young male and one young female of the Linyaari safe in Federation space, as hope for the Linyaari. Meanwhile, the *Balaküre*'s remaining crew worked on coordinating with other teams of volunteer rescuers, in the event it became possible to take a relief mission to Nirii once the Khleevi had been lured away. Distressing transmissions from the Khleevi showed them torturing stoic two-horned beings who were obviously in great pain, but refusing to utter a sound or show any fear at all. Even stranger, Toroona and Byorn, who had been so emotional on their planet's behalf when asking for help, watched the transmissions with the same stoicism. Their emotions showed only when they turned away as the frustrated Khleevi increased their efforts until their prisoners, still silent, died.

Becker and RK enjoyed a brief reunion with Nadhari. She, as security chief, was now second in authority on the Moon of Opportunity only to Rafik Nadezda. Since she was supervising the security arrangements for the evacuation, she had time only for a quick half hug with Becker, and to welcome RK as the cat draped himself around her shoulders while she worked.

As the passengers finished loading onto the *Acadecki*, Miiri and Kaarlye supervised the loading of canisters full of sap into the cargo hold. Hafiz wished to take it to his corporate laboratories for further analyses and study. Should the Khleevi ever attack within Federation space, the Federation would pay well in terms of influence and power, as well as great sums of money, to the holder of a secret weapon against this terrible enemy.

Aari surprised Hafiz by clasping the older man's round synsatin clad form in his own large embrace. "Farewell, Uncle Hafiz. Look after my sister and Thari-inye and our friends and be well. Joh, Khornya, Riid-Kiiyi, and I too will let you know when it is safe to return."

"Er, farewell, my nephew."

Karina gave him a somewhat more effusive hug. "Farewell, Aari, and oh, my, is that a horn you're growing there?" She reached up to touch it and with difficulty he endured what she probably didn't realize was an inappropriate intimacy. "Oooh, I just had a flash. The plan will succeed but there will be difficulty—and danger! Be careful, dear friend—friends!"

Eighteen

eady, Captain," Mac said. The android was in the cockpit of the Khleevi shuttle. It was still in the hold of the *Condor*, which was now orbiting the vine world. The holograms moved below in their randomly programmed patterns. Some of them were speaking, some were not. It didn't matter. The Khleevi wouldn't understand anyway.

Becker rubbed his hands together as gleefully as a landlord about to foreclose on the heroine's mortgage in a vid melodrama. "The trap is set, the bait's in place, now all we need is to wiggle the string a little to make the bait look lively to the rats."

Acorna looked up from the console, smiled and stroked RK's head. "Captain, it occurs to me you've been hanging out too much with RK lately."

"Yes," Aari said. "You are beginning to think like a cat."

Becker shrugged. "I could do worse. Cats are good at strategy. " He flipped the toggle on the ship's intercom.

"Okay, Mac, do your thing," he said, then, recalling how literal minded the android was, added, "I mean, make the speech we discussed to the Khleevi and try to lure them over here."

Acorna frowned. "I wish we were able to wait until the evac ships have time to reach Federation space." She let the words hang in the air. It was a vain wish. All of them had seen the broadcasts of pain-wracked Niriian prisoners being tortured. All of them knew what the planet would look like when the Khleevi were finished. All of them knew that every moment they delayed cost more Niriian lives. They had to act quickly. And really, the evacuation ships would be heading toward Federation space, not near the vine world. There should be no problem at all. Acorna wondered why she remained anxious, nevertheless. When her question popped out, it surprised even her. "I wonder why they do it, really."

"Who, hon?" Becker asked.

"The Khleevi. Why do they torture people? Did you ask the prisoner that?"

"No. I figure it's just cause they're mean mothahs and they enjoy it. Isn't that about right, Aari?"

Aari frowned. "I did not think of them as enjoying anything, Joh. In fact, now that you mention it, I don't believe they *did* enjoy torturing me, as relentless and thorough as they were. It seemed more as if they were very anxious to be wringing from me every bit of pain and fear they could. The few questions they asked me did not seem to be important to them and they did not bother to try to understand enough Linyaari to be able to express themselves. And I am afraid that one thing our observers and diplomats have learned of the

Khleevi is that they *are* very scientific about their torture. The first few of our representatives they captured and tortured died almost at once, so the Khleevi refined their techniques so that they would only cause maximum pain for the longest possible time without fatal results."

He shuddered suddenly and Acorna reached for his hand and held it. She knew from his thoughts that he had been shamed by his fear of the Khleevi, and by the pleading he had no doubt done with them to stop hurting him, natural as such responses were. He did not feel any of the merit Thariinye attributed to him for enduring what he could not escape. Acorna agreed with his assessment. It was pitiable what he had been through, horrible, but did not, in itself, make him a better person. No, he himself did that by his strength of character in facing what he feared most, and with reasons stronger than anyone around him could possibly understand. He faced the Khleevi, and their torture, and examined it to try to find answers and solutions that would help others.

Becker grunted. "Whoever said 'know your enemy' was right, even if he couldn't have known the enemy was going to be big, nasty, alien bugs. If he had known, maybe he would have told us *how* we were supposed to know them."

"Receiving reply from the Khleevi now, Captain," Mac said.

"On our way, Mac," Becker said. The crew clattered across the grated deck plate and down to the hold containing the shuttle. Klackings and klickings emanated from the freshly repaired com unit.

"What do they say, Mac?" Becker asked.

"They are coming here now, Captain!" Mac said.

"Wow, that was fast. Already?" Becker asked.

"The Niriians do not make satisfactory victims, apparently," Mac said. "The Khleevi expressed preference for Linyaari prey. They scream better, apparently. This is a desirable trait in a host race for the Khleevi. They have been quite unhappy with the lack of response from the Niriians, despite their best efforts. The Niriian response has been judged inadequate."

"Inadequate for what?" Becker asked.

Mac said, "I do not know, Captain. I repeat only the—scuttlebutt—I am picking up from their intership transmissions. Shall I ask?"

"No," Aari said. "If you were a real Khleevi, you wouldn't have to."

"True," Becker said. "So, they're on their way. Let's fall back smartly, gang." It had been necessary for them to transmit from the proper physical location to lend verisimilitude to their transmission, but the remote cameras located on the vine world and its moon would provide visuals of the Khleevi invasion. The *Condor* could detect the approach of the Khleevi from considerable distance, thanks to the bank of long-range scanners Becker normally employed for detecting ships in peril, recent disasters, and other juicy salvage situations. Once the Khleevi swarm was all focused on the vine world, the *Condor* could creep back into position for a ringside seat to the "the squishing," as Becker colorfully referred to it.

Once the swarm approached, radio silence would have to be maintained. However, the *Condor*'s shuttle had been repaired and readied to act as a relay between the Moon of Opportunity and the *Condor*, to carry news of the mission's progress. Once the *Condor* was in position on the far side of the vine world's nearest planetary neighbor, their position was transmitted to headquarters on the moon.

The *Condor* lurked, waiting for the Khleevi to become carrion.

When the swarm's vanguard arrived, Becker, who was on watch, let out a whoop. "Mercy gracious, boys 'n' girls, the scanners look like Kezdet's pleasure district on a Saturday night when the fleet's just docked! My oh my oh my!"

Acorna and Aari joined him on the bridge. Mac was still monitoring Khleevi communications from the wrecked shuttle.

The vid screen came to life as the remote cameras switched themselves on to record the landing of the Khleevi fleet. A shark-like school of the mantis-shaped vessels circumnavigated the smallish vine world as if they were the rings of Saturn. From the innermost ring of ships, shuttles shot to the surface, after which those ships spiraled away from the planet to be replaced by others with a fresh supply of shuttles and troops.

"We're going to need something to destroy the ships too," Becker whispered fiercely. Acorna knew why he was whispering. The attack was ferocious. She feared anew for the sapient vines. "If they don't land, the sap can't make contact."

"Perhaps they will land to investigate and infect each other," Acorna suggested.

But they did not.

The vines parted to permit the landing of the shuttles, each of which disgorged an amazing number of ground troops.

At first the vines allowed the Khleevi to pass until it seemed there were as many Khleevi on the ground as there were vines, all marching relentlessly upon the holo compounds.

Acorna trembled at the sight of multiples of herself, Aari, Neeva and the *Balaküre*'s crew, Aari's family, Thariinye and Liriili, going blithely and peacefully about their business while endless lines of Khleevi, ever reinforced by more shuttles dropping through vine-world space in lines of their own, deposited reinforcements.

The staccato klacking of pincers and mandibles was louder than any weapon's fire.

"Why aren't the plants closing on them?" Becker demanded.

"I don't know, Captain," Aari answered. "In the communications we had with them, the mere scent of the Khleevi caused the vine-beings to shoot sap upon the offending objects."

"They're waiting," Acorna said, excitement and awe in her voice. "We knew the plants were intelligent and they're proving it! I think our warnings about the Khleevi were understood much better than we had reason to hope. The plants actually have formed a plan. They want to trap the largest possible number of Khleevi before they counterattack."

"You're kidding!" Becker said, and whistled.

RK leaped onto the console. His fur stuck straight out on his body so he appeared to be twice his normal

size. His tail bristled and switched so fast it slammed
Becker's kaf cup to the floor with one swipe, Aari's with
the next. A low growl from RK's throat grew to a high-
pitched caterwaul that made Becker cover his ears and
Acorna lift the spiky creature into her arms to try to
comfort him. He didn't attack her, but neither did he
calm down. There was nothing to heal in his response.
It was natural and healthy for a Makahomian Temple
Cat to go into battle mode under the circumstances.
Acorna understood this and when the cat remained stiff
and distinctly uncomforted, she set him down again
where he stood with his tail lashing the air like a saber.

The first phalanx of Khleevi reached the holo-compounds and opened fire on the holos, which responded
by breaking up and reforming, continuing the postures,
journeys, movements, and apparent tasks in which they
had been engaged before the attack.

Khleevi klacking escalated to an even higher volume.
Shuttles no longer streamed from the skies. The ground
troops, heedless of the klacks of the vanguard, charged
forward, trampling some of those in front of them.

Mac looked up at the rest of the crew. "The Khleevi
are very frustrated and dissatisfied," he said. The android could have saved the speech. The tone of the
klacks accompanied by the activity of the klackers was
more than eloquent.

Then suddenly, and seemingly simultaneously, the
Khleevi exploded into action, all of them at once diving
into the vines with open mandibles. The attack had
been so typically single minded that it had drawn their
attention—and the attention of Acorna and her
friends—completely away from the plants, which had

been docilely shrinking away from the Khleevi, allowing roots and stalks to be trampled. Even before the Khleevi attack changed course, however, the plants slowly began thrusting upward again, unbending from being trod underfoot, as if reaching for sunlight, all very innocent and plant-like.

But as the first mandibles closed on the first stalk, the vines whipped into action, shooting sap from each fresh wound and from sap sacs hidden in the stalks and under the leaves as well. The Khleevi were surrounded, as they had previously surrounded the holo-compounds.

The cameras became ineffective as sap squirted everywhere. Becker switched to the moon-linked camera. A close-up of the planet's surface showed it glistening with turbulent swells and peaks of slimy sap. The Khleevi shuttle's com unit squealed with high-pitched *eeee* sounds. Acorna reached over and flipped the toggle, and the sound mercifully ceased.

The remote camera showed a handful of shuttles with rapidly dying Khleevi piloting them erratically towards the mother ships. Once the stragglers had been reabsorbed by the swarm, the ships veered off.

"Are they going back to the Niriians?" Becker asked Mac.

Mac flipped the toggle back on again and monitored the noises emitted by the ships. "No, Captain. They are in disarray. This has never happened to them before, I think."

"Predators who prey on pacifists probably don't run the risk of getting beaten all that often," Becker allowed. "So what are they up to?"

"I do not think they know at this time, Captain.

There is talk of returning to the homeworld. They are—unlikely as it may sound—I believe they are very frightened, Captain."

"Of the vine world?" Becker grinned. "They should be. Serves them right."

"Yes, but they are already discussing what might be used to neutralize it. Actually, from what I can detect, I believe they are afraid of returning to their homeworld. That seems odd, don't you think?"

"Maybe the King bug is going to chop off their heads," Becker said with a shrug. "I hope he does and that teaches them not to mess with us again. So, gang, I guess that's it. It's over. We win. Or the plant critters do. End of story."

Acorna could not think of a logical objection to this conclusion, though she felt it was somehow all—anticlimactic. So much horror so easily conquered. Who would have believed it. But she could tell from Becker's tone and his expression that he felt the same. Aari too appeared perplexed and unsatisfied. "What's the matter?" she asked him.

He shook his head, "Perhaps, after living with fear of the Khleevi for so long, it is hard to believe we have put an effective end to them. Perhaps I am merely having trouble adjusting to the idea that they are gone, that our people, and I in particular, no longer have the terror of them looming over us."

"Maybe that's it," Acorna agreed. But she remained uneasy.

No brass band greeted the *Condor*, but everybody looked happy to see it return safely. Rafik Nadezda,

Declan Giloglie, and Nadhari Kando were waiting at the landing bay, as were Aari's parents.

Before the robo-lift had touched the ground, Aari's parents were saying, "We made a significant break-through with the sap! Wait till you see. It's quite simple but very effective."

"That's good," Becker told them. "But I'm afraid we won't be needing it."

He deliberately pulled a long face and Acorna and Aari, picking up their cues from him, tried to keep their thoughts to themselves.

"Why? Didn't it work? What happened?"

"The plants pretty well annihilated the Khleevi army, that's what!" Becker said, grinning. "We—or rather the plants—whipped their buggy butts."

Cheers went up among the reception committee and as the word passed all through the compound. Outlying recreational areas had been closed for the red alert and the main city was bloated with anxious people, some of them bored because their functions had been related solely to the closed areas, some of them pumped with adrenaline, ready to take action against any threat.

The Linyaari delegation pressed forward, the Niriian couple preceding them by a step or two.

Acorna smiled at them and told her aunt, "According to the Khleevi broadcasts, they won't be going back to Nirii either. Mac says from what he can figure out, the Niriians did not make very good victims."

Neeva translated and Toroona smiled beatifically. "She says that's something they can be proud of," Neeva said.

Rafik was smiling too. "Whew. This is a wonderful

turn of events! We had better call Uncle Hafiz at once, Acorna, so he can come back and broadcast a new message taking all the credit!" Acorna and Rafik exchanged knowing grins.

Aari's mother had taken his arm on one side and Acorna's on the other. "And *we* thought we had so much to show *you*."

"We are most interested in your discoveries, Mother," Aari assured her. "While most of the Khleevi army was destroyed, there were still many ships aloft and we are unsure how many troops may have remained onboard."

"Yeah," Becker said. "Besides, they're bugs." Acorna translated.

Kaarlye looked puzzled. "Of course they are insects. Does the captain think we are unaware of this?"

"I believe what he means," Acorna said, "is that insects reproduce rapidly and in large numbers. The danger from the Khleevi is not yet over."

Nineteen

Rafik, dear boy, and my good Captain Becker, this is wonderful news!" Hafiz Harakamian said. The crew and passengers of the *Acadecki* were cheering, holding hands, and hopping up and down, even as Calum reversed course in preparation for the *Acadecki's* return to MOO, as the children now referred to it. "You have vanquished the enemy, saved the Niriian homeworld, made the universe a safer place to do business, brought honor to House Harakamian, created the opportunity for much favorable publicity for the Moon of Opportunity, and all at a relatively low price point! Commendable, gentlemen, most commendable indeed."

The next hail was from the *Haven*. "I presume you've heard the news!" Johnny Greene said.

"We have indeed and splendid news it is!" Hafiz replied. "We are returning to the Moon of Opportunity even as we speak."

"We're within Federation space right now, and I

haven't heard what the general vote was, but the Counsel is pretty sure the kids will want to come back to the Moon, too. Once the vote is in, if that's the case, we'll caravan with you again."

"Very well, Johnny, but tell the children not to dawdle. Uncle Hafiz has a great deal to do now that his staff has made space safe for our new friends and neighbors to travel freely once more."

"Uh—yeah, we knew that," Johnny said. "Catch you in a few."

"So that means we need to wait for them?" Calum Baird asked.

"Yes, indeed," Hafiz said. Laxme and some of the other children made impatient noises.

"Are they going to be long?" Laxme asked.

There was not actually a lot to do on the *Acadecki* and the rations weren't that great either. It wasn't as big as the ships they had come on, and there hadn't been time to prepare properly for a long journey. Nutritious ration bars took up little space, did not require heating or freezing, and provided all of the basic requirements. Laxme knew he shouldn't quibble. Working in the mines, he and many of the others had far less to eat, nothing really, just enough to keep them upright and working. But now that he had tasted enough food, tasty food, lovely desserts and butter for the vegetables and even the succulent meats—he wasn't happy to give that up.

Maati had been indignant at being herded onto the evacuation ship as if she wasn't the former copilot of her own ship, the survivor of two battles, one in space, one on the ground, with the Khleevi. She knew that her parents had insisted she go because they wanted her to be safe, but part of her felt that they really just wanted to be rid of her again, when she had only just found them. And Thariinye was even more impossible than usual. Recently their mutual teasing had been playful and friendly but he was so angry at being kept out of the action again and treated like a child that he took it out on her with deliberately nasty and hurtful remarks. She snapped back just as angrily, and their mood made the other children angry and nasty or depressed too so there was already a lot of fighting on the ship. This didn't improve Calum Baird's temper any either, and Karina Harakamian fluttered about calling for peace and light. When she wasn't hiding in the berth she had to share *only* with Uncle Hafiz.

As for Hafiz, he could not but wonder how he had come to taking leave of his senses so far as to allow himself to undertake a long journey in the company of so many children. He was not a fatherly man, nor, if the truth be known, even an avuncular one unless it proved profitable to appear to be. He could not stand whining children actually.

Of course, the unsettling thing about this lot is that they didn't whine. For the most part they were disturbingly adult. The larger ones seemed to be used to looking after the smaller ones, and even the youngest didn't cry, just looked at him with wide eyes that managed to be hopeful and suspicious at the same time.

Returning to the Moon of Opportunity seemed to please them, and he felt more gratitude than was strictly reasonable that they had perked up so much. Even the two Linyaari young ones stopped scowling at each other to cheer. But as the wait for the *Haven* grew longer, the children became impatient again.

Hafiz did not like the hostile silence. Karina disliked it even more, apparently. Complaining of a headache, she took to their berth.

"What troubles you, my little ones?" Hafiz asked finally, bravely, his own mood at least much improved by relief at not losing his corporate shirt.

"Well," Jana said. "There's not a lot to do here. I think they're bored." She herself, her tone implied, was above boredom.

"Bored?" The concept was not one with which he had much familiarity. Being fabulously rich and imaginative as well, he could usually avoid such unattractive moods.

Calum turned in his command chair and said, "In order to get maximum passenger space, we had to dispense with some of the amenities—there's only one set of phones and goggles for vids, the hardcopy books were offloaded to make room, and I'm getting sick of nutrient bars myself. Of course they're bored. Aren't you?"

"I've been enjoying the rest, frankly," Hafiz said. "And then, my beauteous Karina and I have not been married long."

"Uh-huh," Calum said, rolling his eyes.

"She has her trances and meditations and continuous search for what she refers to as enlightenment to entertain her," Hafiz said. "Perhaps you could tell the children a story, Baird?" he suggested in a helpful tone.

"Or maybe you could, Hafiz. I'm busy skippering this bird," Calum said, turning his back on him again.

"Me? Ah." Hafiz looked around him. "Very well, then. I shall need to employ the remote link to the ship's computer, dear boy."

"To tell a *story*?" Calum asked incredulously.

"Audio-visual aids, homely former senior wife of my illustrious nephew, audio-visual aids," Hafiz said, and clapped his hands. "All young persons wishing to become unbored will now assemble in the hydroponics garden where your beneficent Uncle Hafiz shall entertain you so thrillingly you will completely forget to sulk and fret and otherwise contort your faces and voices into infelicitous conformations."

"That should charm 'em all right," Calum said.

"I shall also require the next meal's supply of luncheon bars and liquid refreshment," Hafiz said.

"Gee, I'd have the chef give them to the maître'd to deliver personally, but they're both busy with this evening's banquet," Calum replied sarcastically. Hafiz knew, very well that if he wanted the damned bars he'd need to take them from the food locker himself. The replicator worked, but even it required supplies from which to manufacture foodstuff and those supplies took up more room than the nutrient bars and caps.

"Very well," Hafiz said, and beckoned imperiously to Jana and Chiura, who were following in the wake of the other young ones headed toward the hydroponics garden, which they would soon, Hafiz knew, come to regard as a garden of delights. "Young ladies, you will accompany me to the food locker and assist in conveying supplies to our destination."

The girls looked at each other and shrugged.

*   *   *

The driver of the Khleevi ship designated by *Fourteen Klacks and Two Klicks* was greatly agitated.

Partly this was from the pain in his sixth foot, which had come into contact with the damaged shuttle pilot who managed to dock aboard *Fourteen Klacks and Two Klicks* before the crew of the large ship realized that both shuttle and the operator of same were infected with an alien substance that ate them. Once they had made this discovery, members of the crew attempted to neutralize the infected personnel in the customary way, by stomping them to death. Unfortunately, this brought feet, pincers, and in some cases other delicate body parts into contact with the alien substance.

The driver really didn't feel well at all and neither did the affected crew members, who could now truly be called a skeleton crew, if not an exoskeleton crew, since the exoskeletons were the first parts eaten away by the substance.

The high-pitched pain sounds they were producing made the driver's brain ache as well as his foot, which he realized would have to be sacrificed before long or it would involve his entire leg. Unlike the crewmembers, he had not done any actual stomping of the infected shuttle soldier. He had merely nudged the soldier with his foot to tag the tainted one for elimination.

He feared that he would be the next to be eliminated. If the disease didn't claim him, he would surely be stomped by the other, healthier ship drivers, or worse, his damaged part would be severed and he would be fed to the Young.

The Young would be even angrier and more ferocious than usual, as they had not received a good feeding in many, many lengthy time units. The Niriians were a stingy, selfish race who kept their pain to themselves and did not beg or plead or weep, no matter how meticulously and slowly they were disassembled. They were so retentive of their feelings that they refused to writhe even under the worst provocation. They also were rather frail things and tended to die. Quickly. Quietly. No nutrition for the Young there.

When the shuttle from scout ship *Fifty-three Klicks and Seven Klacks* reported a juicy colony of the One-Horns, the swarm had been hungry for conquest, and more to the point, the Young had been even hungrier. The lair of the One-Horns had proved elusive and was much sought after, since the members of the race thus far encountered possessed a particularly satisfying capacity for emotional projection. Shock, fear, outrage, loathing, and an unplumbed depth of capacity to suffer and emote anguish when correctly manipulated made even one of these beings a sweet feast for the Young.

But this time the Khleevi had been worse than thwarted. According to the shuttle soldiers who survived, the world was filled with nothing but shadows of One-Horns and their buildings, shadows that could not be touched or hurt or killed and had no redeeming nutritional value to either soldiers or the Young. Worse, there were the growing things with the prominent white sexual organs, similar in appearance to stationary growing things on other worlds. These emitted pheromones of fear which had seemed promising, but when the shuttle soldiers attacked them, the growing things had the temerity to attack back! The entire ground fleet had been lost and many of the swarm ships infected by contaminated shuttles, which nonetheless returned to their ships.

The Young knew. The fear and pain of their own elders had been fed to them as a substitute for the alien food, but it was not enough. So much time had elapsed since a proper feeding, nothing would satisfy the Young now but the actual physical bodies of their elders, whom the eldest of the Young would replace.

This was The Path, the driver knew. In time, the elders, such as him, grew weak and unable to serve, and had to be eliminated and replaced with fresh, fierce Young, who in turn served the even more vicious, malicious, and avaricious *Younger*. So now the swarm would return with nothing to offer but themselves, their own bodies, their own pain and anguish and fear, to be devoured by the slavering hordes of their offspring.

The driver regretted this with a deep bitter regret that the Young would find added a nice tang. He himself had replaced a used up, worn out elder whom he personally devoured only a few brief time units ago. His turn at the Gathering should have lasted many, many more time units. It was not right. It was not fair. It did not suit him. But it was The Path.

Between his agitation and his pain and the lack of attentiveness on the part of the other crew members due to similar distractions, he veered somewhat off course, following several other members of the swarm who were also affected and also deviated from course.

His was the first ship to spot the alien vessel. It did not appear to be accelerating, nor orbiting, nor moving in any way. Nor did it appear to be damaged. The equipment detected life signs. The other ships of the swarm also spotted it. It was still a great distance away and if it was fast, it might yet evade them. But if it was not, here was food to offer the Young, who might be so busy feeding, they would forget to consume a few stringy old elders.

The hydroponics garden of the *Acadecki* now blossomed with exotic flowers of crimson and orchid, lilacs so real they seemed fragrant, jasmine and roses of all descriptions vying with frangipani, plumeria, and lush lotus blossoms floating in a pool of crystal water, fed by a sparkling fountain.

As each child looked at the others, he or she saw not another child but either a beautiful (if rather plump; Hafiz always made his holograms in the images of his own desire) houri or a dashing thief. The ladies were scantily clad in clothing that included many layers of silken veils and skirts, balloon-legged pants with slits down the sides to show shapely limbs, and lots and lots of clanking silver and gold coin jewelry. The thieves were clad in Berber blues, their skins dyed by the indigo in their clothing, or in striped robes colored in the soft golds, saffrons, russets, and browns of a desert most of the children had never imagined. Now it stretched out before them, just beyond the boundaries of the gardens. Each child was alone among fascinating strangers, all of them listening respectfully, attentively to the voice of Hafiz Harakamian. Ouds and doumbeks, tambourines and zills, a whining flute spiraled and curled around Hafiz's words, illuminating each as colored inks adorned the alphabets of ancient holy books.

And that was only the backdrop!

Hafiz's tales came to life between him and the children. The story began, "There was once in days of yore and in ages and times long gone before, on Kezdet, before the Federation, a poor but enterprising lad, by name Habib, son of a lowly designer of inexpensive gaming software. Sadly for Habib, before he had reached his fifteenth year, his father passed into the land foretold by the Three Books and the Three Prophets, and Habib, whose mother had long ago run off with a smooth-talking merchant of space travel insurance, was left alone."

He went on to demonstrate how the young Habib found his fortune in a magic lamp—a lamp that, when used in the sleep pods of space travelers in cryosleep, prevented deaths that had been occurring due to lack of vitamin D. But Hafiz made the lamp look like an ancient magic lamp and coming from it was a genie—in cryosleep.

He was just coming to the next plot turn in this tale when Calum Baird called down, "Hafiz, will you cool it with the special effects? You're draining the power of the ship's computer."

"Nonsense, my boy," Hafiz said. "My holograms take up very little power." Normally, he might have taken Baird's warning under advisement but he had yet to perform his best trick.

Finishing the story, he laid out the nutrient bars on an ordinary table, then had dancing girls in tinkling costumes cover the unappetizing fare with roast swan and hummingbird tongues. Discerning from the puzzled silence that met him, even through the holo-disguises he had cast upon the children, he tapped the computer pad and replaced the swans and hummingbird tongues with burgers, fries, onion rings, milkshakes, soft drinks, and ice cream treats.

The children lunged for the table.

The lights went out.

The burgers, fries, rings, and banana splits and sundaes turned back into nutrient bars and the sloe-eyed houris and sly-faced thieves turned into disappointed children suddenly shivering in the dark.

Soon another light appeared on the circular metal stairway no one used because the lift was more convenient. "Come on back upstairs, everybody," Calum said, "while I get the computer back up. Don't worry. Even if it proves to be difficult, the *Haven* will be here soon and we'll have help.

Unfortunately, the *Haven* was not the next ship to reach the stranded *Acadecki*.

"What do you mean, you lost them?" Rafik demanded of an uncharacteristically flushed and flustered Johnny Greene.

"Just what I said," Greene replied. "After we got the all-clear to return to MOO, we agreed to rendezvous at the *Acadecki's* coordinates. But by the time we arrived, there was nothing there but empty space. We hailed them over and over but didn't get a blip. They just disappeared."

Rafik held his breath for a long moment before he replied. "Johnny, you folks turn the *Haven* around and get back to Federation space on the double. We know the Khleevi left the vine world, but we don't know where they went from there."

"You think they got the *Acadecki*?" Johnny asked. "But—we talked to them just a few hours ago."

"I don't know what happened. But one vessel full of kids has disappeared with Calum and my uncle. We can't risk the rest of you. Go back. Get the posse if you can—after all, Hafiz's baksheesh provides a lot of private schools and widow's and orphan's pensions for Federation forces, and even though this isn't their turf, we are under their protection. I hope."

"Gotcha," Johnny said. "But get word to us the minute you know something, okay?"

"We'll try," Rafik said grimly.

"Saltwater?" Acorna asked. "Is that all?"

Miiri nodded. "Simple saline solution. It breaks down the sap enough for it to liquefy but it doesn't seem to harm the sap's ability to alter to its fungoid form and destroy insectoid tissue. We replicated some of the remaining carapace tissue and the liquefied sap was if anything more virulent than in its original form, just as an acid's potency may be increased by mixing it with water."

"That makes sense," Acorna said. "Though it wouldn't be as tenacious as the sap."

"No," Becker said, scratching his mustache, "but you know if we could have had some in aerosol torpedoes to shoot into the orbiting Khleevi ships, we could have taken out more of them."

Miiri shuddered. "How horrible," and looked at her work as if she had given no thought as to how it would be used.

But Aari said gently, "Mother, these are Khleevi

we're talking about, remember. You've seen them. You say you felt what they did to me."

"Your mother knows, Son," his father said. "It's just not the Linyaari way."

"Which is why you need people like Hafiz and Nadhari and *me*," Becker said. "There are still Khleevi out there. I think it's a good idea, in our copious leisure time, to whomp up a batch of sap and sea water. I can scrounge around here and see if I can find the makings of some aerosol torpedoes. You just never know when that kind of thing will come in handy."

Acorna frowned. "Maybe it would also be wise to return to the vine world and collect more sap there. The plants not only buried the Khleevi in their sap, but also submerged themselves. I'd like to make sure the plants are regenerating properly too. If they need any special climactic conditions to help them grow, perhaps Dr. Hoa could be of assistance."

"Good idea, Princess," Becker said. "But you know RK. He wants to spend a little time with Nadhari before we ship out again."

"I see," Acorna said, smiling. "It doesn't have to be done right now."

But at that moment, Nadhari Kando burst into the lab. "Becker!" she said urgently, then nodded slightly to the Linyaari who were also present. "I have to ship out right away. Sorry."

"I'll go with you," Becker said immediately.

"No. You can't. This is my responsibility. Hafiz hired me to protect him and his people and now the *Acadecki* has disappeared."

Acorna grabbed Nadhari's muscular forearm to get

her attention. "What do you mean, disappeared? Calum was on that ship as well as Hafiz—"

"And Maati," Kaarlye, Miiri, and Aari said at once.

"I know, I know. I should have gone with the Harakamians but he wanted me here to protect his investment," Nadhari said. "But time is wasting. I've commandeered the *Ifrit*. It's the fastest ship in Hafiz's security fleet and well-armed."

She took the time to explain about the *Haven*'s transmission.

Becker frowned. "If they're not where they're supposed to be, I'm not sure fast is going to do you any good, Nadhari. I've got those banks of long-range scanners on the *Condor*. And the Khleevi communications device. And Mac."

"It's too slow, Becker. And you already told me, it's not packing firepower." She hesitated and then said, "Although . . ."

"What?"

"You've had good success defeating the Khleevi without weapons and you do have that unconventional navigation style. Your tactics might come in handy. If you still want to join me."

"No ifs ands or buts about it, lady," he said.

"Good," she said and turned on her heel, as if expecting him to follow.

"Captain," Acorna said. "We can follow in the *Condor* and keep the scanners working and Mac monitoring the Khleevi transmissions. That way if we learn anything, we can transmit to Nadhari's vessel and you'll have the advantages of both ships."

Becker leaned back and gave her a kiss on the cheek

before Nadhari snagged his hand and yanked. "Thanks, Princess. But you can do that from here and we can read you. No sense you taking unnecessary chances. Besides, I need you to make sure the sap shells get made and *Condor*, at least, is outfitted with them. Don't want to get caught with nothing but a tractor beam to fight those klackers again." Nadhari released his arm and threw the door open. He followed her calling, "Hey, wait up, Punkin. Just a sec."

"What?" she asked sharply.

"What about the cat, is he going or staying?"

"He is already aboard the *Ifrit* but wouldn't allow the checkout procedure to proceed. I divined his purpose was that you should be told of the mission."

"I should hope so!" Becker huffed into his mustache. "That's the only reason you came for me?"

"Of course not," she said. "But we will discuss that later. Time—"

"Yes, ma'am. I know. It's of the essence," Becker said, and waved to the others as he allowed himself to be hauled away.

Acorna and Aari conferred with Gill and Rafik.

"Do you think you can locate the materials for making the aerosol torpedoes Becker described?" she asked.

"Are you kidding?" Gill asked. "We have the best engineering help available in all areas."

"And Uncle Hafiz has never been one to turn his nose up at the lucrative business of arms manufacturing," Rafik added. "I can think of at least six of our friendly neighborhood merchants who could supply what's needed immediately."

"Good," Acorna said. "Miiri and Kaarlye cannot be a party to turning the sap into weapons, you understand, but since it's a simple matter of mixing sap and saltwater, there should be no problem with others mixing the formula. We need to return to the vine world. We Linyaari must communicate with the vines, heal them if the Khleevi attack truly injured them."

"Good thinking," Gill said. "Some of the non–House Harakamian merchants may resist having their ships fitted with the torpedoes, but I think from what we've seen, as long as they're in this sector it's really the only smart thing to do. Maybe if we show the vids the moon camera took of the sap's effect on the Khleevi, it will be easier to persuade the skeptical owners to accept the modifications."

"I'll talk to any of them who have reservations and make sure they've seen the vids," Acorna said. "After all, having the modifications made would be useful for their own protection from Khleevi attacks." She paused for a moment. "Of course, it would probably help persuade them if House Harakamian offered to pay for the modifications."

Rafik laughed. "You're beginning to think like a merchant, but not one who's the adopted daughter of Hafiz! However, I'll authorize it if only to aggravate the old boy into showing up again just to tell me off. Meanwhile I'll appreciate any help you can give me persuading the merchants to think like a team, at least during crises. I'm doing my best but I haven't Hafiz's gift for imperiousness."

"I'll see what I can do," Acorna promised. "And Aari and I have a somewhat different perspective on pacifism where the Khleevi are concerned. Both of us will be glad to help supervise the preparation—and maybe the deployment—of the torpedoes and the ships to carry them in case they're necessary to rescue the *Acadecki*," she said, and her voice had a catch in it.

"Of course," Gill said reasonably. "We've no evidence yet to suggest that the Khleevi were responsible for the disappearance of Calum and Hafiz and the kids."

"No," Rafik agreed. "But it's a pretty big coincidence that they should disappear so soon after a Khleevi attack. I think that whether we have evidence or not, we have to be prepared for the worst."

"Of course," Acorna said thoughtfully, "The sap isn't the only thing that will kill Khleevi. For the merchants who can't be persuaded to modification, as long as they are otherwise armed, they have some protection."

"Yes," Aari said. "The Khleevi are used to preying upon people like mine and the Niriians, who do not fight back with any sort of weapon."

Gill grinned. "We all saw that they blow up as easy as anybody if somebody lobs some ordnance at them."

Rafik grumbled into the little goatee he was affecting these days, to make himself look more lordly in the performance of his administrative duties as head of House Harakamian. "True, but the sap works better than anything we've seen."

Acorna and Aari rose. Rafik felt a bit sad. Their little girl was all grown up into a beautiful young lady, and from the look of it, had chosen her mate already. He hoped they'd all live and prosper long enough for him and Gill—and Calum and Hafiz—to have Linyaari grandbabies.

Acorna's voice caught, "I hope they're okay. I can't bear to think the Khleevi have them."

The crash of the computers was a temporary matter, of course, and Hafiz was rather put out with Calum for making such an issue of it. The man's panic had spoiled Hafiz's story for the children, who had been blessedly quiet while Hafiz had held the attention of all, which was practically his favorite way to interact with anyone, especially children.

For two such wizards of the keyboard as him and Baird, not to mention a certain amount of help from some of the children, who were quite talented in that area, restoring the ship's computer to operation was scarcely a challenge. Without the additional load of the hologram programs, the power soon returned along with all of the other amenities.

Including the com screen and the telescopic viewport. Hafiz was making final readjustments to certain navigational calculations when Baird tapped him on the shoulder and pointed at the viewport.

"Yes, yes," Hafiz said, glancing up. "It is good that it is operational . . ." and then he stopped and stared, as a sinister-looking vessel began filling the viewport. "Hut-hut, my boy!" Hafiz said. "Get us out of here this instant!"

"I'm way ahead of you," Calum said. "But we're going nowhere. They have us in a tractor beam."

The children were exclaiming, and some crying. The two Linyaari, the girl Maati who was so talented herself with holograms, and the youth Thariinye, crowded close to the console.

Suddenly the com screen lit up and one of the ugly bug faces leered at them, before being replaced by a scene of the Khleevi torturing a Linyaari prisoner.

"Oh, no, you don't. Not again," Maati said.

The driver of the Khleevi ship designated *Fourteen Klacks and Two Klicks* was the first to put his tractor beam on the vessel containing the life forms.

As soon as he had them, he could not resist looking into their vessel to see what his courage and intelligence had netted. He could hardly believe his luck. The ship was filled with humans—most of them immature! How the Young would love that! And even better, there were two tender One-Horns aboard.

With considerable glee, hampered only a little by the arrival of his fellow stragglers, he began running the demonstration of Khleevi diplomatic methods when dealing with aliens. The Niriians had proved so unsatisfactory that the driver decided to give the One-Horns a little preflight fright by showing what had been done to dismantle the body of the last One-Horn captive.

That should tenderize their youthful emotions, get them ready to scream all the way back to the home-world, providing a substantial emotional appetizer before what was left of them could be physically delivered to the Young.

The driver could not resist, before boarding the ship and scooping out the sweet One-Horns and humans from the hull, taking a look to see their fear and horror at the film he had just transmitted. The smaller of the One-Horns stared back at him, baring her teeth. Then she raised a metal canister of some sort, dipped a gloved hand into it, and pulled out a glob of the horrible, carapace-eating sap, which she smeared across the com screen.

Perhaps the Young would rather extract the One-Horns and humans themselves.

The *Acadecki* had simply disappeared.

Nadhari shook her head in disbelief. "How could it have just vanished?"

"There's a lot of space out there," Becker pointed out, sounding a lot more nonchalant than he felt.

"Of course there is," she said, her voice overly sweet, as if talking to someone with a bad case of stupid. "But the *Ifrit* and the other security ships have the ion trail ID for the *Acadecki* and all of the other ships on MOO. And the trail ends here. Poof!"

"I wish I had my maps to check," Becker said. "Maybe they have a Bermuda Triangle in this quadrant."

"A what?"

"Well, long ago back on Mother Earth, there was this area in the ocean where airplanes and ships disappeared without a trace. It was called the Bermuda Triangle and people thought—"

"Yes?"

"That maybe aliens from outer space were responsible." His voice faded off at the end.

"That certainly stands to reason in this case," Nadhari said dryly.

"Can your ion trail ID thing check for other kinds of ion trails—those not left by Hafiz's or his allies' ships?"

"Like Khleevi ships for instance?" she asked. "I don't

know, to tell you the truth. We only had one encounter with the Khleevi in Federation space and that was rather brief. I'll check for any strange trails however."

She worked at the control panel for a bit, the colored lights bouncing off the planes of her face, and then said, "Got it."

"What?"

"There've been a number of other ships here. Similar trails all. I'm reprogramming so we can follow them but the trails are confused."

"Think it's Khleevi?"

"Who else? It's not us, that's for sure."

"Follow that ion," Becker said.

"What?"

"You have just got to watch more of my antique vid collection, honey," he said.

Acorna and Aari had the *Condor* fitted for the sap shells first. They could use their installation as a prototype to show the others. After a few glitches, which the *Condor* accepted with its usual savoir-faire, the modifications were made and the *Condor* was pronounced Khleevi-ready.

The most effective way to persuade all of the other merchants to go along with the plan, Acorna decided, was to have a meeting and show the vids to all of them at the same time.

Once the vids had finished playing, the boardroom was absolutely still as the lights came up.

Then Holland Barber, the lawyer for Cascade shipping company, which had won the bid to transport merchandise to and from MOO, spoke up. "Ms.

Harakamian-Li," the thin-faced blonde in the abbreviated silver synsilk power suit said, "Your allegation that we need to modify our ships in such a drastic way to deal with an alien race that clearly, from your own film, has been almost annihilated by those sticky things, appears to us to be unfounded. You are overreacting to a ridiculous degree. With Mr. Harakamian missing, there is actually no reason even to suppose that MOO will continue to be operational. Why, therefore, should we risk unnecessary modifications to our ships when we could simply claim because of your lack of foresight in providing a satisfactory business climate, we are no longer bound by our contract? We shall simply withdraw and return to Federation space."

"That is certainly your choice, Ms. Barber," Acorna said sweetly. "But I'd like to remind you that the *Acadecki* has disappeared while attempting to do that very thing—return to Federation space, that is."

The bony blonde gave Acorna a supercilious look and said, "That was one small ship, Ms. Harakamian-Li. *We* control a fleet. I hardly think these cockroaches would consider us as easy a target."

"It's entirely up to your client, Ms. Barber," Acorna said.

At that moment Aari and Mac broke into the meeting. "Excuse us, Khornya. But Mac has just intercepted a transmission we thought would have bearing on this meeting."

"Yes?" Holland Barber, who had yet to sit down, acted as if she were in control of the meeting.

Mac earnestly repeated all of the klackings and klickings he had heard and Aari translated.

"The Khleevi are massing an attack on narhii-Vhili-inyar," Aari said.

"And that is?" Holland Barber asked.

"The Linyaari homeworld," Aari said. "*Our* home-world."

"I can't see that your homeworld, however dear it may be to you, has anything to do with my client," the lawyer said.

"It doesn't actually," Acorna said. "Except that narhii-Vhiliinyar was the primary planet Uncle Hafiz hoped to entice as a trading partner when he established MOO."

"In short, Holland," said Michaela Glen of Hudson Interplanetary Realty, Inc. "Customers. If you want to sit around quibbling about a few modifications House Harakamian has agreed to pay for in order to save your client's penurious corporate butt while these cock-roaches eat some of the most potentially profitable trade partners in the history of the Federation, feel free. But Hudson is willing to follow in the footsteps of our glorious voyageur founders and not only modify our ships to fight, but fight to protect our trade."

The rest of the merchants in the room applauded.

Becker and Nadhari were having a difficult time fol-lowing the ion trail when they received a hail and Acorna's face appeared on the screen. "Captain, Mac has picked up a signal from the Khleevi fleet. They've located narhii-Vhiliinyar."

"On our way, Princess," Becker said. "Your uncles getting those sap torpedoes filled?"

"Yes, Captain. All available personnel have been collecting and diluting the sap and Gill says the engineers have made some very business-like torpedoes and are fitting the ships with them now. The *Condor* is ready to go. Have you found any trace of the *Acadecki*?"

Becker looked at Nadhari. He didn't want to break the news to Acorna.

"We haven't found a trail, Acorna," Nadhari said crisply. "But there are other trails that correspond with those of Khleevi ships. We were about to follow, but it seems we now have a good idea where to find the Khleevi."

"Yes," Acorna said. "Though it's odd that you're finding traces there when the coordinates are so far from those of narhii-Vhiliinyar."

"Those bugs get around," Becker said.

Twenty

*T*he spaceport on narhii-Vhiliinyar took the first hit from the Khleevi missile attack. The third wave took out most of the techno-artisan's compound, including the huge evacuation ships the Linyaari had used to escape their former homeworld.

Due to the Linyaari ability to heal infirmities as well as injuries and disease, even the old were not feeble and the staggered lines of refugees heading for the caves in the hills where the Ancestors lived moved along smartly.

The com-shed officer of the day barely escaped with her life and the portable remote link as her duty station exploded behind her.

Trees were few on narhii-Vhiliinyar but the grasses beyond the primary grazing areas were taller than the heads of the people, and provided visual cover. Council members directed people to the proper path and shepherded them through. The attendants of the Ancestors met the refugees at predesignated places to guide them to the caves.

At first, once the cities and chief settlements were behind them, the refugees faced little danger from the bombardment.

They made their way quietly toward the caves. Only the occasional whimpering of a child or the cough of an elder interrupted the muffled pounding of hard feet and the shush of the grasses as bodies wound quickly through them. The thought that guided everyone was, "Calm. Peace. Go swiftly but silently. Help your neighbors if they fall." The voice in which everyone heard these thoughts was that of the one they loved best and trusted most. The best loved and most trusted heard the thought in the voice of Grandam Naadiina.

Then suddenly the bombing fanned out from the city and ignited the tall grasses, where hundreds of people still travelled. People ran, and screamed, and fell, and some were trampled.

Circling the planet, the Khleevi were pleased at last to feel the terror rising in nourishing waves from the surface. The transmission of it would appease the Young for a while longer, until the ships could land and begin loading the prisoners.

The House Harakamian ships rallied under Nadhari's leadership. Most of the security ships needed only to load the torpedoes in their own bomb bays to be ready to fly into battle. Cascade shipping company's lawyer was overruled by her bosses, although one ship was allotted to take her and some of the other less committed executives and employees back to the company's headquarters. What Ms. Barber had failed to realize, Rafik told Acorna, was that her company was actually a subsidiary of one owned by Hafiz's second cousin, whose holdings were dependent on the backing of House Harakamian.

Acorna and the other Linyaari meanwhile spent time with the plants of the vine world. The vines actually seemed to flourish in the sea of sap they had created, growing from it at an amazing rate and sending forth a pleasant floral smell as if the whole planet was merely a large innocuous bouquet. "Apparently the sap that kills the bugs has regenerative properties for the plants," Miiri said.

"Fortunately it doesn't work that way for the Khleevi," Aari said with a small, tight smile.

Some of the less battle-worthy ships brought up the rear of the makeshift fighter squadron. They formed a supply line back to the vine world to reequip ships that, it was optimistically hoped, would expend all of their sap shells destroying Khleevi and their vessels.

Becker meanwhile was giving the skippers and navigators a crash course in gonzo astrophysics.

"If we use the folds in space as cover, we can pop in and out around the bugs and sap them before they have any idea where we come from. But with this many of us, we have to do it in strict rotation or we'll be ramming each other and lose the battle to friendly fire."

Becker was originally going to return to the *Condor*, flying it into battle and leaving Acorna and Aari with the other Linyaari back on the vine world, which was the only place certain to be safe from Khleevi attack.

But the Khleevi massed quickly around narhii-Vhiliinyar and, instead of sending in ground troops and shuttles as they had before, began a massive bombardment of the helpless planet. Becker stayed with Nadhari as she flew reconnaissance, spying out the Khleevi position, which was basically encircling the planet with ships, as it had done with the vine world.

"You're on your own, kids," Becker told Acorna and Aari in his last transmission to the *Condor* before the battle was joined. "I'll miss my old bucket of bolts, but the *Ifrit* is lighter and more maneuverable and Nadhari needs me with her to weave her troops in and out if we're going to have a prayer against the klackers. Aari, make sure Mac reports to you what he's getting from the Khleevi communications and if there's any break. . . ."

"Lately they've been almost impossible to read, Captain," Aari said sadly. "So many are klacking at once that Mac cannot decipher individual messages. And the sound of the missiles is also disrupting our sensors."

"We're going to start making a lot of noise ourselves pretty quick," Becker said. "Be safe, people."

"Be safe, Joh," Aari said, and touched the com screen.

"Be safe, Becker, and keep the others safe as well," Acorna said.

But she felt so powerless. In the other battle, there had been something she could do to help, but this one, well, it almost went without saying that this was a lost cause. The sap was effective against the Khleevi. Perhaps they could be driven off in time to save the Linyaari people, if not narhii-Vhiliinyar, but it was hard to believe the combination of corporate security and civilian ships stood a chance against the Khleevi hordes.

More immediately saddening was that in the course of their reconnaissance, Becker and Nadhari had seen no sign of the *Acadecki*, and Mac could discern no mention of them from the Khleevi transmissions filling the *Condor* with their staccato.

The driver of the Khleevi ship designated *Fourteen Klacks and Two Klicks* was not, as his non-Khleevi enemies sometimes presumed, incapable of independent thought and action. Quite the contrary. The driver, now trying to control the ship with only five feet, having sacrificed his sixth, knew that once he rejoined the other Khleevi, he would not last long.

When the main swarm discovered the true home of the One-Horns and began bombarding it, the driver was so dismayed he sent an extra jolt of energy to the Young. His wonderful capture, so fortunately come by and so willingly carried to the Young, was about to be rendered insignificant by the might of the swarm. Unless, of course, he and his fellow stragglers delivered their contribution to the diet of the Young before the swarm was able to return with captives.

Some of the other stragglers were little more than dead weight. There had been six of them in his limb originally and he knew for certain that three of the ships no longer contained living personnel. No one was at the com units, and the ships were guided only by the tractor beams attached to the captive vessel from *Fourteen Klacks and Two Klicks* and the other two vessels whose crews still contained some living members.

The only comfort that the driver had was that he knew many of the ships in the swarm were as badly off as his own—as the others of his limb. The communications he received, and ignored, were quite often disordered and nonsensical and he suspected that only the structure of the swarm kept many of the ships in place.

Fourteen Klacks and Two Klicks would not remain in place. It sped, with as much momentum as possible pulling one alien and three Khleevi vessels plus two others whose drivers, he suspected, were suffering more of the effects of contaminated shuttle soldiers than him, toward the homeworld and the Young.

As the bombardment of narhii-Vhiliinyar continued, so did Acorna's healing duties.

The first to show the long-range effects of the damage done to the Linyaari was Aari's mother. Miiri, gathering sap on the vine world, grew more and more distracted and incoherent. Kaarlye said she was receiving telepathic signals from the homeworld, reading the suffering of her people. The time came when she cried out and fainted, falling face forward into a lake of sap. By the time they pulled her out, she had nearly suffocated.

Acorna, Neeva, Melireenya, and Khaari, as well as Kaarlye, all laid horns on Miiri to revive her. But the physical effect of her fall was not what caused her to thrash and cry out in her unconsciousness.

"This is how she was while Aari was a prisoner," Kaarlye said.

"I don't see why," Liriili said. "She's no good to anyone that way."

But as time wore on, and reports were relayed back along the supply channels of the fires in the fields, the decimation of the cities, the saturation bombing of the planet's surface, the bad news took its toll. First Melireenya, then Khaari, then Neeva and finally Kaarlye himself began to succumb to the disorientation and panic that had marked Miiri's decline in health.

Even Aari attempted to use his newly grown horn to soothe his parents and the *Balaküre* crew. He had no more luck than the others.

Acorna had not lived on narhii-Vhiliinyar long enough to develop a bond strong enough to affect her the way it did the others, but she missed Calum, and Maati, Grandam, Hafiz, and even Karina. Not to mention all of the children she had helped to rise from slavery only for them to fall victim to a more deadly peril. Jana would be taking care of the others now, she knew, and Maati would help. So would Thariinye, who was not a bad sort, just a bit callow sometimes.

Calum had helped raise her and at times had been her closest friend. If she were to bond with anyone out there, she thought, it would be with him. But she felt nothing from him. Nothing. Unfortunately, the hard-headed Caledonian, while as pragmatic and ingenious as the best of his race, had not fallen heir to their more magical qualities.

Grandam had lived through much in her long life, but even the Khleevi attack on Vhiliinyar had not been this horrible. The people had escaped then. Now they were ambushed on their own world, their escape routes cut off, the ground quickly being bombed from beneath their feet.

The noise outside her head was no worse than the

clamor inside. Her people were dying. *Dying.* Dead already, many in the tall grasses, and she could do nothing. The keening of death songs in the caves was as loud in its way as the bombing.

Not just bombing either, but ships falling from the sky, huge chunks of them plummeting everywhere, blazing comets of death.

She healed burns and fractures, crushing injuries and shock, all the time trying to exude calm and control, as all the other elders were also doing. But never had she felt so keenly every year of her age. The Ancestors attempted to help, but their energy was older than her own and they were not immune to the chaos and tragedy thundering down upon them.

She felt a sudden jolt of alarm and looked up from the badly burned body of young Hiiri, who had been caught in the first grass fire. One of the Ancestors bolted from an adjoining cave and galloped across the charred stubble that remained of the tall grasses, easily, gracefully leaped the small river fed by an underground spring in the hills, and charged into a remaining stand of tall grasses on the other side. Grandam watched as the grasses parted, and a line of figures, much burdened with cases and cages, bumbled through the grass to meet the Ancestor. (*Aagroni Iirtye!*) Grandam called in thought-speak. (Your laboratory should have been among the first to be evacuated!)

(We could hardly leave all of the new younglings we've been growing from the remains of the animals from Vhiliinyar, could we?) the *aagroni* demanded indignantly. (It took a little time to pack them out but everything has gone very well indeed.)

The Ancestor had gone to offer her services as a pack animal. (Of course, you couldn't,) Grandam replied. (I commend your dedication to your charges.) She turned back to the smoky den behind her to recruit some of the able bodied to assist with the bundles.

The ball of flame flashed across her eyes as she turned and when she whirled back to look, it had landed in the tall grass. She could no longer see the Ancestor or the *aagroni* but she heard the screams and the frantic whinnying of the Ancestor. An attendant ran from one of the caves but he had Grandam's heels before him.

She tried to outrun the flame, circling around it to reach some of the scientists behind it, or the Ancestor. All of these precious beings must not die. So much had been lost in such a short time. This must not go too.

But she could see nothing but fire. She heard the roar of the flames and the screams and she saw the Ancestor leap from the fire with specimens upon her back, her mane and tail on fire before she leaped into the river. Grandam leaped into the river herself and soaked herself thoroughly and then gave a great leap of body and mind and plunged into the flames.

After countless hours of healing work, trying to soothe and sedate Neeva, Khaari, Melireenya, Miiri, and Kaarlye, Acorna was resting. Aari helped by holding the hands of his parents, speaking in a low voice to them of his boyhood, and also remembering some bits of Linyaari spiritual teachings, of how beloved souls returned with the new spirits of the young.

She had finally fallen asleep listening to him herself.

His horn was not mature enough to use for healing, but what he was doing truly helped. More than Liriili, who wrung her hands and demanded that somebody *do* something. She seemed most distressed that all of these outsiders now knew the location of narhii-Vhiliinyar. Irrationally, she was somehow not understanding that the Khleevi had already found the planet. And something *was* being done. The Khleevi bombardment of the Linyaari world was now meeting with resistance from the outside, from the darting mosquito-like attacks of MOO's combined forces. Reports traveled back down the supply channels that the attacks were effective. Once a Khleevi vessel was sapped, it did not remain aloft for long.

On the other hand, another odd rumor was reaching the vine world. Many of the Khleevi ships that had *not* been hit, in fact, even before the MOO ships began their attack, were falling out of orbit and crashing onto the surface of narhii-Vhiliinyar. Direct communication with the front wings was infrequent and terse, so Acorna had not been able to speak to any of the actual combatants about this, but she suspected that some of the Khleevi swarm had been infected with the sap from the swarm's previous attack on the vine world.

The MOO forces had actually been firing a relatively short time—less than forty-eight hours—but the psychic damage from the telepathic bonds between the Linyaari on narhii-Vhiliinyar and Aari's parents and the *Balaküre*'s crew had been occurring since the first Khleevi bomb struck the planet's surface.

Acorna's dreams were fitful and troubled, she was running, hiding, ducking, while the world fell apart all around her. Some part of her mind knew that this was not only a dream. Nevertheless, the bonds of empathy that tied her to her own friends and kin were beginning to drag her into the morass of emotion experienced by the Linyaari under attack.

Suddenly, screams shattered her fragile rest and her eyes flew open. All of the Linyaari, including Liriili and Aari, cried out.

"What is it?" she asked, struggling to her feet.

"Grandam," Neeva cried.

"Grandam," Kaarlye and Miiri echoed.

Aari added, with wonder in his voice. "And Maati."

At the moment Grandam leaped into the flames, Maati was also sleeping. She and Thariinye had their hands full calming children, trying to heal them of fears they shared. It didn't help that Hafiz and Karina were so obviously frightened.

"Look," Maati had told the others. "I think the Khleevi really like it when they scare us. They get some sort of special kick out of it. So the scareder we are, the more they like it. Can we try not to give them the satisfaction?"

Jana nodded her understanding, "Some of the overseers at the mines were like that. And—Kheti said that some of the clients in the pleasure houses were like that, too. They enjoyed scaring and hurting the girls because that was what they wanted really, not the sex."

"I can't help it," Chiura said, cuddling close to Jana. "I'm scared."

Karina Harakamian stopped trembling and tried to rally them. "I know what. We could group sing. Does anyone know the song 'Kum-bye-ya?' It's from an ancient Earth culture and very hypnotic."

Nobody did. Karina sang it with them. It was slow and everybody swayed to it like she showed them to, but it was repetitious. It didn't change their mood or lighten their fears.

Calum Baird, who now had nothing to do, finally said, "That's a nice wee song, Karina, but we've sung it twenty times. Shall we try something else? I know a few. I learned this one from Giloglie one time when we were drunk as skunks. His people were great ones for songs. We used to sing this one and some of the others to Acorna when she was little."

While he taught them, "The Rocky Road to Dublin" and they were all shouting, "One, two, three, four, five! Hunt the hare and turn her on the rocky road all the way to Dub-uh-lin one, two, three, four, five!" Maati and Thariinye were finally able to fall into an exhausted sleep.

And then she felt the flames and heard, for the first time ever, Grandam shriek, and she woke up shrieking too. Thariinye was screeching right back at her. Then Grandam was gone, somehow, but someone else was there, in her mind with her.

"Maati? Maati, where are you? It's Aari. Keep sending. I'm coming to get you."

Twenty-one

(N o!) Maati's thought was loud and clear and Aari and Acorna both heard it, though Miiri and Kaarlye almost immediately lapsed back into their telepathic nightmares. (There's Khleevi ships all around us. They're taking us somewhere.)

(Can you read them, Maati?) Aari asked her.

(A—a little. I know they want to hurt us, but I scared one of them by rubbing sap on the screen.)

(That's good,) Aari told her. (You kept them from taking you off the ship.)

(Maati, ask Calum what your coordinates are,) Acorna said.

(Can't,) Maati replied.

(Is he hurt?) Acorna asked anxiously.

(No, nothing like that. He's doing a lot of clapping his hands and stomping his feet and bellowing. Everybody else is doing it too so I wouldn't be able to make him hear me. But I can read them.) She was silent for a moment, then recited the coordinates.

(Keep sending,) Aari told her. (We're on our way.)

The coordinates were nowhere near those of narhii-Vhiliinyar.

The Khleevi swarm spiraled in rings twenty deep around narhii-Vhiliinyar. Blossoms of red fire bloomed from the inner-most ships as missiles silently connected with the surface of the planet. Then the ships that had fired spiraled back out to the outermost layer to be replaced by fresh ships.

Up until recently, no one who had witnessed this battle formation had lived to tell about it. One hundred percent saturation, domination, and decimation were guaranteed. Usually the innermost ships dispatched shuttles with ground troops instead of bombs, but sometimes the bombs came first, to soften up the enemy before the troops landed. This time the ships themselves intended to land and gather up the prisoners.

The strategy was time tested and utterly perfect against planets without missiles or other defenses of their own. Planets such as narhii-Vhiliinyar.

The attention of every ship was focused inwardly, on the target, though in many cases in this particular formation, individual ships were distracted by a substance brought onboard by disabled shuttles and wounded crew from the battle with the vine world. The substance was as intractable as the Khleevi themselves, creeping, infiltrating, oozing over any and all surfaces, and where it met with susceptible carapace or Khleevi exoskeleton, burning and eating all that it touched, growing ever more rapidly as it fed. Much like the Khleevi. *Very* much like the Khleevi.

The ships that had been infected and remained within the swarm did not request assistance from the other ships. They did not know exactly what was weakening them and causing them to suffer, but they knew that weakness would be met with elimination, so they gave their suffering to the Young and carried on as usual.

Nine Klacks and Seventy-two Klicks had just returned to the outermost spiral ring when its hull imploded and the bridge was filled with burning, clinging yellow sap and the high pitched *eeee*'s of the crew.

Nine Klacks and Seventy-two Klicks was not one of the ships that had been infected on the vine world. But it had seen that many other ships *had* taken back shuttles and crewmembers damaged in that battle. No doubt one of them had become defective. The driver of *Nine Klacks and Seventy-two Klicks* thought in the split second before the liquid sap covered him that this was just the sort of thing that made it necessary to strictly enforce the policy of eliminating the weak.

Seventy-two Klacks and Nine Klicks, on the other hand, had six crewmembers in various stages of being devoured by sap. When *its* hull imploded with ordinary explosive missile material, the driver thought to wonder, just before *he* crashed his ship into sixteen other vessels, which crashed their ships into a like number on the way to the target's surface, how the swarm had known his ship was infected. And why they had not waited to eliminate him until after the battle. But, of course, by then the question was strictly rhetorical.

      ❖   ❖   ❖

"This is like shooting ducks in a barrel," Nadhari complained, but not unhappily.

"More like shooting pool," Becker said. "Lookit that ricochet!"

"Somebody call for Ryk O'Shay?" the com unit asked. "I'm right here with Cap'n Glen in the Hudson IT sapship *Bananas*. And we read you, wing command! One of the bugs just slipped on one of *our* peels and crashed through the Khleevi inner formation taking out, oh, maybe ten or twelve of its little bug buddies, and each of them bumped off at least ten more apiece."

"It hardly seems sporting," Captain Glen opined. "And I wonder if we aren't wasting the sap. Whatever they're hit with, it looks to me as if it's their own tactics that are defeating them. They seem to be totally unprepared for an attack from outside their formation."

"That's a roger, Cap'n Glen," Becker said. The scan scope on the *Ifrit* showed a long view of the Khleevi formation.

"Au contraire, ma capitaine," broke in Andina Dimitri of Domestic Goddess Intergalactic Cleansing Corporation, manufacturers of a multitude of cleaning products and providers of the most comprehensive housekeeping and interior design services in the Federation. "We've been compiling statistics here and according to our figures, the ships hit with sap shells hit three times as many of their companion vessels as the ships hit with conventional ammo. The sap shells are demonstrably superior."

"This is the *Condor* calling the *Ifrit*. Come in, *Ifrit*," the remote link crackled.

"Aari! Acorna, we're kicking butt here. Wish you were here."

"Joh," Aari's face on the com screen was both serious and hopeful. "Khornya and I are taking the *Condor* to find the *Acadecki*. My sister just sent us the coordinates."

"Oh, good, I'm glad they're okay," Becker said.

"They're not okay, Captain," Acorna said. "They're held in a Khleevi tractor beam. Maati is afraid they're being taken to the Khleevi homeworld. But the Khleevi haven't touched them yet."

"Mr. and Mrs. Harakamian?" Nadhari asked. "How are they?"

"Fine, except Maati says Karina has a lousy singing voice. Calum was teaching the kids Gill's drinking songs, Maati said."

"I'll pass it on," Nadhari said. "Keep us posted on the coordinates of the Khleevi vessels."

Acorna's voice was unsteady when she asked, "Do we—know how the people on the surface are doing? Any idea what happened to Grandam?"

"Something happened to Grandam?" Becker asked.

"I forgot you wouldn't know," Acorna said. "All of us felt it. I think maybe she—she's gone."

"We'll check it out as soon as possible, honey," Becker said. "Nadhari wants to shoot something so we gotta go now. Give me those coordinates again," he said. She did and they signed off just in time to hear a very staticky call from Hudson IT *Bananas*.

"What the devil!" Captain Glen called. "Wing command, we've been hit!"

"Fall back!" Nadhari cried, as a missile exploded to the port bow of the *Ifrit*.

"They finally shooting at us instead of the Linyaari?" Gill asked.

"Cloak and shield, people," Becker said. "Do it now."

The mosquito fleet obeyed the command, leaving the space surrounding narhii-Vhiliinyar to the Khleevi, but still the firing continued. The spiral of ships, formerly as tidy and symmetrical as a water ballet, already had gaping holes torn in its pristine formation from the crashes. All pretense of order vanished as the ships on the lower layer fired upward, the ships on the upper layer fired downward, and both hit the ships in the intermediate layers, which crashed. Fire blossomed and ships disintegrated into thousands of pieces, buffeting the shielded ships of the makeshift MOO fleet like a meteor shower.

"Holy smokes," Ryk O'Shay said. "Would you lookit the fireworks."

"Fireworks hell," Becker said, his voice thick with longing. "RK, wouldja look at that *salvage*, and us without the *Condor*!"

Nadhari snorted, "The Khleevi apparently decided what we threw at them was friendly fire—no longer so friendly. I don't know how they could have figured the crashes were deliberate as well but it looks as if they did, and good riddance. They're saving us the trouble of killing them by turning on themselves."

"I like that," Adina said. "It's economical."

"*Bananas*, how bad are you hit?"

"I think we've contained it for now, *Ifrit*, but we'll need a tow back to base."

"Hang on. This will be over soon from the look of it."

It was. In a matter of less than an hour, hundreds of

Khleevi ships destroyed each other. A few managed to flee the scene.

With the ships gone, however, Becker could see what was left of narhii-Vhiliinyar. The planet's surface, once a study in blue-green landscape and charmingly colored cities, was now a smoking black, cratered wasteland.

Twenty-two

The *Condor*'s computers found every shortcut between itself and the *Acadecki*.

Mac, no longer troubled by the cacophony from the fleet, easily picked up the signals from *Fourteen Klacks and Two Klicks* and its cohorts.

"They have injured aboard, Acorna," Mac said. "And they are returning to the homeworld—the captain of the limb, as the six ships are referred to, is attempting to precede the remainder of the fleet to the homeworld to appease those he calls 'the Young' with the sacrifice of the *Acadecki*'s personnel."

The long-range scanners had enabled the *Condor* to stay a safe distance from the limb of Khleevi ships without detection, and now Aari asked, "Shall we close on them, Khornya?"

"Hmm, not yet, I think," she said. "Mac, let us know if you can get the coordinates of the homeworld from the Khleevi vessel—or at least some idea when we're close enough that we have an idea where to locate their homeworld before we free the *Acadecki*."

"Yes, Acorna." Mac said, and returned to his post at the Khleevi shuttle's com unit.

Maati continued to send the coordinates every hour.

(Lots of the kids are sleeping now,) she said. (I told Calum and Hafiz that you were behind us and Calum says please don't get caught. I told him you had sap shells and he's worried you won't use them because of us Linyaari being pacifist and all.)

(A minor technicality in this case,) Acorna said as cheerfully as possible. (Mac can use the launch controls and *he* is no pacifist. But I suppose this is one case where even Liriili might be glad Aari and I are somewhat alienated from mainstream Linyaari culture.)

(Hmph!) Maati sent a picture of herself snorting and giggling. (Are you kidding? If Liriili thought it would save her, *she* would pull the toggle herself.)

(I think you're right about that.)

(Khornya? Do you know any more about Grandam yet? I didn't even say goodbye. Do you think she might think I ran away from *her*? I'm glad I found my—Aari's and my—folks, but Grandam is—Grandam was my real family, you know?)

(I felt what you felt too Maati but I don't know any more about it. We'll just have to go to narhii-Vhiliin-yar when you're free and find out. Captain Becker says the Khleevi mistook MOO's attacks for some kind of internal warfare and turned on each other and blew each other all across the quadrant. I could tell Captain Becker was slavering over all that salvage.)

(*He is coming now, Maati. Riid-Kiiyi is coming, too,*) Aari said.

(*You thought-talk to RK?*) Maati asked.

(*Yes, but you know him. He doesn't listen to me or anyone else. But we have had a special relationship since I helped heal him on Vhiliinyar. Don't tell Joh. He gets jealous. But Riid-Kiiyi just scratched at the door of my mind. He wants you to know he is coming and he will claw the eyes out of the Khleevi and spray their sockets.*)

Maati giggled.

And after a while she said, (I think we're getting nearer. The Khleevi just came back on the com screen even though I scared him off once with the sap. He's showing that—you know, Aari, that vid of you from the *piiyi*, to frighten us again. But we turned the sound off. Nobody speaks Khleevi anyway and many are sleeping now. Calum's songs are very energetic and involve much stomping, clapping, and hollering. He wore himself and everyone else out.)

(I missed those versions,) Acorna said. (Or at least the stomping and hollering arrangements. Gill did sing me an Irish lullaby or two.)

As they spoke, they narrowed the gap between themselves and the Khleevi limb until they were within firing distance.

(Calum says you should know that he thinks each of the ships have a tractor beam on us. But I think at least three of the ships are dead already.)

(That's what I call good news and bad news!) Acorna said. (But I have an idea. Tell Calum to be ready to accelerate and fire upon the Khleevi as soon as the connections are broken. Then to put up the shields and cloak and take you all away as fast as possible.)

(I don't think he will leave you.)

(He must to save the children.)

(They will all feel safer with you, Khornya.)

(That's touching but not helpful. Just tell him, Maati, and wish us all luck.)

She went to Mac's station and asked him, "Can you use the Khleevi shuttle's controls to remotely operate controls on their ships?"

Mac examined the controls and said, "No, Acorna. I cannot find such a mechanism on the shuttle."

"Oh," she said. "Hmm. There are six ships with tractor beams locked onto the *Acadecki*."

"I could try to send them a command to release the ship," he said.

"Three of the ships are dead," she told him. "But if we fire on them to break the beam, I'm afraid we might damage the *Acadecki*."

"Perhaps the other Khleevi ships in the limb will have a remote mechanism to control the tractor beams of the dead ships," he said.

"I suppose there's no harm in trying."

He transmitted command-style klacking and klicking using the identification code from the mother ship of the shuttle.

Four ships fell away from the *Acadecki* at once and when he repeated the command, so did the fifth.

But the sixth ship sent back a message saying, "This is the driver of the ship designated *Fourteen Klacks and Two Klicks*. How is it that you escaped the Planet of Doom, *Fifty-three Klacks and Seven Klicks*, when most of our shuttles were lost?"

Mac shrugged. "What do I say?" he whispered.

Aari had joined them and suggested, "Respond with this message," and he gave Mac a series of klacks and klicks to transmit.

The last ship immediately released the *Acadecki*, which shot away from it and fired a round at each of its captors. Three of the ships were hit at once and flew to bits but the other three maneuvered out of range and returned fire. By then, however, the *Acadecki* had cloaked and shielded, as ordered.

"That worked," Acorna said. "What does it mean?"

"I have no idea," Aari said. "Except that it is not very polite and those in charge seemed to say it when they were particularly annoyed—although with a Khleevi it was difficult to tell, of course."

The other three ships accelerated away from both the *Acadecki* and the *Condor* along the same route they had been following, and were out of range before Aari and Acorna could return to the bridge.

"I am picking up strange signals, Aari," Mac said. "They do not sound like any of the Khleevi transmissions I have heard before."

Acorna and Mac heard a higher pitched sound, containing klicking but also something that sounded more like "snip snip" than a klack.

"However," Mac said, as klick-klacks began transmitting and new blips appeared on the scanner, "*Those* do. *And* they are homing in on us. *Fourteen Klacks and Two Klicks* is transmitting data regarding our position."

"I think it's time to sap *Fourteen Klacks and Two Klicks*," Acorna said firmly. "They have caused enough trouble for one journey."

* * *

The driver of *Fourteen Klacks and Two Klicks* was in agony once more. Behind him the debris of four ships of his limb blew apart. He alone had realized that *Fifty-three Klacks and Seven Klicks* was behaving in an irregular manner. But when the driver called him an eater of his own eggs, he thought the driver must be of very high rank, as such an insult to any but the lowliest inferior was an invitation to be devoured. Thus had he been tricked into releasing his prey. His only hope now was that he would leave the nestworld alive once more.

And then that last vain hope also was eaten.

Another of his crewmembers had become infected while tearing off the legs of one of the previously infected members. Now this crewman crawled up to the driver while the driver was arguing with the false driver of the shuttle from *Fifty-three Klacks and Seven Klicks*. Laying half-eaten pincers upon the driver's carapace, the crewman begged to be slain. The driver obliged at once, but not before the sap began eating through to his internal organs.

Meanwhile, signals arrived from several returning members of the swarm. "Deserter!" their klicks and klacks said, more or less. "The swarm has perished and now you will perish as well." That was the message from behind him.

And just ahead, on the nestworld, the Young were clamoring for their prey, demanding it be brought to them.

On the whole, it seemed easier to oblige them after all. The driver of *Fourteen Klacks and Two Klicks* raised his acceleration and shot for the surface of the nestworld without bothering to initiate a landing procedure.

❋   ❋   ❋

"He crashed it!" Mac said. "*Fourteen Klacks and Two Klicks* crashed his vessel onto the surface of the nest-world. He killed some of the Young. The others seem to be—from what I can tell, swarming over the dead to feast upon them."

"At least it seems we won't have to worry about destroying innocent children when we sap the nest," Acorna said.

"No," Mac said. "But you had better sap them fast and leave. The Khleevi ships behind are gaining on us."

"Khleevi ships to your starboard stern," Calum said. "We'll cover you, *Condor*."

"No!" Acorna said. "Take the children out of here, Calum. Now. You can't risk them."

"This is Wing Command *Ifrit*," Nadhari's crisp and authoritative voice came through. "You heard the lady, *Acadecki*. Move smartly from the field at once."

"Do it," Becker's voice seconded the motion. "We got 'em in our crosshairs, Calum. Vamoose and don't let any salvage hit you in the stern on your way out."

The rest was a bit anticlimactic for Acorna and Aari. The squad from the MOO fleet closed rapidly on the few survivors from the horde's self-destruction and demolished them with a combination of conventional fire and sap shells.

The majority of the sap shells were saved for the nestworld, where the Young had already begun to die from the sap oozing out of *Fourteen Klacks and Two Klicks*.

"Dimitri, Glen, and Giloglie each keep your wing here until you're sure it's over," Nadhari commanded.

"Don't worry, Nadhari," Andina Dimitri said, "I've just the cleanser to take care of this mess."

"Acorna? Aari?" Becker asked plaintively. "I don't suppose you could pick up any of this salvage on your way back to MOO, could you?"

Twenty-three

For the first time since the Linyaari inhabited narhii-Vhiliinyar, hordes of people of other species joined with the Linyaari and the Ancestors.

It had taken much imagination and very precise navigational memory to find the site of Grandfather Niicari's grave. It had once been marked by being located a few steps from the back flap of Grandam Naadiina's pavilion but now all pavilions were little more than pools of molten ash in the lake of such ash that had once been Kubiilikhan.

Neeva swallowed hard and spoke, "Friends and clankin, we are gathered to lay our beloved Grandam, mother, protectress, and wise counselor to our many generations of Linyaari, friend to the outsiders, to rest beside her lifemate, our Grandfather."

Maati was weeping quietly, supported on one side by Aari and Acorna and on the other by a dry-eyed but solemn-faced Thariinye. Miiri and Kaarlye stood behind their youngest, Miiri's hands resting lightly on her shoulders.

Grandam looked so beautiful lying there. The char had been cleaned from her silvery mane, the lines were smoothed on her face, her hands resting peacefully, naturally at her waist. And her mouth was curved in a firm and exultant smile. She had not died in the fire, as it seemed when Maati and the other Linyaari felt first the fire and then the extinguishment of Grandam's life force.

Grandam's leap at the fire had been a complete act involving not only her body, but also her extraordinary strength of heart, mind, and will, as she dragged the river waters from their bed to flood the fires threatening the scientists and the precious new species they had risked their own lives to save.

Never had anyone done such a thing in Linyaari history or fable, as long as any of them could remember. But Grandam Naadiina had lived longer than any two-footed Linyaari and had grown in wisdom and skill with every *ghaanyi* of her life. Unfortunately, her heart, which had grown in the strength of its love and kindness, had not improved structurally, and the strain of her final telepathic struggle to save others had been too much for it.

"Those who were with Grandam at the end said she wore the same smile you see here. *Aagroni* Iirtye, do you wish to add something?"

"I do," he said. His mane was very short and irregular where the char had been chopped off, and he had no brows or lashes. His skin was reddened and peeling, as was that of several people around him. "Grandam died as you were just told, saving me, my staff, and most important, the young we have been growing from cells of species lost with our own beloved Vhiliinyar. I understand that her passing was felt by her foster daughter Maati and Spacefarer Thariinye across several galaxies. I was privileged to be nearest to her at her death and received her last thoughts. They were of you, Maati, full of pride for your bravery in risking your life to save your family and friends, and for all of us, her other children, and most of all, for Vhiliinyar. Just as Grandam knew, somehow, that we would be saved, she also knew that the destruction of narhii-Vhiliinyar was not the end of a Linyaari homeworld. *Visedhaanye-feriili* Neeva?"

"I think Grandam would be pleased and proud now to hear the message brought by my sister-daughter, *Visedhaanye* Khornya, called Ah-khorn-ah by those humans who saved her as an infant, and saved us from the Khleevi. Khornya?"

Acorna gracefully extracted herself from Aari, with a last caress to his fingers and a lingering touch on Maati's shoulder, and knelt beside Grandam to kiss her forehead before standing, quite close to Grandam, and saying, "As some of you know, the Khleevi were defeated by people my Uncle Hafiz brought into this quadrant in hopes that you would trade with them. I want you to know that when these people, merchants, tradespeople, learned that you were in danger, they hastened to help you however they could. Not all could destroy Khleevi. Like the Linyaari, many are good only at building, not at destroying. Dr. Ngaen Xong Hoa, in particular, has long sought to escape from those who would use the weather-control science he developed for martial purposes. He feels a great kinship with the Linyaari.

"He, along with the most expert terraforming specialists available in the Federation, have been brought to House Harakamian's Moon of Opportunity by Hafiz and Rafik Harakamian for the express purpose of helping us restore Vhiliinyar to its former life and beauty.

Her voice lowered for a moment and her silver eyes were covered by their long pewter lashes before she resumed, "I do not recall having seen Vhiliinyar with my own eyes. But in my dreams, since I was a baby, I have seen a beautiful world of rolling hills, snow-capped mountains, tumbling waterfalls and forests, and great tracts of delicious grasses. I am told that is what Vhiliinyar was like.

"Grandam's final sacrifice, which kept *Aagroni* Iirtye and his staff's heroic efforts to preserve native species that would have otherwise been extinguished, was her last contribution to the restoration of this home I have never known, but many of you remember. Her first contribution, of course," and she smiled impishly, "was to have her many children and grandchildren, all of us.

"My adoptive fathers have requested me to ask you if the Linyaari would please direct Dr. Hoa and the other specialists in a joint effort to restore our ancestral home to us. For those of us who require the solitude and seclusion of a peaceful world, Vhiliinyar's location will remain a highly classified secret. My uncles further propose that narhii-Vhiliinyar and Kubiilikhan also be restored as a trade base for Linyaari skills and goods, where our people may interact freely with people of all planets and species so that we may each learn the good the other has to offer."

She knelt once more beside Grandam and, laying her hand upon Grandam's folded hands, said, "Grandam, when the restoration is complete, you and Grandfather will be brought home to join your children on your world."

It was perhaps the first funeral in the history of the Linyaari in which the beloved deceased was interred to sobs of rejoicing and cries of hope for a better world to come.

Glossary of Terms and Proper Names Used in the Acorna Universe

Aagroni— Linyaari name for a vocation that is a combination of ecologist, agriculturalist, botanist, and biologist. *Aagroni* are responsible for terraforming new planets for settlement as well as maintaining the well-being of populated planets.

Aari—A Linyaari of the Nyaarya clan, captured by the Khleevi during the invasion of Vhiliinyar, tortured, and left for dead on the abandoned planet. He's Maati's brother. Aari survived and was rescued and restored to his people by Jonas Becker and Roadkill. But Aari's differences, the physical and psychological scars left behind by his adventures, make it difficult for him to fit in among the Linyaari.

Aarliiyana—A techno-artisan who works on Linyaari spacecraft.

Acadecki—The ship Calum and Acorna journey in to find Acorna's people.

Acorna—A unicorn-like humanoid alien discovered as an infant by three miners—Calum, Gill, and Rafik. She has the power to heal and purify with her horn. Her uniqueness has already shaken up the galaxy, especially the planet Kezdet. She's now fully grown and searching for her people.

Aiora—Markel's mother, now dead.

Almah—Rocky Reamer's wife, now deceased.

Amalgamated Mining—A vicious intergalactic mining corporation, famous for bad business dealings and for using bribes, extortion, and muscle to accomplish their corporate goals or cut their costs.

Ancestors—Unicorn-like sentient species, precursor race to the Linyaari. Also known as *ki-lin*.

Ancestral Hosts—Ancient spacefaring race that rescued the Ancestors, located them on the Linyaari home planet, and created the Linyaari race from the Ancestors and their own populations through selective breeding and gene splicing.

Andrezhuria—First-generation Starfarer, and Third Speaker to the Council.

Andreziana—Second-generation Starfarer, daughter of Andrezhuria and Ezkerra.

Balaave—Linyaari clan name.

Balaküre—The Linyaari ship commanded by Acorna's aunt Neeva in which the envoys from Acorna's people reached human-populated space.

Barsipan—Jellyfish-like animal on Linyaari home planet.

Becker—*See* Jonas Becker

Blidkoff—Second Undersecretary of RUI Affairs, Shenjemi Federation.

Brazie—Second-generation Starfarer.

Caabye—Planet in the original Linyaari homeworld system, third from the sun.

Calum Baird—One of three miners who discovered Acorna and raised her.

Ce'skwa—A captain and unit leader in the Red Bracelets.

Child Liberation League—An organization dedicated to ending child exploitation on Kezdet.

Clackamass 2—An abandoned planet near the Kezdet system, used as a landfill site.

Coma Berenices—The quadrant of space most likely to hold Acorna's ancestors.

Condor—Jonas Becker's salvage ship, heavily modified to incorporate various "found" items Becker has come across in his space voyages.

Dajar—Second-generation Starfarer.

Declan "Gill" Giloglie—One of three miners who discovered Acorna and raised her.

Deeter Reamer—Five-year-old son of Rocky Reamer.

Delszaki Li—Once the richest man on Kezdet, opposed to child exploitation, made many political enemies. He lived his life paralyzed, floating in an antigravity chair. Clever and devious, he both hijacked and rescued Acorna and gave her a cause—saving the children of Kezdet. His recent death was a source of tremendous sadness to all but his enemies.

Des Smirnoff—An unsavory sort, a former Kezdet Guardian kicked out for failure to share the proceeds of his embezzlement with appropriate superiors, now an officer with the Kilumbembese Red Bracelets.

dharmakoi—Small burrowing sapient marsupials known to the Linyaari, now extinct as a result of Khleevi war.

didi—Kezdet slang for the madam of a brothel, or for one who procures children for such a madam.

Didi Badini—A madam on Kezdet who tried to kill Acorna.

Dom—A Palomellese criminal posing as a refugee aboard the *Haven*; a key member of Nueva Fallona's gang.

Edacki Ganoosh—Corrupt Kezdet count, uncle of Kisla Manjari.

Ed Minkus—A companion of Des Smirnoff's who has followed him from the Kezdet Guardians of the Peace to their present employment with the Red Bracelets.

E'kosi Tahka'yaw—Former ally of General Ikwaskwan's, betrayed by him in some manner which he would prefer not to discuss.

enye-ghanyii—Linyaari time unit, small portion of *ghaanye*.

Epona—A protective goddess identified with horses, and by some children of Kezdet, with Acorna.

Esperantza—A planet taken away from the colonists by quasi-legal manipulations on the part of Amalgamated Mining.

Esposito—A Palomellese criminal posing as a refugee aboard the *Haven*; a key member of Nueva Fallona's gang.

Eva—Kezdet orphan training on Maganos.

Ezkerra—First-generation Starfarer, married to Andrezhuria.

Feriila—Acorna's mother.

Foli—Second-generation Starfarer.

Fraaki—Linyaari word for fish.

Geeyiinah—One of the Linyaari clans.

Gerezan—First-generation Starfarer, Second Speaker to the Council.

Ghaanye (pl. ghaanyi)—A Linyaari year.

Gheraalye malivii—Navigation Officer.

Gheraalye ve-khanyii—Senior Communications Officer.

Gürange—Office of toastmaster in a Linyaari social organization.

Giryeeni—Linyaari clan name.

GSS—Gravitation Stabilization System.

Haarha Lürni—Linyaari term for advanced education, usually pursued during adulthood while on sabbatical from a previous calling.

Haarilnyah—The oldest clan amongst the Linyaari.

Hafiz Harakamian—Rafik's uncle, head of the interstellar financial empire of House Harakamian, a passionate collector of rarities from throughout the galaxy and a devotee of the old-fashioned sport of horse-racing. Although basically crooked enough to hide behind a spiral staircase, he is fond of Rafik and Acorna.

Hajnal—A child rescued from thieving on Kezdet, now in training on Maganos.

Haven—A multigeneration space colonization vehicle occupied by people pushed off the planet Esperantza by Amalgamated Mining.

Hünye—Linyaari term roughly equivalent to Galactic Standard term "horse's rump."

Iüliira—A Linyaari ship.

Iirtye—Chief aagroni for narhii-Vhiliinyar.

Ikwaskwan—Self-styled "admiral" of the Kilumbembese Red Bracelets.

Illart—First-generation Starfarer, First Speaker to the Council, and Markel's father.

Johnny Greene—An old friend of Calum, Rafik, and Gill; joined the Starfarers when he was fired after Amalgamated Mining's takeover of MME.

Jonas Becker—Interplanetary salvage artist; alias space junkman. Captain of the *Condor*. CEO of Becker Interplanetary Recycling and Salvage Enterprises Ltd.—a one-man, one-cat salvage firm Jonas inherited from his adopted father. Jonas spent his early youth on a labor farm on the planet Kezdet before he was adopted.

Joshua Flouse—Mayor of Rushima.

Judit Kendoro—Assistant to psychiatrist Alton Forelle at Amalgamated Mining, saved Acorna from certain death. Later fell in love with Gill and joined with him to help care for the children employed in Delszaki Li's Maganos mining operation.

Kaarlye—The father of Aari, Maati, and Laarye. A member of the Nyaarya clan, and life-bonded to Miiri.

Ka-Linyaari—Something against all Linyaari beliefs, something not Linyaari.

Karina—A plumply beautiful wanna-be psychic with a small shred of actual talent and a large fondness for profit. Married to Hafiz Harakamian. This is her first marriage, his second.

Kass—Rushimese settler.

kava—A coffee-like hot drink produced from roasted ground beans.

KEN—A line of general-purpose male androids, some with customized specializations, differentiated among their owners by number, for example KEN-637.

Kerratz—Second-generation Starfarer, son of Andrezhuria and Ezkerra.

Kezdet—A backwoods planet with a labor system based on child exploitation. Currently in economic turmoil because that system has been broken by Delszaki Li and Acorna.

Khaari—Senior Linyaari navigator on the *Balakiire*.

Khang Kieaan—A planet torn between three warring factions.

Khetala—Captured as a small child for the mines of Kezdet, later sold into the planet's brothels. Rescued by Acorna, and now a beautiful young woman.

Khleevi—Name given by Acorna's people to the space-borne enemies who have attacked them without mercy.

Kidaaki—A common waterfowl on the original Linyaari homeworld.

kü—A Linyaari time measurement roughly equivalent to an hour of Standard Time.

Ki-lin—Oriental name for unicorn, also a name sometimes associated with Acorna.

Kilumbemba Empire—An entire society that raises and exports mercenaries for hire—the Red Bracelets.

Kirilatova—An opera singer.

Kisla Manjari—Anorexic and snobbish young woman, raised as daughter of Baron Manjari; shattered when through Acorna's efforts to help the children of Kezdet her father is ruined and the truth of her lowly birth is revealed.

Korii—Melireenya's lifemate.

Kubiilikhan—Capital city of narhii-Vhiliinyar.

LAANYE—Sleep-learning device invented by the Linyaari that can, from a small sample of any foreign language, teach the wearer the new language overnight.

Laarye—Maati and Aari's brother. He died on Vhiliinyar during the Khleevi invasion. He was trapped in an accident in a cave far distant from the spaceport during the evacuation, and was badly injured. Aari stayed behind to rescue and heal him, but was captured by the Khleevi and tortured before he could accomplish his mission. Laarye died before Aari could escape and return.

Laboue—The planet where Hafiz Harakamian makes his headquarters.

Labrish—Rushimese settler.

Linyaari—Acorna's people.

Liriili—*Vüzaar* of narhii-Vhiliinyar, member of the clan Riivye.

Lukia of the Lights—A protective saint, identified by some children of Kezdet with Acorna.

Ma'aowri 3—A planet populated by cat-like beings.

Maati—A young Linyaari girl of the Nyaarya clan who lost most of her family during the Khleevi invasion. Aari's sister.

Madigadi—A berry-like fruit whose juice is a popular beverage.

Maganos—One of the three moons of Kezdet, base for Delszaki Li's mining operation and child rehabilitation project.

Makahomian Temple Cat—Cats on the planet Makahoma, bred from ancient Cat God stock to protect and defend the Cat God's temples. They are—for cats—large, fiercely loyal, remarkably intelligent, and dangerous when crossed.

Mali Bazaar—A luxurious bazaar on Laboue, famous for the intricate mosaic designs that decorate its roof.

Manjari—A baron in the Kezdet aristocracy, and a key person in the organization and protection of Kezdet's child labor racket, in which he was known by the code name "Piper." He murdered his wife and then committed suicide when his identity was revealed and his organization destroyed.

Markel—First-generation Starfarer, son of First Speaker Illart.

Martin Dehoney—Famous astro-architect who designed Maganos Moonbase; the coveted Dehoney Prize was named after him.

Melireenya—Linyaari communications specialist on the *Balaküre*, bonded to Korii.

Mercy Kendoro—Younger sister of Pal and Judit Kendoro, saved from a life of bonded labor by Judit's efforts, she worked as a spy for the Child Liberation League in offices of Kezdet Guardians of the Peace until the child labor system was destroyed.

Midas—Count Edacki Ganoosh's private space yacht, entrusted to Kisla Manjari, used to follow Becker as he searches for the Linyaari homeworld.

Miiri—Mother of Aari, Laarye, and Maati. A member of the Nyaarya clan, lifebonded to Kaarlye.

Misra Affrendi—Hafiz's elderly trusted retainer.

Mitanyaakhi—Generic Linyaari term meaning a very large number.

MME—Gill, Calum, and Rafik's original mining company. Swallowed by the ruthless, conscienceless, and bureaucratic Amalgamated Mining.

M'on Na'ntaw—High-ranking Red Bracelet officer, cheated by General Ikwaskwan in a way that threw the blame on someone else.

Moulay Suheil—Fanatical leader of the Neo-Hadithians.

Naadiina—Also known as Grandam, one of the oldest surviving Linyaari, is host to both Maati and Acorna on narhii-Vhiliinyar.

naanye—Linyaari time measurement roughly equal to a nanosecond.

Naarye—Linyaari techno-artisan in charge of final fit-out of spaceships.

Nadhari Kando—Formerly Delszaki Li's personal bodyguard, rumored to have been an officer in the Red Bracelets earlier in her career. Now a freelance security officer.

[Auntie] Nagah—Rushimese settler.

narhii-Vhiliinyar—Second home of Linyaari.

Neeva—Acorna's aunt and Linyaari envoy on the *Balakiire*, bonded to Virii.

Neeyeereeya—The most populous of the Linyaari clans.

Neggara—Second-generation Starfarer.

Neo-Hadithian—An ultra-conservative, fanatical religious sect.

Ngaen Xong Hoa—A Kieaanese scientist who invented a planetary weather-control system. He sought asylum on the *Haven* because he feared the warring governments on his planet would misuse his research. A mutineer faction on the *Haven* used the system to reduce the planet Rushima to ruins. The mutineers were tossed into space, and Dr. Hoa has since restored Rushima.

Niciiry—Grandam Naadiina's husband, dead and buried on Vhiliinyar.

Niikaavri—Acorna's grandmother, a member of the clan Geeyiinah, and a spaceship designer by trade. Also, as *Nükaavri*, the name of the spaceship used by Maati and Thariinye.

Nirii—A planetary trading partner of the Linyaari, populated by bovine-like two-horned sentients, known as Niriians, technologically advanced, able to communicate telepathically, and phlegmatic in temperament.

Nueva Fallona—Palomellese criminal who posed as a refugee to the Starfarers until she could carry out a coup putting her and her gang in control of the *Haven*. She was defeated by the children of the Starfarers.

Nyaarya—One of the clans of the Linyaari.

Nyiiri—The Linyaari word for unmitigated gall, sheer effrontery, or other form of misplaced bravado.

One-One Otimie—A Rushimese trapper and prospector.

Order of the Iriinje—Aristocratic Linyaari social organization similar to a fraternity, named after a blue-feathered bird native to Vhiliinyar.

Pahaantiyir—A cougar-like animal native to Vhiliinyar.

Pal Kendoro—Delszaki Li's assistant on the planet Kezdet. Brother to Mercy and Judit. Acorna's dear friend, and once her possible love interest—though they didn't, in the end, try to do anything about it. Given that the pair came from different species, it could have been problematic. Currently in love with 'Ziana, the captain of the Starfarers.

Palomella—Home planet of Nueva Fallona.

Pandora—Count Edacki Ganoosh's personal spaceship, used to track and pursue Hafiz's ship *Sharazad* as it speeds after Acorna on her journey to narhii-Vhiliinyar. Later confiscated and used by Hafiz for his own purposes.

püyi—A Niriian biotechnology-based information storage and retrieval system. The biological component resembles a very rancid cheese.

Provola Quero—Woman in charge of the Saganos operation.

Pyaka—A Rushimese settler.

Quashie—A Rushimese settler.

Qulabriel—Hafiz's assistant.

Rafik Nadezda—One of three miners who discovered Acorna and raised her.

Ramon Trinidad—One of the miners hired to direct a training program on Maganos for the freed children.

Red Bracelets—Kilumbembese mercenaries; arguably the toughest and nastiest fighting force in known space.

Renyilaaghe—Linyaari clan name.

Rezar—Second-generation Starfarer.

Riivye—Linyaari clan name.

Roadkill—Otherwise known as RK. A Makahomian Temple Cat, the only survivor of a space wreck, rescued and adopted by Jonas Becker.

Rocky Reamer—Intergalactic vendor of precious stones.

Rosewater's Revelation—Uncle Hafiz's best racehorse.

Rushima—Agricultural world colonized by the Shenjemi Federation.

Saganos—Second of Kezdet's moons.

Sengrat—A pushy, bossy, whiney, bullying know-it-all with a political agenda on the ship *Haven*.

Sharazad—Hafiz's personal spaceship, a luxury cruiser.

Shenjemi Federation—Long-distance government of Rushima.

Sita Ram—A protective goddess, identified with Acorna by the mining children on Kezdet.

Skarness—Planetary source of the famous (and rare) Singing Stones, stones that are sentient, each of which emits a single, perfectly pitched note whenever stepped upon. Collectors usually assemble one or several octave scales of the stones, including the requisite sharps and flats.

Skomitin—Somebody in Admiral Ikwaskwan's past of whom he does not care to be reminded.

Starfarers—Name adopted by the Experantzan settlers who were displaced by Amalgamated's manipulations. They refused unsatisfactory resettlement offers and turned their main ship, the *Haven*, into a mobile colony from which they carried on a campaign of nonviolent political protest against Amalgamated.

Ta'anisi—The Red Bracelets' flagship.

Taankaril—*Visedhaanye ferilii* of the Gamma sector of Linyaari space.

Tanqque III—Rainforest planet; export of its coveted purpleheart trees is illegal.

Tapha—Hafiz's ineffectual son, who made several attempts on Rafik's life before he was killed during yet another murder attempt on Rafik.

Thariinye—A handsome and conceited young spacefaring Linyaari from clan Renyilaaghe.

Theloi—One of the planets the miners had to leave hastily to avoid their many enemies (see *Acorna*).

Theophilus Becker—Jonas Becker's father, a salvage man and astrophysicist with a fondness for exploring uncharted wormholes.

thiilir (pl. thiilirii)—Small arboreal mammals of Linyaari home world.

thiilsis—Grass species native to Vhiliinyar.

Tianos—Kezdet's third moon.

Turi Reamer—Seven-year-old daughter of Rocky Reamer, very business-like.

Twi Osiam—Planetary site of a major financial and trade center.

Twilit—Small, pestiferous insect on Linyaari home planet.

Uhuru—One of the various names of the ship owned jointly by Gill, Calum, and Rafik.

Vaanye—Acorna's father.

Vhiliinyar—Home planet of the Linyaari, now occupied by Khleevi.

Vüzaar—A high political office in the Linyaari system, roughly equivalent to president or prime minister.

Virii—Neeva's spouse.

visedhaanye ferilii—Linyaari term corresponding roughly to "Envoy Extraordinary."

Vlad—Cousin of Des Smirnoff's, a fence, probably descended from Vlad the Impaler.

Wahanamoian Blossom of Sleep—Poppy-like flowers whose pollens, when ground, are a very powerful sedative.

Winjy—A Rushimese settler.

Ximena Sengrat—Sengrat's beautiful young daughter.

Yasmin—Hafiz Harakamian's first wife, mother of Tapha, faked her own death and ran away to return to her former lucrative career in the pleasure industry. After her accumulated years made that career much less lucrative, she returned to squeeze money out of Hafiz in the form of blackmail.

Yukata Batsu—Uncle Hafiz's chief competitor on Laboue.

Zanegar—Second-generation Starfarer.

Zaspala Imperium—Backward planetary confederation, original home of Des Smirnoff.

Dr. Zip—An eccentric astrophysicist.

Brief Notes on the Linyaari Language

by Margaret Ball

As Anne McCaffrey's collaborator in transcribing the first two tales of Acorna, I was delighted to find that the second of these books provided an opportunity to sharpen my long-unused skills in linguistic fieldwork. Many years ago, when the government gave out scholarships with gay abandon and the cost of living (and attending graduate school) was virtually nil, I got a Ph.D. in linguistics for no better reason than that (a) the government was willing to pay, (b) it gave me an excuse to spend a couple of years doing fieldwork in Africa, and (c) there weren't any real jobs going for eighteen-year-old girls with a B.A. in math and a minor in Germanic languages. (This was back during the Upper Pleistocene era, when the Help Wanted ads were still divided into Male and Female.)

So there were all those years spent doing things like transcribing tonal Oriental languages on staff paper (the Field Methods instructor was Not Amused) and tape-recording Swahili women at weddings, and then I got the degree and wandered off to play with computers and never had any use for the stuff again . . . until Acorna's people appeared on the scene. It required a sharp ear and some facility for linguistic analysis to make sense of the subtle sound-changes with which their language signaled syntactic changes; I quite enjoyed the challenge.

The notes appended here represent my first and necessarily tentative analysis of certain patterns in Linyaari phonemics and morphophonemics. If there is any inconsistency between this analysis and the Linyaari speech patterns recorded in the later adventures of Acorna, please remember that I was working from a very limited database and, what is perhaps worse, attempting to analyse a decidedly nonhuman language with the aid of the only paradigms I had, twentieth-century linguistic models developed exclusively from human language. The result is very likely as inaccurate as were the first attempts to describe English syntax by forcing it into the mold of Latin, if not worse. My colleague, Elizabeth Ann Scarborough, has by now added her own notes to the small corpus of Linyaari names and utterances. It may well be that in the next decade there will be enough data available to publish a truly definitive dictionary and grammar of Linyaari, an undertaking that will surely be of inestimable value, not only to those members of our race who are involved in diplomatic and trade relations with this people, but also to everyone interested in the study of language.

NOTES ON THE LINYAARI LANGUAGE

1. A doubled vowel indicates stress: *aa*vi, *abaa*nye, **Khl*ee*vi.**

2. Stress is used as an indicator of syntactic function: In nouns stress is on the penultimate syllable, in adjectives on the last syllable, in verbs on the first.

3. Intervocalic *n* is always palatalized.

4. Noun plurals are formed by adding a final vowel, usually -i: one **Liinyar,** two **Linyaari.** Note that this causes a change in the stressed syllable (from **LI-nyar** to **Li-NYA-ri**) and hence a change in the pattern of doubled vowels.

   For nouns whose singular form ends in a vowel, the plural is formed by dropping the original vowel and adding -i: **ghaanye, ghaanyi.** Here the number of syllables remains the same; therefore no stress/spelling change is required.

5. Adjectives can be formed from nouns by adding a final -ii (again, dropping the original final vowel if one exists): **maalive, malivii; Liinyar, Linyarii.** Again, the change in stress means that the doubled vowels in the penultimate syllable of the noun disappear.

6. For nouns denoting a class or species, such as **Liinyar,** the noun itself can be used as an adjective when the meaning is simply to denote a member of

the class, rather than the usual adjective meaning of "having the qualities of this class"—thus, of the characters in *Acorna*, only Acorna herself could be described as "a **Liinyar** girl" but Jana, although human, would certainly be described as "a **Linyarii** girl," or "a just-as-civilised-as-a-real-member-of-the-People" girl.

7. Verbs can be formed from nouns by adding a prefix constructed by [first consonant of noun] + **ii** + **nye**: faalar—grief; **fiinyefalar**—to grieve.

8. The participle is formed from the verb by adding a suffix **-an** or **-en**: thiinyethilel—to destroy, **thiinyethilelen**—destroyed. No stress change is involved because the participle is perceived as a verb form and therefore stress remains on the first syllable:

enye-ghanyii—time unit, small portion of a year **(ghaanye)**

fiinyefalaran—mourning, mourned

ghaanye—a Linyaari year, equivalent to about 1⅓ earth years

gheraalye malivii—Navigation Officer

gheraalye ve-khanyii—Senior Communications Specialist

Khleev—originally, a small vicious carrion-feeding animal with a poisonous bite; now used by the Linyaari to denote the invaders who destroyed their home world.

khleevi—barbarous, uncivilised, vicious without reason

Liinyar—member of the People
linyarii—civilized; like a Liinyar
mitanyaakhi—large number (slang—like our "zillions")
narhii—new
thiilir, thiliiri—small arboreal mammals of Linyaari home world
thiilel—destruction
visedhaanye ferilii—Envoy Extraordinary

If you enjoyed reading Acorna's World,
then read the following selection from

Acorna's Search,

from Eos Books.

Acorna's Search

*G*iven its location on the star maps, Acorna knew intellectually that the planet under the shadow of their flitter had once been Vhiliinyar, "Home of the People," but it was hard to believe, as they skimmed the surface of this desolate place, that it had ever supported any sort of life.

The planet's remaining sun, "Light of Our People," was an amorphous gray-blue glob of smoky light in the sky, little resembling the brilliant orb she remembered from her dreams and from the descriptions Neeva had provided.

Remembering those descriptions, Acorna realized that some of her recent experiences were at odds with them. She turned to her lifemate—perhaps he could shed some light on the inconsistencies.

(You know, Aari, for a long time I had the impression from the other Linyaari that you were the only one left behind when the evacuation ships fled Vhiliinyar. But I've recently discovered that there were other Linyaari who chose to stay behind rather than leave their homes, as well as scouts who stayed behind to relay information on what the Khleevi were up to. I wonder what happened to them? The scouts claimed that all living beings on the planet appeared to have been killed — that their bones were piled up by the Khleevi as monuments and yet, so far, I have seen no such monuments.)

Beside her, Aari moaned. The memories her question brought back were undoubtedly terrible for him.

(Laarye and I were the only children lost in the chaos, certainly. There were others, mostly Linyaari who were reaching the twilight of their lives, who chose to remain behind on Vhiliinyar, *yaazi,* rather than adjust to a new world. Almost all of them resided in distant settlements. I believe they were exterminated before the Khleevi found me. Certainly the Khleevi thought so. The Khleevi showed me their bones to torment me, but in the end all of the chaos the Khleevi let loose on our world scattered those charnel piles along with the stones of our mountains.)

(You survived. Do you think it is possible we will find others?)

(They would have starved here, with nothing left to eat,) Aari told her. (It was only because our ancestors' graves were near my cave, purifying the blighted land around it and enabling the plant life to continue to grow and thrive, that I was able to find the resources to sustain my own life.)

(I wonder . . .) Acorna said, and toggled the connection to Neeva's flitter.

"Yes, sister-child," Neeva responded. "Is everything well?" Then she added wryly, "Relatively speaking, that is."

Considering the devastation below them, Acorna could understand her aunt's disquiet. "I am as well as can be expected, Aunt Neeva. But I have a question. You once told me that our people had scouts who risked being caught by the Khleevi in order to send back reports to narhii-Vhiliinyar of what happened here following the evacuation. Are the surviving scouts among us now?"

"Just the parents of your lifemate, Khornya. The scouts who stayed behind to see what the Khleevi did to our world sent in reports of conditions on Vhiliinyar as long as they could. But only Aari's parents survived to rejoin us. None of the other scouts were ever heard from again after those initial reports. Because we received no images of them being tortured by the Khleevi, we assume that they made use of the substances they were issued to end their lives before they were captured."

"Oh," Acorna said. She was so distracted by that revelation that she was hardly aware of breaking the connection.

Then Maati pointed out the windscreen and cried, "Lookit! Those long humpy trails, aren't those—?"

"Khleevi scat," Thariinye said, disgusted. "Maybe it is my imagination, or bad memories, but I think I can smell it from here."

"I smelled it back at the cave," Maati said.

Aari snorted. (The stench has not left my nostrils since we first landed.)

(It has been so for me, as well.) Even as she replied, Acorna tried not to broadcast the other disturbing recollection she'd had from the scout reports she'd reviewed. The reports had spoken of Khleevi young being bred in the rivers and streams of Vhiliinyar. She shuddered, recalling her own single encounter with the Young, so voracious and vicious as to form the driving force behind Khleevi conquest. But surely all of the Young were dead now, killed on their horrific home world where they were both protected by and avoided by the adult Khleevi.

Aari picked up her concern and, to her surprise, *he* was the one to comfort *her*.

(I can sense when the Khleevi are close,) Aari told her. (And I do not sense them now.)

Acorna sighed. (Yes, they must have moved on once they had destroyed all the resources here, and returned to their home world. I'm sure you're right.)

(They're gone now, *yaazi*,) Aari repeated. (Nothing of them remains to harm us or others.)

Gratefully, she allowed her special talent for sensing the mineral composition of any substance she chose to probe— something she'd developed while working with her asteroid-miner foster parents—to preoccupy her with the data it fed her senses. Instead of smelling Khleevi scat she smelled, tasted, mentally touched each major mineral deposit in their flight path as they passed above it. This was a vital part of her plan to map the planet. The few survey maps they had were short on biological detail, but extremely precise when it came to mineral deposits. She could take what she learned on their surveys of Vhiliinyar as it existed now and use it to reconstruct the planet topology as it had been before the Khleevi had attacked.

The work was a welcome distraction from the ugli-

ness below her, and from the cold bleakness that over-
came Aari as he withdrew to that inner place where he
found protection when reminded too forcefully of his
ordeal among the Khleevi.

Long stretches of alluvial deposits containing copper,
gold, garnets, agates, and other rare gems indicated
riverbeds, and when Acorna sensed these she noted
their coordinates on the flitter's computer. The distribu-
tion of these minerals and gems would help her trace the
rivers to their origins in the mountains and their endings
in the seas. Limestone deposits in large quantities indicated former ocean floors—even recent ocean floors,
since the Khleevi had diminished as well as befouled the
planet's oceans until they were turgid, lifeless swamps.

Salt deposits provided another indication for the
oceans, and basalt deposits often outlined original
shorelines. Acorna's talent for sensing minerals, a trait
apparently unique among the Linyaari, was invaluable
here. She could use it to help Hafiz and her people re-
verse engineer Vhiliinyar from the mess it had become
and return it, she hoped, to something at least approaching its original beauty and vitality.

The terrain abruptly changed as she increased the
flitter's attitude to avoid the vast ranges of tumbled
boulders before them. This landscape was in constant
motion, like a terrified animal pinned down and
writhing to escape torture. Showers of stones plum-
meted from precipices, landing with puffs of dust on the
hills newly formed from the avalanches. These in turn
were blasted apart by subsequent slides. Plumes of ash
and smoke rose from three vast craters gaping in the
range like festering pockmarks on the planet's face.

After the calderas were some distance behind them, the ground finally stabilized a bit. For the first time they could see vegetation growing, low and scrubby at first, and then a thick parrot-green jungle rising from the battered ground.

At the edge of this jungle, Aari indicated Acorna should set down the flitter, which she did.

"Ouch," Maati said to RK as she tried to pry him from her lap. The cat's ears were flat and his tail was poofed into something that looked like a massive feather duster.

"I don't think he likes it here," Thariinye said.

"But it's *beautiful,*" Maati replied as she was finally able to dislodge RK and dump him onto the flitter's deck. She followed after him, climbing out onto the scarred stone surface of Vhiliinyar. "Isn't this wonderful? This is the first sign we have seen that the planet is finally starting to heal and grow things again."

"Hmmm," Acorna said, noncommittally, "but what kind of things?"

Something scuttled across the edge of the greenery, but disappeared before they could determine its nature. It might even have been an errant breeze moving a plant frond, though the air here was inert and stagnant right now.

Actually, the whole planet was, for the most part, stifling, with much of its protective ozone layer punctured by volcanic explosions and toxic chemical reactions from its unstable land masses and destroyed seas. Add to that the effect of the hazy atmosphere, which served to trap and reflect the energy from Vhiliinyar's sun, and the planet's climate was far hotter than it used to be and likely to get worse before it got better. Acorna suspected that the lush greenery before them was a valiant attempt on the part of this world to restore its own much-depleted atmosphere.

A sudden, happy thought occurred to Acorna. This survey might well have positive consequences for their ravaged world. The presence of the planet's native people might well speed its efforts to recover, even before Hafiz's terraformation could begin. With so many Linyaari horns available to purify the waters and the air and to cleanse much of the poison inflicted upon Vhiliinyar by the Khleevi, the planet might well heal a little each day they were present, just as a wounded creature would heal with the application of the horn's power.

The Linyaari were superb healers, and their horns could detoxify nearly any substance that they came into contact with. The powers of their horns were not unique to the Linyaari, nor had they originated on Vhiliinyar. They were a legacy from their Ancestors, the *ki-lin* of long ago Terra, often called unicorns. An ancient space-faring race the Linyaari knew only as the Ancestral Friends had saved the *ki-lin* from primitive and brutal humans who were hunting them to extinction on Terra, and brought them through the cosmos to Vhiliinyar, where they had thrived once again.

Though the *ki-lin* still existed as a separate race, many of them had blended genes with the Ancestral Friends, and the result of that fusion was the Linyaari people. The powers were the same in the Linyaari as in the Ancestors themselves.

But that was all ancient history—this was now, and they were in the midst of a terrible ecological disaster, one that needed all the healing power the Linyaari could muster.

Maati frowned. The caution displayed by all of her friends, right down to RK the cat, in the presence of the lovely greenery before them confused her. Still new to thought-talk, she addressed the silence of the others with a perplexed protest. "But that forest *is* pretty. And alive! Why aren't the rest of you happier that it's growing things and—and—pretty?"

Aari glowered at her, the first harshness he had shown to his little sister. Thariinye, picking up on Aari's thoughts, pointed out, *(How is she to know what is wrong? She was not born here! She has never been here before. She has nothing but some stories, a few thought-pictures, and Uncle Hafiz's holos to compare it to.)*

(True,) Acorna agreed. To Maati she said, "You remember that place we were in within the holo-bubble, right at the beginning? With the beautiful mountain and the waterfall and lake?"

"Yes. Are we going there tomorrow?"

"We are here now. This is that place," Acorna told her.

"But—it is so flat." Maati said, bewildered. She was not at all stupid, but the concept of total terrestrial destruction was a large one to absorb, especially in the presence of the reality of the thing. This rather savage and uncertain "prettiness," first vestige of life among the ruins of Vhiliinyar though it might be, was a far cry from the deeply spiritual beauty of the mountain with its glorious waterfall and wine-hued lake that she'd seen in Hafiz's holo.

"It's not as flat as it appears. We had to climb quite

steeply to land here. And the vegetative growth is no doubt due largely to the residual moisture from the lake. Perhaps not even the Khleevi could destroy it entirely."

"Its very waters were known to have healing powers akin to those of our horns," Thariiyne said.

"That is clearly no longer the case," Aari said, with a snort to dislodge the stench of the place—a mix of rotting vegetation and who knew what else—from his nostrils.

"The presence of the plants means that there is water here," Acorna said. "We should purify it, but perhaps it would be wise to explore this forest a little at a time at first, until we can analyze just what it consists of, and what pollutants are present in the water and the vegetation."

Aari nodded. "There are chemical combinations that could eat right through what we're wearing before we could purify it with our horns. There are even chemicals the Khleevi developed that ate right through Linyaari horns themselves."

Maati and Thariinye exchanged startled glances. The idea that any chemical could be so strong as to counteract the purifying effects of their horns, and harm the horns themselves, was totally alien to all they knew about their own abilities. And more alien was the thought that such hostile strangeness could exist here, on what had once been the safest place in the universe to be Linyaari.

The pallid sun drooped near the scarred horizon, and Acorna said, "Let's settle in for the night here. For now, we should perhaps use only the water and food we brought with us from MOO."

Her opinion was unanimously accepted, and after a quick meal of water and dried grasses, they spread air mats over the rocks and arranged the flitter's attachable awnings as tents over their small campsite.

The flutter of useful activity served to calm Acorna's nerves, which were, if not exactly jangling, at least on red alert. An air of menace pervaded this spot, the very place, however unrecognizable, that had seemed to be the epitome of peace and serenity in Hafiz's holo. At least she wasn't alone in her concern. Aari was alert to the slightest shift in air currents, the least nuance of shifting current in the miasma of rot and waste simmering around them.

RK, too, that veteran of a thousand adventures, clearly was displeased with the place. He stayed near the Linyaari, slinking with his belly dragging the rocks, his ears rotating constantly, his whiskers and fur bristling, his upper lips raised above his fangs in a snarling expression that uncovered the scent glands on either side of his muzzle. He looked like a creature from a nightmare.

Maati reached out to stroke him. He allowed the small caress after almost taking off her hand. He rubbed it with his head in apology, but continued to slink and prowl about after she released him.

Thariinye, meanwhile, was lamenting, "We could have brought our traveling pavilions if the Khleevi hadn't destroyed so many homes on narhii-Vhiliinyar. They would have been much more comfortable than these makeshift shelters."

"I thought you were the rugged adventurer," Maati chided, "used to surviving in the worst possible circumstances with nothing but your wits, never mind a pavilion!"

"These *are* among the worst possible circumstances, would you not agree, Aari? Khornya? Even with these sleeping pads, we are unlikely to find a rock level enough to rest our flanks upon, much less our shoulders. I cannot imagine that any of us will be able to sleep."

Acorna said, "Nor can I. So I will take first watch."

"Watch?" Maati asked. "Watch *what*? This planet can't sustain sentient life. I thought we'd established that. Well, except for these jungly plants and that scuttling thing and—I guess I see your point."

"I will watch, also," Aari said. "It may be best to do so in pairs for now."

"I might as well watch with you also," Thariinye said, "because I cannot imagine that I will sleep a wink in this place." But he did, and almost immediately. The sound of his snoring soon filled the air. It was a calming, familiar noise.

Acorna and Aari sat, relaxed, each with one knee drawn up to their chins, each with one leg dangling over the side of the largish rock on which they perched. They gazed toward the jungle growth slightly above them, instead of back in the direction from which they had flown. The leaves and fronds of the strange forest were not outlined black against the night, as they might have expected, but instead glowed in the darkness with a greenish iridescence. A small wind stirred the leaves. Otherwise all was silent.

Acorna almost expected to hear a birdcall, or the snuffle of some smaller creature in the woods around

them. Neeva had told her once of the endearing furred
creatures that lived in the forests of Vhiliinyar before
the Khleevi came—but they were no longer here, and
the jungle was nothing but mutated weeds and brush
grown very tall. The creatures of old Vhiliinyar sang in
lovely voices and delighted all who heard. Their beautiful forms entranced all who saw them. Acorna wondered—had *aagroni* Iirtye managed to save specimens
of all those creatures, or even samples of their cells to
clone them from later on? What a wrenching loss it
must be to have known such creatures well, and to lose
them, along with all of the other wonders this planet
had held when it was beautiful and whole.

Absorbed in her thoughts, it took Acorna a moment
to realize she was hearing a noise, a soft snuffling
sound, from beside her. Trails of tears ran down Aari's
face.

She took his hand. (Penny for your thoughts, or was
I broadcasting, and you were responding to mine?)

He sniffed again and turned a chiseled manly coun-
tenance to her. (What is a penny?)

(A primitive coin used by one of the nations of hu-
mankind before it became so devaluated it was not
worth the materials needed to create it.)

He gave a short laugh. (Ah, a coin worthy of my
present thoughts, indeed. Which are that we would
have a better chance of re-forming narhii-Vhiliinyar
into a semblance of Vhiliinyar than we have to return
Vhiliinyar to its former state, as the *aagroni* wishes.
Who would have thought even the Khleevi could so
mutilate the landscape that its own people could not
recognize it? I was wondering where the mountains

were, where the lake was, and the waterfall. I see nothing here that resembles them.)

(And yet they are here. I sense the iron and granite of the mountain, and the plateau — the bones of that formation run beneath us and all through the area. Also the waters of the lake and cascade are here, though there are elements of sulfur and mercury and other contaminants in them. I do not think it will destroy our horns to purify that water. But there is something worrying about those plants . . .)

They heard something then: the thump of paws jumping down and a scattering of small stones beneath soft footpads, the movement of a dark plumed tail hovering at the edge of the plants. RK, Acorna realized, had to relieve himself and he wished to perform his duties unobserved, but he was not happy about the only available cover. The cat emitted grumbling growls and plaintive meows to show what he thought of the feline sanitary facilities available at the campsite. Instead of plunging into the growth, he began to skirt it, his ears still flattened, his tail twitching with frustration, searching for a way to conceal himself without having to actually step between the plants.

Acorna and Aari observed their former shipmate, amused.

(We won't watch), Acorna promised RK.

This produced no visible change in the cat's behavior, but in a moment he disappeared from sight and the Linyaari couple concluded he had found what he was looking for.

Then an earsplitting yowl burst from the greenery several yards to the left of the campsite.

Acorna and Aari jumped to their feet, stumbling over the rocks in the dark. Acorna fell heavily and scraped the skin from her right arm and knee. Aari turned back to her, his horn lowered to help with the healing, but Acorna waved him on urgently.

(This will keep. See to RK. Help him!) she insisted above the cat's caterwauling as she climbed painfully to her feet. (That does not sound like a cat bellyache to me.) She brushed her wounded arm over her horn but the cat screamed before she could touch her leg. Her wound could wait. Something was very wrong with RK. She moved as fast as she could toward the noise. Sounds of thrashing and howling, snarling and more shrieks and screams rang through the night as she limped forward to see one of the tall plants whipping a furry tail back and forth in the air. Nothing remained evident of RK but his furious cries and his tail. A huge green bulbous protuberance on the plant concealed the rest of the cat.

Aari leapt for the lashing tail but it whipped out of his grasp.

They had no weapons handy, no implements or utensils that would be useful in destroying the plant. And RK's cries were growing weaker, strangled, more pitiful. They had to do something . . . now!